"No. *Wrong,*" he said, stepping into the small room beside her. "You knew perfectly well what you were doing. We both did."

"We were just kids," she said.

"Horny kids," he said, a slight smile tilting those damned fine lips of his. She stared at them, her face growing warm again.

"Speak for yourself."

He laughed then, a low rumble deep in his chest. "Not to name names, but I do believe one of us was naked first. And it wasn't me."

"Yes, well, that was then…"

"And this is?" He quirked an eyebrow, the corner of his eyes going all crinkly with humor. He hadn't had those fine lines before. She found she really, really liked them.

"This is now. I'm not a horny kid anymore."

The crinkles deepened. "You stripped in front of me when you got sprayed with a skunk."

"That was different. That was an emergency. I didn't want to bring skunk smell into the house."

"And here I was hoping it was because there was something about me that made you want to get naked."

Half the fun of the game of love is winning...
the other half is deciding to play.

Deal Me In

Cheri Allan

~ Book Four ~
A Betting on Romance Novel

Five Oaks Books

Deal Me In

Editing by Orchard Edits
Cover Image Credits:
Logo image © Elena Elisseeva | Dreamstime.com
Beautiful Couple Kissing © Wavebreakmedia Ltd. | Dreamstime.com
New England Farm © Aaron West | Dreamstime.com
Red Butterly © thawats | Depositphotos.com

Publishing History
First Five Oaks Books Edition, 2016
Print ISBN: 978-0-9904815-7-7
Digital ISBN: 978-0-9904815-6-0

Published in the United States of America

Acknowledgements

Thanks to my amazing editor, Charis, and my beta readers for their lightning-fast work, brutal honesty and support. You keep me looking good. Thanks to Susan and Kathy for their insight into my hero's military background. Any errors or inaccuracies in his backstory are completely my own. Thanks to Susan Wall for being my book birthday partner and sprinkling a little Sugar Falls magic into Lilac Ridge. And, finally, thanks to the many readers and Facebook friends who helped me brainstorm names for my surly waitress and fictional band. You guys rock! Oh, and Angel? Even though you can't see them, I gave my waitress spikey heels, because this girl would never wear flats. ;)

Other Titles by Cheri Allan

Luck of the Draw
Stacking the Deck
All or Nothing

To my dearest Gubby,

I told you if you came back to me I'd catch you.
I'm so glad you did.

CHAPTER ONE

"Jeez, Grace. Get a room. If you'd give me half the passion you're giving that cheesecake, we could be happy together."

Grace McIntyre paused, her fork poised above the cheesecake in question and looked across at her date. "We're happy," she said. "Aren't we?"

Zach's eyes looked a little sad like when he thought one of his students wasn't working up to their potential. "Are we?"

Grace set her fork down. She'd looked forward to this dessert all through dinner. It was the Silver Birch Inn's specialty: cranberry-orange cheesecake with chocolate crust. Seriously worth every calorie. But Zach was talking.

She proceeded to chew and swallow then heard him clunk his water glass down with disgust. "It's like you're making love to that damned thing."

She opened her eyes. "Don't be ridiculous."

"You were *moaning*."

She was? "It's really good."

"I gathered that."

"Well you don't have to sound so peevish. I offered you a bite."

He shook his head. "A bite? *A bite?*" His voice began to rise. Grace glanced over her shoulder at the other diners as a couple of them paused their conversations to more effectively eavesdrop. "I want more than a *bite*, Grace. If you hadn't noticed, I want all of you. The whole package."

Okay, that should have sounded flattering, except he was eyeing her disdainfully, his voice much louder than the modulated tones he typically used. Maybe this was his professor voice.

"But I only ever get a tiny piece of you," he said, gesticulating less than subtly. "You're holding back. And yet, you sit there in that *red* dress which screams sex, by the way, moaning into your cheesecake and I know—I *know!*—I'm not getting any further than second base if I'm lucky and…" He took a deep breath. "I'm okay with that. Mostly. But, do you have to rub my face in it? Do you have to sit there like some porn-star performance right across the table from me?"

Grace's face felt hot as she avoided the now avid stares of her fellow patrons. "I'm sorry. I shouldn't wear red?"

He rolled his eyes and shoved his chair back with a hard scrape on the floor. It echoed across the intimate dining room. "Everyone knows what a red dress is code for but you, Grace. I suppose you're going to tell me now you only wore it because you're getting your period."

"Well, actually…"

He leaned across the table toward her. "Don't. No one gets their period as much as you. Six times in two and a half months? You expect me to believe that?"

"I…" Okay. Maybe she *had* fibbed a bit when he started to get cozy. Was it her fault she liked to take things slow?

He stood and picked up their check. "There are times I wonder if you even *like* men."

She felt heat creep up her neck. "Of course, I like men!"

A passing busboy stopped on his way by. "'Cause if you don't, my sister has always been a bit into you."

"What?" Grace asked.

The busboy nodded. "I could give you her number."

Zach made a disgusted noise and headed toward the exit.

"Um, thanks, but I'm kind of into guys," Grace mumbled before shoving her own chair back.

"I could give you *my* number!" he called after her.

"Zach, wait." Grace stopped her date with a hand on his sleeve.

He shook off her touch. "No, Grace. I'm done."

"Done with dating me or just dinner?"

"Let's face it. You clearly don't want to be with me as much as you want to be with that cheesecake."

An elderly couple sat nearby, openly watching Grace's little drama unfold. The woman sniffed in disapproval. "That's not true!" she said to the woman. She turned to Zach's retreating backside. "That's not true!"

He stopped in the front hall and turned, and she half wished he wouldn't have. His unwavering gaze made her feel very small.

"I didn't believe people when they warned me about you. They said you were an Ice Princess. I told them they were crazy. You were so warm and fun and witty. I was sure they had no idea what they were talking about." He fumbled in his pocket for his wallet. "But they were spot on."

He'd already handed his credit card to their waitress before Grace knew what was happening. He was breaking up with her *and* paying the bill? Guilt crept up her spine, especially seeing as, if she were to admit it, she'd really enjoyed the cheesecake.

"Here, let me" she said, scrounging in her tiny clutch for her credit card.

He paused, his face impassive as he accepted his receipt. "Too late."

"Zach," she pleaded. He scrawled a generous tip at the bottom of the receipt and smiled his thanks to the waitress. "Can't we at least talk about this? What about Saturday? We were going to go miniature golfing with Billy and Cam. We've been talking about it all week!"

Zach stopped at the exit. "Sometimes I think you enjoy spending time with my nephews more than you do me."

"That's crazy," she said to his back.

The door to the parking lot swung closed behind him.

She turned to the waitress. "Could you just wrap up my dessert to go, and I'll be back for it in a minute?"

"Zach, please!" Grace called, hobbling over the gravel parking lot toward Zach's car, the spikes of her heels slipping between the stones. "This is so out of the blue. You need to give me time to process."

He stood in the open door of his car, his trim blazer open, his blue eyes defeated. "Ten dates, Grace. Today is our *tenth* date. I may teach English, but even I can do this math. If you're not into me by now, it's not going to happen."

"I'm slow to warm. I know. That's my problem, but it's not about you at all. I find you very handsome. I do!" She reached around him and hugged him to her. Dang, he was nicely warm, and the air outside had a bite to it. She cuddled closer.

"See? Isn't this nice?" she cooed.

His arms hung at his sides. "Kiss me," he said.

"What?"

"I said, 'kiss me.'"

She must have made a face, because he rolled his eyes and pulled her arms from around his waist. "If you find me so repulsive..."

"No! It's not that, it's just... you took me off guard. I thought we were breaking up. I'm happy to kiss you."

He raised one eyebrow, his chiseled cheekbones and piercing blue eyes every woman's dream. The hate-stares she'd gotten from his female students the one time she'd met him at work told her he was quintessential academic eye-candy. So, it wasn't him.

It was her.

It was happening, again, and it was all her fault.

She moved onto tiptoe and leaned in for a kiss, pressing her lips to his. They were warm, pleasant. Not too fat or too thin. Not too wet. She angled a bit and let her hands hold his face in her palms. *Mmm*. That was definitely nice. His chiseled cheeks felt good under her chilly fingers. She angled a bit the other way and puckered more. His lips shifted under hers and she gave them one last peck before moving away.

There. How could he leave her after that? There was definitely something there, right? "*Mmm,*" she said, opening her eyes again.

He stared at her, his face framed in her palms. "Like kissing my sister."

She dropped her hands. "You don't have a sister. Do you?"

He shook his head and slid into the driver's seat. "No." He ran a hand through his thick, slightly unruly hair. "Go ahead and get in," he said. "I'll drive you home."

She hesitated, pretty sure that kissing like somebody's sister wasn't a compliment. She glanced at the passenger seat and then back toward the restaurant. "I'll... I just need to grab my, um, cheesecake, and I'll be right out."

He gave her a look that said he couldn't believe his ears.

"I'll find my own way home?" she said in a small voice.

She watched as his taillights flickered and blinked into the distance before heading back into the restaurant. Well, that stunk.

Their waitress gave her an unsympathetic look. "Cheesecake don't keep you warm at night. You're crazy not to bang that guy. I sure would."

Grace snatched the handles of the plastic bag from the waitress. "I don't 'bang' guys," she said.

"Maybe that's your problem."

Grace let the door slam shut on the waitress' unhelpful retort and stepped carefully down the walkway.

Okay this... sucked. What had begun as a special night at one of her favorite restaurants had ended rather unpleasantly, but Grace was nothing if not resilient. She'd simply call... someone... and have them drive out here to pick her up and take her home.

Someone who wouldn't judge or ask too many questions.

The mental list became quite short.

She pulled her phone from her clutch and turned it on. It beeped a low battery warning and then went dead.

Crap.

Hiking her skinny purse strap higher onto her shoulder, she returned to the restaurant.

"Excuse me," she said. "I wonder if you could call a cab for me."

"He left, didn't he?" She didn't even have the decency to raise her head.

"He, ah, had an emergency," Grace lied.

The girl raised her head, her lips fighting a self-satisfied grin. "Right." She dragged the word out disbelievingly.

"The cab?"

"I'll trade you. Give me the hunky guy's number, and I'll call a cab."

Grace didn't feel great about throwing Zach under the bus, but he *had* left her here, which wasn't particularly chivalrous of him. Yes, she'd told him it was okay, but she didn't mean it. Was it her fault the cheesecake was to die for? And besides, if she was going to be dumped, she might as well have comfort food in hand.

"Fine." Grace grabbed a flyer from next to the register and scribbled Zach's number on the back.

The waitress tucked it into her pocket and picked up the phone. A minute later she hung up. "Ronnie'll pick you up in a couple hours."

"A couple of hours? Why so long?"

"He don't get off work 'til then."

"Isn't there someone else you can call?"

"In Sugar Falls?" The girl laughed and bent her head again to whatever she'd been doing.

Grace blew out a breath and turned around. "I'll wait outside."

She found herself a spot along the rock wall that bordered the parking lot and brushed the stones with her hand. It was an uncharacteristically raw June evening, but that was New Hampshire weather for you. She sat down. The stone felt cold under her butt, but she was the Ice Princess. She should be able to handle a cold bum.

She hated that nickname, but she knew she deserved it.

A person didn't drive off a guy like Zach without *something* being wrong with her. She shouldn't have even bothered to agree to that first date, but he'd been so charming. But just like all the other times, the more things heated up, the more she felt herself pulling away. It had always been that way.

Well, not *always*. But *that* relationship had ended in disaster, too, so pretty much she was doomed either way. Better to live in a lukewarm world.

The elderly couple stepped out of the restaurant and made their way down the walk toward the parking lot. The man stopped next to Grace and winked. "If it makes you feel any better, I think you look the cat's meow in that dress."

His wife tugged him toward their car. "That wasn't the point the young man was trying to make." She leaned toward Grace. "You'd do well to stop being such a tease."

"I am *not* a tease!"

The woman raked Grace with a speaking glance. "That dress says otherwise."

"What's wrong with my dress?" Grace called after them. "Is it my fault I look good in red?"

She wasn't a tease. She was just hopeful. There was a difference.

She watched patrons filter out of the restaurant, stuffed and satisfied as they strolled hand in hand or arm in arm toward their cars and drove away.

After a while, the weight of the cheesecake got the best of her, and she nabbed one of the kitchen guys when he came outside for a smoke and asked for a fork.

He didn't think it was weird how much she liked the cheesecake.

She ate a few bites and let out a long, weary sigh.

She'd blown it. Again.

And the worst part was the waitress was right. Self-righteous and judgmental, but right.

Grace shivered and rubbed a hand on her arm to warm it. She ate another bite then stood and walked up and down the path for the umpteenth time. A drip of something hit her in the face. Then another.

She closed the clamshell to-go container and looked at the sky. *Seriously?*

The kitchen guy popped open the back door. "Hey, ma'am. We're closing soon. Are you all set?"

Ma'am? Could this night get any worse? She'd gone from a hot chick in a red dress to *ma'am*? "Yes. I'm fine, thank you. I expect my ride will be along any time now."

"Sure. Have a good night."

"You, too."

Another drop landed on her. Then another. Soon a fine sprinkling mist began to fall over the few remaining cars in the lot. To think it was the summer solstice, a time to celebrate the longest night of the year.

Yup. Already the longest night of the year.

At long last, a vehicle pulled in, its tires crunching over the gravel, and Grace heaved to her feet. It was about time! She hurried forward, grateful for the possibility of warmth. She'd tip extra if this Ronnie guy cranked the heat.

But it wasn't a taxi.

Or another customer.

It was a Sugar Falls police cruiser, and as it rounded the parking lot toward the entrance of the restaurant, she got a clear view of exactly who it was.

Ack! Seriously? Wasn't it bad enough to be standing alone, dumped and depressed, in a dress everyone assumed meant something she never intended to convey, clutching half-eaten cheesecake? Did her *ex* have to see her this way?

No. She'd be damned if Jefferson Ward Dayton was going to see her chowing cheesecake in the rain while wearing some red hooker dress. She glanced around frantically for a hiding place and then ducked for cover behind the dumpster.

Yes, ladies and gentlemen, she was hiding behind the dumpster.

The smell of trash hung in the misty air, assaulting her nose, and she rubbed her arms, retreating a bit further into the shadows as the SUV cruiser pulled to a gentle stop in front of the restaurant.

Great. Now he was *stopping?*

Go, she mentally encouraged him. *Nothing to see here.*

She wiggled her nose and rubbed her arms again to get the blood circulating, but her cheesecake bag rustled, so she stilled her hands.

Hurry up and leave. Please, don't get out. Just keep going...

The door to the restaurant swung open, and the mean waitress ran down the walkway, a to-go bag in hand. Jeff stepped out of his SUV, took the bag, all smiles, as he passed over some bills. Grace rolled her eyes.

She huffed out a breath then slapped a hand over her mouth.

Something rustled nearby.

And it was *not* her cheesecake bag.

Grace had that itchy feeling crawl over her skin she got every time something bad was about to happen. She turned her eyes toward the rustling sound and froze.

A small form waddled into view, its distinctive stripe like a neon alert sign flashing under the outdoor spotlight, warning those nearby like the logo on a nuclear reactor. *Warning. Alert. Death this Way.*

Grace couldn't help herself. She gasped.

The skunk stopped and turned, no doubt as horrified by Grace's presence as she was of its.

She held its beady black gaze and moved very, *very* slowly backward. Very, very quietly. As quietly and unthreateningly as she could move, while holding her breath so completely she thought she might pass out...

Then a car door slammed.

After that, it was a blur. Grace may or may not have screamed (a few times, but who was counting?) between gulps for breath, the odiferous cloud stinging her eyes as she stumbled toward the parking lot like a stunned accident victim.

"Grace?"

Jeff leaped out of his cruiser. He took two steps toward her and stopped abruptly.

"You've been sprayed," he said.

"No shit, Sherlock." She blinked, spitting the taste of skunk—who knew it had a *taste?*—ungracefully onto the parking lot.

The waitress chick came running down the front walk. "What the...? *You!*" Her accusing stare pinned Grace like a bug to a specimen board. She wrinkled her nose and threw her hands in the air. "Great. It'll be days before this clears."

"It's not my fault! Someone—" Grace flung an accusatory arm toward Jeff, her cheesecake bag flopping wildly "—slammed his car door and startled it."

"What were you doing lurking around in the dark anyway?" he asked.

"I was waiting for my cab."

His lips twitched. "Behind the dumpster?"

Waitress girl pinched her nose between her fingers. "Ronnie won't be taking you now, that's for sure."

"It's not my fault I was sprayed. It's his!" Grace jabbed a finger toward Jeff.

"Why weren't you waiting inside where it's warm and dry?" he asked.

Grace looked at the judgmental waitress. "She was mean."

Jeff turned with disbelief toward the waitress. "Angela?"

Grace turned toward the girl. Angela was a misnomer if ever there was one. There was nothing *angelic* about her. Were those *skull* earrings?

Angela smiled an evil grin and had the nerve to *laugh.* "Her boyfriend dumped her. It was pretty epic. He accused her of liking the cheesecake more than him."

Jeff turned. "Do you?"

"What?" Grace blinked madly at them. *Really?* They were talking about this *now?*

"Do you prefer their cheesecake over this guy?"

Grace felt the weight of the plastic bag in her hand. "Don't be ridiculous."

"She had us wrap it up after he dumped her," un-Angela blabbed, pointing to the plastic bag.

They all stared at the bag.

Suddenly Grace hated them. She hated the mean waitress and the unhelpful ex-boyfriend and a world where someone could get dumped and sprayed by a skunk all in the span of an evening and *no one* cared.

Grace sniffed in her misery and then instantly regretted the action. She swiped at her nose instead and turned her back on both of them, fumbling with the handles of the plastic bag, which were somehow tangled on her wrists. She stalked over to the dumpster and heaved it in. It wasn't any good *now*. The cold misty fog plastered her hair to her face, and her eyes stung, but she wasn't sure it was from the skunk spray as much as abject humiliation and soul-deep misery.

When she arrived back at the parking lot, mean waitress was gone.

Jeff stared at her. "I suppose you need a ride home now."

"Yes." She didn't want them to, but she knew her lips wobbled.

He compressed his mouth, assessing. "Don't take it personally, but I asked Angela to bring me some plastic bags. I'd rather you not sit directly on my seats."

She nodded, looking up so no tears would spill over in front of him. "I don't blame you."

Angela came down the walkway, her nose pinched between her fingers again, and handed a box of trash bags to Jeff.

He pulled a couple out and held them toward Grace. "You can change behind the dumpster while I prep the backseat."

"What?"

"Well, you can try, but I doubt Angela will let you back in the restaurant in your present state."

Angela raced back up the walkway. Grace heard the sound of a deadbolt clicking into place. She turned to Jeff.

"You expect me to ride in your cruiser wearing nothing but a plastic bag?"

"How about two plastic bags?"

Grace snatched the trash bags from his outstretched hand. At least they were waterproof.

A few minutes later, she met him at the cruiser, one bag with holes torn in the top and sides for her arms, another pulled on like a skirt. She'd decided to toss the dress in the dumpster. She hated that dress now. She might never wear red again.

"Very chic," he murmured, laughter in his voice.

"Not to be ungrateful, but I'm not ready to see the humor in any of this. Please just take me home. You probably need to get back to the station anyway."

"Nope. Shift's over. I'm on my way home myself. Just picked up dinner." He frowned. "I may put that in the trunk, though. No offense."

Grace rolled her eyes and waited as Jeff moved his precious dinner. While she'd changed, he'd spread a handful of bags over the back seat like she were nuclear waste or something. She sat, the bags squeaking under her.

He walked back to the restaurant, presumably to return the unused bags.

As the minutes ticked by, she wrapped her arms around her for warmth. Come on! What was the hold up? Wasn't this evening hellish enough? Did he need to drag it out?

Eventually, he returned, threw something into the trunk and eased into the driver's seat.

She saw his grimace in the rear-view mirror. "I promise, I'm not making fun of you, but would you mind if I crack a window or two?"

She swallowed her humiliation and shook her head, welcoming the cold, wet, fresh breeze that flowed in as he pulled onto the main road, shivers be damned. If she froze to death it would all be over.

"I just have to make one stop."

She sighed. Was it too much to ask that he take her straight home so she could shave her head, take a four-hour shower and go to bed?

He pulled into the local grocery store lot and cut the engine. "Be back in a minute," he said.

She should be grateful he was taking her home and not being too much of a jerk about it, but she couldn't quell the resentment flowing in where all her good karma was flowing out. Hadn't she forgiven him after all this time? Hadn't she forgiven herself?

She'd thought so... right up to the moment she'd seen him again after all the years he'd been away in the Army, but then there he'd been, back in Sugar Falls, standing there in this very grocery store of all places, staring at a display of apples. She'd stopped dead in her tracks, unable to breathe or think as the wave of all their shared history had washed over her, overwhelming her. She may or may not have bruised her mango as she clutched it in her hand. Damn him. Damn him for still having that *something* that called to that place inside her that only spoke in sighs.

That had been nearly two years ago. She'd successfully avoided him for two years. Why, oh why, did fate pick *tonight* to throw them together?

Grace leaned forward and hung her head in her hands, the tears welling up despite her best efforts to hold them in.

It was bad enough Zach dumped her, but this? The plastic bags chafed parts of her body that, frankly, were not used to being encased in plastic.

She raised her head when the cruiser door opened again.

"All set," he said.

Fifteen minutes later, they pulled into her driveway. She didn't bother to ask how he knew where she lived. He was a cop. She supposed that was his job.

He held open the door, and she slithered out, clutching her makeshift skirt and handbag. "Thanks for the ride."

"Hang on."

She turned, a bit alarmed by the fact that he was unbuckling his seatbelt and opening his door. "No offense, but I plan to leave these outside and go shave my head, so if you'd just go ahead and leave, that'd be great."

He had the nerve to chuckle. "I actually thought I might help."

"Thanks, but I've got this." She turned toward her door.

His car door slammed behind her. "Grace, hang on. No need to do anything crazy. I called the vet's. They told me what to do."

She stopped. "The vet's? When?"

"When I returned the trash bags to Angela. They told me what supplies to pick up. Now we just need a bucket and your garden hose."

"I fail to see how a bucket and garden hose would make this evening less of a disaster."

"I'm serious. They said it works, but it's messy and you probably want to do the initial treatment outside to keep the odor from getting in the house."

"It's barely fifty degrees out here. I'll freeze to death!"

He pulled the plastic bag of grocery items out of the front seat and dropped it on the walkway. "Okay. Your choice. Have a good night."

He made it to the driver's side again by the time she forced the words out of her mouth.

"Fine. You can help."

His lips tilted at the corner. "How gracious of you."

She shivered and looked at the bag. "That doesn't look like much tomato juice."

"Actually, it's not." He pulled out a couple of bottles of peroxide, some baking soda and some dish soap.

"That's it?"

"And some deodorizer for my cruiser."

She turned her back. "The hose is over by the garage."

"I'll need a bucket or something to mix this in," he called out.

Grace pulled open the side door to the one-car garage and found a bucket. By the time she met him again at the side of the house, he'd hooked up the hose to the faucet.

"All right. We mix it in the bucket then lather it into your hair."

Grace handed over the bucket. She clutched the neck hole of her trash bag closed while he rolled up both his sleeves and measured out the ingredients. "So I just dump this all on my head?"

"Pretty much. Just don't get it in your eyes, she said."

The mixture foamed ominously. Grace fumbled the bucket as she tried to pour with one hand and hold the trash bag tight to her neck with the other.

Jeff lifted the bucket out of her grip. "You'll dump it all over the ground if you keep this up. You hold your bag, and I'll do your hair. Just... bend backwards or something so it doesn't go in your face."

She leaned back and Jeff poured with one hand while working the vile smelling liquid through her hair with the other.

She closed her eyes, the heat of humiliation replacing the shivers of cold. He shook the remainder of what was in the bucket onto her scalp, spreading the foamy mess over her head and hair until he stepped back to pick up the hose to rinse off his hands. "There. Now we wait."

Grace kept her eyes screwed shut and straightened a bit to ease the kinks in her back. "What do you mean, wait?"

"The vet said you'd want to leave it on for a bit. She didn't say how long, but it helps neutralize the odor if you let it sit before rinsing."

"I think that's long enough." She heard his chuckle. She hated that chuckle. It sent warm tingles over her chilled skin.

"Do you want this to work or not?"

"I'd rather not freeze to death."

She heard footsteps retreating, and then the sound of the garage door opening and closing. A few moments later, he'd obviously returned, because something bumped her shoulder. She cracked one eye open. "What are you doing?"

"Wrapping you in a tarp to keep you warmer."

"Just kill me now," she whispered.

"That would be against the law," he said.

"Laws are meant to be broken."

"It's not that bad."

She opened both eyes now. "I'm dressed in trash bags and now— God help me—a *tarp*, standing outside my house at midnight, and I reek of skunk. Please tell me how it could possibly be worse."

"It could be raining harder," he said.

She sighed and held the tarp more tightly around her. "True."

She swiped at a dribble of goo seeping down the side of her face. "How long do I have to stay like this? For real?" she asked.

"Ten minutes maybe? She wasn't specific."

"This peroxide smells worse than the skunk."

"No it doesn't."

She gave him a quelling look, but the haughty expression probably didn't work particularly well seeing as she was currently sporting the latest in tarp-chic.

"I can't wait to take a hot shower."

He grunted and looked at his watch. "Seven minutes to go."

She sighed and decided if she couldn't make him go away, she'd retreat to her mental happy place. The only problem was her happy place tended to feature this man. And fewer plastic bags. She could hear him breathing, slow and steady, as if having her naked, plastic-wrapped body so close to his did nothing for him while she... She blew out a breath. "So... you get take-out from there often?"

Jeff glanced up, his dark eyes unreadable in the dim glow of her solar butterfly outdoor lights. "You're not the only one that likes their cheesecake."

She pressed her lips together. Talk of her lost cheesecake made her depressed.

"So what happened?" he asked.

"Well, I was waiting for my ride, and then you slammed your door..."

"Not the skunk. With your date."

"Oh. Him." It was probably telling that she'd already forgotten about Zach. "We broke up."

"And he left you stranded?"

"I told him he could leave."

She didn't have to see Jeff's face to know he was probably rolling his eyes.

"So what did you do?" he asked.

"What did *I* do? What makes you think it was my fault?"

One dark eyebrow rose at her.

"I didn't do anything. We just decided we weren't compatible."

"*Hmm.*"

She frowned. "There's no *hmm* about it."

"I just find it interesting that Angela had a much different take on things."

"I see. And you'll take her word for it over mine? A woman who bribed me for Zach's number just so she'd agree to call me a cab?"

"Did you give it to her?"

"Yes. They deserve each other." He snickered. "What's so funny?"

"She's married, you know."

"What?"

"She was only screwing with you. She has a funny sense of humor"

"I don't think she's funny at all. What did I ever do to deserve that?"

His body grew tense beside hers. They both knew what he was thinking. He leaned over and picked up the hose again. "Brace yourself. Time to rinse."

Even though she clutched the tarp tight around her, she could feel little rivulets of cold water sliding down her bare skin, her scalp going numb from it.

Jeff worked quickly, thank God for small miracles. Grace screwed her eyes shut and clamped her lips closed against errant drips.

"There." He shut off the sprayer. She heard it clunk on the ground behind her. "That's probably good for the first try. I'll stick around until you're done with your shower in case you need a second treatment."

And here she'd barely survived the first treatment. She swiped her face, avoiding looking directly at him as water slithered down between her shoulder blades. "Can you wait in your cruiser?"

"I'd rather not." He pressed his lips together. "I think it could stand to air out a bit longer."

She swallowed as he stared at her, all massive, solid male. Despite the cold water dribbling down from her hair, parts of her grew warm. "Fine," she said, "but avert your eyes. I'm not planning on taking these plastic bags inside with me."

One eyebrow cocked as his gaze slid down her tarp. "That's indecent exposure," he said.

"Only if I'm seen. So turn around."

He turned, eventually. Still, something about the way he was standing made her feel incredibly exposed.

She let the tarp slide to the ground. Then her makeshift skirt. Last, she pulled her arms inside of her remaining coverage. "Are you sure there's no one around? No cars coming?"

"Just us ghosts."

With one last peek to be sure he was behaving, she tore off the last trash bag, grabbed her purse, and bolted to the front door. She fumbled the keys in her cold fingers but finally managed to get the door unlocked and made a mad dash to the first floor bathroom.

She had her back to the closed door, her naked skin sticking to the wood paneling when she heard the front door close down the hall.

"I'm just going to leave the supplies outside the bathroom door in case you need them," Jeff called through the paneling.

She popped the bathroom door open. He was bending over, setting the bag on the floor. His dark eyes grinned up at her. She huddled back a bit.

"There's soda in the fridge if you want one," she said before slamming the door in his face again.

"I didn't think you drank soda."

She reached into the shower and turned on the tap to warm it up. He wasn't supposed to remember little things like that. "I don't. They were for Zach's nephews." She opened the bathroom door again and reached a hand out, groping for the plastic bag of supplies. She felt the handle loop over her wrist and shivered. She'd thought he'd gone to the kitchen.

"Can't hurt to dose yourself twice," he murmured as she shut the door again.

He was right. She still stank a little. Or it could be that the skunk smell was permanently stuck in her nose. She wrapped herself in a towel and leaned over the tub for another peroxide treatment before finally, gratefully, taking the long, hot shower she'd craved.

A half a bottle of shampoo and a generous amount of body soap later, she stepped out of the shower feeling almost normal. She dressed in the robe she had on the back of the door, wrapped a towel turban-style around her head and went in search of her rescuer.

She found him in the living room.

Jeff stood by the window, fingering the butterfly sun-catcher she had dangling there. He dropped his hand without turning around. "Better?"

She nodded, figuring if he knew she was behind him, he must have eyes in the back of his head to see her response. "Yes, considering."

She took another step closer. "Could you just, um, smell my hair?"

He did turn then, his body all stiff with surprise. "I don't think…"

"Please." She pulled the towel off with a hard yank and shook her head. "Just sniff it, okay? I want to know if I need to de-skunk it again."

He walked closer, his throat working as he swallowed. She looked away and held her breath. He leaned toward her and inhaled.

He pulled back abruptly. "Seems fine now."

"Are you sure?" She lifted a big hunk toward her own nose. "All I seem to smell is skunk."

"It'll dissipate. You're on olfactory overload."

"If you say so." She grimaced. "Thanks. For helping. I'm going to go get dressed and stuff."

He frowned and cleared his throat. She stepped back to give him a clear path to leave.

"Sure," he said. "Have a good night."

"Goodnight." She walked him to the door and only breathed freely again when he was on the other side of it.

She returned to the bathroom to dry her hair.

A few minutes later reality set in.

Suddenly the front door slammed against the wall behind it. "Grace?"

"I'm fine!" she lied through the bathroom door. Apparently she must have screamed for a second time that evening.

He didn't even bother to knock, just burst in on her. "What is it?"

"It's…" She was about to say 'nothing' but that would be a horrific lie, as horrific as the skunk streaks running amok through her hair. So, she pointed and winced, waiting for his response.

"What?"

She looked at him. "What? Do you not see? Look what your skunk remedy did to my hair!"

"What? It looks good."

"Good? I'm all streaky! I look… I look like a *skunk!*" She turned back to her reflection. "How could you do this to me?"

"Relax. I'm sure it'll grow out."

She glared at his reflection in the mirror, sure that if she looked at him directly, her gaze would burn hot holes of wrath through his skin. "It'll grow out? That's all you have to say?"

"It doesn't smell like skunk anymore, does it?" And then he did the unthinkable. He laughed.

"Oh, I brought you this." He held up a plastic bag.

"I don't need any more of your quack remedies." She sniffed. "I'm fine. Just…" And then all the anger and humiliation left her, and she simply felt hollow. "Go. Please? Just go."

"Sure," he said.

She didn't watch him leave this time, just let the tears flow silently as she turned off the bathroom light and went in search of her slippers.

She saw the plastic bag sitting on the floor just inside the door.

"I told you, I didn't need your quack remedies," she mumbled, but she frowned when she realized it wasn't a bag from the grocery store. It was a plain white one like from the restaurant. She peered inside and popped open the clamshell. A pristine piece of fresh cheesecake lay inside.

She clamped the container shut again, and was about to take the bag and put it in the fridge when a paper napkin floated to the floor.

She picked it up and couldn't stop the sob that gurgled up in her throat. Tears flooded her vision, and she slid down the wall, clutching her knees.

The bastard. How could he? How could he rub it in her face like this?

She looked at the napkin again, the two words written there making her want to lash out and curl in a ball all at the same time.

Happy Birthday.

She crumpled the napkin in her palm, hurled it at the wall and wept.

CHAPTER TWO

Grace pulled into the library parking lot the next afternoon and parked in her usual space.

The Sugar Falls Civic Pride Committee met every Wednesday to plan parades, Founder's Day and First Night celebrations and carve approximately three million jack-o-lanterns every Halloween.

As an area business owner, Grace had been invited to serve on the committee. (She would have begged off—committees weren't really her thing—except her grandmother, Ruth Pearson, was chair of the committee and had threatened to stop inviting her to her spaghetti dinners if Grace didn't 'do her part.')

Erg. And now she was late. Her shop, *Currents*, had been busy all morning with customers buying graduation gifts or dashing in to escape the on-again, off-again rain they'd had all day.

Grace grabbed her oversized tote from the passenger seat and hurried up the brick walkway of the sprawling, Victorian-era library. It had once been the private residence of one of the town's founding families and dated to a time when the old mill along the river still produced textiles instead of housing a bagel shop, condos, and small stores. When she'd been a girl, they'd built an addition out back to hold the library's growing collections so they didn't crash through the parquet floors into the basement. Grace loved the dark-paneled front parlors and upstairs ballroom with its narrow, arched windows. The old rooms gave her wonderful arm shivers, as if the people who'd passed through them were still there somehow. There were times she could almost picture her father flirting with her mother over the skinny, oak card-catalog drawers still on display near the front desk.

Some might call such musings wishful thinking on her part, piecing together what little she'd learned of her parents over the years and imagining likely scenarios from their lives, like little silent movie vignettes. Grace knew it was more than that. She could feel her mother's presence every time she passed under the Ladies' Craft Guild quilt that hung in the entrance with the lilac-appliqued square her mother had contributed.

She checked her watch as she entered the 'morning room' and made her way toward her usual spot in the corner. It had a lovely view of the gardens, and just a few weeks ago, the heady scent of lilacs had floated through the open windows.

But she didn't smell lilacs now. She wrinkled her nose.

A balsam tree air freshener lay on the table in front of her.

"Har-dee-har-har," she said, pushing the air freshener aside.

Snickers rippled around the table punctuated by a poorly muffled snort or two.

News traveled fast, apparently.

Joe Sedowsky, heir-apparent to a local medical supply business, pulled a chair out for Grace and murmured a hello. Joe had unwittingly stolen her first kiss when she was sixteen, so Grace always felt on guard around him, as if he'd lunge toward her all these years later and try for lip-lock number two.

She nodded and shifted her knee away from his hot leg under the table as she took her seat. Who wore shorts in the rain?

He leaned toward her. "You don't smell at all," he assured her.

"Um, thanks."

He grinned, his perfectly spaced, perfectly white teeth like a PR photo in an orthodontist's office. For some strange reason she found the unnatural symmetry of his smile disconcerting, like they were a Trojan horse of dentistry potentially hiding all sorts of evils. Possibly halitosis.

Meg Daniels nudged her with an elbow from her left. "*Psst.* I can fix your hair if you want to swing by the salon tomorrow," she whispered.

Grace nodded gratefully. She'd pulled her hair into a low, messy bun to make the peroxide streaks a bit less noticeable, but they were definitely more concentrated on the right side versus the left. And that didn't even address the strangely bright section just below her right ear.

Lydia Sweet, owner of a local consignment shop and one of Grams' friends, passed around a plate of cookies. Technically, she wasn't supposed to serve food in the library, but no one said anything, because she was an excellent baker and she made sure to make the chewy varieties so as to minimize crumbs.

Grams cleared her throat. "Well, let's get started. We have less than two weeks left before the Independence Day parade and several issues to iron out. Ah! And here's Officer Dayton with the agendas."

Grace's breath caught in her chest as Jeff Dayton strolled in and set a stack of papers at the head of the table.

What was *he* doing here?

She made a herculean effort to appear unfazed as she searched in her tote for something to write on. And with. Because she was a business woman at a business meeting and not a sixteen-year-old girl wearing this man's concert t-shirt.

She pulled out a pen and held it above her notepad with as much casual professionalism as she could muster.

Jeff's lips quirked at the corners.

She glanced down.

Oh, Dear Lord. *A tampon?*

Grace shoved the tampon back into the depths of her tote again, the memory of Zach calling her out on her fibs making her cheeks flush hot.

Grams carried on. "Chief Russell sent over Officer Dayton to help us rethink candy distribution at the parade in light of safety and litter concerns."

"Rethink? Does that mean he doesn't want us to distribute candy?" asked Meg.

"That's one option," Grams said.

"But we've distributed candy for years. It's a tradition," said Grace.

"I've always been a bit worried about Amy, to tell the truth," said Meg. "The little kids get carried away and forget about the parade vehicles, and sometimes the big kids grab the candy out from under them."

"And we certainly don't need the liability issue of running a kid over," said Joe.

Okay, that was… graphic.

"Why not hand it to kids directly?" asked Grace. "Would that satisfy everyone?"

Jeff accepted a cookie from Lydia, but didn't sit. Instead, he ate, one arm propped on the aged white marble fireplace mantel, looking for all the world like the lord of the manor enjoying a macaroon.

Grace grabbed a cookie from the plate on the table and took a bite, hoping no one other than Jeff had noticed her waving a tampon over her notepad. She hated how sexy-hot he looked in head-to-toe navy. Honestly, it didn't even make sense, because monochromatic dressing wasn't even sexy unless you were a UPS carrier, and even that stereotype had its exceptions. It wasn't as if she got all hot and bothered and weak in the knees when she saw Sully in his mechanics coveralls. Not even *she* could pull it off. The one day she'd tried to rock head-to-toe black, Trish had asked her who'd died.

So, it wasn't fair that Jeff should look *good*. Plus, why wasn't he sitting? Standing was so… so… overbearing. Was it some sort of power play?

Meg shrugged. "Maybe we shouldn't even distribute candy anymore given the whole childhood obesity and diabetes concerns nowadays."

"Fine, we'll distribute non-food items, like glow-sticks," said Grace.

"In the middle of the day?" Jeff scoffed. Fine, maybe it wasn't a scoff, per se. Maybe it was more of a gently spoken reminder that she was the idiot waving around tampons as if they were writing implements and no one should listen to her.

"It's probably a good idea to at least have alternatives," Joe said, "for the kids with allergies. We don't want to exclude anyone."

Thank you, Joe.

Lydia nodded. "Ooh! Brainfart! We could have people dressed as gumdrops! Wouldn't that be fun? Then the kiddies would know who to get their treats from!"

"I believe you mean 'brainstorm,' Lydia, and where would we find gumdrop costumes at this late date?" Grams asked, as if *that* were the pertinent issue.

"Plus they'd be hot," said Grace knowing if anyone would be 'volunteered' to dress as a sweltering gumdrop it'd be her.

The candy discussion lasted another ten minutes before they'd ironed out the details.

They all nodded heads in agreement.

"Officer Dayton?" asked Grams of the silent sentry in the corner. "You've been awfully quiet. I think we've all agreed to table the discussion about candy versus non-food treats, but do you think it will make the chief happy if we were to distribute the candy directly to the children this year versus tossing it?"

Jeff shook his head. "No disrespect, Mrs. Pearson, but I don't think any of you folks grasp just how many safety issues an event like this raises."

Grace sighed and bit into another cookie. She'd skipped lunch. "I don't think we need to overthink it. We've been doing the parade for years without any problems."

"Just because you've never had an issue doesn't mean you won't. You're so caught up in whether or not you give out Tootsie Rolls versus lollipops you're forgetting the real concern is you've got a whole lot of people in one area and no surveillance or real oversight. Anyone could tamper with the candy… or run their car into the crowd… or drop a pipe bomb in a knapsack outside Lucky's... How are you going to stop a terrorist when you're dressed as gumdrops?"

Grace watched as Lydia blanched, her silver bangle bracelets chiming their dismay as she covered a gasp with her palm.

Well that was harsh! Sure, Grace wasn't a fan of the gumdrop costume idea, either, but how dare he mock and frighten poor Lydia!

"This isn't Boston," Grace pointed out. "No one is going to bomb our little parade."

"She's right," Grams said, patting Lydia's arm. "The odds are next to nil that anything like that would happen here."

"There are fanatics and crazy people everywhere," Jeff said.

Everyone went silent, as if they were imagining the horrors of the world visiting their small downtown streets.

Grace set down her cookie. "Oh for Pete's sake! The whole point of this committee is to bring the town together. We can hardly do that sitting in our own homes, regardless of how safe that might be. We can take reasonable precautions without caving to Mr. Killjoy."

Jeff turned to Grams, his jaw tight. "I'll let the chief know what you decided."

Grams cleared her throat. "Thank you. Well, look at the time! I'm sure you all have places to go and things to do, so I'll see you again the Wednesday after next. Thanks for your input, Officer Dayton. Definitely points worth, uh, thinking about. Meeting adjourned!"

Well, *that* had been less than uplifting.

Grace stood and shoved the air freshener into her tote and thanked Meg again for the promise of a do-over at her salon.

Jeff lingered by the exit as the others filed out.

Grace crumpled her cookie napkin and tossed it in the trash. "I suppose I have you to thank for the hilarious air freshener joke."

He shook his head. "I'm guessing that was from your grandmother. Must have heard it from one of your relatives."

Grace sighed. Gotta love family.

"You okay today?" he asked.

"Yes. Why shouldn't I be?" His expression shuttered, and she hated how sharp that sounded. Okay, he'd been less than a cheerful presence at the meeting today, but he had gone out of his way to help the night before. And it wasn't his fault she'd been dumped and skunked on her birthday. She just had a hard time getting past how he'd been so... so... distant. It was one thing to have a past with someone, another thing entirely to realize you weren't entirely over that someone and have them treating you like they felt nothing toward you.

28

Under other circumstances she might have fooled herself into believing that the slice of cake and the birthday well wishes he'd left for her were a sign he still felt something for her. But she was under no illusions. He'd barely spoken to her over the years, had openly laughed at her unfortunate situation the night before, and now was clearly frustrated with the fact that she'd dared to question his hypervigilant tendencies.

Well, she could be mature and show him that she wouldn't stoop to taking jibes at him just because he was her ex. She'd grown. Maybe some of her inner serenity would rub off on him.

"I suppose I should thank you," she said. "What I mean is: thank you. For helping me out and for the cheesecake. That was nice of you."

He gave a curt nod. "No problem."

"I hope your cruiser doesn't smell too badly because of me."

His lips tilted a bit. "I might borrow your air freshener tree."

"Here." She sifted through her tote and held it toward him. She couldn't stand the chemical smell of the thing anyway.

His fingers brushed hers as he took it, sending a jolt of awareness up her arm.

"I'm not trying to rain on your parade," he said after a moment.

"What?"

"You all looked at me in there like I'd just outed Santa Claus."

"You might have been a little less... graphic... in making your point," she said.

"Sometimes people need to be shocked out of their complacency."

"Sometimes people need to lighten up a bit."

"It's not like Sugar Falls insulates you from what's happening in the rest of the—"

"Lydia's niece was running the day of the marathon! She's not insulated, you ass. She's traumatized!"

Jeff swiped a hand over his face. "Christ. Why didn't you say something?"

"Because we all knew." She sighed. "She wasn't badly wounded, thank God, but it was hours before we knew where she was or even if she was okay."

He exhaled, the sound heavy with regret. "I guess that's my point. No one expected that either. These days, we have to be on guard."

"I know. But we're not going to check every kid's Hello Kitty backpack."

He frowned. "I never suggested that, but—"

"Sometimes we just have to accept that life comes with risk."

He seemed about to reply, but Meg opened the door again. "Grace! I'm glad you're still here. Oh. Sorry if I'm interrupting."

"Not at all. We're done." Jeff said a curt goodbye and pushed out the door.

Meg winced. "Sorry. That looked intense."

Grace shook her head. "It's nothing. What's up?"

"I just remembered I had a cancellation right before I came here, so I can fit you in around five o'clock today if that'd work for you." Meg eyed Grace's head critically. "But be prepared. We may need to do some strategic trimming."

"It can't look any worse," Grace replied.

~ * ~

Late that afternoon, Grace settled into a chair at Meg's salon.

"It wasn't my fault," she said, having a flashback as Meg slid a black cape over her shoulders that, frankly, too closely resembled a trash bag for Grace's comfort. "Jeff Dayton slammed his car door and startled it."

Meg *mmm-hmmed* as she lifted and dropped Grace's hair and eyed it critically.

"Of course, that was after Zach and I broke up. Just the icing on the cake of my worst birthday ever."

"What?" Meg stopped lifting and peering and popped back into view. "I heard about the skunk, but not that. What happened? Didn't you wear the red dress?"

"Don't talk to me about that dress. It currently resides at the bottom of a dumpster. And, the usual happened," Grace waved her hand vaguely. "We were at different stages in the relationship, that's all. Mismatched."

"*Hmm.*" Meg said, her full lips twisting a bit. She wasn't looking at Grace's hair now.

"What?"

"I don't know. It's just… I thought you two were getting along really well. He seemed nice."

"He is nice. Was nice. He just wasn't The One."

"Oh, honey, are any of them?"

Meg went back to lifting and assessing. "I hate to tell you this, but you did some damage with that de-skunking. I can deep condition, but if we don't trim some of this out, I'm afraid the breakage will only continue. How do you feel about layers?"

"I like cake."

Meg grinned. "I promise to only take what I think is absolutely necessary. For the most part, given your natural auburn color, it looks sun-kissed, but we can do a little color correction on the side and maybe a little more blending if you have the time."

"Do it. I don't have Healing Circle until tomorrow."

"You still do that?"

"Yup. You should stop in again. That weird guy isn't coming anymore."

"I don't know what I'd do with Amy." Amy was Meg's kindergartner. Cute as a button and mischievous as all get out. "Besides, not to be critical, but don't you think you should spend less time with a group of middle-aged women and more time trying to meet men your own age?"

"What's your point?"

"You just scared off another one, and there was a long dry spell before that. Things aren't looking good for the home team."

Grace squirmed a bit in the chair. "Maybe I'm not the dating kind. My life is full. I'm good. I don't need a man to complete me."

Meg frowned and turned on the tap on the faucet to warm it up.

"I'm not talking about completion. I'm talking about companionship. Maybe if you didn't press yourself to be intimate with these guys, you'd find you enjoyed their company, and the intimacy would naturally follow."

"Okay, Dr. Ruth. I'd like my haircut now."

Meg pursed her lips. Clearly she wasn't finished. "There's always Joe Sedowsky. He's definitely got his eye on you."

Grace frowned as Meg spun her away from her reflection. "I know what you mean. Don't you think it's kind of creepy?"

"That he likes you?"

"No, the eye. Even when he's not looking, it's like he's still looking at me."

Meg laughed. "I never noticed. He's got a nice smile."

"If you go for that sort of thing." For some annoying reason, the slightly imperfect smile of a certain local cop popped into her mind. She had always liked that Jeff's teeth were even without being *too* even. Like being effortlessly hunky.

Drat. Meg wasn't talking about Jeff, was she?

"Would you listen to yourself? You've got a guy who owns his own business, volunteers for the community, has a gorgeous smile *and* likes you, and you're making up excuses not to date him."

"I own my own business. What's so special about that?"

"I give up."

Meg threw up her hands, tilted the chair back and shoved Grace under the faucet.

CHAPTER THREE

Jeff pulled into his mom's driveway, the small, neat cape looking much as it had for the last two decades. Since he'd come back to Sugar Falls, he'd tried to make a point of stopping in from time to time. He knew she'd missed him while he'd been deployed, and even when he'd been stateside, he'd only visited briefly, torn between the pull of his hometown and the desire to leave unpleasant memories in the past where they belonged.

He let the screen door slam behind him, the scents of pot roast and garlic potatoes wafting from the small kitchen in the back of the house. Oh, crap. Pot roast and potatoes? That could only mean one thing. *Dad was here.* Jeff glanced at his sister on the couch. "Hey, Mauri."

Maureen sat on the edge of the floral sofa, her slim navy skirt and matching heels indicating she'd come straight from work. "Did you know about this?" she hissed.

Jeff could only assume she referred to the damning scent of pot roast. "No. She left a message about needing help replacing the bulb in the spotlight over the garage. Promised dinner."

Maureen rolled her eyes. "Men are so gullible."

"I'm not the only one here."

"She told me she needed advice on her investments. Wanted to talk to me about reallocating her retirement savings. It seemed plausible."

It was Jeff's turn to roll his eyes.

"Hey? It's what I *do*. Not such a stretch."

Jeff folded himself into the matching stiff-backed wing chair. "Well, we're here now. So where are the lovebirds?"

"Out back. Mom was showing him where the ladder is kept." Another eye roll.

Jeff sighed and leaned his head back. "This could take a while."

He and his sister were probably the only children of divorce on the planet that dreaded seeing their parents getting along. Awkward moments of catching their parents canoodling in corners inevitably led to tense fighting, tears, stormy departures and the uncomfortable and protracted conversations about 'what went wrong this time.' Hint: the same things as last time. You're not a match. You're too different. There was a reason you broke up before I was even born. He's a leather-jacket-wearing, rock-and-roll-playing product of Irish and Italian immigrants from South Boston and you're a floral-couch owning Special Ed teacher whose ancestors rode the Mayflower.

"I hate it when Mom giggles," Maureen whispered.

"She's happy," Jeff said, knowing exactly what she meant.

Maureen sighed and pulled her cell phone out of her briefcase. "For now. It never lasts."

They sat in silence as the back door slammed shut. Muffled giggles and low murmurs floated in from the other room.

Maureen winced and glanced over at him. "If they start having sex on the kitchen table, you're hosting Thanksgiving this year."

"As long as you call a caterer, I'm all in."

"Deal."

Their mom poked her head around the kitchen door. "Oh, Jeff! You're here! Dinner is ready. Can you kids set the table?"

Mauri sighed as their mom slipped back into the kitchen. She slid her phone back into her briefcase. "Kids?" she muttered. "I bring back multi-million dollar businesses from the brink of ruin and she's still calling us kids?"

Jeff unfolded himself from the uncomfortable chair and stood. "Relax. It's a term of endearment. Everybody knows you're a big shot."

"A big shot with big plans."

"Buying another company?"

Mauri hid a grin. "Bigger than that."

"Dinner will be cold by the time you kids get in here." Their mom now stood in the dining room doorway, the picture of grinning domesticity. She had the warm demeanor, bright eyes and cheery dimples one associated with people who had more than their fair share of optimism or a less than recommended grip on reality. Jeff and Maureen stepped into the room. Their father stood by the opposite wall under a family portrait of Jeff, Mauri and their mom as if he could insert himself into the photo twenty years after the fact.

Achoo! "Surprise!" their mom said, yanking a tissue out of a crocheted tissue box holder on the side table. "You're father has come for dinner, and—*Achoo!*—he has *news!*" She blew her nose and stuffed the tissue into the pocket of an apron emblazoned with red kissy lips and the cringe-worthy words 'make me late for dinner.'

"Oh, God help us," Mauri muttered as she slid into her seat. Jeff grabbed a stack of plates from the cabinet and handed them to his sister. He turned back for utensils and napkins.

"We'll be using cloth napkins tonight, Jeff," their mother chirped as she dove for another tissue. "Special occasion! I'll go get the roast. Oh, if anyone sees my bottle of antihistamine, let me know. My allergies are going haywire with all this damp weather."

Jeff set a light green napkin and a fistful of utensils at each place setting and nodded to their father. "Rodger," he said.

"Jeff, you're looking good. Maureen." Their father nodded awkwardly and grimaced.

Peggy Dayton returned from the kitchen, a large pot cradled in her mitted hands. "Oh, Rodger, have a seat, for heaven's sake."

Maureen pushed back her chair. "I'm getting some white wine. Can I get anyone anything?"

"We're having beef," their mom said. "You should really drink red with that."

"I didn't realize this family worried about appearances."

Their mother sighed and gave Jeff a pained expression. "Must you be so unyielding, Maureen? I'm trying to help this family move forward." She wiggled her nose and sniffed.

"You know they say the definition of stupidity is trying the same thing and expecting a different outcome."

"Maureen!"

"Your mom doesn't deserve that attitude," Rodger said.

"I'm thirty years old. I don't need you to coach me on my attitude."

"I'm still your father."

Maureen stood by her chair, her eyes darting between her parents before shaking her head in defeat. "I wish I were an orphan," she muttered, then she disappeared into the kitchen.

Their mom swung toward Jeff. "What's that all about?"

"Maybe she's worried because we've seen this all before. Pot roast is the beginning of the end. Dad comes back to town like the prodigal son, you whip up pot roast and potatoes, everything is hunky-dory for a few weeks, and then it devolves again in a sea of tears until he disappears again."

"Is that what you think happens?" she said.

"In a word: yes."

She shook her head with disappointment. "We're all adults here. It seems to me we can have one meal together without it becoming a *thing*." She huffed and cast an apologetic glance at her ex-husband. "I'm sorry. Being outside has triggered my allergies. I'm going to see if I can find that antihistamine."

Maureen pushed back into the room, a clear beer stein filled with white wine in her hand.

Jeff raised an eyebrow. "I certainly hope you're not driving home after this."

Maureen leveled her eyes at him as she drank then set the mug on the table with a *thunk*. "Scott's picking me up. We have some social media strategy to review."

"Nice to know you'll be coming at it in the same frame of mind as most of your readers."

"Back off, Jeff. I may be your baby sister, but I'm not a baby. You celebrate family reunions in your own way. I'll celebrate them in mine."

Peggy returned and stood by her chair, popping a pill and swallowing. Rodger leaned toward her.

"I can go, Peggy," he murmured, his hand on the small of her back. Jeff stared at the contact, willing his father to step away before anyone got hurt. Mom was too gullible, too trusting. Too damned optimistic that history wouldn't repeat itself.

"Maybe that's best," Jeff prompted.

"No." His mother's lips compressed into a stubborn line. "You won't drive him away again, and you won't drive a wedge between us. I've planned a lovely dinner, and by God you are all going to sit here and enjoy it!"

She sat down in her chair as if shocked by her own outburst and laid her napkin across her lap with shaking fingers. *Achoo!*

"You've upset Mom," Mauri said, glaring at their dad across the table.

"No," their mom said, angrily fishing for another tissue in her pocket, "*you've* upset me. Both of you. I invited you here tonight, because your father has some exciting news he wanted to share. I thought for once we might try to simply be happy for one another. Is that so much to ask?"

Jeff folded himself into his chair and glared at Mauri until she did the same. "No," they said in near unison.

"Rodger, please serve the pot roast."

His father nodded and doled out the food, handing it around. Jeff took it wordlessly and ate in silence.

"This is delicious, Peggy," Rodger finally said.

"Thank you, Rodger."

Jeff set his fork down to take a drink. "So, what's your news?"

Rodger swallowed his bite and took a swig of water. "Well, you all probably heard that Bobby Andrews had a stroke last year."

Maureen shrugged and shook her head. Jeff nodded. His mom's eyes grew glossy.

"Anyway, he's out of rehab now, and, well, we're going back on the road. We're calling it the 'Live Free or Die Trying' Tour."

Maureen's mug hit the table with another *thunk.* "What?"

"A tour!" their mother repeated like a groupie who'd just heard her favorite band was getting back together. "Throughout New England and then up and down the East Coast! They'll even be playing Atlantic City!"

Maureen shoved her chair back and lurched to her feet. "I've heard enough. Thanks for dinner, Mom. Delicious. Warn me the next time you plan to yank the rug out from under me, will you?"

"What? I thought you'd be excited for... *Maureen!*"

Rodger put a hand on Peggy's wrist to hold her in her chair as the front door slammed. For some reason seeing Rodger touch his mother made Jeff want to haul off and slug the guy. That would probably be frowned upon, and then he'd only be burdening his coworkers with more paperwork, so he shoved his own chair back and went in search of his sister.

Maureen stood on the front porch, furiously texting.

Jeff let the door slam behind him. She didn't even flinch.

"You want to explain what that was all about?" he asked.

Maureen pressed 'send' and let her hand drop to her side. "I can't believe he'd do this to me now."

"By 'this' I assume you mean more than accept a dinner invitation from Mom?"

Maureen brushed her chin-length bob behind her ear and swallowed hard. "I told Scott we were in a good place. I *assured* him I was 110% focused on the future, and now *this* explodes in my face." She glanced at the porch ceiling as if she were fighting tears. "I cannot believe that stupid band is getting back together."

"*That's* what you're upset about?"

Mauri turned to glare at him. "This is not me acting out because I'm embarrassed about dad's shenanigans. I'm not a petulant child no matter what you all seem to think. People depend on me. My staff. My constituents. I have a political career to think about."

"You won your senate seat, Maureen. You're in. Relax. Dad's band isn't going to negate all the work you've done there."

"Relax? This is what you have to say to me? You don't understand. The senate seat is just a first step. Scott says I have what it takes to take it further. He thinks—no, *I* think—it's time I threw my hat in the ring. I plan on running for governor."

"Seriously? That's fantastic! You'll be a shoe-in."

"Not if *The Jolly Rodgers* get back together. Dad has threatened for years to get back in touch with the old bandmates, and thank God he hasn't. Why *now?* I mean, Atlantic City, Jeff! The gambling capital of the East Coast! Seriously? The 'Life Free or Die Trying' Tour? What kind of a message is this sending about our family? About our politics? How can he do this to me?"

"My guess is he doesn't even know you're thinking of running for governor."

"How could he not?" she cried, throwing her hands up into the air. "Why would I have spent the last decade of my life working to grow my consulting business and political connections and running charity races for wounded veterans and cancer survivors if I *didn't* plan on parlaying that into a political career? This couldn't happen at a worse time. I'm already at a disadvantage because I've put my career first before starting a family. And now, this is all I've got."

"That wasn't your choice."

"Yeah, well, I can only ride the sympathy wave of losing Christopher for so long. At some point the voters expect me to move on."

"You don't get over your first love that easily. That PR guy of yours seemed to think it worked in your favor to have a fiancé killed by a drunk driver last time you ran for office."

Tears pooled in Mauri's eyes before she blinked them away. "Yeah, well, it turns out I'm only allowed to mourn for so long. After a certain point, even though it wouldn't do for me to go on dating sites, it also doesn't skew well for the conservative voters that I'm still single. I'm in a Catch-22. I *need* my family to be, for lack of a better word, *normal.*"

"Good luck with that."

"That's not helpful."

"What do you want me to do? I came back to New Hampshire and passed up that job in California. I did everything you and your PR guy asked of me. I covered my tattoos, stopped going to Lucky's so much. I became a model citizen. Hell, I became a *cop* for that guy..."

"His name is Scott."

"All I'm saying is, I played the part. Hell I'm still *here* because of you, so don't act as if nobody cares."

Mauri's face softened, the gratitude clear. "And I can't tell you how grateful I was—*am*—that you came home. It gave me the courage to keep moving forward when Chris..." her voice caught, and Jeff found himself folding her into his arms.

"I know," he said. He hadn't planned on leaving the Army. What had once been merely a stepping stone had become the destination. But then Christopher had died, and his baby sister had asked him not to re-up. So he'd come home.

He'd intended to spend a couple of months visiting in Sugar Falls before heading to the job a buddy had lined up for him, but when he'd seen Mauri again, seen how hard loss had been on her, he'd hesitated. She was thinner than she'd ever been, and when she spoke of the future, she twisted her engagement ring round and round her finger as if she didn't know whether to keep it on or take it off.

She said she wanted to run for the state senate—even hired a PR guy that would 'sell' her to the voters. Could Jeff help?

So he'd cheered for his baby sister, distributed flyers, taken a job at Sugar Falls PD and done most everything that little suit-wearing PR guy had suggested. And, hell, if he were completely honest, after having his every move—right down to what he ate—decided for him for so many years, leaving the Army had felt like an unmooring. A part of him was grateful for the familiarity of family and somebody else calling the shots for a while.

Mauri pushed back to look at his face. "I don't like being needy. I didn't want to ask you to stay, but I'm glad you did. I'm sorry they didn't hold that job for you."

Jeff shrugged. "You snooze you lose. There'll be other opportunities. In the meantime, I've got a paycheck. I'm all right."

"And I'm not asking you to give that up. I'm not asking for you to sacrifice the next opportunity for me, either. I'm stronger now. I just need to know you and Mom will help represent this family in a positive light until I can get a foot in the door, until the voters can learn who I am without associating me with Dad and *The Jolly Rodgers*. You and Mom—you're like made to order perfect for my image. A lifelong school teacher of special needs kids? The hometown hero turned police officer with an honorable discharge from the military? It doesn't get any better than that. But Dad... Ugh. Are we absolutely sure he's our real father?"

"We're the spitting image of him."

Maureen let out a heartfelt sigh. "Damn his dark Irish/Italian genes. At least I can thank him for good hair." She pulled away and glanced at her phone then back at him. "Chris and I were going to do this together, you know. We were going to be that political power couple. Now that I'm on my own, I need you. I don't want to, but I do. You've always had my back. I just need to know you still do."

"I don't know what more you want from me, kiddo."

"I want you to keep Dad off the radar for a while longer. Convince him the band hasn't played in years and why start again *now*? I can't worry about him *and* the campaign. Give me another six or nine months to campaign before he comes back on the scene."

"I don't know if I have that kind of influence."

"Can you please at least try?"

"Sure," he said.

She grinned, the smile transforming her features. "You always were my hero," she said.

He grunted. "You should look for a different kind of hero. I can't save everyone."

CHAPTER FOUR

On Friday night, Grace pulled into her cousin's gravel drive and cut the engine. She climbed out of the hot car, grabbed her laundry bag and shut the door with a clunk. A few bits of rust chipped away from the bottom edge of the door like dull confetti, sifting onto her bare toes. She wiggled her flip-flop to shake it off and looked out over the quiet waters of Whisper Lake. To think that less than a week ago she'd been struggling to stay warm as Jeff hosed her down in her side yard and tonight she thought she'd melt from humidity. Welcome to New Hampshire in June.

She hitched the bag over her shoulder and looked at the small, oddly sprawling cape with the mismatched dormers and sloping porch. Rachel and Doug lived here now, but this had all once been hers, too, as much as Rachel's, all the cousins crowding onto the small dock on hot summer days while Grams mixed up powdered lemonade in the tiny kitchen. Now the cousins were all getting married and having babies and Grace lived in daily fear that she was one rescue cat away from becoming the stereotypical crazy cat lady.

She glanced down toward the empty, weathered dock as it jutted out over the water. Her t-shirt clung to her with sweat and she half wished she'd thought to bring her swimsuit. Maybe she and Ella would come out and dip their toes in the water before ordering pizza. No doubt, despite the warm air temps, the lake water would still be too cool for swimming.

A warm breeze swept over the lake, lifting her hair, the new cut sending wispy strands floating around her face. She smacked her flying hair down and tried not to be envious of her cousins and siblings as she walked toward the low-slung porch of the cottage Rachel now called home. After all, it only made sense that Grams would offer the small cape to Rachel and Doug now that they'd moved back to Sugar Falls.

Grace eyed the neighboring house through the lilac bushes, the one that used to be her other cousin, Jim's. He was married to Kate now with a houseful of kids and had, in an ironic twist, moved into the home on Blackberry Hill her brother, Ian, had built for himself before deciding he wanted something smaller.

So in the game of house-swapping roulette her family had begun to play, her brother Carter and wife, Liz, had moved into Jim's old place next door.

Grace thought about the half-house across town she'd been renting since she'd moved out of Joan and Pops, which seemed to fit her half-life as a half-woman. Funny how being the youngest growing up she'd always felt the center of attention. She knew they didn't mean to exclude her now, but the very fact that everyone seemed to be getting married and starting families made her feel like she'd been drifting further and further away from shore, like a raft no one had bothered to pull high enough onto the beach.

It used to be she and Ian at least had the quirky single status thing going on until he'd gone and fallen in love. Now he was engaged and rehabbing the big old barn outside of town, and Grace was the lonely holdout, the one everyone tried to throw the bouquet toward at weddings. As if the pity hurling through the air at her wasn't enough, she had to pretend she *wanted* to get married and have kids. But the truth was, there was only one guy she'd ever thought about marrying, and the prospect of kids terrified her.

Sure she *liked* kids, it was the having them that made her want to turn tail and run. And ever since Kate had had Lily and then the twins, it seemed all anyone wanted to talk about was babies and how they ravaged ones' body. As if this were somehow a selling point.

Grace inhaled again, the scents of early summer heavy in the air. The only heavy thing in the air lately at her place was the scent of an overworked septic system down the road.

She thought about her rental across town, the one with no laundry facilities, and suddenly she felt too old to be hauling her dirty laundry around town in a sack.

Rachel met her at the door, one earring dangling from her fingers as she wiggled her feet into heels. "Thanks for coming over on such short notice. Ella's in her room gathering friends for your TV party, there's pizza money on the counter, and the movie is all cued up."

"No problem. Ella and I always have a good time." Grace pulled her laundry bag into the entry and nudged it to the side like the elephant in the room they all pretended didn't exist, as if it were Grace's love life trailing around behind her. Smelly and pathetic.

"Oh! You probably want to run down and start that," Rachel said, eyeing the sack and hopping into her other heel. She lurched toward the stairs. "Ella! Gracie is here! Doug, we'll be late!"

"Coming!"

Rachel's husband, Doug, pounded down the steps, looping his tie around his neck as he said a passing hello to Grace. He threw open the coat closet. "Rach! Where are my dress shoes?"

"In the bedroom."

He turned around toward the stairs again, stopping at the entry. "Did she leave you pizza money? She was going to leave you money."

"Yes. It's fine. We'll be fine."

He pounded back up the stairs as Rachel pushed a wrinkled piece of paper and tiny floppy stuffed cat into Grace's hands. "Here's the number where we'll be, my cell number, Doug's cell, the number for poison control and the red button on the phone is pre-programmed for 9-1-1."

Okay, that seemed a bit excessive, but for how long it took Rachel and Doug to conceive Ella, it was understandable they'd be a bit helicopter-y.

Rachel kept talking. "I've cut up some mango for dessert, but if you need to bribe her, there are popsicles in the basement freezer. Make her sit in her high chair if she eats one though, because she makes a mess. Oh, and don't lose Boo. Whatever you do. She won't sleep without him these days."

Grace nodded and stepped out of the way as Doug rushed back down the stairs. "We've got to go, Rach, or we'll be late."

Rachel grabbed a shoulder scarf and her purse off a hook by the door. "Doug's boss is having some big-wig meeting tonight about some changes—"

"*Rachel*. Later, please."

Rachel stopped at the door. "Did you tell Ella we were leaving?"

Grace called up the stairs. "Ella, your mommy and daddy are going for a boring drive in the car. You want to watch a movie?"

Ella's bright little face appeared at the top of the stairs. "'Kay! Bu-bye!" She waved cheerily as she started tossing little stuffed animals down the stairs.

Doug waved and pulled his wife out the door.

Grace bent over to collect an armload of animals. "Who are all these critters?"

"Fwens!"

"Friends, huh? Okay. Are there many more?"

Ella ran off and then back again with another armload. She tossed them and then made her way carefully down the stairs on her bottom.

"Doesn't that hurt?" Grace said.

Ella grabbed a pink horse off the bottom step. "No."

They brought their friends to the sofa and arranged them carefully so everyone could see the television. Grace watched as Ella grabbed Boo and swung him around by his tail. "Boo fwy!" Ella laughed. She let go and the little cat flumped onto the coffee table and tumbled to the floor. Grace picked up the stuffy and pet its little fabric head. "Aw. You want to be gentle with animals, sweetie. Cat's don't like to fly."

Ella snatched her lovey back. "Boo wike it." She swung the stuffed cat once more. It landed on the laundry bag.

"Okay, hon. I'm going to start my laundry and then we'll order the pizza for dinner. Sound like a plan?"

Ella nodded and picked up the phone and held it toward Grace.

"Oh, not yet, sweetie. Soon."

Grace hefted her laundry bag and hauled it down the basement steps to the washer and dryer. She ducked under the low ceiling toward the far corner where the washer sat wedged against the wall of the old root cellar. The space felt creepy and claustrophobic, but it beat making small talk with the weird guy doing an entire load of underwear at the laundromat. She pulled open the washer's pedestal drawer for laundry soap, pushed it closed and began loading the drum.

Ella wiggled down the basement steps behind her, Boo swinging from his tail in one hand, the phone gripped in her other.

Grace shut the washer and turned. "Ella, sweetie, don't swing Boo like that. He doesn't like it."

"Boo fwy!" Boo swung into the air again and Grace caught him in her hand.

She grabbed Boo's tail and swung him to demonstrate. "Boo gets dizzy when he swings like this. So—"

"Boo!"

Grace watched in horror as Boo's body detached from his skinny tail. He sailed over the washer and into the dark space behind it. Grace glanced at the scrap of tail still in her hand and quickly shoved it into her shorts pocket.

"Boo!" Ella cried again.

"See?" Grace said. "This is what happens when Boo flies. He gets into trouble. Don't worry. I'll get him back." Grace hefted herself onto the washer and peered into the dark space behind it.

Yup. There was Boo, flopped on his side, his little glassy eyes accusing Grace of unspeakable abuse. "I'm sorry. I'll get you soon," she muttered.

She pushed herself off the washer again and looked around for a step stool. "I see him, don't worry. I just need to find something to boost me up so I can reach."

She spied a plastic bucket with some gardening tools. Emptying the tools out, she set the bucket upside down. She stepped up and reached down behind the washer with her right hand and swept with her fingers. Missed. Hitching herself up a little further, she stretched her arm out again. "Almost there!" she called out. "Almost. *Oh!*"

The bucket kicked out from under her toes, unbalancing her. Her knuckles scraped on the foundation wall as she caught herself. Something tickled her bare leg. She shrieked and jerked away, falling forward onto her right palm.

"Ella! Don't touch me! You scared the crap out of me!"

Great. Now she was doing a one-armed handstand behind the washer. And, okay, maybe saying 'crap' wasn't the smartest thing to say to a two-year-old who'd been soaking up new words like a sponge lately, but Grace wasn't fond of heebie-jeebie critters, and Ella's little fingers had felt like a hairy spider if ever there was one. At least it brought her within reach of Boo.

Grasping the toy with her left hand, Grace pushed off with her right.

Nothing happened.

She pushed again, trying to lurch herself back onto the top of the washer. She smacked her head against the foundation stones instead.

A curse word may or may not have slipped through her lips.

"Ella, honey?" Grace whispered. "Are you there?"

A tiny feather-touch tickled her ankle again. Grace couldn't help it. She lurched.

A curse word definitely slipped through her lips that time. It wasn't 'crap.'

"A simple yes or no would have sufficed," she grunted.

Okay, *think.* Grace tried not to panic as the blood rushed to her head in the narrow, dark, claustrophobic space. She was stuck, there was no denying it. Stuck in a creepy spot, upside down, behind the washer while a two-year-old ran amok. Not good. This was *not good.*

If she turned her head just so, she could just make out a sliver of toddler peering back at her through the crack between the washer and dryer. "It's okay, sweetie, I just need a little help boosting myself here..."

"Help?" Ella asked.

Grace nodded. She smacked her head on the wall. *Ow.*

"Yes, honey. I'll be out in a jiffy." The blood pounded in her ears. Maybe if she worked her way toward the dryer...

Grace turned her head toward the crack between the appliances again to check on the toddler. Ella was fine. She—

"Ella, no! Not the red button!"

"Nine-one-one Sugar Falls Emergency Dispatch. What's your emergency?"

~ * ~

Jeff stepped out of his cruiser, surprised he was the first on the scene. He had assumed Rachel's cousin, Carter, would have responded already, seeing as he lived next door. Must not be home.

Jeff rapped on the front door a couple of times and then opened it. "Sugar Falls Police!"

A little wide-eyed face stared up at him.

"Hey there," he said, crouching down. "I'm Jeff. I'm here to help. Can you show me where the basement is?"

The little girl nodded and walked down the hall, pointing to an open doorway. "Thanks, sweetie. You're doing a good job. Can you hold this for me?" He pulled out his whistle and handed it to the girl. "Just stay *right here* and hold that for me until I come back, okay? Don't move."

She nodded again, and he ducked down the narrow steps hoping the old, 'hold my stuff' ploy would keep the tot occupied until he could get her mom freed.

Rounding the corner at the base of the stairs, he paused as he came face to, er, bottom with a pair of candy-red shorts and long legs.

"Officer Dayton from Sugar Falls PD," he called out. "Just hang tight, and I'll have you out in a minute."

The legs wiggled, so did the bottom. "Jeff?"

Jeff stepped closer. He knew that voice. "Grace?"

"Yes," came the muffled reply.

"Where are Rachel and Doug?"

"Dinner."

"I see. And you are…?"

"Babysitting." She shifted again. "Could you stop laughing at my expense and get me out of here? The blood is rushing to my head and my stomach hurts."

"I'm not laughing," he insisted, grateful she couldn't see his face right at that moment. "I'm assessing."

"Well assess quickly. This isn't comfortable."

"All right. I'm going to try to lift you up. Can you find something to push off of to give you some resistance?"

"I think so, but can you grab Boo first?"

His eyes landed on her rear. "Um, what's a boo?"

She wriggled and grunted and then a dusty little cat face appeared near her right armpit. He grabbed it and a delighted shriek rose up behind him.

"Boo!"

The little girl snatched the toy out of his hand and grinned, then shrieked again. "Boo! Boo hav boo-boo!"

"He's all right!" Grace yelled from behind the washer. "I can fix him!"

"She says she can fix him," Jeff repeated helpfully.

"Could we get me out now?" Grace grunted from behind the washer.

"Sure." Jeff stepped toward Grace's legs. "Just, ah, stop kicking."

Her legs stilled. He sucked in a breath and reached forward to wrap his hands around her waist as professionally as he could given the circumstances.

Her skin felt smooth and soft beneath his fingers where her shirt had ridden up, and he hated himself for noticing. But, damn, it was impossible *not* to notice. Impossible not to remember how other parts of this woman felt in his hands even after all these years. He told himself he was only adjusting his grip as his fingers spread wider but other parts of his anatomy knew better. He was touching. Definitely touching. He should write himself up for this. It might even be worth the paperwork.

He closed his eyes and took a calming breath. It wouldn't do to rescue her only to get slapped with a harassment charge. He needed to cool it.

"On the count of three. One, two..."

"Rachel?"

Heavy footsteps pounded down the basement stairs. Grace's muscles stiffened under Jeff's palms and her body curled away as if she were *trying* to disappear behind a major appliance. "Who's that?" she whispered.

Jeff turned to see Grace's brother bounding down the stairs. "Carter," he replied.

"I can't let him see me like this. Get me out of here quick!"

"Three!" Jeff pulled up as Grace convulsed her way out and onto the washer like a giant fish on the deck of a ship. She pushed her cobweb-tangled hair out of her eyes and grabbed Jeff's shoulders like a human shield. Carter whipped out his cell phone.

"Don't you dare," she squeaked.

A light flashed. Carter shrugged. "Oops. Reflex. Won't happen again. Sorry I wasn't here to help."

Grace smacked Jeff on the shoulder. "Why is he even here?"

"It went out on the scanner. He must have recognized the address. And no assaulting an officer."

Grace pushed herself off the top of the washer and stumbled as she landed on the floor. Jeff reached out to steady her.

"I got it," she insisted, batting his hand away. "I got it."

The little girl ran toward Carter. "She bwoke Boo! She bwoke Boo!"

Carter scooped up his niece who proceeded to cry wrenchingly into his shoulder and shoot accusatory glances at Grace.

Grace pulled something out of her pocket. "Don't cry, Ella. Look! I have his tail right here. I'll fix him."

Ella cried harder after seeing the tail, blubbering about 'mean Gracie' until Carter stepped forward and took the tail then assured the tot he'd protect them both. He carried her upstairs, leaving Grace and Jeff alone.

Grace sighed and swiped her hands on her shorts. Her arm had a long red scrape along one side, her shirt was askew, and she had a large cobweb tangled in her hair.

Jeff reached without thinking toward her hair. She stepped away abruptly.

"What are you doing?"

"You have something in your hair," he said, reaching forward again, but instead of holding still, she paled, shrieked, and hurled herself back atop the washer.

"What the—? It's only a spider web."

Grace flicked at the web. "Not that," she said. "*That!*" She pointed behind him as something slithered behind a bucket.

"That?" He craned closer to the bucket for a better look. "Would you look at that? It's just a little snake. Harmless. Just hop down and go upstairs."

"I can't," she whispered.

He turned around. She was crouched atop the washer, arms hugging her knees.

"Don't be ridiculous. It can't hurt you. It's more afraid of you than you are of it."

"I highly doubt that."

"What? Are you going to spend the rest of your life sitting on this washer?"

"Maybe."

He let out a breath. "Do you need me to carry you up the stairs now?"

She pursed her lips together. Swallowed. "Don't be snarky. Phobias are real things. Just like—*aargh!*" She shrieked again and leaped, flinging herself at him. She landed across his chest, her fingers digging into his shoulders.

"You could have warned me," he grunted, grappling with a maniacal woman.

"There's another!" she yelled, as if her mouth wasn't mere inches from his ear.

"It's probably the same one." He kicked the bucket to show her.

Baby snakes darted in three different directions.

Another shriek pierced his eardrum.

"Would you relax? I'm the one standing in the snake pit," he said.

"Not funny," she gasped, her arms now clinging to his head and threatening to separate it from his body. "How many are there?"

"I don't know. Three?"

"Three?" And then she crawled up his chest, over his shoulders and lunged for the washer-top again.

"Cool it. They're just little ones. We probably disturbed a nest."

"A nest?"

"Everything okay down there?" Carter's voice carried down the stairwell.

"Just a few garter snakes," Jeff said.

Carter's laughter could be heard. "Nice knowing you, Grace!"

"Very funny!" she shouted back.

Jeff glanced back at her. Her eyes were wide, her body shaking. He actually felt badly for her.

He grabbed a pillowcase from the top of the dryer. "Relax. I'll try and collect them. All right?"

She huddled. "That would be really, really appreciated."

He stepped closer to the corner they'd come from. *Ah.* A small drainage hole. He pulled a cement block in front of the hole. That ought to keep any more from coming in. A dark slither moved in his peripheral vision. He lunged and made contact. He grabbed the snake and tossed it in the bag. "One down."

"Good." Grace pointed. "There's another!"

Miraculously, he caught the second one, albeit with a scrape of his knuckles on the concrete floor.

Grace shrieked and pointed to a third.

Jeff whirled and reflexively stomped toward the snake with his boot.

She shrieked again. "Be careful!"

He looked over his shoulder. "It won't bite me," he said, stomping madly. Dang. These suckers were quick!

"You might hurt it!"

He stopped and turned as the snake slithered around the bucket again. "Huh?"

"I said be careful you don't hurt it."

"This from a woman planning to live out her days from the top of a washing machine?"

"I want it gone, not *dead.*"

He looked at the pillowcase in his fist. "What did you think I was going to do with these?"

"Release them outside?"

"Seriously?"

"Seriously." She visibly paled. "You weren't?"

"Well I wasn't going to keep them as pets."

"I can't be a part of this, she said.

"I'm sorry for misinterpreting the long-term plan for these guys. I wasn't the one jumping around and shrieking in the 'death to all snakes' dance."

"I'm in my bare feet!" She slid off the washer, clearly not doing the math that there was still one snake at-large. "Just because I don't want it near me doesn't mean I want it *dead.*"

"I give up. Your priorities always were screwy." He headed for the stairs.

"What's that supposed to mean?"

"Never mind."

You'd think after all the intervening years they could look at each other and shrug and move on. But old wounds were slow to heal. It bugged him that she was more worried about a stupid snake than him. He'd returned from his first tour of duty, desperately needing the familiarity of Sugar Falls—and her—yet she'd refused to even return his calls.

Yeah. She might look smokin' hot in those red Daisy Dukes, but he wasn't enough of a masochist to want anything to do with Grace McIntyre. She was hot, but fire burned. And he'd been burned by her before.

He kept walking, ignoring Grace's sharp intake of breath. She lunged for the bottom step and dashed up the stairs ahead of him. Jeff followed more sedately with the pillowcase.

Carter set down the purple unicorn he'd been dancing with. "Everything okay down there?"

"No offense, but your sister's a piece of work."

"He almost killed one of them," Grace said from behind him.

Carter sighed. "You didn't realize Grace is from the catch-and-release camp?"

Jeff stepped aside to let Grace go by. "I never would have guessed that about her."

Grace pushed past him, a wounded look on her face. She eyed the wiggling pillowcase warily.

Carter grinned at his sister. "Did you thank the nice policeman for saving you?"

Grace glanced up at Jeff. "Thanks."

"If only I'd gotten here sooner," Carter sighed. "That definitely would have made the Christmas card this year."

Grace paled. "Show's over. Go home," she said. "I have Boo's boo-boo to mend."

Carter ruffled Ella's hair as he headed for the door. "All right. Just don't go hurling yourself over any more appliances. Next time, I might take video."

"Har-dee-har-har."

The door clicked shut. Grace turned to Jeff. "I know you guys like to joke about this stuff, but please don't make this one of those hilarious police reports we read in the paper."

"That's more Dee's specialty."

"Thanks. I don't want my butt the topic of conversation."

He had no reply that wouldn't land him in hot water with the chief, so he stayed silent.

Grace reached up to brush the hair out of her face. Her hand shook. "Well, thank you for getting me out of my pickle. Again."

"It's my job," he said. She didn't have a right to look hurt, but she did. He didn't want to feel sorry for her, but he did. She'd always been one to wear her heart on her sleeve. He'd learned long ago doing so made it an easy target.

"I wish…" Her words trailed off. He watched her throat work as she swallowed. Her large eyes looked up at him. "I wish things weren't so awkward between us."

"We're exes for a reason," he said.

She nodded and glanced away. "Right. I'll try not to do anything else that requires rescuing."

"That's probably for the best." He reached for the door.

"I'm sorry," she said.

He stopped, his back to her, not entirely sure what she was sorry about. There were so many things, really.

"For overreacting. I just hate… feeling responsible for things dying."

He looked over his shoulder at her, her hazel eyes luminescent and sad, and any thoughts about how beautiful she looked standing there in her bare feet with her hair all lush and tousled were overshadowed by her words.

"I can't imagine why," he finally said.

~ * ~

Grace watched from behind the curtain as Jeff walked to his cruiser and pulled out of the drive.

He hadn't looked back. He hadn't said anything else, and she was glad of it, because his words had cut her like no knife ever could.

To think that after all these years, she still somehow imagined that he'd understand how wrong he was about her. She'd done them both a favor by putting on the brakes when they were too young to make commitments before either of them really knew themselves, much less each other.

To think she'd believed he was The One.

Time had proven otherwise, hadn't it?

Two hours later, after pizza, a Wiggles movie marathon and a quickie mending job on Boo, Ella lay sprawled on the sofa, her little arm dangling off the side. Grace tucked Boo under the blanket she'd wrapped around her niece and pushed the coffee table over so Ella wouldn't accidentally roll off. She glanced at the clock. Rachel and Doug would probably be out another hour, at least. She'd have Doug grab her clothes, and she'd just hang them to dry.

Grace went to the kitchen to start the kettle for tea. Her side still ached from her nose-dive behind the washing machine, and she didn't think she'd ever recover from the humiliation of being face-planted behind a major appliance.

Her cell beeped with a text. She fished it out of her pocket.

Dee: Heard u were practicing ur dumpster diving techniques again. Need photo evidence!

Grace: I'm suing the SF police for breach of privacy.

Dee: No such thing. I'm off duty anyway. Wanna hang?

Grace: Can't. Babysitting. :(

Two seconds later, her phone rang.

"Babysitting who? Not that kid who eats pennies. Hide your change purse." Grace could hear the rustle of a snack food bag on the other end.

Grace sighed and pulled a mug from the cupboard. "No. Rachel and Doug are at some dinner. I'm with Ella. She's asleep though, so I'm just relaxing now."

"Break out the boxed wine."

"I'm driving home after this."

"Okay. I'll drink for both of us." More crinkling on the other end. "So," Dee said, letting the word trail off. "Not to be a busy-body or anything, but what did you say to Jefferson?"

"Don't let him catch you calling him that. And nothing. I didn't say anything to him."

"Well you did something. He came back to the station all grumpy. He cursed at the vending machine."

Grace ripped open a teabag. "I fail to see how that's my fault."

"Oh, come on. I'm not an idiot. The whole town knows you two have been hot and cold for each other since the beginning of time. Just, for my sake, can you put whatever happened between you two behind you? He needs to get laid. So do I, for that matter."

"Well don't look at me! For either one!"

"You're not my type."

For some reason, Grace found that slightly insulting. "Why not?"

"Please. I'd squash a bug and you'd break up with me. Who needs that drama?"

"He told you about the snakes, didn't he?"

She could hear Dee's laughter on the other end. "Pantomimed, really. It was quite entertaining. Then he called you a fruitcake."

"That's not the first time."

"Why are you so hung up on him, Grace? It's obvious you two are like oil and water. Just... move on. Don't you think it's time?"

"Yes." Definitely. It was *years* past time to get over him. "I should start dating again."

"Good plan. Get right back out there. I hear Zach is already dating some T.A. from the Biology Department."

"It hasn't even been a week!"

"Men are resilient that way. Unlike you who molders like old bread forgotten in the drawer."

"I do not molder. I dated Zach for over two whole months."

"Uh-huh, and that's only because the only date you'd had before that was last August."

"You're forgetting that guy at Carter's wedding."

"Grace, walking down the aisle with some random guy in a tux isn't a date."

"He was cute."

"He doesn't count. He flew in from Phoenix. You can't even make it work with people who live in the same zip code."

"Fine. I'll ask someone out."

"That's a girl. Who?"

Grace turned off the kettle and poured water over her teabag. Hmm. Good question.

"How about Matt from the co-op?" Dee asked.

"The man eats sausage. I don't trust him."

Dee sighed. "Omnivores are people, too, Grace. It doesn't make him suspect."

"Plus, he has a beard. I don't like bearded men. What is he hiding behind all that hair? I read a study once that the average beard contains the same contaminants as the average cell phone, if you know what I mean."

"Ew."

"Exactly."

"Then who?"

"Meg suggested Joe Sedowsky, but I don't know. I tend to remember him before his growth spurt when he was young and dorky. Plus we kissed once a long time ago. Doesn't that make things weird?"

"No. That's first base. You're already on the field there. I'd totally date him if I were straight. He brought over traction gear for my dad when he tore his rotator cuff. He seems nice, and word on the street is he's single and looking for love."

"Not a selling point."

"Come on. My neighbor, Trudi, recommended him."

"To you?"

"Yeah. She's a little slow on the uptake. I forgive her, because she makes amazing meatloaf. You should call him."

"Now? You expect me to call him out of the blue? Doesn't that send kind of a weird message that I'm on the prowl?"

"Aren't you? How long has it been since you've done the deed anyway? Months? Years?"

Grace wasn't going to reveal that 'decades' was the word Dee was searching for. Somehow, stated that way, it didn't sound noble and virtuous just... sad.

"Anyway," Dee went on, "you've got to start somewhere."

Apparently 'rock bottom' was as good a starting point as any.

CHAPTER FIVE

It had been nearly a week since the disastrous dinner at his folk's house, and Mauri had already left Jeff a half a dozen texts asking if he'd spoken with their dad. Lord only knew why she thought Jeff would have better luck getting Rodger to change his mind about things, but Mauri lived on the seacoast—if a twenty-six mile stretch of rocky shoreline and sparse beaches qualified as such—and thought an in-person approach would be most effective.

Jeff assumed she'd settled nearly two hours from Sugar Falls so she wouldn't run the risk of running into their father, but if he were feeling charitable, it was probably more to do with the fact that the population there favored her political agenda and tended to be less conservative than other parts of the state.

So the unpleasant business of talking sense into their dear old dad fell to Jeff.

He pulled into the rutted drive. His dad's place wasn't a dump, but it wasn't the Taj Mahal either. A rustic-looking log cabin slung low and looked as if a child had plunked their Lincoln Logs in the middle of a forest. There was no lawn to speak of, which was just as well, because his father wasn't much one to spend a lot of time hanging around doing yardwork. More often than not, the place stood empty while Rodger and however many band members that could make it performed at state fairs and the occasional music festival. In between, Rodger lived off the income of the band's two albums and took fishing trips.

Jeff didn't bother to knock on the cabin door. He could see the lights on in the separate garage out back.

He let himself in the side door of the garage and pulled it closed so as not to let in any of the moths darting around the outdoor spotlight. His father crouched beside his beloved Harley, old jeans torn at the knees and a weathered tee making him look like a greying, overgrown teenager. He stood when he saw Jeff, his face creased in a wary grin as he wiped his hands on a rag that hadn't seen clean in years.

"Well, hey," he said. He motioned to the bike. "Just getting the ol' girl ready for the season."

Jeff nodded. "Looking good," he said.

There was once a time Jeff had ridden that very bike, a time he'd had fond memories of riding along the back roads of Sugar Falls, his girlfriend clinging to him from behind.

Now he drove around town in a four-door cruiser, and the only time in recent memory a woman had wrapped her legs around him had more to do with a snake phobia than lust.

His dad stepped around the bike and let his breath out long and slow. "I take it your sister sent you."

Rodger reached down to the small dorm fridge he kept under the workbench and pulled out a couple of cans. He handed one to Jeff.

"Soda?" Jeff asked. "You've turned over a new leaf."

"Bobby's stroke was something of a wakeup call."

"I imagine."

His dad took a long swig, his mouth twisting as he swallowed. "She wants me to cancel the tour, doesn't she?"

"Or postpone."

His father shook his head, his scraggly few days' growth of beard tinged with silver. Jeff wondered when that had happened. He'd always thought of his dad as a perpetual teenager.

"You'd think she would have grown out of being embarrassed by me by now."

"Embarrassed? I think it goes beyond that, don't you? Embarrassed is thinking your parent dresses badly. You and the band..." His words trailed off. Really? He even had to explain this?

"Last tour you were trailed by groupies half your age. You routinely get calls from neighbors for noise violations because of 'practices.' Dennis smashed his guitar on the stage at your last concert and got a three-inch splinter through his thumb. Not to mention Johnny's 'Better Living through Chemistry' mantra..." He cursed. "It's not like you're a twenty-year-old anymore. People expect you to grow up and if not become respectable at least become responsible. Mauri has goals. The least you can do is clean up your act long enough to support her."

"I should've known this day would come," his dad said. "I blame your grandparents, God rest their souls." The last was said with a wry, slightly sarcastic twist to his mouth.

"I'd hardly place the blame of Maureen's political aspirations on Grandma and Grandpa."

"No? That man was so straight-laced, I'll bet he wore a tie to bed. And your grandmother! She was the only woman on God's green earth who *hoped* she'd be picked for jury duty. Always carrying on about civic duty... Always following the rules..."

"Always obeying the law. These aren't faults."

Rodger shrugged. For some reason this pushed Jeff's buttons more than any sarcastic retort.

"Not everyone can be the perpetual teenager," Jeff said. "I'd say Mom raised us right." It was a less than subtle dig at a father who hadn't always been around, and Jeff could tell by the slight tightening of Rodger's grip on the can of soda that the barb had hit home.

"Don't let her fool you. Your mother wasn't always so straight and narrow." A small, wicked smile crossed his dad's features. "When she and I eloped, that was mostly her idea, you know."

"That's funny. Growing up, I believe she generally referred to it as 'that time I lost my mind.'"

Rodger chuckled, then his eyes grew serious. "We were good together."

Jeff set his soda down, its overly sweet flavor tasting like the fake childhood he'd never had with this man. "You mean until you guys had me and Mauri."

Rodger shook his head. "It made it harder having kids, true. Mostly on your mom."

"Seeing as she was alone."

Rodger grimaced and tossed his empty can toward a bin in the corner. "I know you and Mauri like to paint me with the good-for-nothing father brush, but it's not that simple. I wish you could understand that."

"I understand that responsibility became too hard for you. And now you've got a daughter trying to do something for herself, for her constituents, and you're putting yourself first again. She's—*I'm*—asking you to put her first for once."

Rodger's eyes went dark.

He'd pissed him off? Good. Jeff was pissed, too. It could be like that sometimes. There was once a time he enjoyed hanging out with his dad. Fishing. Hiking. Now, it seemed the slightest thing could set them off.

"You don't know shit." Rodger pinched his fingers in the air. "I was *this* close to leaving the band when we got hitched to the *Rising Stars* on their last tour. We were just the warm-up band, but when *Tears on My Pillow* hit the top of the charts, people took notice of us. It was our big break. We were getting calls and opportunities we'd never dreamed of before then. We got signed for our first record deal. But then your sister was born...

"I tried to make it work, but your mama decided it was harder not knowing when I'd be home than it was being a single mom."

"And divorce was easier than giving the band up for your family?"

"I didn't want a divorce. That was your mother's idea. I just went along, because I wanted her to be happy."

"You think raising two kids on her own made her happy?"

"She wasn't alone. She had her folks. Anyway, it is what it is. No changing the past."

"I'm not here to talk about the past. I'm here because Maureen is asking you now, for her, will you just let this reunion tour go?"

"No."

"You won't even consider it?"

"I gave up my marriage and my kids for this band. They're my family. Maybe that pisses you off, but it's the truth. Bobby almost *died* after that stroke. It's a miracle he can even play again. He's like a brother to me. The *Rising Stars* are on their farewell tour. At my age... I'm not going to be one of those old rock stars that cling to performing long after they're dried up husks of themselves. I've got more pride than that.

"This is our last chance, Jeff. Our last chance before it's all over... I can't let this go by. If I pass this up, we'll never be anything but that band people had play at their cousin's wedding. You can't ask me to give this up."

"I just did."

Rodger gave a curt nod. "Tell your sister I said hi."

"Tell her yourself."

"Perhaps next time she can speak to me herself."

Jeff almost turned to leave but then stopped himself. It often ended like this, them getting at each other and leaving in a huff. It was stupid of Mauri to have sent him, but coming herself was worse, because the frustration of it all made her cry. And Mauri hated anyone to see her crying. It shows weakness, she always said. And she was living in a man's world. "When will you stop living your life as if you were the only one that mattered? There are other people's futures at stake here."

Rodger shook his head. "Don't you see? I only ever wanted for myself what I wanted for each of you—the freedom to go after your dreams."

"Right. You're the regular poster child for misunderstood absentee fathers everywhere."

His father's face grew hard. "Now hold on. I'll admit I wasn't your typical dad, but I did what I could to support you and your sister. Didn't I send her to that model congress thing where she met Christopher? Didn't I take you on all those hikes, just the two of us?

"Ever since you rescued that couple off the mountain, I've been a hundred percent behind your dream to go into search and rescue. I even had Brad Thompson talk to you about the Army. I've supported you. Don't I deserve the same?"

"Shows what you know about my dreams."

He wasn't sure where that had come from, but it was out there now. It wasn't as if he hadn't wanted to pursue a career in search and rescue, but he didn't like his dad acting as if he knew that much about him. He'd blown Jeff off one too many times in favor of the band.

His father frowned, frustration and confusion warring on his face. "I can't ever win with you," he said.

"You don't get it, that's why. The only reason I ended up helping that couple is because you weren't there. You were at a gig in New York."

"It turned out all right. You knew what you were doing. That night is what made you the Hometown Hero."

"I never wanted to be that."

"I never wanted to divorce your mom."

"I suppose it's too late for both of us then, isn't it?"

"No. It's never too late."

Jeff stared at his father, too many words bubbling up inside him. The truth was, it *was* too late for a lot of things. He turned to leave, throwing the door wide, moths be damned, then stopped. "You're wrong. Some things we have to get right the first time."

He let the door slam behind him.

CHAPTER SIX

Hot July sunshine poured into the shop windows at *Currents*, and something wonderful just walked in her door.

Grace watched from behind the counter as the man crossed over to the wind chime display, his neatly pressed khakis and pale blue button-down suggesting he wasn't local. Most of the guys around town wore old t-shirts and jeans or whatever they happened to pull out of their hamper. When the man turned and smiled and wished her a "good morning" in a lazy southern drawl, she nearly swooned in a very unprofessional manner.

"Good morning," she smiled back. She could do this. Flirting was never the hard part. Who knows? Her oracle cards that morning had told her to expect the unexpected today. Who expected a sexy southerner on an average Wednesday morning would be shopping a new-age shop in Sugar Falls, New Hampshire? Plus, she had gotten the arm shivers as soon as he'd walked through the door. She knew it was the universe's way of telling her to pay attention.

"Looking for something special? For your wife, perhaps?" she asked.

Good grief. Had she really asked that? Talk about obvious! Heat flooded her face. But desperate times called for desperate measures. After a decade of being single, she'd pretty much run through the available men in town, so it was either this guy or Joe Sedowsky. Maybe that question hadn't sounded as obvious as it felt. She pretended the heat was getting to her and fanned herself with a random inventory list she'd had lying on the counter.

Who would blame her, anyway? She was tired of being the odd one out. Tired of going home to the same four walls and wondering if she should just go ahead and get another cat. She had four now. What was one more?

A lot. Five cats was a lot.

The man, God bless him, didn't seem to notice her less than subtle query. He glanced away with a rueful smile. "No. I'm not married. Just browsing. My sister might like them, though."

Ooh! He had a sister! She'd read somewhere that men with sisters were better boyfriends and husbands because they understood women. This was *very* promising!

Of course, thinking on it, that bit of wisdom was clearly bunk, because Jeff Dayton had a sister.

"Let me know if I can help you choose something. If you have any questions, I'll be out back," she said.

There. That was low-key but professional, right? She'd give him space, and if he were interested, he'd let her know.

Grace spent fifteen minutes idly rearranging CDs in the back of the store before she decided, perhaps, she needed to actually *see* him to see if he was interested.

She walked back to the register and popped the *Nighttime Woodlands* soundtrack into the player. An owl hooted over the sound system followed by rustling leaves.

Grace turned.

The man was staring at her. "Maybe I could use some help after all," he said.

"Certainly." *Yes!* Hope sprang to life again inside her.

"I'm only in town for a short time," he said, effectively yanking her back down to earth, "but there's a little girl whose birthday is coming up..." He glanced away and back again, his warm eyes self-deprecating. "The truth is, I want to win someone over, and her daughter's birthday is coming up, but..."

Hope shriveled to dust at her feet. Oh. So he was taken. Grace stifled a sigh. And he was clearly special, because how sweet was he? "So you need a gift that a little girl will love, a mother will be okay with, and it can't be too extravagant."

"Exactly. Thank you. Do you have that?"

"How old is the little girl?"

"She'll be six."

"All right. I think I have just the thing." Grace walked over to the front window display. "I have this crystal unicorn ornament and a solar-powered hook that rotates it so the room will be filled with rainbows. It's one of my best sellers."

"I'll take it," he said. "But make it two."

"Two?"

It was his turn to blush. "One for the mother, too."

Oh, criminey. Why couldn't she find a handsome southern gentlemen to buy her sweet gifts? "Gift-wrapped?" she asked.

He nodded. "Please."

So much for happy shivers of intuition. Maybe she needed to turn down the air conditioning again. Grace pulled out tissue to wrap his purchases and made tentative mental plans to visit the local Humane Society.

"So, are you enjoying your visit?" she asked.

He grimaced, although it only had the effect of making him look more charming. She'd always had a weakness for soulful eyes. "It's had its ups and downs."

"I'm sorry to hear that. I hope things will improve for you."

"It's not me. I'm fine." He shook his head. "My sister has experienced a spot of trouble. I'm here to bail her out."

Sister? So this wasn't for a significant other after all? Hope flickered to life again inside her; although, in a tempered way, because—hello—he was only in town a short time and she'd been on an internal roller-coaster ride ever since he's strolled through her door. Still… how gracious was he? She *experienced a spot of trouble.* How discreet and vague. It sounded… quaint. And yet, he looked uncomfortable. She wondered what sort of 'trouble' would warrant a brother to travel all this way.

"It's good of you to help her," she said, realizing her internal thoughts had left an awkward pause in the conversation.

A bubble of sound that might have been laughter erupted from him. "Tell her that. I've become the interfering older brother in her eyes, but she refuses to talk to the rest of the family, so here I am."

"Well, I'm sure your niece will enjoy the unicorn; although, I can't say whether it will help with your sister."

He frowned. "I don't have a niece." Then his face grew pink, and Grace realized her mistake. Ah. So he was trying to sweet-talk someone local while *also* rescuing his sister. Hope fizzled entirely, and yet…

The hair on the back of her arms tingled again. It was like that every time she got a premonition about something. It wasn't a bad feeling, more of excitement. Awareness.

Because she tended to act first, think later, she reached into the counter display and pulled out a blue heart-shaped stone. "Here. Something tells me you could use this."

"A heart? My sister would probably agree with you on that count."

"Don't be too hard on yourself. Mercury won't be out of retrograde until the first, so it's no wonder you've been having communication issues."

He blinked at her. Hmm. She was never sure how much to push with people. They either accepted her gift or doubted it, but the fact that he was in her shop…

"This is sodalite," she explained. "Hold it in your hand or pocket when you most need to communicate, and… it will help. I promise."

He waved it away. "Oh, I don't—"

"No charge." She dropped the stone into the bag and looped the handles together. He'd have to untangle them to refuse her now, but something told her he was willing to give anything a try. "I insist."

He offered a small smile. "Thanks. I'll let you know if it works."

"It will. My feelings are never wrong." Confusing, even disappointing sometimes, but never wrong.

~ * ~

"I'm off to my Civic Pride meeting again. I'll be back in a couple of hours." Grace slung her tote over her shoulder and took a quick glance around the shop. Trish, her part-time help, sipped her coffee. Grace often wondered why Trish went through the trouble of balancing daycare and after-school schedules to work at the shop, but perhaps it had something to do with having four kids. Grace often found Trish standing in the aromatherapy corner with her eyes closed.

"I'll hold down the fort, don't you worry, boss. Have fun."

Grace shook her head. "Fun is probably not on the agenda. This is the pat-on-the-back, point-the-finger-of-blame parade recap, but if all goes well, we'll have a little respite before we have to start planning for Halloween."

Ten minutes later Grace pushed open the door to the library and made her way to the morning room.

Grace pretended not to see Jeff masquerading as a sentry by the fireplace and settled herself into one of the overstuffed chairs by the windows. If Jeff was going to pretend he could lounge about the periphery and take jabs at their hard work, she could relax while he did it.

Meg, Grams, Joe, and Lydia had already arrived.

"Sorry I'm late," Grace said automatically. She wasn't, actually, but everyone else was of the 'arrive ten minutes before your appointment' crowd. Joe gave her a forgiving nod from his seat at the long table. Such magnanimity.

Grams shuffled some papers. "Meg has a client at two o'clock, so we need to keep on task today. If you'll each take an agenda, we can run through the recap and be on our way."

Grace was the last to receive the stack of agendas, having to lean forward out of her seat to grab them from Joe. She reached behind her without looking and held one out to Jeff. She didn't have to look. She could feel his tension from four feet away.

The paper slipped out of her fingers, and she compressed her lips. As if he could ignore her.

Grace scanned the agenda and glanced up. "You're nixing the Beetle Brigade next year? People loved them!"

"They were disorganized," Grams said. "And two of them were late. It made it difficult to weave them into the parade."

"It was their first year. I don't think we need to cut them from future parades over a couple of stragglers."

"Well, I'm just making note of it for next year," Grams said, pointing to Lydia to make a note of it in the minutes. Lydia scribbled dutifully then gave Grace an apologetic glance.

Meg sighed. "I'm sorry to say, the donated food collection didn't work well. The kids thought we were handing out treats instead of collecting, and a lot of people said they hadn't heard about the donation thing, so…" she trailed off.

"It was our first year," Grace said. "We'll advertise better next year."

"Maybe you're trying to do too much," Jeff said from behind her. "Why not create a kid-safe, pedestrian-only zone along the parade route where parade volunteers can walk close to the kids and hand out candy, but the rest of the route where there are vehicles is candy-free?"

You'd think the man had just invented cheese for how everyone fell all over themselves liking his idea. Fine. It *was* a good idea. It would have been even better had he had it a couple of weeks ago instead of alarming old ladies about the threat of terrorists in their midst.

Grams tapped the table in front of Lydia with her index finger. "Make a note of that for next year that we unanimously agreed to make a kid-safe candy zone per Jeff's suggestion."

"Really? You need to say that he thought of it?" Yes, she felt childish asking, but come on!

"Well, if we need to follow up next year to get a better idea of how it would work, I think it makes sense to note whose idea it was," Lydia said.

Oh, sure. Make her look foolish.

"Wish we'd thought of that a couple weeks ago," said Joe.

"No kidding," murmured Grace.

Joe turned to smile at her. He had a nice smile. Warm. Albeit weirdly perfect. Grace turned her attention back to the agenda. They'd gotten to 'Other Business' which, thank God, meant they were done.

Grace pushed herself out of her chair. "Great job everyone! Looks like we're done until after Labor Day. I've got an amazing jack-o-lantern idea planned, so be prepared to be wow—"

"There's one more thing," Grams said, folding her hands on top of the table.

"There is?"

"Yes. Chief Russell is seeking our suggestions. Apparently, despite our little issues, the Independence Day Parade is very popular. As is the Founders' Day celebration, the tulip planting days and all the other events we organize. He thinks very highly of us."

Grace sat in her chair again.

"Unfortunately," Grams continued, "he reports that Homecoming has devolved into a series of pranks and underaged drinking parties, and he's asked us to brainstorm ways of making it a more community-friendly event."

"You mean like another parade?" Meg asked.

Jeff moved over to the windows. Did the man never sit down? "No. The parades tend to attract families with young kids. Teens not so much."

Everyone grew silent.

"We could do a band competition!" Lydia said.

"We only have one marching band," Joe pointed out.

"How about a pet show?" Meg said.

"Sounds like a liability nightmare," said Joe. "Remember what happened when they hosted that pet vaccination clinic on the common?"

Grams looked around at the various expressions of deep thought and annoyance. "Well, perhaps we should reconvene another day to give ourselves time to mull it over."

Grace bit her lip. She had those arm tingles again, but she wasn't sure why. "Isn't Homecoming the end of September or early October, right around the time of the Harvest Moon? Maybe we could do something around that. You know, shift the focus away from football and make it more of a festival celebrating the season."

Jeff let out what sounded like a snort. "I don't think some moon dance thing is what the chief had in mind."

"Don't be patronizing. I'm thinking outside the box. We could still do a bonfire, which the teens love, but make it a more family-friendly event with old-style fair activities, maybe some live music…"

"I like it," Grams said. "I like it a lot." She turned to Jeff. "What do you think? Would the chief approve?"

Jeff shrugged. "You can run it by him, but sounds like a lot of work."

"We can do it!" Lydia exclaimed. "I'm behind Grace one hundred percent!"

"What?" Grace nearly bobbled the to-go cup of iced chai tea she wasn't supposed to have in the library. "I was just throwing out an idea. I wasn't volunteering to spearhead it or anything."

"Didn't you know that's how these committees work?" Jeff murmured from behind her. "Rookie mistake."

Grace let out a breath. "I think Grams is right. We should give ourselves a week or two to think it over. I'm sure there are lots of good ideas—"

"I think you should run with it," Grams said, throwing her under the bus.

"I love it," Meg said. "Honestly. Please still be my friend after this."

Lydia had clasped her hands, her silver bangles chiming their clenched excitement.

Grace looked at all their hopeful faces and sighed. "Fine. I'll do it. Who knows? It might even be fun. We can meet again same time, same place next week to brainstorm the details, but you are *all* in this with me."

"Deal!" Lydia cried.

"Adjourned!" Grams declared. "Although the Ladies Auxiliary has this space Wednesday afternoons the rest of the summer. How about seven o'clock? Can everyone make that?"

Everyone nodded.

"Seven o'clock it is," Grace said. She pinned Jeff with her eyes. "Except you. You don't have to come. I promise not to plan any knife-throwing contests or anything overly dangerous."

"Actually," Grams said. "Officer Dayton is on the committee now."

"What?" said Grace.

"The chief wanted a representative from law enforcement to help us plan for traffic, crowd control, security, that sort of thing. You can never be too careful these days."

Perfect. So now she had to plan this thing with Mr. Gloom and Doom casting negativity shadows at her every step of the way?

Jeff stepped abreast of her, his mouth tilted up in a cocky way that made Grace's insides go all hot and tangled. "I suggest you leave your Hello Kitty backpack at home."

Nothing had ever made her want to own a Hello Kitty backpack more.

CHAPTER SEVEN

The next night, Grace ran to the corner deli after work for a salad and wolfed it down before jogging back to *Currents*. Each Thursday she hosted what had become known as Healing Circle afterhours at her shop. It started informally with a few friends gathering to try out a new meditation CD and had grown organically from there. Now, each week, Grace closed the shop to customers, and an hour later welcomed anyone who wanted to drop in for a time of casual mingling, relaxation exercises and other activities designed to help reduce stress and encourage balance in their lives. They'd had men come a time or two, but random comments about hot flashes and hysterectomy scars soon put an end to that.

Those who attended now were an unlikely mix of women from various ages and backgrounds, small business owners and housewives to retirees. Healing Circle, as a result, was seldom dull.

"I haven't had dinner yet, so I brought snacks." Grams dropped a foil-covered tray onto the counter by the cash register and let the strap carrying her yoga mat slide down her arm to plop at her feet. She took Healing Circle very seriously.

After what had happened at the Civic Pride Committee meeting the previous day, Grace wasn't feeling the warm fuzzies toward her Grams. The woman could have warned her about the whole police presence on the committee before saddling her with heading up the festival.

"We can eat at break," she offered. The other women could be heard chatting in the back of the store. Snacks? There had better not be pepperoni on that tray. Grams was notorious for trying to sneak meat protein into Grace's diet even if it were filled with nitrites. She always told Grace she was too thin. As if that were even a thing.

"I even made some of that quinoa you like so much." She pronounced it 'kwin-o-ah'. This did not bode well for whatever was hidden under the foil.

"Sorry I'm late! Hi, Ruth." Linda Andrews pushed through the door, her mass of curly red hair wild around her plump cheeks as she greeted Grace and Grams. "Jerry never remembers I have commitments other than making him dinner. Are those brownies?"

"No," Grams said. "I'm trying something new this week."

Grace picked up Grams' yoga mat and handed it to her. "Why don't you go ahead and get settled. We're still waiting for Sandi."

"And somebody named Peggy," said Grams. "She's a client of Sandi's who's having allergy issues. Sandi thought we might help."

"Grams, Healing Circle isn't a medical…" Grace cut herself off. Arguing with Grams was like spitting into the wind, ill-advised and unpleasant. "Never mind. You all make yourselves comfortable, and I'll get the lights and cue the music. Chants or nature sounds tonight?"

"Chants set my teeth on edge," Linda said. "Sorry. They do. But I like crickets!"

"*Meadow Songs*, it is," said Grace. She cued the music, dimmed the lights and waited by the door for the remaining stragglers.

"Hi, Gracie. God, you look cute tonight. Love that skirt! My last blow-out ran over." Sandi Adams plopped her yoga mat and pillow on the counter to let her large purse sag to the floor. "This is Peggy Dayton. I mentioned some of your local honey and apple cider vinegar remedies for allergy sufferers when she was at the shop this week, and I figured I might as well invite her to Healing Circle, too."

"Ah, sure." Grace went rigid, realizing her face had probably frozen into anything but a welcoming expression. She forced her features to relax and motioned for them to join the others. She locked the door and flipped the sign on the door to 'closed.'

Lovely. Just lovely. Jeff's mother?

Meg knocked on the door, and Grace let her and Toni, V.P. of the local bank, scurry in. Meg pulled a beach towel out of her tote. "Sorry we're late. Amy's with her grandparents, so I'm here!"

Grace assured her it was fine. It was a comfort to have friends around her after the surprise of seeing Peggy Dayton of all people.

But she could do this. She was a professional after all.

Grace stepped across everyone to her usual spot on the far side of the Healing Circle area, which consisted of a large area rug in the back corner of the shop near the Himalayan salt lamp display. She would have moved her mat, but everyone was settled, including Jeff's mother directly to her right.

Grace avoided eye contact and settled herself, legs crossed, palms up on her knees. She could do this. "Everyone, this is, uh, Peggy." She leaned toward Jeff's mom. "We're very low-key. Enjoy this time to just relax or feel free to participate at whatever level feels right to you." Peggy Dayton nodded. "We'll start with some deep breathing," Grace announced.

She led the group through the routine, quietly speaking. She inhaled through her nose and exhaled through her mouth, letting the stress of everyday life float away on the imaginary breeze implied by the nature sounds CD.

It had been years since she dated Jeff. His mother probably didn't even remember it, right?

Grace sucked in another deep breath. "No matter our backgrounds or beliefs, we allow the white light of love and truth to surround us. May no negativity from the world enter this space and none of our own negativity enter the world." She nodded to herself, hyper-aware of the new woman beside her. She didn't want to feel biased against anyone entering the circle, but she felt somehow invaded all the same.

No, that wasn't right. Vulnerable. She felt raw, as if the woman who had given birth to the man who'd stolen her heart all those years ago would sense the weakness within her. She took another breath and pushed the negativity away, clawing her way back to a sense of peace.

"When you are ready, I invite you to speak of what is heavy on your heart this week. Large or small. Give it voice so we may focus our love and positive energy toward you."

Linda sighed, no doubt thinking of Jerry. Sandi nudged Peggy Dayton.

Peggy cleared her throat. "I, ah, have bad allergies."

Grace nodded encouragingly in what she hoped was a professional and not a 'I once had sex with your son' sort of way.

Grams leaned forward. "Tell us about them."

"Well, they keep me up at night." Murmurs of understanding and sympathy rippled around the circle as if Peggy had just confessed she had a terminal disease. "And my ears feel so itchy I want to scratch out my brain through my ear drums."

Sandi snickered. "I doubt that's the best approach."

"I end up taking allergy meds that knock me out and make me feel drowsy the next day. I'm at my wits end." She rubbed her ear as if to illustrate.

"Are they bothering you now?" Grams asked.

Peggy nodded.

Toni yawned. "Try yawning. Opens the eustachian tubes. Can't hurt."

Toni demonstrated a wide yawn. Then Grams did. Soon all the women were emitting groans of release and enthusiastically flapping their jaws.

"Massage along your jaw bone as you yawn," Toni suggested. "It feels really good."

Peggy gamely yawned and massaged along with the other women.

Meg was the first to giggle. "Toni, if I swallow a fly, I blame you."

"It's actually helping," Peggy said with a bit of surprise. "Thank you."

Grace smiled serenely and looked around the circle. "Anyone else?"

They offered up worries, stresses and fears and held hands in the silence, the calming sounds of nature washing over them.

Grams's stomach growled.

Grace decided that was a sign to wrap things up for the evening. "Remember, as women, we love and cherish one another. We are connected and interconnected. When one feels pain, we all feel pain, and when one is joyful, we all rejoice. Go, knowing that you are beautiful and strong and gifted. And may our mutual nurturing help each of us be our best selves. Namaste."

Usually they rose and gathered their mats, saying their goodbyes or, in Grams's case, eating.

Today, Grace heard the quiet sound of weeping in the opposite corner. "Linda?"

Linda quickly swiped the back of her hand across her nose and pretended to search for something in her tote bag.

"Linda, what's wrong?"

"Nothing," she lied.

"Honey, you're not crying because you can't find your Chapstick," said Grams. "Spill it."

Linda set her tote aside and sniffed. "I'm sorry. I know we're not supposed to let the negativity of the world intrude on this time."

Grace crawled across the area rug to grasp Linda's hands. "Oh, sweetie, that's not what that means at all! If something is weighing on you, that's a burden to share."

Linda pulled her hands away and smoothed the hem of her t-shirt. She grimaced and glanced away. "Jerry doesn't... think I'm attractive anymore."

"What? Since when?" Toni demanded. "He was just singing your praises last Tuesday when I ran into him at the grocery store. Said you were a Hot Momma making him Mexican for dinner and he needed to bring home the cilantro."

"Are you not having sex?" Grams demanded as if she had every right to know these intimate details of Linda's private life.

Horrified that her low-key healing circle had gone rogue, Grace sat back on her heels and tried to redirect. "Linda, you don't need to answer—"

"No. I mean, yes," Linda said to Grams, blushing. "But he doesn't... touch me. Not like he used to. It makes me feel ugly."

"WHAT?!" Sandi cried. "Don't be ridiculous. You are *not* ugly. You are beautiful inside and out."

Linda placed a hand on Sandi's arm. "I'm not being ridiculous. I love you for sticking by me through everything—when I had to ask you to shave my head, I don't know who cried harder—but I have to face the truth. I have my hair back, and I've never felt stronger, but I don't *feel* beautiful. I feel like, like some shipwreck survivor that's washed up on shore. Alive but battered. I don't blame Jerr for not being attracted to me anymore. I have battle scars instead of my gorgeous breasts..." She looked down at herself. "...and they were magnificent."

Grams and Sandi nodded in agreement. "They were," Grams assured her. "So perky. Lydia and I always said so."

"But they were going to kill me if I didn't get rid of them, so I had to say goodbye. And I've made peace with that." She brushed a tear off her cheek and tried to smile through it. "But how do I make peace with the fact that I'm no longer the woman my husband married?"

"Oh, honey," Sandi said, wrapping her in a hug. "You're twice the woman you were. Jerry knows that."

"Have you talked to him about it," Toni asked.

"Have you tried sex toys?" Grams wanted to know.

"Grams!" Grace cried. "Inappropriate!"

Grams rolled her eyes and shrugged.

Peggy looked like she wanted to bolt, except she was still wedged in the corner with Sandi and Linda hugging in the center of the circle space weeping over lost breasts and insensitive husbands.

Grace turned to her, still choked up over Linda's confession. "I'm so sorry," she whispered. "Healing Circle rarely gets this, er intense." She'd been about to say 'intimate' but that would have been a flat out lie after last week's discussion about vaginal dryness.

"It's all right," said Peggy. "I'm honored you all feel comfortable enough with me to be so honest. It's a refreshing change."

Linda sat back, a tissue Sandi had passed her crumpled in her hand. "Your home life not quite this in-your-face?"

Peggy chuckled. "Hardly. I live alone and have adult children. My daughter, especially, likes things to be very low drama, but her work keeps her in the public eye, so I don't blame her for being conservative. I does make things a bit awkward with her father, though."

"Why so?"

"He's part of a rock band."

"*The Jolly Rodgers,*" Grace supplied.

"Yes," Peggy said, smiling. "How did you know?"

It hurt, that one little question. It hurt, because Grace had fallen so deeply in love with this woman's son, she had once imagined spending a lifetime with him, and this woman didn't even realize it.

It felt freeing almost, but in a skydiving without a parachute sort of way. Inevitably, you'd smash back into reality, your emotions crushed and broken.

Grace swallowed. Well, *that* wasn't a very uplifting mental image.

Peggy lightly touched Grace's arm. "I remember now. You were friends with Jeff way back when, weren't you?" She smiled warmly as if it were a fond memory they'd shared milk and cookies over. Her hand slipped away again. "I'd love to try some of the local raw honey Sandi told me about."

Grace willed her chest wall to hold in the heaving thudding of her heart. "Of course. I'm out at the moment, but I'm expecting another delivery soon. You can leave your number before you go, and I'll be happy to call you when it comes in."

"I'll do that."

Grace stepped over Linda and Sandi, ready to eat whatever was hidden under the foil to escape spending another moment near Jeff's lovely, oblivious mother. "Well, everyone, shall we see what Grams, er, Ruth brought?"

CHAPTER EIGHT

It had rained for three straight days.

Jeff tied on his sneakers, stretched his hamstrings, and resigned himself to another soggy run. He set out toward the outskirts of town, the soft rain sticking his tee to his chest as he settled into a steady pace.

Truth be told, he didn't mind the rain. It sure as hell beat the gritty memory of a foreign country where fine sand and dust made its way into everything. Food. Hair. Underwear. At least the rain felt clean. Some of the things he'd seen, felt... Hell, there were times he couldn't imagine ever feeling clean again.

He rounded the bend toward the river and sped up as he saw the familiar flash of hazard lights through the drizzle, quickly processing the scene. Only one car. Probably a flat tire or something. A lean figure stepped out of the driver's side, facing away from him, a bright pink-hooded slicker pulled up over her head. She popped the trunk.

Jeff slowed to a walk and frowned.

He knew that car. Knew those tags.

Knew that pink-hooded woman.

"Got car trouble?"

Grace jumped. The shovel she held knocked against the trunk hood with a loud *thunk*.

"Jeff? What are you doing here?"

"Running."

"In the rain?"

"I'm water repellant." He eyed the shovel. "What are *you* doing?"

She avoided his eyes. "Nothing to worry the good men and women of Sugar Falls' finest."

"How about I decide that?"

She stood, the shovel head pointing skyward like she was recreating that old painting of the farmer with the upright pitchfork. "Is it illegal to park on the shoulder here?"

He glanced around for fire hydrants, no-parking signs or nearby intersections. "No."

"Then, I'll thank you for giving me some privacy."

He eyed the shovel again. "You know you can use the restroom at Lucky's. It's a half mile from here."

She looked at him. Then the shovel. Then at him. "*Ew!* No! I do not have to... no."

She looked so flustered, so damned adorable with her dark red curls poking out around the tightened hood, he gave in to a smile. "Just tell me what you plan to do with that shovel, Grace. You know I'll find out eventually."

"This is invasion of privacy."

"This is me making sure you're not burying any dead bodies. We of Sugar Falls' finest frown on that sort of thing."

Her face grew pale before two high spots of color appeared on her cheeks.

He frowned. "You're *not* burying a dead body, are you?"

"Define 'dead body.'"

He swiped a hand over his wet face. "Oh, geesh."

She turned and walked toward the front of the car. He followed.

He winced. "*Oooo.* Not a good day for being a gopher."

She ignored him, instead stepping through the tall weeds at the side of the road and positioning the shovel. She jammed her foot down onto it.

"What the hell do you think you're doing?"

"Burying it."

"May I ask why?"

"I can't just leave it like that for people to just keep hitting its poor little body. It's the least I can do after being responsible for..." Her words trailed off. She sniffed.

"Why not just toss it to the side of the road and let nature take its course? The carrion birds need to eat, too."

She glanced up then continued digging. "That's disgusting. I've never done that."

He chuckled, then paused.

"Wait a minute. You've done this before?"

She didn't answer.

He stepped closer and looked at her growing hole. "Have you done this before?"

He looked up and down the road imagining all the dead chipmunks and squirrels and porcupines that might have been there. But weren't. "Tell me you don't drive around with a shovel in your car burying roadkill."

She swiped an arm across her brow as the water trickled down into her eyes and gave him an annoyed look. "We planted annuals along Main Street last month. I never took the shovel out."

"That doesn't answer my other question."

She stopped. "Fine. *Once.* I've done this one other time. Satisfied?"

"You are fruitier than a fruitcake."

Her eyes flashed up at him. "Caring about living things doesn't make me a fruitcake."

"It's beyond caring, Grace. It's dead."

"I realize that." She pulled a rock out of the hole and kept digging.

He eyed the dead gopher again. "So the other—dead body—it wasn't like a dog or a deer or something, was it? Because Fish & Game would have something to say about that."

Satisfied with her handiwork, she hiked back down to the roadway toward the gopher. "No. I call Deanna at the station when I see anything bigger than a breadbox."

"Thank God."

She scooped the gopher up with the shovel, carefully balancing it. The carcass wobbled, and she bent to steady it with her hand.

"Don't touch that!" he barked.

She dropped the gopher, the shovel bouncing on the pavement. "*Ack!* Oh! Look what you made me do! The poor thing!"

He retrieved the shovel from the pavement. "Grace, you can't handle a wild animal with your bare hands."

"It's not going to bite me."

"Yes, but it may have rabies or other disease. Don't you have gloves?"

She shook her head.

He wordlessly handed her the shovel then reached around to the runner's pouch behind him and pulled out a sealed packet.

"You have gloves? And not a rain coat? Who's weird now?"

He ripped the packet open with practiced hands and pulled on the gloves. "They're for emergencies. I always carry a pair." He bent down and carefully lifted the gopher. "You never know when you'll happen upon an accident... or a crazy woman burying roadkill."

After he'd settled the animal in the makeshift grave, Grace quickly refilled the hole and then picked a wildflower and laid it over the top. She turned and started hiking back toward her trunk.

"That's it? Don't we say a prayer or sing or something?" Jeff asked.

"Don't be ridiculous," she said. "It's raining." The shovel landed in the trunk with a thud and she slammed it closed.

She'd already closed her door by the time he made it back to the roadway. She rolled down her window. "Thanks for the help, officer. I'll be on my way now."

"Grace…" Jeff stood at her open window. He watched the rain dance off the hood of her car. He wanted to talk to her. Wanted to figure out this woman that cared so much about a dead gopher but had cared so little for what they'd had together, she'd done the unthinkable.

But the words wouldn't come, and he found he really didn't want to figure it out after all. It was enough to know he'd escaped when he'd had the chance from tying himself to a woman loony enough to bury roadkill.

He stepped back from her vehicle. "Drive safe."

She didn't roll up her window, just drove away, her taillights winking at him until they disappeared altogether.

CHAPTER NINE

Later that day, Grace caught herself rearranging the pens in the cup by the cash register for the third time and dropped her hand to her side, purposefully flexing her fingers. She watched out of the corner of her eye as Jeff Dayton picked up another doodad, turned it over in his hand, and set it back down in the display.

A customer skirted by him, nodded a polite 'thanks but I'll be on my way' look at Grace and dashed out the door.

Grace blew out a frustrated breath. "Would you stop skulking around my shop in your Magic Mike costume? You're scaring the customers," she whispered. She pressed her palms flat on the countertop as yet another customer left without buying anything.

The sign outside her shop welcomed the "thinkers, dreamers and peace travelers of the world," and she worked hard to make the shop a sensory oasis away from stressors and outside distractions. The last thing she needed was brooding Officer Jeff Dayton staring everyone down as if they were her next shoplifter.

"I'm not skulking. I'm looking." Jeff turned back to her and raised one expressive brow. "And this isn't a costume; it's a uniform." He squared his shoulders in that annoyingly superior way officers of the law are probably trained to do.

"Well, it's intimidating." And distracting. The man clearly worked out. A lot. Sheesh. You'd think he'd be developing a paunch by now. Or at least a chink in the armor.

He spoke again in that low, slow baritone. "I'm only intimidating to people with guilty consciences."

Grace watched as he scanned the shop again in silence, all brooding alpha male with his crisp navy uniform and close-cropped dark hair. She refused to think of him as Officer Dayton. He would only ever be Jeff to her.

"So this is *Currents*," he said, looking around. "Interesting."

Grace nodded. She thought so. She glanced from the wall of Himalayan salt lamps glowing near the back of the store, across to the Tibetan singing bowls and collection of chimes, to essential oils, her spiritual reading room, CD rack and indoor stone fountains. "I like to think of it as a place to reconnect with earth, ourselves and each other."

"Huh," he said.

He fingered a wind chime briefly on his way by and glanced down at a basket of muffins by the door. "You got a health permit to cook food for sale?"

"They're not for sale. Have one. They're all-organic sunflower zucchini muffins."

He made a face. "Thanks, but I just had lunch."

"Great for people who tend to be bound up."

"Excuse me?"

"Wound up. Stress relieving. Are you afraid to let go of your stress, Jeff?"

"It's Officer Dayton, and the only stress I feel is coming from whatever the hell you're playing on that sound system."

"They're Gregorian Chants."

"They're giving me a headache."

She turned the volume down a smidge. "Better?"

"You don't really like that stuff, do you?"

"It's meditative. Better than that rock music you used to listen to."

Something came over his expression. Something like regret. "Yeah. I suppose you wouldn't have fond memories of anything we shared."

She swallowed, took the Gregorian chant CD out and popped in *Ocean Waves*. Truthfully, she didn't love Gregorian chants either, but she'd felt in a penitential mood ever since the whole roadkill incident. "Things have changed since then," she said.

"They sure as hell have." He scowled. "Your store layout makes no sense. Why do you have soap in two places?"

Oh, Good Lord. Of all the ridiculous... Surely he wasn't in her shop to critique her organizational systems! "It only makes 'no sense' to rigid black-and-white thinkers. My customers are intuitive, experiential people. They like to browse."

"Ah. So they're aimless."

"No. There *is* an order to things; it's just not obvious to you. I've arranged everything according to the elements: earth, wind, fire and water." She walked over and gestured to the displays just inside the door. "This is the earth and body section, so crystals, chakra aids, herbs and teas are here. Then drums, singing bowls, wind chimes, CDs, essential oils and scented soaps are here in the air and aromas section." She flipped a switch, and a wall of glowing lamps and nightlights warmed the dark, windowless back corner. "Then we move into fire, hearth and home with salt lamps, candles and such and finally we come to water with indoor fountains, ocean wave CDs, sound machines and, okay, yes, more soaps."

"See? Redundant." His lip actually smirked at her, the rest of his face stony hard.

"It's because you use soap with water." He raised that blasted eyebrow again. "Fine, I know it seems silly, but if you have people in the water section ask where the soap is enough times you'll give in and set up two displays, too."

"You missed a section."

She exhaled. She was hoping he hadn't noticed. "That's the Third Eye area. Tarot cards and medium aids, motivational materials, books and, of course, angels." She gestured to the shelves of books, a wall plastered with signs and desk placards with everything from single words to whole quotes, prayers and blessings on them, and in the center of it all were tables crowded with an entire heavenly body's worth of angels. She carried everything from squat porcelain cherubs to stained glass wall hangings to elegant, hand-blown art glass and rustic wooden figures. Strips of silvery white tulle wove among the merchandise like frothy, ethereal clouds. Grace loved the effect. Loved that she was surrounded with all that kept her grounded. Hated that Jeff was eyeing it all with a dubious air.

"Angels?" he said.

She wasn't even going to tell him that it was some of her most popular merchandise. "Some like to imagine a physical form to the spirits in their lives. It helps them feel… connected to those whom they've lost."

His eyes pinned her like she was committing perjury on the witness stand. "You mean ghosts."

"That has such a negative connotation to it. I find my customers prefer the words 'spirit' or 'angel.'"

"You mean how I prefer the word 'uniform' over 'costume?'"

Before she could stop herself, her eyes slid over the navy fabric pulled taut over his broad shoulders and tucked crisply into his trim waistband. She forced herself to glance away before her gaze slid lower. She flipped her hair over her shoulder.

Jeff's eyes focused on the movement like a hawk sighting prey.

She dropped her hair-flipping hand and blew out a steadying breath. She'd like to pretend his presence didn't affect her, but his energy was palpable. It had always been that way.

He strode toward the register again. "Well, as fun as it is to listen to you talk about your friends in other dimensions, I'm actually here to pick up some things for my mother."

"I know. I spoke with her earlier." Grace pulled a bag from under the counter.

He peered inside the bag. "This is it? A jar of honey and a *rock?*"

"It's organic local honey. And that's not just a rock. It's a pink quartz crystal. It has a nice, clear energy I think she'll find healing. But if she doesn't like it, tell her to let me know."

He went to pull the quartz out of the bag, but she batted his hand away. "Don't! It'll soak up all your negative energy."

His lips tilted slightly at the corner again. "You've gotta be joking."

She rang up the order. "I'm perfectly serious."

"*I* have negative energy?"

"You're too..." She'd been about to say 'hard' but bit her tongue before that double-entendre had a chance to erupt like so much Freudian lava from her mouth. "Let's just say, you'll muddy things for her. She's still learning."

She told him the total. He frowned. "For two little things?"

"Crystals are not cheap."

"I'll say."

He handed over his credit card and eyed her shop again. "Who knew there was so much profit in this Voodoo stuff of yours?"

She slid his receipt toward him without comment. Then impulsively grabbed something out of a bowl she kept under the counter and tossed it in the bag.

"What's that?"

"Sage. Tell her I'll call her later to tell her what to do with it."

Jeff took his big, intimidating broad-shouldered self out of her shop, and Grace slumped onto the stool she kept behind the counter. She pulled out a hair-tie to corral her flirtatious hair into a ponytail. Not even the soothing sound of ocean waves rolling from the surround-sound speakers could ease the jittery, restless feeling the man left in his wake. Och. She'd carefully avoided him for two full years since he'd moved back to town. Now, it seemed he was everywhere she looked. Like some incredibly hunky version of Whack-A-Mole. Clearly the universe was telling her they had unfinished business. Sometimes she hated the universe.

The bell above the door jingled again and Grace stifled a groan as she saw who it was. Now what? Grams and 'the ladies', as the grandkids had taken to calling them, bustled through.

They entered the shop with purpose, flanking Grace, their expressions serious, lavender talcum powder and old lady perfume assaulting her senses.

Grace slid Jeff's receipt into the cash drawer and folded her hands in front of her. "Yes?"

Grams pursed her lips and set her bag on the countertop. "I'll not beat around the bush. I'm replacing you as lead on Harvest Festival planning."

"What? Why?" Could she even do that?

"Your interpersonal issues are causing discomfort with the other members."

"What interpersonal issues?"

Lydia Sweet leaned toward the counter, a crystal window ornament dangling from her fingers. "Does this come in pink? And she means your *thing* with Officer Dayton."

Grace shook her head. "What? So now that Jeff Dayton is on the committee I have to get off? I have an entire page of ideas I was going to present tonight."

Grace looked for support from her grandmother's other friends. Claire shrugged. "Don't look at me. I've no idea why we're here. I just heard we were getting lunch."

Grams squared her shoulders. "I'm sorry, but with your history of entering into childish and inappropriate bets with Officer Dayton—June can back me up on that one—I think it's best we ask someone else to finish the job. I bet Meg would step in if I asked her."

Grace couldn't believe they'd bring up some silly incident from two years ago. Okay. *Fine.* She would admit that accepting the bet to 'shake her booty' while riding the Gifts for the Greater Good float during the Independence Day parade a couple of years ago was not a shining moment for her, but she hadn't gone through with it!

Lydia met Grace's eyes. "You can't run from destiny forever. You and he will keep crossing paths until you learn the lessons from one another you need to learn."

Grace instantly regretted selling Lydia that book on 'Linked Destinies.' The woman was convinced she was linked with her garbage man and that's why he'd not missed a Tuesday morning pick-up in six years. It had nothing to do with it being his *job*. Plus, Grace hated when the universe felt the need to ram home a message like a sledge-hammer. She got it. Unfinished business. Must address. *Sheesh!*

Claire snorted. "What's this about destiny and lessons? I'm starved. Leave her be, Ruth. Let them duke it out. If I don't get some food in me my blood sugars will go off."

June Hastings, grandmother to Grace's sister-in-law, set down the bottle of essential oil she'd been sniffing and rummaged in her purse for her wallet. "There's nothing wrong with your blood sugars, Claire, and we were talking about the festival situation. Grace here is not making things any easier for that poor Joe Sedowsky to get a foot in the door, and if you'd been paying attention the other night when Ruth was telling us about it, you'd know things have come to a head with Jeff."

Grace turned to her grandmother. "Things have come to a head? What's that supposed to mean?"

Grams glared at her friends and then turned back to Grace. "Fine. I'm going to lay it out there. Sitting around a conference table with you two is as pleasant as an overcast day in black fly season. You're ignoring opportunities right in front of your face; you're letting your personal feelings interfere with your duties, because you practically sneer every time Officer Dayton makes a perfectly good suggestion; and you're all-around making life very uncomfortable for everyone."

"Me? *I'm* making everyone uncomfortable?" Grace ignored the 'opportunities' jab as her eyes grew round in disbelief. "I'm not the one that nearly made Lydia cry! If he had his way, we wouldn't have a festival at all."

"I'll admit he doesn't mince words, but he does make some valid points," Grams said.

Lydia rested a hand on Grace's arm. "I appreciate your trying to protect me dear, but I'm made of sterner stuff than that. He just surprised me."

"What if I told you Chief Russell said Jeff is grumbling about you, and it's giving him a headache?" Grams asked.

Grace folded her arms over her chest. "Again. Not my fault. Jeff Dayton will just have to grow up, suck it up and deal with it. I won't let us be held hostage by some over-inflated worries over things that are less likely than *actual* cats and dogs raining from the sky."

Grams huffed out a breath. "Fine. I was hoping we could avoid any more unpleasantry and address it before the fact, but it's clear you are as stubborn as always."

"I am not stubborn. I'm principled."

Seven o'clock that night proved her a liar.

~ * ~

"That's terrific," Grams enthused despite having tried to stage a coup just hours earlier. "This is a fantastic start. The Burgess's farm will be the perfect spot to hold it, too. Grace, you've outdone yourself."

Grace nodded, feeling vindicated for not simply rolling over and passing the baton to Meg. As if Meg even *wanted* the festival planning job. She was up to her eyeballs organizing some over-the-top birthday party for her daughter.

Besides, Grace hadn't spent untold hours over the weekend brainstorming what the heck they might *do* at a harvest festival that would be both fun for teens and families alike for nothing.

It had involved a lot of staring out the window and petting of her cats, which was not easy given how often images of a hunky, stubborn local cop kept invading her thoughts.

Grace thanked everyone and adjourned the meeting. She pulled away from her chair, her thin shirt sticking to her back, and excused herself to get some water as the others gathered their things to leave.

Jeff followed.

"I'm just getting a drink, Officer. Nothing to see here."

He reached out and gripped her arm, or rather touched it, but it seared through her body like a lightning bolt anyway. "Grace, hold on."

She stopped but refused to turn around for him. "What?"

She heard the slow, heavy release of breath behind her and then he took the two steps forward to look her in the face. "Can we be adults here?"

She felt her eyebrows pop up to her hairline. "Excuse me? I'm not the one who tried to get me kicked off the committee."

He frowned. "I never tried to get you kicked off. Who told you that?"

"My grandmother. She said you were complaining to Chief Russell." He frowned again. They both looked back toward the room. Grams was *such* a meddler.

"Anyway," Grace said, "if you did have a problem with me, I'd hope you'd address me directly."

The muscle in his jaw tightened. It did that when he was trying not to say something.

"Spit it out," she said. "You'll get constipated holding things in like that."

He raised one eyebrow, his lips twitching on one side with humor.

"Really?" is all he said.

Heat crept over her cheeks.

"I wanted to tell you, my mom says thank you. She said the honey made her throat less scratchy," he said.

"Oh. Good. I'm glad." Grace felt a bit nonplussed by the unexpectedly civil remark.

They stood there awkwardly for a moment, not speaking, the heavy air like all their unspoken history weighing down upon them. Grace fought the urge to pull her sticky shirt away from her chest. She didn't want to draw attention to herself.

And yet, perversely, she did.

That was the problem with standing in a quiet hallway feeling all hot and unsettled next to the one and only man she'd ever done *that* with. She resented the fact that he knew things about her no one else did... and also that he wasn't willing to do them again.

"Unless there's something else," she finally managed to say, "I was getting a drink."

She moved past him and swung her hair into her hand to lean over and drink from the water fountain. When she stood again and turned toward him, he had an odd look on his face that disappeared behind his stony mask.

She let her hair fall again and wondered if she'd imagined it. It would be nice to know she still had the power to throw him off as much as he did her.

"What?" she asked.

"Don't take this the wrong way. I like most of your ideas, but I think the llamas might be a mistake."

"Good thing you're not in charge of llamas."

His jaw tightened. "Goodnight, Grace." And with that, he turned crisply on his heel and walked away.

Grace pursed her lips, hating that she cared what he thought, and feeling very, very childish for being so ungracious.

The problem was she always felt at a disadvantage around him. He knew things about her. Remembered things. And while she knew and remembered things about him, that just felt like so much baggage as opposed to having the upper hand.

Everyone else had gathered by the library entrance by the time Grace returned, hurrying to be on their way before the thunderstorms predicted for the evening hit in full force. They said their goodbyes, peered at the dark sky and scurried to their parked cars as rumbles of thunder rolled down the valley and a few hot splatters of rain hit the pavement.

"Allow me."

Joe Sedowsky popped open a giant green and white golf umbrella and held it over Grace's head as the skies opened up as if on cue.

"Oh, I can make a run for it," she said.

"I wouldn't hear of it." He smiled, even white teeth beaming at her. They glowed a bit in the half light.

"Um. Thanks." She allowed him to escort her the thirty feet to her car and then turned to thank him.

The rain fell heavily, splatting on the umbrella, splashing her feet. The air underneath the umbrella felt hot and close. *Joe* felt hot and close.

She remembered the heat and proximity of a different summer rain.

Joe smiled, and she wished the urge to flee wouldn't take over every time this man drew near. Surely that wasn't a *good* sign? Maybe it was because he was so horribly *earnest*.

"Grace, I wondered if you'd do me the honor of," he paused and swallowed, "joining me for dinner tomorrow."

"I'm sorry. I can't. I've got my healing circle tomorrow night."

"Then Friday?"

She shook her head. "I'm babysitting."

He let out a frustrated breath. "Wednesday?"

"This is Wednesday. I've already eaten."

He flushed. "Is there a day in the future that you *would* join me for dinner?"

'Never' leapt to mind, but that seemed pretty harsh for a guy who had slogged through rain with an umbrella so she wouldn't get her hair wet who owned his own business and had all his teeth even though, once, a long time ago, he'd left her and she'd ended up falling in love with the man who'd broken her heart. After all these years, surely he deserved a second chance to get it right. Surely they both did.

The truth was, there was nothing *wrong* with Joe. Even the lazy eye was less pronounced somehow than she remembered it being in high school. And Meg and Dee both spoke so highly of him; although, neither of them knew about that night on her sixteenth birthday. Maybe it wasn't what was wrong with him, but something wrong with *her?*

"How about coffee tomorrow morning? Nine o'clock?" she found herself saying. "I don't open the shop until ten."

"I look forward to it. Shall we walk from the shop?"

"Sure." She beeped her key fob.

He reached behind her to open her door. "I'll see you tomorrow then."

"Tomorrow!" she said with false brightness.

Grace ducked into the car and shut the door before he could say anything more. She waved as he walked to his own car, closing her eyes for a brief second. Ugh. Another poor guy to let down. Who knows? Maybe Joe wouldn't turn out like the others. Maybe he'd understand. Maybe her problem was being *too* attracted to her dates, and that made her have performance anxiety or something.

Maybe he'd understand that the woman on the outside wasn't anything like the one on the inside. All men seemed to see was long, dark auburn hair and a somewhat tall, lean, yoga-limbed body. They complimented her bright eyes and clear skin and blah, blah, blah.

As soon as they got to the third date and expected something more than the peck on the cheek goodnight, that's when the cow poopy hit the fan.

It usually wasn't long before they threw words like "tease" and "flirt" at her... among other less flattering phrases.

The air inside her car felt hot and stifling and she cracked the window open despite the threat of rain pouring in. A face suddenly appeared at her window. She let out a little squeak.

"You have a taillight out. Passenger side. Get it fixed." Jeff strode away, all superior officer attitude, and Grace had the overwhelming urge to honk her horn at his retreating tight-assed backside.

To think she'd once imagined that Jeff Dayton was The One.

Pfft. As if.

CHAPTER TEN

Grace rolled over in bed and sighed. She couldn't forget she was meeting Joe for coffee.

After her morning yoga routine, she pulled a few items out of her closet, decided they were the most 'so casual can we even call this a date?' clothes she could manage and hopped in the shower.

Joe was right on time.

"Good morning." He beamed as she walked toward him as he waited on the sidewalk outside her shop. The morning air was comfortable and breezy and tangled her skirt around her legs. She wished she'd worn something shorter.

"Good morning."

He held out an elbow. "Shall we?"

She rested her hand on his arm, which felt a bit awkward and fussy for a trip around the corner to the coffee shop, but it was a gentlemanly gesture, so she accepted.

"Thank you for coming," Joe said.

"You're welcome."

"Congratulations, by the way, on your shop."

"Oh, thanks. You know it's been open for a while, right?"

"I meant, I hear it's doing well."

"Who told you that?"

"My mother. She likes to keep tabs on the eligible single women in Sugar Falls."

"How helpful." And how very Mrs. Bates of her.

He grinned then, his teeth flashing like a newscaster's. "Not so much so, but I don't blame her. I'm an only child. And, as she likes to point out, not getting any younger."

He ducked his head, heat staining his cheeks. "Sorry. TMI I imagine."

Definitely. "No. It's fine. It's better than hearing you've been stalking me on social media."

"No. That would be my mother. Feel free to block her."

Grace laughed then, relaxing a bit as Joe flashed her a self-deprecating grin. He'd always seemed awkward and earnest as a teen. Trying too hard. It was nice to see he had a sense of humor.

"I didn't think you'd say yes," he admitted, holding the door to the coffee shop open.

"You didn't?"

"After what happened back in high school. I guess I figured I'd be lucky to have another shot."

"I believe in second chances. We were both very young then."

"I was especially. My sincere apologies for that. At least nothing bad happened that night."

No, nothing except hooking up with a man who would later break her heart, but who was she to quibble?

"So, what'll you have?" he asked as they reached the front of the line.

They placed their orders and then chose a table by the outside wall to sit.

"You look beautiful, by the way. I admire a woman who's confident in her natural beauty."

"Um, thank you?"

"Sorry, I didn't mean to make you uncomfortable."

"No. It's sweet of you."

They sipped their hot drinks, blessed awkward silence filling the void.

The lazy eye had improved somewhat with time. She seemed to recall some talk of surgery and a pirate look he'd sported for a while. And he'd had a growth spurt at some point, so now they were at least eye to eye.

Grace cupped her latte and wracked her brain for pleasant but benign conversational topics.

"So, how's business?"

"Excellent. We just launched a new line of commodes with a lift-assist that are selling like hotcakes."

Joe's family ran a medical supply company. He told her how he'd run with some ideas he'd had with a start-up manufacturer... but frankly the details became a bit fuzzy. Truth be told, she zoned out a bit. It was tough to maintain interest in the latest wheelchair technology and medical-grade padding. There was such a thing?

Maybe it was because they'd been in this coffee shop for a full thirty-seven minutes, and not once had she gotten *that feeling*. She crunched her almond biscotti and nodded.

"I think about that night sometimes."

"What night?" she asked.

"Our date." It was more of a set-up, but whatever. "I didn't handle myself well, but thank goodness you had Jeff Dayton—a future cop no less!—to drive you home."

"I think we all learned some lessons that night," she said.

"Definitely. Never mix beer with hard alcohol."

Never trust your heart. "Yes." she smiled. "I assume you made it home all right? We never did get a chance to talk after that. Those were some storms."

"Tommy gave me a ride. I think. It's all still a bit fuzzy. And wet as I recall. There were sandbags involved. And Jell-O shots. But here I am now." He grinned. Were those crowns? "And here you are."

"Yes."

Joe looked at her expectantly. Hopefully. She took another sip of latte to hide her grimace. She shouldn't fight this, she'd promised herself last night in a moment of weakness fueled by loneliness and too much *Outlander* to give Joe a shot.

She'd known The One once. She'd had the tingles that ran over her skin and made her heart beat like a living thing in her chest, and it had ended badly. The spirit cards she'd read that morning said she must prepare for big changes. They said she needed to let go of old thinking in order to embrace what was on the horizon. Her spirit guides were watching over her and her purpose and path would be revealed, but only after a period of upheaval and transformation.

Sometimes she wondered what sort of sick sense of humor her spirit guides had.

The door jangled and Grace's attention shot to the man walking up to the counter. A different kind of energy filled the small space, and she had trouble taking a breath for a moment like she'd been sprayed by a skunk all over again. He did that to her. EVERY. DAMN. TIME.

Jeff walked up to the counter, oblivious to the fact that she was sitting there, in broad daylight, having coffee with an attractive, eligible man.

Well, fine. Maybe if she forced herself out of her comfort zone and made herself move forward, she could finally put this *thing* with Jeff to rest.

"You know what?" Grace placed her oversized mug on its saucer with purpose and sucked in a breath. "I think we should consider dating."

Joe spewed his decaf onto the table in front of her and quickly mopped it with his napkin. He grabbed hers, too, and cleaned the dribble off his chin. "What?"

"I know this is probably a surprise given my less than enthusiastic responses to your many overtures, and the fact that you thought me so indifferent you didn't think I'd even agree to share coffee with you. But if I'm going to be honest, you seem like a decent guy. I didn't put my all into my last relationship, and I think it's time I dive in, you know? To dating, I mean, not necessarily a relationship. But I'm fine, you know, if it *leads* to a relationship. I'm not afraid of commitment. And everybody deserves a second chance, even you, right? Not that what you did was so horrible, and it was so long ago... What I mean is, let's give this a shot, shall we?"

Joe nodded as if he understood her frightening monologue and this was all perfectly normal.

She held her breath. "So... what do you think?"

His eyes still bugged out a little, the soggy napkins crumpled in his palm. "Wow. Still taking this all in. I thought we'd start with coffee and see if we hit it off."

"I'm sorry. I... Maybe I misunderstood. I just didn't want you to wonder where I stood. We don't have to—" Cripes. Really? He was going to rebuff her here? *Now?*

"How does dinner Saturday night sound?" he asked.

"I'd love to," she announced a little louder and more brightly than necessary. She stroked her fingers through her hair and gathered it to pull over her shoulder, willing Jeff to notice that she was openly hair-flirting with another man with amazing teeth.

Joe grinned and gripped her hand, pulling her attention back to him. "Terrific. I'll pick you up, say, seven o'clock?"

She gulped and nodded. This is what she wanted, to move forward. Why did it feel like she might have just gotten in over her head?

But Joe was there, willing to give her a shot—even though she was the Sugar Falls Ice Princess. There was something comforting about that. Maybe her problem was wanting everything to be dynamic and exciting. Maybe she needed to learn that that passion only left you burned and licking your wounds in the end.

Jeff still hadn't turned around. "Seven o'clock it is," she said.

~*~

Jeff's jaw ached from the tension he held rigid inside him. *Really? Joe*

Sedowsky? She was doing that goddamned hair twirl for Joe Sedowsky? That had to be a new low. He grabbed his coffee, gave Melody, the barista, a curt nod and turned to exit.

The lovebirds were already there.

"I'll see you Saturday, then," Joe said to Grace, his smarmy hand gripping her elbow. Jeff had the unholy urge to bend each finger back until it broke, which was probably not the best approach considering he was supposed to uphold the peace and law of the land. He reached out and held the door for them instead.

"Oh, Jeff, I didn't see you there." Grace was lying, of course, because her pupils were dilated and she was making an extra effort to hold his gaze. He watched her pulse jump at the base of her throat. She blinked. Repeatedly. Yup, lying.

"Just heading to work," he said. "You?"

"Um, yes. The shop opens in ten minutes." She turned her back on him, throwing her hair over her shoulder like a scarf of disdain. "Thanks, Joe. This was lovely." Then she leaned forward and *kissed the man's cheek.*

Joe ducked his head, grinning like a goddamned fool, and mumbled something about being late for an appointment with the commode rep. Jeff willed him on his way.

"Don't burn a hole in his back with your laser-stare." Her words drifted up to him as they exited the shop, Joe hurrying in the opposite direction.

"I'm doing no such thing."

Grace headed toward her shop. Jeff fell into step beside her. "And stop stalking me," she said.

"I'm hardly stalking you. We happen to both be walking in the same direction."

"After getting coffee at the same time?"

"I always get my coffee at this time."

"Oh."

He took a sip. Still hot. "Hmm. Maybe you're stalking me?"

"You wish."

"I forget. That's not the Grace McIntyre M.O. is it?"

"I wasn't aware I had an M.O."

"Sure you do. You date a guy a couple of times and then move on to greener pastures. I guess I should feel lucky you kept me around as long as you did."

"I do not do that. But, I see no sense in stringing someone along if it's not working. That would be cruel."

"Right." He dragged the word out a bit and took another sip. Walked.

"Anyway, I didn't realize my love life was any of your concern," she said.

"It's not. Not for quite some time."

"Definitely not."

Her skirt tangled with her legs as she walked, billowing around them. It reminded him how long they were. Somehow she appeared graceful and fluid despite the shapeless clothes.

"So, this is your first date attire? Kind of bland isn't it? You late getting up?"

"Joe said he likes the natural look."

"He's a liar. Guys only say that to make the woman feel better about having not made an effort."

"Excuse me?" She stopped in the middle of the sidewalk, her eyes flashing. "You think I haven't made an effort? And who are you to tell me whether I should or shouldn't make an effort?"

"I seem to have touched a nerve."

"Stop talking to me. It agitates me."

"Does it now?"

He was being a dick and he knew it, but he couldn't stop poking at her. He needed to know she was just as agitated by his proximity as he was by hers.

It had always been that way. Ever since the day she'd stolen his better judgment with her artless flirting and large, expression-filled eyes.

Ever since he'd stolen from her that which he could never give back.

"You didn't always mind my company," he murmured.

She glanced up at him and away again, started walking. "That was before. It's ungentlemanly of you to mention it."

"I didn't mind you, either," he said.

"Well, that was before."

"I don't mind you now," he said.

She stumbled then, an almost imperceptible hiccup in her stride. "You don't?"

Damn. He wasn't sure why he'd said that. Somehow it had slipped out. He usually had far more control over his speech. He was careful.

Except when it came to Grace.

"I find you entertaining," he said. "And occasionally smelly."

Her delicately arched brows frowned at him. "Har-dee-har-har."

"I find you... intense," she said, walking again. "Why are you always hovering and standing places?"

"I don't know. Maybe I find it easier to place my coffee order when I can see over the counter."

"Not that. At the Civic Pride meetings. You always stand in the corner."

He sipped his coffee and avoided her eyes. "I don't like to sit."

"Why?"

"I like to see all the exits."

"But there's only one door. Doesn't take a lot to keep it in sight."

"There are other ways in and out of that building than the door."

"Yeah, I don't think you'd fit in the book return slot."

Her gaze bounced off his shoulders and away again.

"Civilians never see things we do." He ticked off each egress as he named them. "There are windows facing both the parking lot and the street. The skylight in the new wing. The cellar entrance..."

She stopped. "The skylight?"

He made an impatient noise. "You don't see them as access points, because you're not trained to see them, but that's my job. It's my job to be aware and do everything I can to anticipate risk."

"But a skylight? You think somebody is going to rappel down through it like some Bond movie? I think the odds of that are relatively low. They'd slide off the metal roof into the shrubbery."

"There's nothing stopping some old lady from jumping the curb and plowing right into the Morning Room. Think about that the next time you give me the evil eye for watching your back."

She paused then, the snark leaving her expression.

"You know we're safe there," she said quietly.

"That's what you think. Until some whack-job with grandpa's hunting rifle and a grudge against the new librarian gets it in his head to charge in and start shooting the place up."

Grace rested a light hand on his arm. He fought the urge to shake it off. He found her calmness unnerving.

"We can't prevent everything."

"No, not everything," he said.

He pulled his arm away.

"So we should just live our lives in fear?" she asked.

"There's a difference between being afraid and being prepared."

"You make it sound as if there's no third option."

"Is there?"

"I believe so."

He wanted to believe it, too, for the sake of the hopeful, vulnerable look in her eyes, but he couldn't let himself. It was his job to be ever vigilant so the doe-eyed idealists who thought they lived in a rose-colored bubble didn't have to face the realities of life.

"Listen, I don't want to alarm you," he said, "But we've had some reports of businesses in and around town getting broken into—mostly back doors or side entrances while the owners are elsewhere in the building. No damage or anything reported missing, but it may be the thieves have been spooked. Just keep an eye out and let me know if you see or hear anything suspicious. Could just be kids getting a thrill. Could be someone looking for cash more than merchandise."

"Why would anyone break in during the day? Seems the risk of getting caught would be pretty high."

He glanced down at her. "The penalty is steeper for crimes committed after dark. Right now we're treating these as attempted burglaries. Just keep an eye out."

"Sure." She said, her hand now on the door to her shop. "Thanks for the warning."

CHAPTER ELEVEN

That afternoon, Grace begged Trish to cover the store so she could go visit *Second Chances,* Lydia's vintage clothing and consignment shop. Like so many things, it was hit or miss, but Grace had always enjoyed Lydia's company if not her personal style choices, and she felt the need for something new for her date with Joe the next night. Her recent run-ins with Jeff only cemented her determination to Move On with capital letters.

"Ooh. I like that one. Very nice color on you." Lydia busied herself behind the glass display counter arranging the estate jewelry she'd bought at auction the prior week. Her ever-present silver bangles tinkled like wind chimes on her wrist.

Grace held the Asian-inspired dress in front of her and looked in the mirror. She fingered the rich, ruby brocade with the black piping around the edges. "I don't know. I like it, but I was told red sends a certain message."

Lydia snorted happily. "Ed always liked me in red."

Grace grimaced. "I don't know if it's first date material. Maybe it's too forward?"

"Just try it on. It's better than that 'kindergarten teacher slash hippie slash bored housewife' look you've been trying out lately."

"Excuse me?" Said the woman who favored muumuus and animal prints!

"Oh, don't take offense, but you sometimes look like you've dressed in the dark, and this is from a woman who likes to keep things interesting."

Grace eyed Lydia's snakeskin patterned blouse and flowing pink skirt. Yeah. *So* not taking fashion advice from this woman.

But maybe she should consider spicing things up a bit. Wasn't she trying to turn a new leaf by mindfully pushing herself out of her comfort zone? She should consider the Zach break-up a wake-up call. She couldn't take her future happiness for granted.

She slipped into the dressing room.

Sigh. Of course, the dress fit like a dream.

It would be wrong to discard it simply because some people had ridiculous notions, right? Plus it made her legs look fantastic.

She waited, perusing the jewelry, while Lydia rang up her purchase. "Very pretty. Is that one sapphire?"

"Hmm?" Lydia paused and peered at the rings on their velvet display board. "Yes. Beautiful, isn't it?"

"Yes."

Something about the delicate band of tiny gemstone flowers drew Grace toward it and made her feel inexplicably sad all at the same time. "May I try it on?"

Lydia set the velvet board on the counter and turned to put the dress in a bag.

Grace slid the ring on and held it up.

"A bit unusual for a wedding band, but it suits you."

Grace blushed. "It's the only finger it fit on." She slid it off again. "Pity. I don't think it would resize well." She set it back in its slot on the display board.

Lydia passed over the dress bag. "I have a good feeling that finger won't be empty long. And you know my feelings are usually right." She waved her hand like a magic wand, her bangles tinkling excitedly.

Grace rolled her eyes as kindly as she could. She didn't want to hurt Lydia's feelings, but it'd take a miracle to change her trajectory from bumbling singleton to marriageable.

"I thought I'd found The One once, too. Clearly feelings can be wrong."

"Our feelings are never wrong," Lydia insisted. "But sometimes our timing is."

CHAPTER TWELVE

"She's going out to dinner with Joe Sedowsky tonight," Lydia said. Poker night was at her house this week, and she'd made extra nibbles. For some reason September always made her feel melancholy, and she wanted her friends to linger.

"Oh good God!" Ruth Pearson muttered. "That boy needs a twit not someone like Grace. He'll bore the life out of her."

"She said she needed to get back in the dating game."

"Was she ever in it?" Claire sniffed and popped a roast beef and cream cheese roll up into her mouth. "Seems to me, she keeps her legs too tightly crossed."

"Claire!" June Hastings admonished. "Really!"

Claire swallowed and picked up her gin and tonic. "What? It's a compliment! I'm just saying she's choosier than most. That's not a bad thing. In our day they didn't have killer STDs."

"Oh, dear Lord," Ruth muttered. "They did, but that's beside the point."

"They call her the Ice Princess," Claire said.

"Where? Who says this?" June wanted to know, as if it were her granddaughter being maligned and not Ruth's.

"I heard it from Trudi who heard it from her grandson. Says she's a hopeless flirt who, and I quote, 'never puts out.'"

Ruth sniffed and added a photo to the pot in the center of the table, not even looking at it. They never played for money but played using family photos. The winner got to talk about whatever they wanted. Lately, they'd been talking a lot about great-grandchildren. Maybe that was why Lydia felt melancholy.

"Well, there are worse reputations one could have," said Ruth. "What do they say about Joe Sedowsky?"

"He's very prompt," said Claire.

"Oh dear."

"Nobody has gotten a royal flush in hearts in months," said Lydia.

"Oh, for Pete's sake," said Claire. "Are we on that again? Can these kids not get matched up without us believing some nonsense about a royal flush in hearts being some magic spell that causes it to happen?"

"It's *not* nonsense," Lydia said. "It's happened *three* times now. I was just thinking it was time for another match."

June tossed a photo of her granddaughter's twins into the pot. "There aren't many singles left to match up anyway."

Lydia sighed and stared at the photos her friends had already anted up. Ruth's little great-granddaughter, Ella, splashing with brightly-colored toys in a bathtub, grinned back at her from the top of the pile. Lydia looked away.

Or maybe this malaise hanging over her was because September was when her friends had all, so many years ago, first revealed to her that they were pregnant. Lydia stuffed her mouth full of roast beef roll-up and pretended it was enough to fill the empty ache inside.

Had they all forgotten how incredibly lucky it was to find that one special person you want to spent your life with? To live and love and have babies and grow old with, God willing?

She looked back at the cards in the pot. Every photo was of a great-grandchild or grandniece or nephew. Every. Single. One. And the hard part was the others had forgotten how amazing each child was, what a miracle they were. Here they were not even *looking* and their hands fell on an adorable photo.

Lydia reached into her box. It held the same edge-worn photo of her and Ed at the Grand Canyon she'd been using for years, a shirtless fireman holding a kitten—some booze advertisement she'd pulled from a magazine—and Grace's business card which she'd thrown in at the last Healing Circle, because she'd written her grocery list on the back.

Lydia read the list:

Ensure

Ham

Tapioca

Lydia tossed the business card on top of the pile.

Claire frowned. "Lydia, that's not even a photo."

"It has a pretty picture on it." She pointed to the lotus flower floating in a brook with the word *Currents* in elegant script over it.

Claire turned to the others. "Lydia's in a funk, and I need more than miniature food. I missed dinner." She scooped a handful of the roll-ups Lydia had painstakingly prepared and tossed them on her plate, their toothpicks toppling every which way.

Lydia gasped.

"Relax, Lydia. You know how Claire is. Claire, behave." This from June as she reordered her cards.

"Just because I don't have grandchildren doesn't make my card inferior. For your information, I've always thought of Grace as the daughter I never had."

Ruth blinked. "That's very sweet of you, Lydia. I'm sure Grace would be flattered to hear that."

Lydia nodded. She hadn't said it to flatter. She hadn't meant to say it at all.

The roast beef and cream cheese formed a blob in her stomach. She took a quick swig of her cocktail. She should be over this, stronger than this. Nobody wanted to see the old woman lose her cool and start babbling. They put people away who started to do that. Especially people of a certain age.

It wasn't her fault she'd always been eccentric.

"I think I'd like to try salsa dancing," she said.

Claire coughed into her shoulder. "Excuse me?"

"The ballroom above the library. I hear they're offering salsa lessons. Who's with me?"

They stared at her in shock, but maybe that was aspirated roast beef on Claire's part. "Fine. I'll go by myself."

"It sounds fun, actually," June said. "What? I don't promise to be any good, but I enjoy dancing. Always have."

"Count me out," Claire said. "I have two left feet."

Lydia turned to Ruth. "Well?"

Ruth looked around at her friends and shrugged her shoulders sheepishly. "I've been going every Monday since *Happily Ever After* went on summer break. Just a warning, whatever you do, don't pair with Chief Russell. The man will dance your socks off."

CHAPTER THIRTEEN

"You look stunning tonight." Joe held Grace's chair for her, his teeth flashing bright in the soft light of the candle-lit lantern on their table.

She hadn't had the heart to inform Joe that she'd rather eat cat food out of a can than show her face at the Silver Birch Inn again. She told herself to suck it up and be grateful the skunk smell was gone.

"Thank you." She sat down and did that awkward humping thing women do so he didn't have to scrape the chair across the floor to get her into position. Joe was nice and all, but he didn't appear to have all the upper-body strength of some men she knew.

Not that she was at all thinking about Jeff Dayton.

Joe seemed satisfied she was in far enough and took his seat opposite. She shuffled herself demurely the rest of the way so she could at least reach her water glass.

He grinned and unfurled his napkin, draping it precisely over his lap. His dark gray suit and matching tie made him look a bit like a middle schooler dressing up as a secret service agent.

He waived the waiter down, requested a bottle of merlot by name and turned to her.

"So, you look beautiful."

"You said that."

He paused. Blinked. "I suppose I did." A self-deprecating grin creased his features. "It bears repeating."

Smooth. And very smarmy. No! She had to stop thinking about it that way. It was sweet. She could do this. She could stop obsessing over the effortless hunkiness of men like Jeff Dayton long enough to give this perfectly eligible man a chance. Yes, Joe might seem a bit... bland... at first blush, but maybe that was better than the sharp current of awareness that shot through her every time she was near Jeff.

Jeff was too... intense. The man *throbbed* for heaven's sake.

And Joe... Joe was like reading a sweet romance novel. Nothing too spicy. Nothing too dangerous. Just predictably... pleasant.

"I hear you may be taking over your parents' business soon," she said.

A cloud of sadness shadowed Joe's features. "Unfortunately, since my dad's heart attack, it's likely I'll be stepping in, yes."

"That's good isn't it? I mean, not the heart attack part, that's awful, but the other thing?"

He shrugged. "Yes. I just wish it were under different circumstances."

"Of course."

She drank her water again.

He cleared his throat.

"Your business doing well?" he asked even though she was pretty sure they'd covered that topic over coffee two days before.

"I've added a mix-your-own aromatherapy counter, which is doing well."

"Have you?" He leaned forward on his elbows like a talk show host.

"Um, yes. I found a woman at the Farmer's Market who creates her own essential oils. She even designs and makes these really beautiful aromatherapy pendants. So far they've been selling as fast as she can supply them."

"Yes. Yes," he nodded, as if repeated affirmations could carry a conversation.

Grace took another sip of water and glanced around. Her stomach growled.

"Would you like an appetizer?" he asked. The waiter arrived with the wine and poured for them. "We'd like an order of Oysters Bruschetta," Joe said, winking at her as if she'd be pleased he'd just asked the waiter to deliver a plate of sea slugs on toasted baguettes to their table.

She blanched. "Oh, none for me. I'm vegetarian."

"You are?"

"Yes. Have been for years." Thank the Lord.

He frowned, and ordered a fruit and cheese platter instead. The waiter soon returned, set a rustic wooden cutting board of artisanal cheese and sliced fruit on the table and took their entrée order.

She and Joe chatted about rotator cuff injuries, the Civic Pride Committee, the weather. Basically, boring stuff.

"So what made you open a shop like *Currents* anyway?" he asked.

Grace paused in the process of stuffing her mouth with brie-topped pear. "It seemed a natural fit. I've always been interested in the metaphysical, spiritual, nature..." She waved her hand vaguely hoping that would satisfy him. She'd found people tended to fall into two camps where her shop was concerned: those who thought it odd and suspect and those who naturally understood. Joe clearly didn't have a clue.

He nodded nevertheless. "I imagine being an orphan will do that."

She grimaced. Ugh. She'd forgotten the third camp—those who felt it was some sort of psychological commentary, as if her interests and therapy were necessarily intertwined. Plus, she hated when people referenced her family history so casually, as if it were a random factual statement instead of a devastating childhood tragedy.

"You know about that?" she hedged.

He lifted his shoulders. "Everyone did. My mother volunteered with your mom at the library, or so I'm told."

Grace stopped, a hunk of cheese hovering near her mouth. "I didn't know that."

"Yeah. Mom has been pushing me to 'friend that poor McIntyre girl' for years."

She laughed and ate the cheese. "I think I did know that."

He chuckled, and she found herself relaxing. He did have a nice laugh. It made her feel... safe. Unthreatened. She wondered why she'd shied away from him for so long. The vaguely lazy eye and unfortunate night back in high school notwithstanding, he seemed earnest in a kind way. Like a puppy.

Soon the waiter delivered their entrees. Fettuccine Alfredo for her, filet mignon for him. She took a bite, her eyes closing of their own accord.

"Holy crap," she breathed. "You've got to try this." She dug her fork into the mound in front of her and shoved a bite into Joe's mouth without thinking.

His eyes flew wide as he grimaced and chewed the mouthful she'd just forced on him.

"Amazing, isn't it?" she asked.

"Delicious," he nodded. He smiled and took a sip of wine. Then another. He cleared his throat.

He drank more wine.

"So, what do you do for fun?" she asked. *Hmm*. She normally wasn't a red wine fan, but whatever he'd ordered was really good. Joe seemed to think so, too, because he drank again.

He licked his lips. "What?"

"What do you do for fun?"

"I, ah..." He shook his head, glancing around. "I need to go," he said, abruptly pushing back his chair.

"To the bathroom?"

He shook his head, yanking his color-coordinated tie from his neck somewhat desperately. "To the E.R."

Grace dropped her fork. "Why?"

"I think… I'm having a reaction."

"*Ohmigod.* Really? Okay, we'll… I mean *I'll*… get help." She pushed away her chair and ran as fast as her three-inch heels could carry her to the front desk. "I need an ambulance. My date is having an allergic reaction."

"You just can't keep 'em, can you?" the cashier said, looking up from her cell phone. *Great.* It was Evil Angela. Did she never have the night off?

"I'm serious. Please, dial 9-1-1."

"I'm dialing. I'm dialing…"

Grace rushed back to the dining room where Joe was currently slumped in his chair again, a small crowd of concerned diners gathered around him. "Does anyone have an epi pen?" she asked. "Do *you* have one?"

His face was pale, and he shook his head.

Oh God. He was going to die. Lips were *not* supposed to be that color! Why didn't he have an epi pen? Shouldn't medical supply people have that sort of thing?

She knelt on the floor next to him, gripping his hand, murmuring inane words of comfort until she heard the commotion of paramedics arriving. She stumbled aside, wincing as they produced an epi pen, stabbed Joe's thigh, and bundled him onto a gurney.

She hurried after them, unsure of what to do. Or how to do it.

"Don't be thinking you'll get out of here and stiff your waiter," Angela said.

Grace whirled. "Really? At a time like this?"

"Just kidding. Hope he's okay. Your track record ain't the greatest. You might want to ride with him so he doesn't get away."

"Har-dee-har-har," Grace whispered as she watched them load Joe into the back of the ambulance.

Then she realized he'd driven them to the restaurant. And he still had his car keys.

A Sugar Falls police cruiser pulled into the parking lot. The window rolled down. Jeff leaned across the seat to peer out at her. "I should have known you'd be in the middle of this."

"It's Joe Sedowsky. They're taking him to the hospital. He ate something…"

"Hop in. I'll give you a ride over."

She hurried down the walkway. "Thank you."

Blessedly, Jeff didn't speak on the way to the hospital. They pulled in behind the ambulance. Grace threw open her door and rushed forward, her heels dangling from her fingers. "Is he all right? He's going to be all right, isn't he?"

Joe's eyes met hers above his oxygen mask as they wheeled him through the doors and into the bowels of the hospital. The doors to the E.R. closed in her face.

She felt a hand on her shoulder. "Relax. There's nothing you can do from here."

Grace glanced up into Jeff's brown eyes, taking comfort from his stoic demeanor. He'd always been calm in a crisis. Even when things were at their very worst.

"I know." She sighed. "I just feel like I should be *doing* something." She stilled and met Jeff's eyes. "I should call his mom."

She pulled her cell phone from her bag, looked up the number and dialed. A few minutes later, she slid it back again. "She's on her way. Thankfully, she's not far."

Jeff nodded and flipped open a note pad. "So I'm assuming you were there when the subject started showing signs of distress."

"Yes. We're on a date."

Jeff glanced toward the closed E.R. doors. "*Were* on a date." He made a couple notes. "Can you tell me what happened?"

"We'd just been served our entrees when he started having trouble breathing. It all happened very fast."

"I see. Did he eat anything unfamiliar?"

"No. He ordered the filet mignon, which he said was a favorite of his, so I'm assuming that wasn't it."

Jeff made an *mm-hmm* noise. "Anything else?"

"Some cheese and a piece of pear. And red wine. Oh, and a bite of my pasta."

Jeff glanced up. "He ate from your plate?"

"Well, not exactly. I offered it to him."

"And he took it without asking about the ingredients?"

Grace felt herself go cold. "Um, I kind of took him by surprise."

"Surprise?"

"It was so good, I gave him a bite without thinking. Besides, I'm sure it's unlikely to be my pasta. He's allergic to Chinese food, not Alfredo."

"MSG. He's allergic to MSG."

"How do you know?"

"He had a medic alert bracelet on."

"Oh."

"They use MSG in sauces, Grace."

"Oh." She glanced up at him as the outside hospital doors burst open and a small, frantic woman rushed in. *"Oh."*

"Where is he? Where is my Joseph?"

"Mrs. Sedowsky?" Jeff turned, saving Grace from having to speak.

Dear God. She'd just poisoned this woman's son?

Jeff stepped forward. "He's in the E.R. I'll let the nursing staff know you're here."

After the hospital staff ushered Mrs. Sedowsky away, Jeff took a few moments to speak with the paramedics before walking over to Grace again. She sat slumped in one of the stiff plastic chairs near the window.

Great. Another disaster Jeff Dayton had a front-row seat for. She might have expected this sort of turbulence if Mercury was still in retrograde, but needing 9-1-1 twice in one month? Clearly the universe thought these opportunities to humiliate her were too good to pass up.

"I assume you need a ride?" Grace glanced toward the double doors of the hospital as Jeff spoke. "Thought you might want to leave before his mom comes out. She might not be feeling too warm and fuzzy about you after you tried to kill him."

"It was an accident!"

"I'm kidding." Jeff had the nerve to chuckle. "They'll probably keep him overnight though, so there's no point hanging out. You can check on him tomorrow."

She nodded. "Sure."

She followed him out the doors, the night damp and overcast.

He opened the passenger door of his cruiser.

"I appreciate your taking me home," she murmured. She felt awful. And hungry. And really, really guilty.

"No problem. My shift ended ten minutes ago."

He pulled out of the hospital parking lot.

She darted a glance at him and then away again.

"You must think I'm a magnet for trouble," she sighed.

He didn't look at her, although his mouth quirked up on one side. "It does seem to follow you."

"I had no idea. He didn't ask the waiter about ingredients or anything."

"He probably called ahead so he wouldn't make an issue with you there."

"That backfired."

"Hey, it could have happened to anyone."

"Especially me."

He laughed outright then. "I wasn't going to say it."

She sighed again. Her stomach grumbled loudly.

"Hungry?" he asked.

"A bit. I had a few bites of cheese and fruit, but I was so busy today I skipped lunch."

His gaze skimmed her profile before returning to the road in front of them. "And you all dressed up for the evening."

He slowed, checked his rearview mirror and pulled a quick U-turn.

"What are you doing?" Grace said, grabbing the dash as they spun around.

"Getting you food."

"I have leftovers in my fridge," she said, albeit weakly.

A few minutes later, he turned off the road, tires crunching on a gravel lot.

Grace moaned. "Oh, no. Not here. They hate me here."

"Come on. They'll want to know he's okay."

"Seriously. This is the scene of the crime. No—*two* crimes. I'll go hungry before I go back in there."

"Suit yourself, but I plan on having dinner, so I might be a while." He swung open his door and slammed it behind him.

She stared mutinously out the window for all of three seconds. Then her stomach growled. She was out by the time he'd rounded the car. "I'm only eating because I'm hungry, and because I should probably pay our bill before your Angela comes after me with a pitchfork."

His eyes crinkled with humor. "I wouldn't expect anything else."

She hung back by the door as Jeff approached Angela who had probably already posted damning pictures online of Grace force-feeding Joe. Jeff held his arm out behind him, waiting for Grace to step forward.

"Angela, Grace here would like to finish her dinner, and I'm just off my shift. Any chance you have a table for two?"

The girl gave Grace the hairy eyeball but then smiled at Jeff. "You're in luck. Some woman poisoned her date so we do have a table free."

Grace followed them into the dining room again. Thankfully, most everyone who had been in the restaurant earlier had finished their meals and left already. Still, she slunk in as quietly as she could wearing a red brocade dress and spiked heels.

"Thanks, Ange." Jeff took his seat and watched with an amused expression as Grace grabbed a menu and held it like a shield in from of her. She knew his expression was amused, because she could hear him laughing.

"No one is even looking at us," he said. "Relax."

"Easy for you to say. By the time I'm done here, Mrs. Sedowsky will probably have a hit out on me. Plus, Angela hates me. She'll probably spit in my food."

"I doubt it. I think she actually respects that you have the guts to revisit the scene of the crime."

She dropped the menu. "Must we call it that? It was an accident. A terrible, horrible accident."

"So you want another order of Alfredo?"

Grace frowned. "No. I'll have the vegetarian lasagna. I'm not sure I can bring myself to eat Alfredo ever again."

Angela approached their table, set a couple glasses of water down and took their order. Jeff leaned back in his chair and took a long drink before setting his glass back on the table.

"Why are you being nice to me?" Grace blurted.

"Am I? You look like you'd rather be anywhere else but here."

"I would, but that's because of nearly killing my date here. And, um, the skunk thing."

"I've learned it's best to face your fears head on. You can't run from this place forever. For one thing, you'd miss their cheesecake."

She sighed. "True."

"So, I'm doing you a favor. Plus, I was hungry. Win-win."

Grace picked up her water and sipped it. She didn't feel like a winner.

"You look great tonight, by the way. That dress suits you."

"Oh, here we go…"

"What?"

"You're not going to say, 'but that color sends a certain message?' Am I the only one who didn't know that rule? And now you're thinking, 'did she really want to get lucky with Joe tonight?' Which isn't fair, or accurate, because maybe, just maybe, I *like* the color. It's vibrant. And strong. And—"

"Were you?" he interrupted, which she was relieved about, truth be told. She tended to run at the mouth when she was nervous or upset.

"What?" she said.

"Hoping to get lucky with Joe?"

"Lord no. I mean, none of your business."

He snickered, which, thankfully, was less appealing than the cocky grins he'd been flashing her way. "Thought not."

It annoyed her that he was right. And that he knew it.

He leaned back with his arms crossed. "So, Joe Sedowsky, eh? Wasn't he the guy that ditched you for that party the night we—"

"Is that why we're here?" she interrupted. "To take a trip down memory lane together? Because, I'd rather not if it's all the same to you."

He nodded, looking a bit less relaxed. "Me either."

"Besides, if either of us doesn't want to revisit our past, I'd think it would be you."

"Why me?"

She made a dismissive gesture at him. "You're clearly all yellow."

"You think I'm sunny?"

"No. Yellow means you're blocked up. You're stifling your energies."

He snorted. "Huh."

"Don't believe me if you want. I'm not the one suffering."

"I feel perfectly normal."

"So you're chronically blocked? Not surprised."

He leaned across the table toward her. "Maybe you're projecting. I feel perfectly open. I'm not hiding from the truth."

She looked away. "I'm not hiding anything." Much.

He leaned back again. "Liar," he said.

She frowned. "I've never lied to you."

His lips hitched up on one side. "Maybe that's our problem."

She leaned back as their entrees were set before them and mumbled a thank you. "No, lying was never our problem."

~ * ~

After a reasonably successful dinner, meaning they hadn't come to blows and no one left in an ambulance, Jeff drove Grace home. He opened the passenger door for her. She got out with a frown, which seemed unnecessary seeing as he *had* just bought her dinner.

"Why are you looking at me that way?" she demanded. "Stop it."

"How am I looking at you?"

"Menacingly. Stop playing cop at me. It makes people uncomfortable."

Menacingly? How about hungrily? he thought. "I'm not *playing* cop, Grace. I *am* a cop." He shook his head. "*Police officer.*"

"Can't you just be a guy for once? What happened to the guy who scaled an eight-foot security fence to pick flowers for his girlfriend? The guy who rode a motorcycle and had tattoos? It's like you've sanitized yourself since you've come back to town. You're... different."

"It's been years. You've changed, too." He meant that in a good way—that she was as mesmerizing as a flame in the dark—and yet he could see she wasn't sure if he were paying her a compliment.

"You used to be... relatable," she said.

"I see. So, because you can't see my tattoo you don't recognize me? Who knew long sleeves made me invisible?"

Something lit up in her eyes. "So you still have them?"

"There was only the one."

"Prove it. Show me there's some piece of the old Jeff behind the badge."

"I'm not taking off my..."

And that's when the woman who'd kept him up nights for more than a decade began to cluck like a chicken.

He wasn't sure what happened, how they shifted from standing outside his cruiser and sparring to sharing something just as electric, but he found himself unbuttoning his shirt nonetheless. He watched her eyes go dark as he freed the bottom hem from his waistband and pulled it down and off his left shoulder, exposing his torso and arm.

"Hey old friend," she whispered, staring at the tattoo on his bicep.

He couldn't read her expression, and for some inexplicable reason, her eyes grew moist before she swallowed and blinked and threw her hair over her shoulder in a careless gesture.

He pushed his arm back into his sleeve unsure of what to say. "I'm still me," he said.

She offered a wry half-smile as if remembering something forgotten. "Still you."

"Grace, for what it's worth..." He let out a long breath. "I forgive you for what happened."

Her expression shuttered. "You forgive me?"

"Yes." He reached out and brushed her hair from her cheek. "I'd like to put the past in the past. You were young..."

"*We* were young," she corrected.

"We were young... and we made mistakes."

"Yes we did," she repeated.

"But I'm hoping we can let that go. Don't you think it's time to move on?"

She pressed her lips together. "Yes, but I don't know if that's possible."

He let out a grunt of frustration. "I've said I've forgiven you. What more do you need from me?"

She shook her head. "You could start with a little understanding."

"I'm being understanding," he grated. "I'm all friggin' blocked up with understanding here."

"I think we have different definitions of the word."

"So tell me your definition, because we're too old for these games."

"That's just it. I was never playing games with you. Never."

"Then can we at least call a truce between us? We live in the same town. We're on the same damned committee. It'd be nice if we could at least promise to be civil with each other."

"Fine. I promise to be civil."

He wanted more than that. A hell of a lot more, he wanted to push her or himself out of this godforsaken limbo he'd been living in too long, but she had her arms crossed in front of her, her chin held high, and he knew there was no way he'd talk her into anything.

So it was a damn good thing he didn't want to talk.

He snaked a hand out to cup her cheek. A muscle vibrated in her jaw under his palm. He stroked her cheek with his thumb.

"God help me, I want more than that."

He didn't bother to smile.

"I miss you, Grace," he admitted, whether to himself or her he wasn't sure, but he felt her lean toward him ever so slightly at the confession, and he chose to capitalize on that small toe-hold. "I know it would be easier for both of us to just move on and pretend we didn't have something once, but I don't want to."

"You think it's easier to move on?" she said.

"No. No, I don't."

He didn't say anything more, instead taking that half-step closer to press his body against hers and dip his head to taste those wide, ripe lips once more.

She shuddered as they made contact, like a wave of something held tight had found involuntary release, and then she reached up and slid a soft hand up his neck and into his hair to hold his lips to hers.

He groaned and pressed against her harder, drinking from her mouth as if he'd just finished a twenty-mile run in full combat gear. He felt dizzy and light-headed, then remembered to breathe as she made tiny sounds of surrender.

He'd forgotten this about her, this all-consuming electricity like a current that only flowed when he was physically connected to her. It pumped through him now, sending his pulse into overdrive. Every nerve ending was acutely aware of her body against his. Hell, even his toes could feel that his lips were kissing her.

It had been this way the first time, too. She'd touched him, a slight graze of her fingers, and he'd felt the jolt through his body like lightning.

A man would do almost anything to feel this way with a woman. He'd forget himself. His principles. His place. His convictions. He'd be drawn under her spell like a riptide pulling him out to sea, and he'd thank the siren song even as it led to his being pulled under.

His hands found their way down her body, remembering her through touch, astonished that so much felt familiar even though she'd grown into her woman's body. All the proportions were there, just richer, fuller than before. It was Grace still, only more so.

He gripped her waist, exploring her mouth so deeply, she bent backward slightly like a willow in his arms, strong but flexible.

He prayed she could survive the storm inside him, because he'd lied about forgiving her. A part of him still pushed at her, the pained, wounded piece of him he'd buried inside so many years ago. It pushed up and out like a stone working its way toward the surface of the earth. Eventually, he wouldn't be able to deny it.

But now... now he pretended it wasn't there, the hard, unyielding remains of what they'd once been to one another. Now, he let himself take what she so freely gave. To just feel.

Until she pushed him away, her palms flattened against his chest, a slightly panicked look in her eyes.

"I'm sorry," he said, even though he wasn't.

"For what? What are you sorry for, Jeff?"

He faltered. It felt like a test. He wanted to get the answer right—but he had no idea what she wanted to hear. He was just sorry in a vague, all-encompassing sort of way. Sorry he came back. Sorry they kept butting heads at committee meetings. Sorry he could see her every day but not touch her like he once had. Sorry that a feeling this goddamned good existed in the world, but he couldn't keep hold of it. Of her. Just... sorry.

"I'm sorry I don't understand," he tried.

She took a small breath and stumbled back a step. She blinked, eyes suddenly bright. "Well. I'm sorry for that, too." And then she grabbed her purse and ran to her door.

CHAPTER FOURTEEN

_____

It had been four days since the disastrous 'Date of Death' as Dee had jokingly begun to refer to it. Apparently, she'd gotten the full scoop from Jeff.

Well, hopefully, not *all* of it.

Joe had been discharged Sunday morning and had, bless him, called to ask to reschedule their date for the coming Saturday. Grace had hedged and suggested they might take a wait-and-see approach, not wanting to kick the guy while he was down. Better to let him fully recover before breaking it to him that it just wasn't going to work no matter how hard she tried to push on the end of that string.

At least he'd begged off the Civic Pride meeting, because she couldn't look him in the eye knowing she'd nearly killed him, accidentally or not.

Grace hauled her tote over her shoulder and braced herself for the meeting ahead. She could do this. She could walk into that library, do the job she'd been volunteered to do, and keep herself whole and composed in the process. She could.

She lifted the hot cup of cappuccino she'd brought to keep herself alert—because Lord knew she hadn't been sleeping well the last few nights—and pushed through the library doors.

They were all waiting for her when she got there.

"Good evening, everyone," she said, studiously avoiding any eye contact with Jeff. She might never be able to look the man in the eye again after their disconcerting lip-lock. "I think we're in good shape, so I'll try to keep us on track and let you get on your way."

She pulled out a stack of agendas and passed them to Lydia for distribution.

"As some of you may have heard, Mr. Larson had an unfortunate run-in with a fork over the weekend and lacerated his tongue, so the *Sugar Falls Jazz Ensemble* had to cancel. I've taken the liberty of booking *The Jolly Rodgers* in their stead."

"You've got to be kidding me."

Grace glanced up at Jeff. "No. Is that a problem?"

"Shouldn't you have consulted the committee?"

"There wasn't time." She turned back to the others. "Do I have approval to book *The Jolly Rodgers* for the festival?"

Heads bobbed around the table amid murmurs of approval. Jeff shook his head from his usual spot by the mantel.

"Then it's settled. Moving on to sanitation stations, the llama-petting zoo, and face-painting volunteers. Meg, do you have a report on those agenda items?"

The meeting moved swiftly from that point on and was, thankfully, wrapped up within a little over an hour.

Grace thanked everyone and starting gathering her papers.

"Can I talk to you?" Jeff asked.

"I'm really tired," Grace said, picking up her tote bag and empty to-go cup.

"I have to warn you. My sister isn't going to be happy sharing a stage with *The Jolly Rodgers*."

Grace pursed her lips. "Sometimes we have to accept that things don't always go as we'd planned."

His expression clouded. "This means a lot to her, announcing her candidacy here in Sugar Falls. Surely we can find someone else to entertain at the festival."

"On such short notice? I don't think so."

He sliced the air with one hand in frustration. "Why not? You managed to call my father on short notice. Just call someone else."

She stopped, one foot over the threshold. So close to escape. "For your information, I didn't call anyone. Your mother arranged it, and I was grateful for her help. If you're going to be mad at anyone, be mad at her."

She turned and stalked across the parking lot. She could hear him breathing behind her.

She beeped her car door.

"Jeff, I'm tired. I'm in no mood to hear you criticize me."

He turned her with a hand on her shoulder. "I'm not. I'm trying to help. You don't want to put yourself between Mauri and my dad. Trust me, it's a hell of a crappy place to be. I'm trying to save you from—"

"Maybe I don't want to be saved!" she cried, stepping toward him. She pushed the air between them with her palm. "Why won't you just... go away? You can't be that jerk in my past *and* my hero at the same time. We need to walk away from each other and accept that we're over. It's like you keep dragging me over the same coals, and I can't do it anymore."

The air whooshed out of her lungs. "We've had over a decade to get over us," she whispered. "I think that's long enough."

She turned and opened the car door.

"I'm not trying to fight with you, Grace. Jesus, when will you figure out, we're not in competition against each other? I'm on your side."

She got in her car, too overwhelmed to let herself sink into whatever he was offering. The risk was too great. The potential for pain unimaginable.

She at least knew this limbo she was in. She knew how this felt. She could still get up each morning. She could still breathe in and out. She could at least *exist* like this.

She wasn't sure if she could if she let herself believe they could make it work between them... and it didn't.

CHAPTER FIFTEEN

Grace touched her lips for the three-thousandth time since they'd made contact with Jeff Dayton's five days ago. She could still feel the lightning bolt of awareness that had shot through her, stunning her when he'd kissed her. The shock of his touch had short-circuited rational thought, and for a few brief, brilliant moments, she had been sixteen again, kissing him for the first time, the future a broad expanse of bright light.

She knew now that was just the explosion of her hopes and dreams rising up to the heavens in a great big old mushroom cloud of disaster.

Needless to say, she was a hot mess.

She dropped her hand from her lips and let out a silent sigh as a couple more ladies entered her shop. Normally she looked forward to Thursday evenings, but she already felt drained, and she wanted nothing more than to go home and snuggle with all four of her cats, snarky comments be damned.

Grams, Lydia and Linda crowded around the CD player.

"Oh, no. Not the waterfall CD. It makes me need to pee." Sandi Adams plopped her yoga mat onto the counter by the register and yawned. "And crickets make me sleepy."

Grams huffed out a breath and put down the *Meadow Songs* CD. "What would you like to listen to?"

"That rain forest birds one is nice."

"Fine. *Birds of the Amazon* it is." Grams popped in the CD and set the volume.

Personally, Grace found this particular soundtrack a bit unnerving. She always had the urge to duck her head when it got to the startled flock section. She'd simply have to envision a protective canopy of leaves.

The ladies settled themselves in the back, chatting about global warming, the weather and the rumored closure of a local clothing store. The door to the shop jingled again. Dee walked in.

Grace looked up in surprise. "Dee! What are you doing here?"

"Is your healing thing tonight?"

Grace came around the counter to greet her friend. "We're just about to start."

"Good. Someone at work suggested I might need to de-stress a bit." Dee rolled her shoulders uncomfortably and looked around. Grace was pretty sure who 'someone' was. Huh. Maybe he thought more highly of her work than he let on?

After introductions and opening circle, the group chose silent meditations followed by supported revelations.

Or, as Linda liked to refer to it: 'The Airing of Grievances.'

The usual litany of health, social and home appliance complaints out of the way, Dee cleared her throat.

"I'm worried about my dad," she mumbled. The admission sounded a bit like a secret shame. She rolled her shoulders a bit, her lips twisting. "He's been kind of 'off' ever since mom died. Heck, ever since he retired."

The ladies around the circle murmured their sympathy. Grams reached across and patted Dee's knee, which earned her a startled look. "Grief can do that sometimes," she said. "Men don't handle it as well."

The others nodded their agreement, but Dee looked uncomfortable with that.

"What do you mean by, 'off?'" asked Grace.

"I don't know, he's just not as on top of things like he used to be, you know?"

"He probably has a lot on his mind," Lydia suggested. "Men aren't used to fending for themselves."

Grace frowned. "He doesn't have to fend for himself. He lives with Dee now."

Dee swallowed. Twice. Her face twisted into a grimace.

"Dee? Honey? Tell us what's really going on."

Dee's head shook back and forth as if some truth she was trying to bury inside her was attempting to shake itself free. "He just seems… lost."

"Depressed?" Linda prompted gently.

"Forgetful," Dee finally forced out.

"You think he's got Alzheimer's, don't you, dear?" whispered Sandi.

Dee nodded, blinking furiously.

"Oh, honey," Grace said, wrapping Dee's rigid body in a hug. "Why haven't you said anything?"

She shook her head again and shrugged. "I haven't wanted to admit it."

"Maybe it's depression," Linda suggested. "Or an infection. Both of those can appear like dementia sometimes."

"Are there any other symptoms?" Grams asked. "Lord knows we all get forgetful over time."

Grace frowned. Grams was still sharp as a tack. Forgetful? The woman was an elephant.

"I think he's been sleep walking," Dee said. "I keep finding things out of place in the mornings. Nothing major, but it's happening more lately. And when I ask him about it, he gets defensive."

"He may well be sleep walking," Linda said. "Stress can do that. I'd take him to the doctor. You never know."

"Yesterday, he went for a walk and forgot his way home," Dee blurted.

Everyone went silent.

"Oh, honey," Grace said again, pulling Dee into another hug. Tears burned the backs of her eyes but it would do her friend no good to get all mushy when she needed solid help. "I'm so sorry."

Dee nodded and sniffed. "We'll have to do something," she said. "I know we'll have to do something. Thank God, Kevin works second shift and can come over when I'm at work. Our neighbor has been helping, too."

"But you guys have to sleep," Grams said. "What's to prevent him from trying to cook scrambled eggs at three in the morning and starting a fire?" She looked around. "What? It happened to Whitney Piper's dad. Remember?"

"I'll lock his door," Dee said.

"What if there were a fire and he was locked in?" Lydia said.

Dee bit her lip. "I don't know."

Grace patted Dee on the shoulder. "It's okay. You don't have to figure it out tonight, but please know we're here for you"

"We're all here for you," Linda insisted.

Dee smiled gruffly through her tears. "Thanks. You guys are awesome. Wow. Great therapy session. How much do I owe you?" she gave an awkward laugh.

Grams motioned to a basket on a shelf behind them. "There's a free-will offering if you'd like to support the local animal shelter. We do a different charity every week."

Dee stood to toss a couple bills in the basket and wandered off, mumbling something about a tissue.

"Speaking of support," Sandi said, turning toward Linda. "How are things with Jerry?"

Linda made a sound of disgust. "Don't even bring him up this week."

"Why? What's happened?" Meg asked.

Linda rolled her eyes. "Nothing, that's what. I suggested we might do it with the light on the other night, and he said the light, 'hurt his eyes.'" She sniffed, her own eyes welling up a bit. "I've half a mind to rip my shirt off in the supermarket some day and declare myself free of his judgment and just tell him, 'This is me now. Get over it.'" She gripped her loose, sequin-embellished t-shirt in her fists as if she were ready to rend the fibers right there.

Grace grimaced, wishing she could think of some way to support Linda. Dee had disappeared into the bathroom. Probably just as well.

"We could hold a survivor's rally." This from Peggy as she sat cross-legged at the edge of the rug, eyes closed. She looked like she'd just returned from a round of golf at the Sugar Falls Country Club in her fine-knit polo and matching skort. "I know my daughter's senate office would be happy to support that sort of thing. She has press people that would help spread the word."

"I don't know," Linda said. "It sounds kind of depressing. I know I'm not supposed to say that, but frankly, it's a club I never wanted to be a part of. I don't feel like a spokesperson. I don't want to be 'that woman who had breast cancer.' I just want to be... I don't know...*normal*." She glanced down as if suddenly aware of the fact that she were twisting her shirt into knots. She let it go and shrugged. "Besides, who would come to that but a bunch of frustrated middle-aged women like me? It'd probably feel like sitting in the oncology waiting room all over again. Thanks but no thanks."

"I'd go," said Sandi.

"Me, too," said Meg. "I know it feels like you're the only one struggling, but you're not. There are lots of survivors out there looking to move on after serious illness or injury."

No one said anything. They all knew Meg was well aware of the hard road back from injury. She'd spent two weeks in a medically-induced coma after the car crash that ended her husband's life and nearly hers, too. If anyone understood where Linda was coming from it'd be Meg.

"My friend works in the Pediatric Ward," Meg went on, "so she'd be able to promote it at the hospital. I think you'd be surprised at the turn-out."

Sandi nodded. "And it wouldn't all be patients. Sometimes it's the friends and families who are feeling alone."

Linda grimaced. "What would we *do?* Just stand around and compare scars?"

"Of course not," said Grace. "It would be a cheerful, uplifting, celebratory event."

Linda forced a small smile. "I know you all mean well, but it sounds like a lot of work, and you're already planning the Fall Festival. You don't need a rally added to your plate."

"Nonsense," Grams said. "We'll just combine the two."

"Brilliant idea!" said Peggy. "I'll speak to my daughter, Maureen, about it right away. She's already going to be making a big political announcement at the festival, I'm sure she'll be happy to support us. Ooh! Maybe we should have special badges or t-shirts made as a fundraiser item! Donations could go toward support for patients and families... What's the name of that non-profit that provides housing to families with critically-ill children? Is it New Horizon House or something? I can never—"

Grace was about to name the charity in question when Linda hiccupped loudly. Then sniffed.

Everyone fell silent.

"Linda?" Grace prompted. Good heavens. They were like a runaway bus. The poor woman was probably feeling overwhelmed. Hadn't Linda said she wasn't sure about the idea? And here they were already printing t-shirts. "Honey, we only mean to help. We don't have to do any of this."

Linda nodded, overcome for a moment as she fumbled in her bag, presumably for a tissue. "You are... helping. It's just..." She raised watery eyes to Peggy, her face crumpling. "You said *us*."

Peggy smiled warmly. "So?"

"It... you'll think I'm silly, but... it makes me feel less alone."

Grace crawled across the carpet and hugged Linda. "You're never alone. *Never*." She pulled back and patted Linda's round shoulder. "We don't have to make this into some big public thing if that doesn't feel right. We can nix the whole rally thing and just do something together. Just our group."

"Like what?" asked Linda.

"Maybe we could hold a special Healing Circle—like at the Harvest Festival. The moon is said to have special healing power that night. What do you think of that?"

'You mean hold Healing Circle outside?" asked Meg.

"Why not? There's nothing magic about these four walls. In fact, being out under the stars, with the moon, and the glow of the bonfire... it might give us all a new perspective on things. Let's take this on the road!"

"I can't sit too close to the bonfire," said Sandi. "My hair extensions aren't flame retardant."

"We'll put you a safe distance away," said Grace.

"What will this do again?" asked Linda.

"It will say to the world that we are united in your fight to live after cancer, and we join you in celebrating your courage and strength."

"And after that, we can burn your wig," said Sandi. "What? The bonfire will be right there."

Linda harrumphed. "You know what I'd rather throw in the fire?"

"Jerry?" asked Lydia.

"No. My old bras. They just lay in my dresser drawer like collapsed fish bladders, reminding me of what I used to be. I'd like to burn them all."

"Let's do it!" said Lydia, alarmingly excited about burning things all of a sudden.

"Yeah," said Linda. "Let's do it!"

After that, they all needed tissues as they crushed around Linda, group-hugging, half-laughing and whole-sobbing about sisterhood and always having each other's back like drunk girls at a break-up party.

Grace finally pulled free, mopping her eyes with the back of her hand as the others herded Linda toward the stockroom's kitchenette for a cup of juice and a cookie, as if she were a preschooler that had bumped her knee and not a middle-aged woman who'd lost pieces of her body to cancer. Dee stepped out of the bathroom and was swept up in a new tide of weepy hugs. Grace's heart ached for Linda and these beautiful women but in all the right ways. It felt good to be there for Linda and Dee and the others, to support them. Healing Circle had helped that happen.

Grace swallowed the lump that threatened to close off her throat as she stood apart, watching. She told herself it wasn't regret or jealousy that made her hold herself away.

It was simply the wish that, the night she'd lost a piece of herself, she'd had a group of women like this to rally around her to make her feel whole again.

~ * ~

"We're all cleaned up, sweetie. Thanks for another lovely evening." Lydia stood at the front counter, a hastily-rewrapped platter of brownies tucked under her arm, Grams' baked cheese bites long gone. "Don't worry. I left you some brownies out back for tomorrow."

Grace forced a smile. "Thank you. That was very thoughtful."

"You can take it more than me." Lydia patted her belly and winked, her blue eyeshadow smeared a bit under her eyes from all the crying and laughing they'd done. It didn't matter to Grace. Lydia had a perpetual brightness to her eyes, an innocence Grace couldn't imagine still having at that age. Hell, she'd lost her innocence a long time ago. It cheered her to see someone in the world at peace with their lot.

"I don't care if nobody's gotten a royal flush. I think it's a good omen you're dating again." Lydia snuck a hand under the plastic wrap to pinch off a bite of brownie. She didn't seem in a great hurry to leave.

Grace cleared her throat. "I'm not sure 'good omen' is how I'd describe my last date."

Lydia chewed and pulled back the plastic wrap a bit further. "That's disappointing. You should enjoy that body while you're young or you'll be an old woman eating brownies and doing a whole lot of 'remembering when.' Oh, if only Gene Kelly were still alive. And not gay, of course."

Grace frowned, struggling to keep up with all of the older woman's conversational tangents. "Gene Kelly wasn't gay."

"He wasn't? Oh, that's a relief." Lydia snagged another chunk of brownie.

"Anyway, I should close up. I've got a busy day tomorrow, you know, with work and stuff..." Perhaps if she babbled enough about needing to wrap things up, Lydia would stop talking and let her leave.

Because, okay, yes, she'd shared a kiss with Jeff, and while it had occupied most of her waking (and non-waking) thoughts as she'd obsessed over its meaning, the fact of the matter was: it was only one kiss.

It didn't mean they were getting back together. If *that* were going to happen, it would have by now. Jeff hadn't even called. His behavior wasn't that of someone that wanted to start things up again, whereas Joe... Joe was clearly ready to forgive and forget, God bless him.

Had she been too quick to cut him loose like all the others?

It didn't take a psychic to detect the open, smooth path the universe was laying out for her. As much as she was drawn to Jeff *physically*, could she ignore the many signs that she was supposed to give Joe a shot? How many of her friends had brought Joe's name up independently of one another? That had to mean *something*.

"So the date with Joseph didn't go well?" Lydia asked, as if reading Grace's thoughts.

"I've had better."

"Did you wear that pretty dress you picked up the other day? A dress like that tells a man you mean business."

She was afraid to ask. "Business?"

"Well, at your age, you'll be wanting babies soon."

Grace's gut clenched as if she'd been punched.

Lydia's hand paused in midair, a bit of brownie falling to the platter beneath it. "Oh, sweetie. I'm so sorry. I forget sometimes."

Grace forced a nonchalance she didn't feel. "Forget?"

"Well, you know..." Lydia said it meaningfully, looking at Grace's midsection before glancing away.

Grace's hand fluttered over her belly button before she dropped it purposefully to the side. "No, I don't. Thanks for coming tonight."

Grace turned toward the door to open it for Lydia when she felt a soft hand on her shoulder. "I never had babies, either, you know."

Grace closed her eyes. Yes, but Lydia had had a husband, and they'd *wanted* babies. It wasn't the same at all.

"I think I need a cup of tea," Lydia announced, the brownie platter clattering atop the nearby countertop. "I don't suppose you have anything to go in it?"

Grace turned, letting a deep sigh ease out of her. "No."

Lydia shrugged and toddled toward the back room. "Some conversations are best had sober anyway."

Grace could hear Lydia opening and closing the cupboard doors looking for supplies, filling the electric kettle and setting mugs on the counter. She reluctantly walked toward the back room.

"Lydia, I appreciate whatever you're trying to do here, but I'm beat."

Lydia ignored her and walked over to peruse the angels display. After picking up and admiring the figurines for a few minutes, she picked up a small figure of an angel watching over a baby in a basket and turned to Grace. "Tell me about him," she said. "I do love a good love story."

"Who?"

Lydia raised one silvery eyebrow and turned to gently set the figurine back in its place. "You know who I'm talking about."

Grace shrugged even though Lydia wasn't looking. Yes, she did. "There's not a lot to tell."

The teakettle whistled, and Lydia bustled to the back room again. "I'll get the tea, then we'll sit and you can unbottle what's all bottled up inside. You'll feel better after, I promise." Her head peeked out of the back room. "And grab me another brownie, will you? Then you can tell me how it all started."

How it all started?

Grace swallowed again over the clog of dread that lodged in her throat. What could she say? That Jefferson Ward Dayton was the beginning and end of everything wonderful and awful that had ever happened in her life? That she blamed him for stealing her innocence and belief in happily-ever-after? That she blamed herself for not wanting what they had together enough to see it through?

Except she wasn't sure any of that was true. Maybe no one was to blame. Maybe the simple truth was: it happened. It sucked. And, thankfully, it was all in the past.

She'd fallen under the spell of the throaty saxophone music he'd played for them off his phone, the rhythmic rain drumming the roof of the motel, and the white noise of the A/C as it drowned out the sounds of them making out, and… and… it happened.

That's what she'd tell Lydia. Nothing more to it than that.

Except she somehow found herself sitting in the corner of the Healing Circle area, a giant flowered mug of herbal tea cupped in her palms, lights low, spilling her guts like roadkill.

Just the idea of an animal smeared across the pavement, its entrails spilling over like so much messy stuff revealed in all its horrible truth, truths that nobody wanted revealed even though they all knew they were there, hidden and ugly, made her want to cry big, hot tears into her mug.

"It's not like I *planned* on losing my virginity in a seedy motel on the edge of town on my sixteenth birthday," she said.

No, she hadn't *planned* it, but when you're an orphan, you learn early on to carpe diem and all that. She'd carpe'd the hell out of that diem.

Lydia, thank God, remained silent.

So Grace began. Because even though the story was engraved on her heart like words on a tombstone, she'd never spoken them aloud. To anyone.

"It all started with ice cream…"

CHAPTER SIXTEEN

(Grace)

Thirteen years earlier...

I was at the *The Scoop* waiting for Kristen to meet me when she got off work. She had a part-time job at Lamont's clothing store and had snagged the fancy beaded tank top I was wearing for which I was eternally grateful. So there I was, minding my own business, sitting at the counter when none other than Jeff Dayton walked in and sat beside me.

He ordered vanilla. I don't know why I found that intriguing, maybe because it seemed so unapologetic. It wasn't trying to be anything but what it was.

Just like him.

He didn't know me from Adam, of course, but everyone knew the Hometown Hero. He was the guy who'd saved that couple up in the White Mountains *all on his own.* Plus, he was hotter than the surface of Venus, and I knew this because I was up on both my astrology *and* my astronomy.

He nodded at me, politely, probably because he'd caught me staring at him, and ate his ice cream. I drank my water, my arms *singing* with awareness, and I knew how our 'how we met' story would play out the moment I chose not to ignore the drip of ice cream on his shirt.

I'd seen all the scenarios flash across my mind like a movie reel: I could ignore the drip and never see him again. I could giggle and point him to the men's room. Or, I could silently put my hand on his bare arm—the lightest touch—to get his attention, and without a word, I could reach across him to the napkins—casually, breezily. I could bring the napkin toward my lips to draw his attention there, purse them and then pretend to chuckle to myself as I licked my lips and lowered the napkin instead... down... down... Down past my emerging cleavage in my white gauze tank with beaded trim... and dip the napkin into my ice water. Just a quick dip, mind you, and then I'd reach over and carefully dab at the spot on his chest. When I was satisfied I'd gotten it all, I'd smile like a

Cheshire cat, lick my lips one more time, because that flavored lip gloss really did taste like Dr. Pepper, meet his eyes and then reach forward with my right hand to sip out of my straw as if nothing. Had. Ever. Happened.

That's how I mapped it out in my head in those few seconds after I noticed the spot.

This is what actually happened...

I grabbed a napkin, two more spilling out after the first, and I fumbled a moment to shove them back into the dispenser. Undeterred, I brought the napkin near my lips and pursed them, but I must have done it wrong, because Jeff frowned at me like I'd swallowed a lemon. I smiled, and ducked my head away as I dipped the napkin in my water, but instead of a quick dip, someone bumped me from behind, and my whole hand slammed into the glass, hooking the top and pulling it over onto the counter as I yanked my hand out of the icy liquid. Water splashed down my front, ice cubes skittering on the floor, and I leaped back in surprise and landed on Jeff's foot. *Hard.* I rocked atop his foot, horrified and thrilled all at the same time, as he grunted in my ear, holding me up by my armpits, no doubt to relieve the pressure on his instep. I gasped and scrambled away, the soggy napkin breaking free of my fingertips and landing with an audible 'plop' on the floor between us.

Oh, where the hell was a lightning strike when you needed one?

I'm sure my face flamed three shades of crimson.

"Thirsty?" he finally asked. His eyes were laughing at me, his lips tilted in humor, and I wanted to curl up and die for being the butt of his joke.

"You have ice cream on your shirt," I said.

His face lost its humor and he reached up with his hand. "Where?"

I swiped at my sopping front with my left hand and waved toward his chest with my right. I was less concerned now about his spot when my own, hand-wash-only top was sucking itself to my bra. "There."

He licked his thumb and rubbed it over the spot until it disappeared.

"Thanks," he said.

His voice was edgy, dark and delicious, like Dr. Pepper, and I took a half-second breath to savor it before turning toward him. "Hmm?"

He gestured toward his chest. "Most people would have just handed me a napkin... unless you were planning to mop me with your shirt."

I ducked my head, feeling like an ocean wave had crashed into me. Ohmigod! He was flirting! "Then it's a good thing I didn't act on my first impulse." He raised his brow on cue, and something cut loose inside me, and the words spilled out. "I thought about licking it off, but who knows what might have happened then."

He laughed then, his head tilting back, and I almost didn't mind standing in a puddle of ice cubes. Or my wet shirt. His voice was beautiful when he laughed.

"We'd probably both be on the floor then," he said.

I nodded and grabbed a wad of napkins to dry my shirt. I pictured us on the floor. I imagine my mental picture was a lot less clumsy looking than his. I frowned and blotted more frantically.

"It's just water. Don't worry about it," he said.

I held my tank away from my body with pinched fingers, my face growing hot again. "Yes, but until then…"

He glanced down, his eyes finally registering my predicament. He threw a few bills on the counter to pay for his ice cream then wrapped his fingers around my elbow. It sent a rush of something hot and electric up my arm. "Let's walk down by the river. The sun will dry you off in no time."

I wiggled my feet back into my purple flip-flops, mumbled my thanks, and let him lead me out the door.

This was definitely not how I'd envisioned things going, but he'd been gracious enough not to comment or look excessively at my drenched self, I'll give him that. I wasn't confident enough to want anyone to see the outline of my bra, which was just a thin layer of t-shirt material and made me look like a college girl on spring break. Not even the darkly gorgeous Jeff Dayton. So, I held my tank off my skin and allowed him to lead us down the path toward the river, the sound of the water calming me. I'd always loved the falls. I glanced up at the long, brick mill buildings across the river.

"You can let go," he said. "I promise not to look."

"Oh." I dropped my hand, looking up at him through my lashes, knowing my face was bright red again.

"We'll just stand here for a bit." He said it while facing away from me, looking toward the river, but his lips curved like he was enjoying some private joke. He had really fantastic lips, and a strong jaw that belonged on a magazine cover. He was that hot.

"Sorry you got doused like that. You could have just dabbed at it with your finger." He slanted a quick glance at me. "Or licked it off." He looked away, the grin wider now.

"I was afraid you might misinterpret that."

"How might that be misinterpreted?" he asked.

"The truth is… I just really like ice cream."

He made a strangled little sound in his throat as his eyes slid to my lips. I tasted the Dr. Pepper again. His eyes crinkled. God, they were lovely. He was lovely. My skin hummed. "So you thought drenching yourself was preferable?" he asked.

I let the weight of my breath ease out of me, feeling light and full of possibility. "That's to be determined."

He smiled. His teeth were straight without being perfect. I loved that. Loved that he was naturally dreamy. "Oh, drenching yourself was definitely the right move."

The words hung between us, heavy with promise, and suddenly I didn't care anymore that my tank clung to me like a second skin. I didn't want to hide from this. Or him. I turned to face him.

His eyes dropped to my chest, burning a hole through me before clawing their way back to my face. I watched him, my nerves humming. This was gloriously uncharted territory, and I was eager to map it with him.

He cleared his throat and turned away. "Let's walk," he said, his back rigid through his dark tee. It had a giant pirate ship emblazoned across the back with his father's band's name depicted in a flag. I wondered how cool it would be to have a father who was a real live rock star. Heck, to have a father. All I remember of my own father was a wedding photo of him and my mom looking impossibly young. Joan and Pops kept it on the mantel growing up to remind us we were family, too. I sometimes wondered if it had come with the photo frame, they looked so... perfect together.

Mom died trying to rescue dad. I wanted a love like that. A Nicholas Sparks kind of love, amazing and transcendent but maybe without the death part.

I watched Jeff's shoulders bunch as he walked, as if he were trying to shake something lose.

I trailed after him, careful with my footing on the uneven ground. "So, plans for the summer?" I asked hoping we weren't just going to hike until my shirt dried.

"Um. Yeah. Sort of. You?"

"Lifeguarding."

"Nice."

"So, um, what are your plans?"

"I've been talking to recruiters."

"College?"

"Military. I want to join the Army."

"Wow. Really? Like G.I. Joe or something?"

He chuckled. "Or something. It's a good way to get experience for what I really want to do, search and rescue.

"You mean like when they go in and rescue captured troops?"

"More like searching for lost hikers, rescuing people after natural disasters... You know those commercials with the guys rappelling out of helicopters to rescue people stranded on their rooftops during floods?"

"Yes?"

"Like that."

I nodded. Wow. That was... serious. I eyed him sidelong, feeling both safer knowing I was in the presence of future rescue personnel and a bit unnerved by it. Suddenly the fact that I was flirting with someone planning his career made me feel very young. And naïve.

I heard voices coming up the path along the river at the same time Jeff stopped in the middle of the path. We were still around the bend and out of sight, but before I knew what he was doing, Jeff pulled his tee over his head. He shoved it behind him toward me. "Put this on."

"What?" I grabbed the tee. It was still warm from his body.

He looked at me over his shoulder, his eyes gone dark. "Put it on. Unless you want whoever's coming to see you like that?"

I glanced down at my still transparent tank and fumbled with Jeff's tee to pull it over my head moments before the others rounded the bend. Oh God.

It was Chip Otterman, Dan O'Connell, and a couple of other guys from school. All of them were upper-classmen. I was sure I flushed a thousand shades of crimson.

"Whoops!" Dan smirked. "Sorry if we're interrupting something."

Jeff turned on them with dark, piercing eyes. Dan had the presence of mind to back off a smidge.

Dan gave me the hairy eyeball. For some reason he'd never liked my family, particularly my brother, Carter (which, given that Carter always referred to him as 'Dan-the-Jerk-Jock-O'Connell' kind of indicated it was mutual.)

"Not at all," I said with more bravado than I felt. "Just catching some rays."

"Come on," Jeff said to me, "these boys have better things to do than hang out here. Don't you?" He emphasized the word 'boys' although maybe that was just in my head.

"Damn straight," somebody said. I couldn't see who spoke, because I had moved to the other side of Jeff. I pulled out my bun, pretending to work out a particularly unruly knot. I heard them shuffle off, talking and goofing around.

I glanced at Jeff.

He had an odd look on his face. Then he gathered my hair in his hand and set it carefully behind my shoulder.

I couldn't breathe.

His arm hovered in the air for a moment, then moved back to his side, and that's when my eyes settled on his left bicep. I glanced up to him. "You have a tattoo?"

He looked down at himself as if surprised. "Oh. Yeah. Got it when I turned eighteen."

It was an eagle. Simple. Black. Sort of tribal. Staring at it made me feel completely and utterly underwater.

Lifeguard? I'd be lucky I didn't drown myself in lust.

"You're awfully tan for so early in the summer," I said.

Jeff grimaced. "Yeah, my mom is always telling me to wear sunscreen, but I end up just sweating it off. I work construction for the state. For now."

Something about that sounded very... manly. My mouth watered even though I wasn't hungry for food, and I could feel a hot aching somewhere inside. I inhaled, and the scent of him rose from his tee to my nostrils.

"Thanks for stepping in," I said. "I appreciate it."

His lips hitched up at one corner. "You would have been all right. I have a feeling you're tougher than most people probably give you credit for."

"Why do you say that?"

"For one thing, you didn't shriek when you poured ice water down your front."

I glanced up at him through my lashes. "Maybe I was in shock."

"Naw." His eyes danced. "If you lifeguard at Whisper Lake, you're not afraid of a little cold water."

"You got me there." I grinned up at him fully now, the easy banter filling my veins like liquid sunshine. "Thanks for the loaner," I said, fingering his t-shirt. It was soft as butter. I hoped he'd never ask for it back. "I should get going, my friend is probably wondering what happened to me."

"No problem."

We stood there, the hot sun beating down on us, and I smiled, because I knew this was just the beginning. And I almost didn't mind when Kristen appeared at the top of the embankment, hands on hips saying, "There you are!"

~ * ~

That afternoon, I curled up in the hammock at the edge of the yard, hidden by the lilac bushes, the sweet, floral scent of the last lingering blooms like the warm hug of an old woman.

I liked to imagine my mother smelled of lilacs, and that she was nearby each year on my birthday, hugging me in that hammock.

I looked out over Whisper Lake, the water dark, the sun glinting off the surface. It made me feel guilty thinking about and yearning for a mother when I had a perfectly happy home with Aunt Joan and Pops. But maybe that's why, because Joan always insisted Ian, Carter and I call her that. *We're not here to replace your parents*, she would say, as if she didn't want the job, but I knew that wasn't true. It was just her way of being respectful to her dead sister-in-law.

Still.

Maybe because it was my birthday or the summer solstice, but I felt like I was on the cusp of something. On the edge. Or maybe I just didn't want tomorrow to feel like today despite the monumental bliss of lying in a hammock wearing Jeff Dayton's t-shirt. It was as if something *big* needed to happen or it would feel like the same old slide from one dawn to the next, always waiting for something important to change, and then feeling disappointed at the quiet entrance of a new day. Like a promise that keeps coming but never comes to be.

Or maybe that's just what adolescence is like for everybody.

Anyway, I told Joan and Pops I was staying at Kristen's for the night. We were going to hang out and watch movies. The usual. Maybe that's what had me feeling in a funk. I was turning sixteen at 11:58 p.m., wearing *Jeff Dayton's* t-shirt feeling like I was on the edge of *something,* but I knew I'd spend the night in Kristen's smelly basement eating over-buttered popcorn and watching movies while her little brother pretended to be a dog and tried to lick my bare ankles.

Except, that's not what happened at all.

I should have known it wouldn't be the same when Kristen called, breathless and excited, telling me she had the *best* birthday surprise ever (she was that good a friend) and that I was spending the night at her house.

This didn't seem a particularly spectacular birthday surprise seeing that was already the plan until Kristen told me that, in fact, her new upper-classman boyfriend (Tommy Daniels) had broken up with Meg again and they were all going on a double date to THE QUARRY!

Anyone who was anyone knew the quarry was where the cool kids went to underage drink and blast their car stereos and disappear into the surrounding woods for *we all knew what*. Which is why Kristen and I had never been. We were goodie-two-shoes. Kristen's mom and step-dad made her eat at the dining room table every night. They followed up on homework assignments and had already started looking at colleges on weekends even though Kristen was only a sophomore.

And everyone knew I had two older brothers who would kill anyone who even looked cross-eyed at little Gracie McIntyre. (Apparently this excluded Joe Sedowsky's lazy eye, but I'll get to that.)

"This is *huge!*" I breathed into the phone. "When? And how do we get there?"

"Wait," I said. "Double date? With who?" Not to look a gift horse in the mouth, but…

"Joe Sedowsky."

"*Joe?* How come him?"

"Why not him? He's kind of cute, and he's rich as Bill Gates."

"He's shorter than me. Plus he has that lazy eye."

"It's not so bad," Kristen said.

"It's always staring at my chest."

"You're imagining things. We'll pick you up at eight."

With the details worked out, I took especial care on my hair and makeup. After stabbing myself in the eyeball for the third time, I decided mascara was over-rated anyway. I swiped on some deep rose lip-gloss, dusted on some blusher and patted concealer on those annoying acne spots. There.

I was often told I looked like my mother—all long-ish limbs and dark auburn hair. I'd always felt a bit gawky and had matured faster than the boys (height-wise) without anything else coming along for the ride until the past year when (thank you, Jesus!) I actually began to have my chest interfere with the view of my toes.

That was when I began to notice the boys noticing *me*.

Tommy and Joe were late picking us up, but I didn't mind. I grimaced, slid into the back seat of Tommy's Volvo, my hair sticking hotly to my neck. I should have put it up, and regretted not having thought to bring a hair tie. I usually wore it up, though, and I'd wanted to look different tonight. Because I *felt* different.

I felt… on edge.

Distant thunder rolled across Whisper Lake, echoing and tumbling over the surrounding hills as we drove out toward the edge of town. Pop-up storms had threatened here and there, but I didn't mind. The electricity in the air only added to the hum of excitement running through me. It was a night of possibilities.

"Here's the thing," Tommy said. He had one hand on the wheel and the other on Kristen's thigh as he drove. I watched it slide back and forth on Kristen's flesh and wondered what that would feel like, having a man's hand on you.

Not that Tommy was a man, per se, more a large boy. He was a football player, though, and he had the hopeful scratch of stubble on his cheeks he stubbornly refused to shave.

It looked a bit like troll hair on his chin, but I kept that to myself.

"Cops are going to be out at the Heights tonight, because we've all been spreading the word about a party there, but if they do show up here, you two haven't been drinking. Got it? They can't bust you if you're clean. We're just up enjoying the social side of things."

I nodded and looked out the window wide-eyed as if I'd just been debriefed for a top-secret spy mission. So this is what the cool kids did on the weekends.

It didn't sound like much.

"So," Joe said, as we watched Tommy's hand slide back and forth on Kristen's thigh. "You must have Mrs. Dayton for Health this year. Is she still doing that 'Beautiful Body' series?"

"Um. No. I think the school board put the kibosh on that."

"Too bad."

Joe's eye skittered away and focused on the headrest beside me. "I'm glad you're here. Must be quite the treat to be out without your bodyguards."

"My what?"

"Your brothers. That's what everybody calls them, you know."

"Carter and Ian?" I snorted and then realized he was serious. "You're serious."

"Not that I blame them."

Creepy. He grinned and stretched in something that wouldn't pass for subtle in any language and lay his arm across the seat behind me. He had to stretch his body up to reach, which was rather funny, but the smell of his hot armpit was anything but amusing.

I shrugged my shoulders. He didn't get the hint.

"I thought we were going to the quarry?" I said, leaning toward Tommy and Kristen to get away from The Eye and The Armpit before Joe developed any more alarming body parts.

"We are," Tommy said. "I'm taking a back way."

I stifled a groan and held myself away from the back of the seat, which was awkward as hell as we bumped over the rough back road. Thunder rumbled in the distance.

"Are you sure that's a good idea? Won't these roads get muddy when it rains?"

I was still wearing the t-shirt from Jeff. I'd put on a fresh tank top underneath, but couldn't leave it behind when I went out that night. He was an older man, and by older I mean college-aged. Almost as old as Ian, who as my eldest brother had already graduated. Jeff had real facial hair, a deep voice, and shoulders like nobody's business. I bet he used jackhammers.

Even though we'd only actually spoken to one another for the first time that afternoon, I felt there was something solid about him that felt like an anchor in stormy seas, as if the world could wash away around me, but I'd still be safe.

Joe did not make me feel that way. Joe was a slightly sticky spot on the counter after you've eaten pancakes, which you're pretty sure is a benign splotch of maple syrup, but you aren't *quite* sure, and then you lean your elbow in it and hurry to wash it off, because it's uncomfortable and icky and something that in some circumstances (like on your pancakes) is good, but not when you find yourself confronted with it on your bare skin.

Then he touched me. His fingertips did this 'not quite casual' feathery thing on my arm that felt like ants crawling on my skin. I shivered, and he took that to mean I was cold, because he smiled and pulled me closer. *Ack!*

Kristen!

I screamed in my head for her to do something, but of course Kristen was oblivious to my horrified thoughts as Tommy's hand crept a bit higher to slide under the edge of her skirt. *Hello? We can SEE you!*

How to get out of this???

Tommy pulled to a stop in the middle of nowhere and cut the engine, turning to smile at Joe and me in the backseat. "We're here," he grinned, as if this was welcome news.

"Where exactly is here?" I asked.

Kristen made eye sex with Tommy for a moment. "Just a couple hundred yards from the quarry," she said as if she'd been here before. Wait. She'd been here before? Why did I not know this?

As I pondered the secret double life Kristen may or may not have been leading, Joe squeezed my shoulders again. "Close enough to have fun, but far enough away we can disappear if the cops show up."

Terrific. Now I was expected to hike through the woods during mosquito season wearing my best flip-flops *and* outrun cops? I burned a hole in the back of Kristen's headrest with my eyes.

Joe's arm slid off my shoulders—thank you, Jesus!—and he popped open his door. "Come on. Let's leave these two lovebirds alone."

Really? Who says that? Plus, um, *no thank you.* Safety in numbers and all that. More thunder sounded in the distance, rumbling over the lake to the south. "Yeah. Um. I didn't bring a flashlight. Or hiking shoes. I think I'll hang out here."

Joe's lazy eye pointed toward the front seat. The windows were already fogging from the inside. *Ew.*

"Maybe a little walk," I said. "But this is just so they can have some privacy. Clear?"

The eye winked. "Crystal clear."

He reached for my hand. I pretended not to notice (which was tricky, seeing as I had to physically shake mine out of his grip under the guise of swatting a bug.)

"So, you looking forward to taking Algebra II this year?"

I sighed. Small talk? Happy birthday to me. "Not especially." Seeing as this was the beginning of summer, I was just grateful to be done with school for a while.

"I got a 102 average in that class, you know."

"Wow. Congratulations." You are officially the geekiest guy I know. He reached for my hand again. I quickly scratched an imaginary itch.

"How far to the quarry?" I asked as much to make small talk as to see how far before I might find deliverance. Surely someone there would save me.

"Not far at all. Just follow the edge of the trees here."

The sound of voices and music carried in the humid night air. I pushed the hair off the back of my neck and stepped out into the open toward the vehicles clustered near the edge of the quarry.

Guys. It was all guys.

Unease snaked up my spine as I nodded to the gathering of upper classmen and recent grads. These weren't the guys I typically saw, but I knew them. Or, more specifically, knew *of* them.

The voices stopped, and one of the guys I recognized as Ethan-something-or-other tipped his bottle toward his lips. "Welcome," he drawled. He passed the bottle to his other hand and took a long draw off a cigarette. I watched the end glow.

"So, this is where the party's at, huh?" Joe said. Suddenly it struck me just how young and awkward Joe seemed. These were not his peeps. And Ethan was looking at me like I was fresh meat thrown into the lion's cage.

Somewhere out of sight, I heard a girl's laughter. She sounded drunk. I felt sorry for her and a little creeped out all at the same time, like I'd stumbled into a brothel and there were loose women laughing upstairs while men did things to them that made me slightly sick to think about.

"Joe, I think I'm gonna head back to the car," I said, grabbing his hand for a change. My sixth sense was screaming at me to *run*. And fast. His sixth sense seemed to be in a stupor.

"Aw. Don't leave yet. We're just getting the party rolling, aren't we guys?" Ethan looked around at his buddies. "Somebody hand this girl a drink."

I didn't want a drink. Or to party.

"Grace, don't be such a dork," Joe said, turning on me. Dork? *Really?* This from the guy that just three minutes ago was spouting off about his 102 average?

"That's me," I said, shrugging. "Just a dork." I took the bottle someone held toward me and handed it to Joe. "You have fun, though. Don't let me spoil your party."

I backed away, waving casually like I'd just remembered a commitment I needed to keep. I stumbled a bit, my flip-flop catching as I moved toward the parked cars further along the edge of the quarry. A few couples clustered around their cars, talking loudly, drinking beer and groping each other.

I skirted them, glancing back over my shoulder and stepping behind a clump of trees when I heard a mumbled 'oof' and a curse. A hand shot out and grabbed my arm.

"Don't move," the voice said, "or we'll both embarrass ourselves."

I froze, my bare arm tingling despite the fact that the hand that had briefly touched me had disappeared again.

I heard the distinct sound of a fly being zipped and nearly died. Oh, dear God. I'd stumbled into a guy pissing in the woods.

When I dreamt of something new and different in my life, this wasn't what I had in mind.

I mumbled an apology.

"Grace?" The voice spoke, and I recognized its rich baritone. It made my insides shudder oddly. Then my face grew hot, because I was still wearing his t-shirt. I prayed he wouldn't notice in the dark, except it had a giant skull and crossbones across the front. Kind of distinctive.

Jeff Dayton grimaced as he stepped from the trees. "What are you doing here?"

He looked at me then around the quarry. "Are you with your brothers?"

Ack! "My brothers? Are they here?"

"Not that I know of. How did you get here?"

"Friends."

Jeff frowned, his dark eyebrows forming a disapproving line. "Good. You shouldn't be wandering around alone out here."

"Tell me about it."

He caught my arm again. I found I didn't mind. "What's that mean?"

"Nothing. I'm fine. Relax."

I rolled my shoulders and lifted the hair off my neck for a moment to catch a breeze. The air was positively cloying. "What are you doing out here?"

He shrugged and looked uncomfortable.

Heat swarmed my face. Pissing. He was pissing out here. Duh.

"I meant at the quarry. Not that you need to account for yourself," I quickly said. "You're out of school now. You're an adult. I mean, you have a job." I bit my tongue to stop babbling, but just thinking about the fact that he'd be making plans for his life not just a few months kind of blew my mind. The thought of the future as an open horizon made me feel full of possibility.

"Yeah." He didn't seem excited about that, which seemed odd. Everyone I knew was excited about graduating and life as an adult. We'd had a big party for Ian even and then set off fireworks over the lake.

"I envy you," I said. "You can do anything now. You're free."

"That's one way of looking at it."

I thought about Health class and Algebra II and suddenly I felt very young and unsophisticated.

"Well, maybe you can stop in at the beach some time. I could, uh, set you up with a paddle board or something."

He nodded noncommittally.

His dark eyes slid down toward me. He was tall. Older than the crowd out here at the quarry. I wondered why he was here.

"Or not," I said. "No pressure."

"Sounds good," he said, but he wasn't looking at me, his dark eyes scanning the clusters of teens.

He heaved a heavy sigh. "Well, it's been nice talking to you, but I think I'm gonna head out."

"You're leaving?"

"Yeah. I was looking for someone, but she's not here. You take care."

"Yeah. Sure thing." I watched him lope away and wondered what girl would make him so distracted he wouldn't even notice I was still wearing his shirt.

A few new cars arrived, teens tumbling out into the dark with their laughter and music. Somebody started dancing and singing along, a long arm and bottle reaching for the sky, and a part of me longed to join them. Wait. "Rachel? Rachel!"

"Grace?" My cousin, Rachel, turned guiltily. She was a grade ahead of me, dating Doug who was going to be a senior in the fall and who was spending the summer interning for a lab at some biotech outside of Boston.

Rachel pulled me close. "What are you doing here?"

"I'm with Kristen. And Tommy."

Rachel's eyebrows skimmed her bangs. "Meg and he broke up again?"

I shrugged. "What are you doing here?"

"One last hurrah until Doug goes away for the summer. Looks like rain, so we thought we'd hit the late show at the theater. Wanna come with us?"

And be a third wheel? "Thanks, but I'm good. We probably won't be staying long either."

Laughter carried across the quarry. Somebody threw a bottle and it shattered in the dark. More laughter.

"We're heading out," Rachel said. "See you at home?"

"I'm staying at Kristen's tonight."

"Okay. See you tomorrow. Be good."

I rolled my eyes and watched Rachel and Doug drive out.

Thunder rumbled again, the wind swaying the tops of the trees.

I decided it was time to head back toward the car.

A stick cracked nearby. I glanced up sharply. "Joe, what are you...?"

His lips tilted oddly, or maybe that was just how it looked as he held his phone up like a flashlight. "Awful lonely out here."

"Yeah. But, I'm headed back now."

"Easy. You'll get a stick in the eye if you aren't careful. You were gone so long I was getting worried."

"You were?" Okay, that made me feel bad. He'd come to check on me?

"Kristen and Tommy ditched us. I thought maybe you were upset. But it's cool. I've found us another ride."

"She wouldn't ditch me..."

"They pulled out about five minutes ago. Don't sweat it. Some of the guys invited us up to the Heights. Turns out there's a party there after all on account of the rain coming."

I pulled out my cell phone. Zero bars. Figures. "Listen, I appreciate the offer, but I'll figure something out."

"Sure thing." He held a branch aside for me. I smiled my thanks and brushed the hair off my neck again. "Warm?" he asked.

"Yeah."

He reached out and gathered my hair in his hand, lifting it off my nape. "Better?"

I shivered. "Um, it's fine. You don't have to…"

He smiled again, "Just think of it as me holding your tail."

My back was to him. "I can't walk like this. It's very impractical."

He turned me around with my hair. He wasn't shorter than me like I'd thought, more my height, he just seemed short compared to how I'd had to look up at Jeff just that afternoon.

Joe's eye shifted toward my hairline. "Grace…" he breathed, and then his mouth was on mine, his lips fat and wet, his tongue invading my mouth and I gasped and pushed, the taste of his beer on my tongue gross and bitter.

"Get off! What are you doing? *Get off!*" I shoved—hard—and stumbled away, bile rising in my throat, and ran back through the woods, adrenaline rushing through me.

And then it came, like a wave across the treetops, the sudden rain drowning out all other sound, sifting through the branches above us. I broke free of the trees, the rain sheeting over me, lightning brightening the sky, Jeff's shirt plastered to my chest as people shouted and laughed and rushed to their cars. Leaving. *They were all leaving.* I glanced around frantically as Joe burst out of the woods behind me.

"Grace," he said. "Wait."

"No."

"It's not what you think."

Really? And how had I misconstrued the sudden and unwanted invasion of his tongue in my mouth? I wanted to spit, to hock up the disgusting taste of him and expel it from my body. I was glad of the rain, pictured it washing the feel of his hands off of me. He'd had no right. No right at all.

I turned to face him. "You stole my first, and that's unforgiveable!" And as much as I hated it, my eyes felt hot, my throat tight as I thought of what he'd taken.

"What?" The jackass had the nerve to seem genuinely confused.

"Nothing. Go away."

"Grace." He grabbed my arm again, and although he didn't do anything else, I fell to the ground in a defensive move I'd seen on TV, the rich scents of wet earth and rain filling my nostrils. He fell to his knees next to me, breathing on me, and instead of escape, I felt suffocated and panicky. Everyone had gone into their cars. Everyone was leaving or waiting the storm out. No one would hear me even if I tried to scream.

My hands slipped on the wet ground as I struggled to leverage myself up and away. "Leave me alone."

"Grace, I'm only trying to help—"

But his words died as two leather boots came into my vision, a large palm thrust toward my face. "Need a hand?"

Jeff stood over me, and without speaking, I let him haul me off the ground. I didn't bother to swipe at my clothes. Or his mud-smeared t-shirt. He dropped my hand.

Ethan and his buddies pulled up alongside us, their windows rolled down. "Hey, we're leaving. You guys coming?"

The back door swung open as the couple inside shifted into the far corner of the backseat, and Joe stepped forward like an eager puppy. "Grace?"

Jeff tensed beside me. "I'll make sure she gets home," he said.

Joe's shoulders twitched, as he glanced at me and what I'd guess was his first invite into higher society. "Grace, I don't know if I feel comfortable leaving you here."

I tried not to choke on my disbelief. Seriously? I wasn't comfortable staying with him.

"It's okay. I know Jeff. Looks crowded. I'll see you there?"

Ethan honked the horn impatiently as other vehicles roared out and Joe hurried into the back seat before they changed their minds.

As soon as they were gone, Jeff turned away. "Okay, sweetheart, time to go home."

"But..." I hurried after him, my clothes heavy and hot on my body. "Aren't we going to the Heights?"

"Nope."

I stopped. "Why not?"

He turned, a slight lift to his shoulders the only indication he'd sighed. "Because the cops are crawling all over the place looking for parties tonight."

"How do you know?"

"Because it's graduation weekend."

"Then why aren't they at this party?"

"They came through an hour ago. I expect they'll be back through soon. Why do you think everyone's leaving?"

I stilled, the taste of Joe's illegal beer still in my mouth. "I haven't done anything wrong."

"Yep. And let's keep it that way." He started walking back across the quarry. I hurried behind, my feet splashing in the dirty puddles before I could see them.

"Could you slow down? What's the hurry?"

"I'm trying to get out of here before this place turns to a mud pit."

Oh. Well that seemed smart.

We reached his truck, and he hauled his door open with a rough creak, waiting for me to climb in ahead of him.

I almost did.

I almost climbed up and across the seat and let him drive me home like the good girl I'd always been. Like a smart girl. And maybe I should have.

But I didn't.

I thought about Kristen ditching me and Joe's fat, yucky tongue and Ethan's leer… and I froze.

I froze with my back to Jeff, in the cage of his arms as he held the door with one hand and rested his other on the cab of the truck, waiting. I didn't know what I was going to do, but I didn't want *this* to be the memory I had of my sixteenth birthday. I didn't want to look back one day and remember that I'd lost my first kiss to Joe Sedowsky, been left behind by my pseudo-best friend and then let the hottest guy on the planet drive me home and drop me at my door like so much soggy leftovers.

No, thank you. That was *not* the memory I wanted to look back on.

"I can't," I said, backing up from the open cab.

"Grace, just get in. It's pouring."

"Not yet."

"Why not?"

I could hear the impatience in his voice, but I could also feel the energy pouring off him, like he was all humming masculine beauty behind me. I turned around and pushed my hair back from my face where it stuck to my cheek. I knew I must look a mess, but it was so dark, I figured it didn't matter. "Kiss me," I said.

"What?"

Like he hadn't heard. "Please, just kiss me, and I'll get in the truck."

"Now?"

No, in three years. Yes, now! But I didn't say that. I just waited, my heart clogging my throat, my pulse hammering in time to the now steadily falling rain. Waiting.

His dark head leaned toward mine, and I could hear his breathing, could feel the warm puff of it against my temple just before he pressed his lips to my forehead... like I was a little kid with a crush he was humoring.

But I wasn't a little kid, and I didn't want to be humored.

"Not like that," I said. I swallowed the nerves that threatened to steal my voice. "Like you mean it."

I could feel the heat of his lips hovering near my skin. "I don't think that's a good idea," he said.

Oh, dear Lord. A wave of humiliation washed over me as the skies opened up for a second time. I could hear the water splashing onto his dashboard and truck seat as we stood there, unmoving, and I pushed away and under his arm and ran back into the night across the quarry.

He cursed and slammed the door shut behind me. "Grace, wait!"

I was pretty sure this was the moment that I would remember—this moment of utter rejection and humiliation as I hurried toward what I thought was the trail leading back to the main road. Lord only knew what I'd do once I got there, but if I walked far enough, I could get cell service and call one of my brothers. Not that I wanted to explain any of this to them, but better that than sitting in that truck with Mr. Gorgeous knowing he *didn't want me.*

"Grace!"

It didn't take him long to overtake me, his large body looming in front of me. He didn't touch me—gee thanks—just put his hands up in front of him to block me and make me stop before dropping them to his sides. "What are you doing? Let me drive you home. It's pouring."

The rain slicked my hair down my back and stuck it to my arms. I blinked. "I don't care. I'm already wet."

He looked down at me, and he went rigid. "You're still wearing my shirt."

Oh, sure. *Now* he noticed. His gaze came up and locked with mine.

"I suppose you want it back now," I said, and it made me angry that he didn't say anything. We just stood there in the pouring rain, and he just stared at me with this funny look on his face I could only see when lightning flashed across the sky. And something inside me snapped.

I grabbed the edge of his shirt and tugged. "Fine. If you want it, you can have it."

His face grew panicked, and he grabbed my hands before I could tug the wet and clinging fabric any higher. "What are you doing?"

142

"Giving it back!" I twisted away, pulling at it, my wet tank underneath clinging to it like a wet swimsuit on damp skin.

"Grace, stop."

"Why?" I was half-sobbing now, and I hated how pathetic that made me. "You obviously aren't attracted to me. And no one else is here. I think I'm safe. Take your damned shirt."

His hands gripped mine, fisting in the shirt, his knuckles grazing my stomach. "Who said I wasn't attracted to you?"

"All I asked for was a single kiss," I said. "And you *refused*."

His breath escaped in an exasperated huff. "I didn't refuse because I'm not attracted to you." His grip tightened, his thumb brushing across my skin until I shivered. "I refused, because I knew if I started, I wouldn't be able to stop at just one."

My chest felt light, like I'd swallowed a balloon, and it was lifting me up. "Who said it had to be just one?" I let the lightness fill me, lifting me up on my toes, as his warm hands spread out against my skin and slid to my bare back to pull me up and into him.

He kissed me then—like Ryan Gosling and Rachel McAdams in the rain kind of kisses. And all I remember about it was that it filled me, as if everything male about him poured into everything female in me, and I pushed up and toward him as if I could never, ever get enough.

I could have kissed him like that forever, the rain pouring down our faces, my hands sinking deep into his hair, and I'd probably still be standing there if he hadn't pulled away, the crack of lightning hitting a nearby tree warning us that, perhaps, standing out in the open in a lightning storm was not the best idea in the world.

I let him pull me by the hand back to his pickup, crawling over the seat, the air inside all hot and expectant. I grinned at him and let him start the truck, throwing it into reverse, the tires slipping a bit on the muddy ground.

I didn't want to go home, but as he pulled the truck out onto the main road, I tried to make peace with it. I'd had the most amazing kiss of my life. If it ended now, I'd be grateful for that. Joe Sedowsky was a distant memory.

My hand crept across the seat, and he shook his head with a rueful grin. "Better not, sweetheart, or I'll drive us off the road. This weather is wild tonight."

I peered into the faint light of the headlights, his wipers pounding at top speed, and let the thrill of it all wash over me.

He'd called me *Sweetheart*.

The sight of blue lights throbbing in the distance was the first sign of trouble. Jeff slowed to a stop, a police cruiser askew across the road. An officer, rain sluicing off his hat, stepped toward Jeff's open window. "Sorry, road's closed."

"Can I get through Miller Brook way?"

The cop shook his head. "Flooding. Your best bet is to go north of town and wait it out. We had a microburst come through. Trees are down all over."

I heard Jeff swear under his breath as he put the truck in reverse.

He shook his head, driving in the direction we'd come from, the rain easing a bit, but there were branches down all over, the wind skittering bark and leaves across the pavement. I wondered whether the others had made it to the Heights before the road closed.

"What'll we do now?" I asked.

I wished I could see his face better in the dark cab. "Head north, I guess, then take the interstate back," he said.

I nodded even though he wasn't looking my way and let him concentrate on the road. Now that the rain seemed to be lightening up a bit, there really wasn't any reason not to head home.

"Damn."

My head came up at his whisper. The truck slowed. The top of a large tree hung across the road, electrical lines tangled in the branches.

"Now what?"

"There was a motel a half mile back." I could feel his gaze glance my way.

I caught my breath. A motel. "That sounds responsible."

He snorted. I think I knew what we were both thinking.

Miraculously, the motel had power, the streetlight outside shining off the puddles in the nearly empty parking lot.

I hung back by the door while he talked to the owner. The owner kept glancing my way, a frown creasing his brow. "We don't rent by the hour," he said disapprovingly.

Jeff squared his shoulders. He might have been younger than the owner by a good twenty or thirty years, but he had a quiet confidence that made me glad I was with him. Who knew where everyone else was at this point? Kristen's house was out by Miller Brook. She wasn't likely to be making it home tonight either.

Jeff turned and gave me a reassuring glance. "That's okay, because we're here for the night. Roads are closed all around town. I'm surprised you've still got power." He turned back to the owner. "I've got cash."

My eyes bulged a little as he laid a stack of crisp twenties on the counter, probably the only dry things on his body.

The owner harrumphed and pulled a key off a peg-board behind the desk, clearly less concerned about the threat of our eternal damnation than the fact that someone was willing to pay good money to sleep in his dive.

I gave the guy a dirty look for not being more charitable and followed Jeff back outside.

We were number seven. Lucky seven. Jeff opened the door and flipped the light. "So, um. Why don't you dry off? I'm going to hit the gas station next door and get something to eat. Want anything?"

"I'm thirsty."

"What do you want?"

"Surprise me."

He nodded and shut the door. The air smelled a bit like stale cigarettes, so I turned on the A/C to high and kicked off my flip-flops. My feet were so filthy, I looked like a Lost Boy from Peter Pan.

By the time I heard Jeff return, I was freshly showered and wrapped in a towel, my clothes hanging over the shower rod, grateful for the small blow dryer stashed under the sink so my hair at least wasn't sopping.

Jeff knocked on the bathroom door. "I bought some sandwiches if you're hungry."

I glanced back at my clothes, still dripping onto the side of the tub and looked at my reflection in the mirror.

Joe Sedowsky had stolen my first kiss tonight. I suddenly realized it could happen like that. In an instant, the future you'd envisioned for yourself could be stolen away. Gone.

Just like my momma.

It occurred to me that I didn't want to risk another Joe Sedowsky moment. I mean, here we were, trapped in a motel for the night, clearly attracted to one another...

"I got you a Dr. Pepper." Jeff spoke from the other side of the door again, his deep voice warming places inside me I hadn't known were cold. "I hope that was all right."

"Perfect," I said, even though I didn't really like soda, because it was Jeff, and he'd done something sweet for *me*. Without even knowing how, I *knew*, without a doubt, that this was a first I'd remember for the rest of my life.

I opened the door.

I dropped the towel.

I can't honestly tell you what his first reaction was, because my eyes were squeezed shut.

"I won't make you a one-night stand," I heard him say. I opened my eyes. He had a death-grip on the plastic bag from the convenience store and was staring at my left shoulder.

My feet felt nailed to the floor, as if I'd somehow forgotten how to make them move. "It's not a one-night stand if we do it again," I whispered.

He laughed then, a sort of choking sound and tossed the bag onto the dresser and took two urgent steps toward me.

His eyes migrated south for a millisecond, and then he jerked them away. "Why?" he asked, his heartbeat jumping in his throat. I could see it there, pulsating at the base of his neck. It was the only thing about him moving. "Why me?"

"You're the Hometown Hero. Isn't that enough?"

I must have said something wrong, because he frowned and looked away.

His eyes darted across my skin again, burning a streak across my flesh, and he cursed. "I can't talk to you like this." He grabbed the corner of the coverlet from the bed and tried to wrap it around me.

I squiggled away. "Ew! Don't do that! Don't you know that's covered in pee?"

He stopped and stared at me. "What?"

"I read it on the Internet. They never wash those coverlets. They're covered with disgusting body fluids."

His eyes burned into mine. "Grace…"

"I'm serious. I don't want it touching me."

He dropped it, his hands fisting at his sides like he didn't know what to do with them. "Grace, you don't want this. You're not this kind of girl."

"What do you know about what I want?"

I wasn't sure where that throaty voice came from, but it seemed to be working for me. And as I stood naked in front of him, completely exposed, I suddenly felt… free… like I had nothing to hide except an ill-advised farmer's tan I'd gotten on Founder's Day. "All I know is that at any moment life can change. Everything you once had can be taken away without warning or your consent…" *Like your first kiss!* "And I don't want to regret letting this chance slip away."

"*Jesus*," he breathed, and I could tell that he thought I was talking about my parents and the fire all those years ago, and part of me felt guilty for not clarifying that my mind was actually on more recent events, but what did it matter? I still felt the same way. I *wanted* Jeff Dayton like

I wanted chocolate or a thick, meaty Reuben—with every fiber of my being.

I stepped over to the dresser, pulled out the can of Dr. Pepper and popped the lid, drinking down huge, sweet gulps of liquid courage, the bubbles tickling my nose. I knew he was staring at my bare ass. I could *feel* his eyes on me. I took it as a good sign and took my time letting the bubbles rise up and pop silently in my throat.

I turned, trying with all my heart to stand tall and confident and not shake with nerves, because I could tell if I showed even a moment's hesitation, he'd walk out and sleep in his truck without me. And I'd be the same as always.

I didn't want to be the same. I didn't want to have tomorrow blend seamlessly into yesterday. I wanted… him.

"I've never met anyone even remotely like… you." he whispered, although the way he was looking at me made me think he meant it as a compliment. "It's like you don't give a damn what anyone thinks. You speak whatever comes into your head. You see something you want, and you go for it."

I set the can on the dresser. "That's where you're wrong. I do care what you think. But I'm hoping it's the same thing I'm thinking. So, will you kiss me? Please?"

I didn't think he was going to. For one endless, excruciating moment, I thought he was going to turn me away and go sleep in his truck, but then he reached out and slid his palms up my bare arms, fisting his hands in my damp hair as he pulled me toward him.

And we kissed.

A long… long… *long* time.

I forgot all about Joe What's-His-Name.

Finally, he pulled away. "Are we really doing this?" he asked.

I nodded, and he yanked his t-shirt over his head.

He grinned at me, his jeans the only thing separating us now, and I fumbled with his belt buckle, the sudden realization that *this was happening* making my hands shake. "I'm never going to be able to drink Dr. Pepper again without getting a hard-on," he murmured, and he brushed my hands aside and sucked in his already tight abs to unhitch his jeans.

I laughed a little at his joke, but it turned into a gurgling sound when he pulled off his wet jeans.

His underwear pulled down with them, and I watched as he kicked them both away, his *you know what* standing tall and proud.

I'd never seen one for real. Not like that, anyway.

I wasn't nervous, but I wasn't sure what came next. The movies I'd watched only ever showed people rolling around under covers or less-than-subtle cuts to images of disembodied hands gliding over skin, fingers interweaving suggestively.

An image of a train rushing through a tunnel flashed in my head, and I tried not to giggle.

Logistically, I had gotten us as far as I knew how to go before shifting into bad sexual imagery-land. I didn't know what to do next.

But Jeff did.

He touched my cheek with his thumb, and a slow, hot vibration hummed to life deep inside me. He bent to kiss my lips, and I held myself very still, reminding myself to breathe as his mouth drifted lower to places only I had ever touched.

And I let him.

I let him.

~ * ~

When it was over, he kissed me, once, very sweetly, on the forehead and once more on the lips and pulled away.

"We need to talk," he said.

I kissed him back, savoring the sense of weightlessness in my muscles. "*Mmm.* Later."

"No. *Now.*" He pulled out of me, sat naked on the side of the bed and ran a hand over his face.

I sat up against the headboard and heaved a sigh. "If I told you I was a virgin, this night would never have happened."

"Damn right it wouldn't have."

"That's why I didn't say anything."

He shot me a look. I tried not to shrink into the pillows. "They call that a lie of omission."

"Not necessarily. You never asked."

His eyes grew hot and piercing. "The next thing you'll tell me is you're not on birth control."

I thought it best to stay quiet on that.

He cursed, running an agitated hand through his hair. "Anything else I should know? Is today really your birthday? How old *are* you?"

"Yes, today is my birthday." I glanced at the clock to be sure. 12:03. "I'm sixteen."

"Christ. *Sixteen?* Shit." He said again.

"There's no need to keep swearing."

"I just had unprotected sex with a virgin. A *sixteen-year-old* virgin! I think I have the right to swear!"

"Consensual sex. And it was *wonderful*. Thank you."

"I'm sorry. Why are you so relaxed about this? I just... deflowered you!"

"Did you just say 'deflowered?'"

"Yeah. I don't know where that came from."

I sighed. "You're perfect, you know that?"

"I'm not! I just stole your virginity on your birthday."

"You didn't steal it. I gave it to you. Think of it as a birthday gift."

He jumped up to pace. "This is so messed up."

"Look. I've been wanting to lose my virginity for a while (okay, that was a bit of an exaggeration) but not just to any old slob, and then you became the Hometown Hero, and the more I learned about you, the more I knew you'd be perfect. Meeting you at the ice cream shop today, I mean, yesterday was just as I imagined it. Mostly."

He stopped. "Wait. You *stalked* me?"

"No, not exactly. More, profiled you. And when you approached me today, I took it as a sign that this was meant to be."

"Meant to be? You *wanted* to lose your virginity to a virtual stranger in a cheap motel?"

"You're not a stranger. Not anymore, and I know way less pleasant places to lose your virginity. Trust me. At least we had a bed." I stretched long and happily, like a satisfied cat, and stood up.

His face blanched. "You bled."

I glanced back at the bed. I hurried to strip the sheet off. "Don't worry, I'll clean it."

His hand grasped mine to stop me. He closed his eyes. "Wait. Just... wait." He looked at me again and pulled me into a hug, his warm arms encircling me deliciously, his parts already pressing hopefully against me again. "You shouldn't settle for this. You should set your sights higher than this. If everything goes as planned, I'll be headed for basic training soon. You need to understand that. You deserve more than a brief fling with some guy..."

"I'm not settling for anything," I said against his chest. I pulled back to look at him. "And this isn't a brief fling. And you're not just any guy."

He shook his head. "Now you sound like a stalker again."

I shook out of his embrace. "Forget it. When you figure out we're meant to be together, you'll let me know."

"I'm sorry?"

I shrugged. "You heard me." Then I grabbed the wadded sheet, flicked on the bathroom light and shut the door behind me.

I was bent over the tub holding the sheet under running water when he pushed the door open. "We just *met.* And for the record, I didn't approach you, you came on to me! Yes, we had sex in a bizarre sequence of events that is making me think you've expertly manipulated me ALL DAY and yet *somehow* you *are* a virgin and it's your birthday and I'm NOT supposed to feel like I've just walked onto the set of Fatal Attraction? *Meant for each other?* Jesus. You're delusional. Seriously, *hotly* sexy on a level I've never before dreamed of, especially bending naked over the tub like that, Good God! Could you stop that for a minute? But delusional just the same! If you think we have a future—"

"*Stop.*" I turned off the water and stood. "Are you even listening to yourself? You've just had what you, yourself, describe as sensational sex, I am not even asking you for a second date, and yet you're having a hissy fit?"

"Hissy fit? *Hissy fit?* How can you stand there with your breasts staring me in the face—my God, it's like they defy gravity!—and tell me you don't want a second date?"

"I never said that. I said I wasn't *asking* for one, that's all. I have my pride."

He stared at me, his gorgeous dark eyes boring into mine. "Pride and no sense *whatsoever.*"

"It's called faith. When I feel that happy buzzy feeling, I know I'm on the right path. It's destiny. When you touched me in the ice cream shop, I got that feeling. I'm surprised you didn't feel it, too, but not everyone is aware of their sensitivity."

He blinked at me. "Are you on drugs?"

"I don't do drugs. I'm high on life." I reached behind him for a towel.

"You're a fruitcake."

I smiled, because my whole body was buzzing now and we weren't even touching. He was *so* The One. "You'll figure it out," I said. And I wrapped myself in a bath towel, went back to the room and turned on the TV.

CHAPTER SEVENTEEN

Grace didn't say it all out loud. At least she hoped not. She hoped what had come out of her mouth was something along the lines of, "The summer after my sophomore year, Jeff and I ate ice cream and then had sex…" but she guessed that, based on Lydia's expression, she hadn't glossed over it all to quite that degree.

"Yes, I know I seemed young, but it was totally my idea," she said, raising her mug to her lips and realizing it was empty. She set it on the carpet beside her and raised her chin a bit. This was her past, her reality, her mistakes. She could own it, even if it hadn't turned out the way she'd imagined it would.

"He freaked, of course, but by the next morning, I'd convinced him he was overreacting. We started dating. Lots of kissing and hand-holding but none of the other stuff. Jeff told me we were going to take a step back. Too much too soon and no need to tempt fate, he said. But that was okay. I knew I was in it for the long haul. It was a gorgeous summer. Idyllic. We were together every spare moment.

"He talked to some recruiters, and we had it all planned out. He'd go off to basic training in the fall, I'd finish high school, and then we'd go from there. No hurry. No worries. We knew we were meant to be together."

She toyed with the handle of the mug as Lydia sat silently beside her. "Of course, I think you can guess that's not how it worked out."

Lydia nodded. "So when did you know? Did you take a test?"

Grace dropped her hand, her lips pursing at the memory. "I didn't need to. I knew I was pregnant even before I took the test…"

CHAPTER EIGHTEEN

(Grace)

Thirteen years earlier…

It was the second week of August, and I'd gone home with Kristen after lifeguarding. I told her my suspicion, and she scrounged up a pregnancy test right there on the spot, something about her sister I didn't want to know.

I drank two giant glasses of juice, I think it was cranberry, then I went upstairs.

I didn't need to read the little paper flyer that came in the box to know it was positive.

It was weird. Surreal. A part of me was probably in serious denial, but as I stood in Kristen's tiny bathroom with its salmon-pink and black tiles, used towels hanging off the shower-curtain rod and makeup scattered on the sink, a sense of something larger and more important than me took over. Life. I was carrying *life*.

I felt simultaneously the wonder of being chosen as a vessel for new life and the urge to throw up.

The urge to throw up won.

"Well?" Kristen sat on her bed, a look of gravity weighing down her features when I finally emerged.

"It's positive."

"Are you sure? Let me see."

"Ew. I peed on it. Trust me, okay?"

She looked unsure but nodded. "What are you going to do?"

I stared at her. I truly didn't understand the question. At this stage, pregnancy was not an active process. At this point, I was just along for the ride.

"I don't know." Shock. I was in shock. That would explain the numbness, the feeling of cold that washed over me.

"Well, you'll have to tell him."

"Right." Except, I couldn't even think yet. How could I form the words to tell the father of my child that I was pregnant?

Which meant I would become a... "I need to sit down," I said. I fumbled for the edge of the bed and sat, gingerly, as if I would break if I weren't careful.

"You have options," she said, that serious look back on her face. It looked odd. Like a child pretending to be a grownup.

I felt like a child pretending to be a grownup. Suddenly I thought I would suffocate if I stayed inside any longer. I needed to get out. To think. To figure this out. To *leave*.

"I need some time to myself," I said. Kristen nodded. She looked a bit relieved not to have to discuss it anymore, like I had just announced I had some deadly virus she was afraid of catching.

I grabbed my backpack and hurried out without even returning her mother's wave.

I burst out into the late afternoon sunshine and hurried down the road.

I had no idea where I was headed, but I needed air. I needed a way out.

I don't know when I started crying, when the fear and enormity of it all over-swept the dams inside and began spilling over.

It wasn't until I heard the familiar rumble of a motorcycle behind me that I came to myself and swiped desperately at my face. Damn that interfering Kristen. Who was she to call him?

"Hey, Beautiful."

I tried to smile and pretended I had a bug in my eye to hide my tears. I kept walking.

"Grace. Hang on. Kristen said you were upset about something."

I shook my head, letting my hair fall forward. I didn't trust myself to speak.

I could hear him cut the engine and engage the kickstand. His boots crunched the gravel shoulder of the road. "Please."

It was just one word, low and soothing, and I turned and buried my face in his t-shirt and let myself soak in his warmth and inhale his scent as I struggled to find the words to tell him I'd screwed up. I'd made a mess of my life.

And his.

"Hey," he whispered, wrapping his fingers around my arms to hold me steady. "Whatever is going on, I'm here."

This only made me cry harder. What if he left? What if I told him and he got angry? Could I blame him?

153

"Is there something going on with your family?"

I shook my head.

"Something at work?"

Oh God. If only.

"Grace, I can't help if you won't tell me what's wrong."

I took a long, shuddering breath and let my gaze glance off his earnest brown eyes. "You can't help even then."

"Tell me anyway," he said.

I screwed up my courage. "I'm pregnant."

His grasp grew a little tighter on my arms. "What did you—?"

"I said, I'm pregnant."

"Are you sure?"

"I have the stick to prove it."

He swallowed, his Adam's apple working as if he could force the truth down with enough effort. I watched him blink. He blew out a breath.

"I'm sorry," I whispered. I was. *So*, so sorry.

He stared over my shoulder, down at the ground, back at me. I wondered what he must be thinking.

"It's yours," I said.

He met my eyes then, a familiar slightly bittersweet tilt to his lips. "I guessed that, seeing as you were a virgin and all."

"Right. Not an Immaculate Conception or anything."

The ironic tilt to his lips lingered, and it gave me hope that if he could find humor in this, our darkest hour, we might be okay after all.

"Are you okay?" he asked after a minute. "Feeling okay, I mean?"

"Yeah. Mostly. Yeah." I shrugged. "I was just late. Kristen had a spare test. From her sister! I don't know why you'd care about that. Anyway. I just took the test."

"How long?" he asked distractedly, his hand sliding through his hair and leaving it all askew.

I shrugged. This was all new to me. How was I supposed to know? Twenty minutes ago maybe? Why did that matter? Oh. Wait... "Since that first night. So, almost two months."

"You'll start showing soon."

I nodded reflexively. Another truth to wrap my head around. My body, this body I was only beginning to know and appreciate was going to change in ways I'd only read about in fifth grade biology. It was as if I'd been abducted by a sexy alien and impregnated with his pod child.

Except I'd done this to myself. I'd chosen this path. I had no one to blame but myself.

"I guess I have some decisions to make."

"*We* have some decisions you mean."

I frowned and swatted a bug for real. "Yeah. We."

~ * ~

That Saturday I agreed to meet Jeff out by the hiking trails to talk. I won't lie. Since I'd last seen him, I'd spent a lot of hours in my room crying. I wanted to be mature about it, but inside I wanted to run away and hide somewhere, curled up with my stuffed animals, watching Disney movies, and pretending my future was full of happy endings and Prince Charmings and not some horrible reality TV mash-up of *Sweet Sixteen* and *Knocked Up*. I didn't want anything to change, and yet I knew it was. Irrevocably. I felt like I'd been swept out to sea and if I didn't swim, I would die.

But most of all, I wish I'd never, ever put my toes in the ocean.

"Hey, Beautiful."

I tried to offer him a smile. I knew he was trying to keep my spirits up, but we hadn't talked since the other night. I didn't know what to say. I didn't know what more *could* be said.

"How are you?" he asked.

"Same." I wasn't sure what he wanted to hear. Still pregnant. Still panicky. Still not sure whether you'll speak to me ever again. Desperate to have you hold me and tell me it'll all work out, even though I know it's a lie. A beautiful lie.

We walked for a while in silence, him holding my hand in his broad warm palm. We stopped in a clearing, the feathery branches of a hemlock sliding back into place behind us like a secret room.

"I've got something for you," he said.

He looked a little shy and ill at ease, and I wondered what could make him nervous now that the specter of impending fatherhood wasn't already doing. He pulled something out of his front pocket and held his fist toward me.

I held my hand out, and he dropped something into it. "A necklace?" It was silver, oval. A locket. It made me want to cry, because it was the kind of gift a guy gave a girl right before he left her. Probably a piece of his hair was in it, which was both creepy and sweet all at the same time. But I wanted him to leave. We'd planned for him to leave.

"Open it."

I popped the latch, and my breath caught. In one side was a picture of us, a bit blurry, smiling. In the other side, he'd taped a piece of paper with a question mark drawn on it. I looked up questioningly.

"For when the baby's born," he said.

I stared into the locket at our faces, trying to imagine the third face there. The three of us. A family. My vision blurred a little. I half wished the damn thing had hair in it.

"Thank you," I said. "It's beautiful."

It was. But it scared me.

I didn't know what to do with it. The waves were crashing over me now. I couldn't see land. I didn't know which way to go, so I clung to the only thing I thought might keep me afloat. I reached out and let Jeff hold me. I let him believe I was as confident in our future as he was.

I let him believe that the image of our family together gave me comfort, but it only made me more panicky. I was too young to make a family.

I was too scared to be a mother.

I had a life I wanted to live, and I hated that question mark, because it was like every uncertainty opening up before me. It was the great unknown of my future.

We had plans. *Jeff* had plans. Jeff was going to go into the military and become a ranger, but now… now would he stay in Sugar Falls, with me?

No. I didn't want that, did I? I didn't want him to have to give up his dreams for my mistake.

I didn't want my future, *our* future reduced to nothing more than a question mark.

After a minute, he stepped back and took the locket out of my numb fingers and fastened the necklace around my neck.

The locket sank to my chest like lead.

"Whatever happens," I said, "I love you."

He frowned a bit and kissed my forehead.

"I love you, too," he whispered.

I wish that hadn't been the first time I'd said it. Another first I'd regret the timing of.

I held the locket in my fist, a little away from my chest and tried to keep from suffocating.

It was a beautiful gift, and I hated myself for not appreciating it more. But I hated what it represented.

The loss of innocence.

I sometimes wonder if my mother had still been alive, if things would have turned out differently. I fantasized about confiding in her and having her wrap me in her arms and tell me she'd take care of everything. But she wasn't alive. And I needed to take care of this mess myself.

Jeff took a deep breath, the kind a person sucks in right before they give you really bad news.

"I've been thinking," he said. Which seemed obvious. My thoughts had been doing nothing but whirl round and round in my head for days. "I should push up my timeline."

"I don't know what that means," I said.

"I'm saying, I think I should enlist sooner than later."

"But why?"

"The sooner I get in, the sooner I get out. This baby will already be four by the time I can come home again for good. It was one thing thinking you'd be half-way through college, but now… I don't want to miss my kid's first day of kindergarten."

I didn't know what to say. What *could* I say? I hadn't even started showing yet, and he was talking about kindergarten!

"We should probably consider getting married, too," he said.

"I'm only sixteen! I can't get married at sixteen!"

He winced. "You can. With parental consent."

"Oh, God." I hid my face in my hands. I didn't want to think that far ahead. I hadn't even told anyone yet, and he wanted to get *married?*

"I looked it up," he said. "I'll get more pay if I'm supporting a family, and you'll have good insurance this way."

Insurance. Family. The words spun around in my head. How did I go from being a sixteen-year-old getting her first kiss to talking about things only middle-aged people should have to worry about?

"I can't think about all this right now," I said.

"You'll have to think about it sometime."

"Don't you think I know that?" I didn't mean to turn on him. He was my anchor, but right now it felt like he was pulling me out to sea and sucking me to the ocean floor.

"You can't just go on pretending this isn't happening, Grace. At some point you need to grow up and accept responsibility for your actions."

I swallowed. "*My* actions?"

"Our actions," he corrected. But it was too late. I knew what he really meant.

"Fine. Then I choose *not* to make a decision about this right now," I said. "Let's just let things play out for now…"

"Maybe I'm not comfortable with 'letting things play out.'"

"I don't see that you have a choice."

I was wrong.

When Jeff called the next day, I told him I wasn't ready to marry him, and that if he insisted he was going to enlist, he'd have to do it as a single person. Marrying him would mean I needed to tell Aunt Joan and Pops, and I couldn't bring myself to do it. Not yet.

The next thing I heard, Jeff had left for basic training. He didn't even say goodbye.

CHAPTER NINETEEN

It must mean something that my love affair with Jeff began and ended with ice cream. The universe was telling me to enjoy it while it lasted… before it all melted away.

He called me when he arrived at the base. I'll give him that. It was a hurried, stilted conversation. We were both still angry with each other, but I felt alone, too, like he'd chosen to leave me when I most needed him. And yet, he was doing what he'd always planned to do, and who was I to get in the way of that?

He'd call me on weekends, when he was allowed, he said. It'd be over before I knew it.

How right he was.

A few weeks later, I knew something was wrong. I could *feel* it. Or, rather, it was more what I *didn't* feel. I felt dead inside.

And then I knew: she was gone.

I didn't know if it was a *she*, but I called her that. I asked her not to go. I begged her in my mind to stick with me. I'd figure things out. I knew she didn't mean to make my life complicated. It wasn't her fault.

But she didn't stick around. Even before I went to the bathroom and saw those first brown stains on my underwear, I knew it was too late.

It didn't happen right away. I kept telling myself it was nothing. I'd never been pregnant before, so what did I know? I read on the Internet that light spotting was perfectly normal. Sometimes.

Two days went by, and then Rachel and I went for ice cream. As we stood in line at *The Scoop*, the place my love affair with Jeff had begun, Rachel thought I was sick, because I doubled over and raced to the bathroom. It smelled bad in there, and I was crying before she even closed the door, and I felt something… shift… *down there*, like a letting go. I told her I had to use the toilet.

She put her hand on the doorknob.

"Please don't leave me. Please don't leave me…" I whispered over and over.

Rachel thought I was talking to her.

When I pulled down my jeans, blood streaked my thighs. I barely made it to sit when I felt it—*her*—fall out of me. I asked Rachel to flush. I couldn't watch, couldn't make myself do it. It seemed wrong. I remember looking in the bowl, bloody paper towels on the floor from where they'd dropped from Rachel's shocked fingers, trying to figure out what part of the swirling red was baby. It didn't look like a baby. Not anymore.

Then the pain came. All of a sudden. Wave after wave of pain slammed into me as blood filled the toilet. I flushed. Again. And again. I remember crying, because it hurt *so bad* and Rachel just held me and let me sob and rock back and forth until it was over.

And just like that, it was.

As quickly as it all began, it ended.

Like a storm that had passed.

Someone knocked on the door and Rachel told them her friend was sick and they'd need to go somewhere else.

I loved Rachel then. I owed her.

She begged me to go to the hospital, but it was too late, and I couldn't bear for anyone to see me like that. So she nodded, eyes wide and worried as she mopped the floor. Then she rinsed my underwear in the sink and wrapped them in paper towels.

As if I'd ever wear them again.

Neither of us had any sanitary pads, so Rachel broke into the vending machine for diapers on the wall with her car key, and we laughed at the irony of it even though it made my heart hurt so bad I wanted to curl into a ball in the corner and never stop crying.

And yet, a part of me was relieved. It was over. I didn't have to tell my family. I didn't have to be a mother before I'd become a woman. I hated that part of me. It felt like a betrayal of my baby.

Like I'd lost her because I hadn't wanted her enough.

Rachel slipped out and left me alone to run a comb through my hair and to wash my face as if the life force hadn't just been flushed out of me and down the drain. I stuffed the wet, bloody underwear blob in my purse, patted my face dry, steadied my breath, and stepped out.

My cell phone rang. Rachel answered it. She held the phone toward me. "It's Jeff."

I backed away from it, my mind spinning. Not here. Anywhere but here. "Tell him to call back in ten minutes," I begged. I asked her to take me to the trailhead of the park. I needed to be where he and I had felt right together before I broke the news to him. "It's more private," is what I told her.

On the way over, Rachel looked at me worriedly. "You'll have to tell him."

I nodded, still too gutted to speak, feeling dizzy and off-kilter. She was right, of course, but how? I fingered the locket at my throat as Rachel drove and felt very, very old. As miserable as I felt, he'd be happy. And if he was happy, I could be happy. We'd be able to find our way back to the way things had been before...

"I can leave," Rachel said. We were there. She opened her door to get out, but I grabbed her hand and shook my head.

"I need the fresh air," I said.

My cell rang again, and I pressed it 'on' with a shaking finger. "Hello?"

I got out of the car and went to sit at one of the picnic tables there. The diaper felt large and awkward in my jeans—an awful reminder of what I was about to tell him.

"Hey, I don't have a lot of time, but I wanted to check in—" he said.

"She's gone," I blurted, hugging my own body. I felt cold. And tired. So, so tired.

"Who's gone? Speak up. The reception here is crappy."

"The baby," I whispered.

There was a long pause.

"When?" So he'd heard.

"This afternoon. Now." I shook my head. It was hard to speak, as if the act of putting thoughts together was something I'd never done. "It's all over," I said. "I thought you'd want to know."

"Just like that? It's all over?"

"Yes."

"Gone," he repeated.

"They didn't need to do a D&C after all."

"*Jesus.* I don't need the details."

"Anyway," I said, "I thought you should know. As the father..."

"Gee, thanks." His voice sounded dark. Black. I'd never heard it so... hard. "And you didn't think to tell me about this earlier because...?"

I shook my head, confused. It would be so much easier in person. "I wasn't sure."

He laughed, a hard sound that wasn't about laughter at all. "Thanks for including me, you know, as the father. Is this payback for enlisting? Trying to make plans for us?"

"What?" How could this be payback? I didn't understand his reaction. It made no sense. "I thought you'd be happy. Well, not *happy*.

Relieved. Don't you see? At least now we can go back to how things were. Back to our plans—"

"Maybe you can go back. This," he choked out a word I won't repeat, "this changes things for me."

"It doesn't have to!"

"Grace, you just killed our…" He swore again. "I gotta go."

And he hung up.

He hung up on me.

And it was only then in the awful, damning silence that followed that I knew what he meant.

I knew.

Dear God. He thought I'd had an abortion? I felt gutted for a second time that night. How? How could he believe that of me? How could he *think* that?

I was so sick and drained and angry and sad all at the same time, so *hurt*, that I began to cry, big ugly tears that rose up from down where there was no baby anymore, where there was no *us*.

And I hated him. In that moment, I *hated* that he assumed the worst. I hated that the one person I'd been looking forward to comforting me had instead turned on me in my darkest hour.

"I guess you're free now," I said, even though the phone was dead. "There's nothing tying you here. Nothing tying you to me."

Nothing except for the love he'd professed to have for me, but after this, I knew 'we' were done. Dead.

Just like our baby.

I held my head in my hands.

"What happened?" Rachel asked.

"I think we broke up," I said.

"Now? He broke up with you *now?* How could he?"

"He thought I had an abortion," I said.

"What? How—?"

"It's what he wanted to believe." I swallowed and looked up at the sky. A thousand brilliant stars lit the sky. Stars he'd told me were wishes come true.

"You can't let it end like that, Grace. He deserves to know the truth!"

"Stay out of it, Rachel." She didn't deserve it. I knew I was being shitty to her, but I didn't care anymore. Anger and pain boiled inside me.

"You have to find a way to get in touch with him to tell him the truth! He'll be hurting."

"Don't you think I'm hurting?" I shouted.

I shrugged my purse off my shoulder, the weight of loss heavy inside it. "I'm sorry. It's just... You can worry about giving Jeff warm hugs later. Right now, I have something I have to do."

She nodded. "Do you want me to come with you?"

I let out a weary breath. "No."

I turned and hiked up the path, the cool night air oddly soothing. I knew my way. Jeff and I had come here a month ago. A lifetime ago.

When I reached the small clearing where he'd given me the locket, I stood and looked up at the sliver of moon high above. She had no name. Her body was flushed away. All I had left of my baby was wrapped in paper towels in my bag, a pale red reminder of a life that was but would never be.

I kicked at the ground with my toe harder and harder until the dirt flew in clumps and I had a hole big enough to bury what was left of her.

I hated that her life was reduced to this: to random body fluids, hers and mine. At least in that small, ugly way we were still together. The loss tore through me again as I dug with my bare hands, the tears falling like rain into the dark hole, and I gave her the only gift I could. I gave her my sorrow. My regret. The tears from my body. I cried, harsh, wrenching sobs that tore my throat until I had nothing left to give.

But she wasn't just of my body, and as hurt as I was, I couldn't separate us. We were—had been—if only for a little while, a family.

So, I reached around the back of my neck and unclasped the locket.

Even though he was an ass, she deserved to be laid to rest with a part of her daddy, too, and I set it in the hole and pushed the dirt back and patted it down, the earth cool and gritty against my palms. I found a smooth stone nearby, brushed it with my sleeve, and set it on top.

There. Done.

"Faith, you're with my momma now." I said her name, the name I'd given her, because that's all I had left of her.

I stood, slowly, as if the weight of the world had settled upon me and dared me to ever stand again. I looked at the pale slice of moon, so cool, so beautiful, so silent.

"I wish you were here," I said.

She didn't answer, of course, because Momma was dead.

Just like my baby.

~ * ~

I didn't expect to hear from Jeff again. What was left to say? You can imagine how shocked I was to answer my cell a couple weeks later.

"Hey," he said.

"Hi."

We made ridiculous, pointless, awkward small-talk as we danced around the elephant in the room.

"Listen," he finally said. "I get why you'd… do what you did."

"But, I didn't—!"

"Please," he said, cutting me off. He sounded weary. Worldly. "Let me finish." Another deep breath. "You're only sixteen. *I get it.* Everything was too fast with us. Too much. And I'm to blame for that. I let it happen. But now… now that the baby's gone, there's nothing tying us together."

Nothing but the love he'd professed to feel for me.

He wasn't done. "This way… you can… get on with your life." Someone in the background was talking to him, telling him to hurry up.

"But—" I said, a bit desperately.

"Grace, you said it yourself…you're too young to get married. Or have kids. Or hitch yourself to one guy for the rest of your life. I've been talking with the other guys… It's better this way."

"It doesn't feel better."

"I think it's best we put some distance between us for a while," he said. "I've asked for immediate deployment."

"Deployment?" Wasn't this far enough? Did he feel I was so much of a threat he needed to put the whole damned Earth between us? "Why?"

"Because…" He made a gruff, impatient sound. "Never mind. If we keep talking about it, we'll only end up hurting each other more."

He was wrong, of course. There was no way he could hurt me more.

"Goodbye, Grace. Take care."

The line went dead.

CHAPTER TWENTY

Grace came back to herself then, slowly aware of a pile of damp tissues crumpled in her lap, a rough catch in her throat, like coming out of the dream-state of deep and wrenching emotion she'd experienced after watching that Japanese movie about the diabetic guy and his seeing-eye dog where they all die in the end, including the dog. God what an awful movie. 'Heartwarming' indeed. Her eyes felt puffy. She snerfled. Lydia handed her another tissue.

"The funny thing is," she said, her words barely a whisper, "it wasn't even a break-up. More like a break-off. We just snapped in two. And then, I guess, we both assumed we could never be put back together again."

She blew her nose into the tissue, mopped her eyes with the hem of her shirt and took a ragged, cleansing breath. "I've never told anyone that," she said.

Lydia pressed her lips together and nodded. "Well, it was about time you did."

Grace stood, her legs wobbly beneath her. "I'm sorry to burden you with it."

Lydia unfolded her legs from underneath her and accepted the hand Grace offered. "It's no burden, my dear. We all have our pasts to lug around. And they only seem heavier when we're the only one doing the lifting."

"That's for sure."

"Of course, I knew about the pregnancy. I just didn't know the rest of the story." Lydia patted Grace's hand and turned to retrieve her own mug from the floor.

"Ah. I forgot about your 'gift,'" Grace said. Lydia had a knack for knowing when a woman was pregnant—often before the happy mother-to-be.

"Yes, well, I've tried to tone it down after I nearly got myself in trouble a couple of times." She sniffed and shrugged her own shoulders. "But really, I don't see why that Betsy Currier had any right to complain. I wasn't the one cheating on my husband. How was I to know he was impotent? People don't talk about that sort of thing at potlucks, you know."

"No. I don't suppose they do. They don't talk about miscarriages, either."

Lydia's face grew quiet. "No, they don't, do they?"

"I wonder why we do that to ourselves, bottling it up inside."

"Because we feel guilty. And flawed."

Grace nodded. It was true. "For the longest time, I blamed myself..." She let the words trail off. She walked to the back room to rinse her mug. "I suppose you think I'm silly to have named her."

"No."

"She would be thirteen now," Grace murmured.

"Fifty-two," Lydia said.

Grace turned. "What?"

A small, sad smile graced Lydia's face. "My oldest would have been fifty-two this year."

"But you never had children," Grace whispered.

Lydia's smile faltered. "None that walked this earth, no."

When she understood what Lydia meant, she stumbled forward. "Oh, Lydia!" Grace hugged her then, hating the fact that she'd carried on about herself when this woman was carrying her own loss. "I had no idea!"

Lydia gave Grace a squeeze and then brushed her arms away. "No surprise. I never told anyone."

"Not even Grams? Or June?" She didn't ask about Claire. Claire wasn't the touchy-feely type you confided in.

Lydia shrugged her round shoulders. "No."

"Why not?"

"They were happy. And there was nothing to be done. My babies weren't meant to be."

"Babies? *Plural?* How many did you lose?"

"Five that I know of. I stopped counting the times I was late."

She gave another small smile as if she were trying to convince herself it wasn't so bad after all, and the full impact of the burden this woman had carried for so long stole Grace's breath. "Oh, Lydia. I'm *so* sorry..."

"Aw, don't feel too sorry for me, dear. I admit it hurt at the time, but Ed and I enjoyed the trying. And, after a while," she shrugged again, "I guess I gave up wishing for it."

Grace swallowed her grief. Good lord. *Five.* "I wish you would have told someone. It's not right that no one knew."

Lydia made an indelicate *pfft* sound. "It only makes people uncomfortable."

"Because no one ever talks about it!"

"You've never talked about it."

Grace set her mug in the sink. She'd clean it later. "No. But I should have." She turned back to Lydia. "And I am now."

"True. Phew! I'll admit, it feels good to share that after all these years. I always did feel a little guilty that people assumed poor Ed was shooting blanks, but it wasn't him, God bless him. It was me."

"No! You mustn't blame yourself."

"Pot calling the kettle black? As if not wanting a child enough would end a pregnancy. That's hogwash, and you know it."

Grace sighed, knowing Lydia was right. "I wonder why it's such a taboo. We admit other things, but this…it's very isolating, isn't it?"

Lydia looked pensive. "Maybe it's because when you lose a baby you find yourself included in a group you never wanted to be a part of. Like AARP."

Grace laughed. "Too true." The humor didn't last, though, and she found herself searching her carefully arranged displays of uplifting placards and frolicking angels. "I always wondered if I had gone to the clinic sooner, if they could have done something. But when I called and told them I was spotting, they wanted me to come in so they could listen for a heartbeat. I remember asking what if they didn't hear one…" For a moment the words clogged up inside her again and it was only Lydia's hand on her arm, her old, shaky fingers digging into her flesh as she tried to pull her to a chair. "They wanted to scrape it out of me," Grace whispered, "like my baby was some sort of unwanted thing I needed to exfoliate."

She met Lydia's eyes. "But I wanted her. I was scared to death, but I wanted her, you have to believe that."

"You could want her and still have been relieved she wasn't born."

There. Right there was what she'd waited years to hear.

Grace nodded, unable to respond. She wanted more than anything to believe that was true, but she wasn't sure. She didn't dare, for a moment, let herself off the hook that easily.

She sucked in a long, shaky breath. "Well, I think I should head home. I appreciate your support more than you can imagine, but life goes on, right?"

"Yes," Lydia sighed. "Except when it doesn't."

CHAPTER TWENTY-ONE

They'd gathered at Ruth's for Friday poker night, because Ruth was trying out nibbles recipes for the upcoming Ladies Auxiliary luncheon.

"First of all, I said I wouldn't say anything," said Lydia.

Lydia pulled her cards up one by one off the table in front of her. Bugger. A jack of spades. Two threes. A seven of diamonds and a five of hearts. She slid the seven and five facedown toward Ruth and prayed for more jacks.

Claire smugly held onto the cards she'd been dealt and sipped her gin and tonic. "If you said you wouldn't say anything, I'm not sure why you're bringing it up."

"Animal, vegetable or mineral?" June asked. She shrugged when Claire gave her a look. "What?" June said. "She said she wouldn't say anything, she didn't say we couldn't *guess*."

"Does a person count as an animal?" asked Lydia.

June nodded.

Lydia enthusiastically nodded back.

"Oh, for Pete's sake," said Ruth. "This will take forever. Is it someone we know? Someone we're related to? A son or daughter? Grandchild? My grandchild? Granddaughter?"

"So something about Grace," Claire said after Lydia's pantomimed answers turned her into a life-sized bobblehead. "I'm guessing it's about her and Jeff Dayton."

Lydia nearly knocked herself over nodding.

"So?" June asked. She slid four cards forward toward the dealer. Huh. Worse than a pair of threes? "Grace and Jeff are old news."

"Not what I know," Lydia couldn't help but murmur.

Ruth frowned. "Lydia. Come clean. It's time to stop hiding behind ridiculous head-nodding. We're liable to pass on before you tell us your news."

Lydia took her new cards. Another three. A queen. She pursed her lips and set her cards on the table. "You're right. It's time to come clean." She took a deep breath. "I had a miscarriage."

Claire blinked uncomprehendingly. "Recently?"

"No! Not recently!" Ruth interrupted, slapping Claire with her fanned cards. "Don't be ridiculous!"

Claire glanced back to Lydia. "Then when?"

Lydia smoothed the front of her blouse trying to assemble the courage to finish what she'd started. "Obviously it was years ago. I feel silly even bringing it up now. Forget I said anything."

"Nonsense!" June said. "Of course you should say something. You should have said something then. When? How far along?"

Lydia willed herself to stop fussing with the tiny pull she'd discovered on her shirt and dropped her hand. "It was right after you all had Anne and Walter and James. I was eleven weeks. I thought it would take that time. But it didn't."

"Oh, Lydia!" said June. "You poor thing. There were other times?"

"I was late a few times, but by the time I worked up the nerve to go to the doctor's, it was clear I wasn't."

"What shitty timing," Claire mumbled.

Ruth looked alarmed at Claire's language. "Yes. Horrible timing. And to think we were so caught up in our own lives we didn't notice anything was going on with you. I'm sorry."

"We're all sorry," June agreed. "Oh, honey, don't cry."

But she couldn't seem to stop. The tears seeped from her eyes, sliding silently down her cheeks, and she let them. "I don't even know why I'm crying. It was so long ago."

"I can't believe we didn't know," June said.

"It happened while Ed and I were away. We'd gone to the Grand Canyon for our second honeymoon. He knew I'd be feeling down about all of you having your babies, so we'd planned to get away. I found out I was expecting about a month or so before we left, and I couldn't wait to come home and make my big announcement knowing by then you'd all be holding your little ones. Only, it didn't turn out that way."

"Oh, Lydia," June said again.

"At least I had my Ed by my side. No matter how it all turned out, I was blessed to have him."

"You were," June said. "You certainly were."

"And I was happy. I've had a good life," she said, the tears starting up again in earnest.

"We all have," Ruth agreed. She set the cards aside. "To think we were all mothers after all."

Lydia's tears became sobs.

"What's wrong now?" Claire asked.

"I've never—*sniff!*—thought of myself as a mother!" she said.

June pushed her chair back and circled the small card table, the game forgotten. "Oh, honey. You're a mother the moment you lose your heart to any child God brings you. And I know for a fact you loved that precious baby a lifetime's worth of love for as long as you carried her."

Lydia let herself be enfolded in June's arms, the shaking of her sobs echoing the shaking of June's frame as she held herself awkwardly over Lydia's chair to hug her.

"You said, 'her,'" Lydia said, pulling back a bit. "I always thought of her that way. In my head, I named her Grace."

"Oh, crap," grumbled Claire. "Now you're going to make *me* cry."

"You named her Grace?" Ruth's eyes shined with her own tears. Then she smiled. "No wonder you were thinking of her tonight."

Lydia decided to let Ruth believe that. It was easier than explaining the truth about Jeff and Grace and all those years ago. One giant revelation was enough for one evening.

"Thank you," she said, mopping her eyes with her cocktail napkin. "I can't tell you how grateful I am for all of you."

"Well, if we have nothing else—" Ruth began.

"—we have each other," June finished.

They all looked toward Claire. "What they said," she said.

And they laughed, declared all their hands garbage and decided it was time for dessert.

CHAPTER TWENTY-TWO

The next evening, Grace flipped the sign on the shop door to 'closed' and let out a long, shaky exhale. So it was September seventeenth again. You'd think that after so many years, this night would be like any other, and yet she had struggled to get through the day without remembering—the word 'faith' popping up at her all day like some televangelist pounding home his message.

"As if I could ever forget," she murmured.

She'd gone home after her grand revelation and spent the rest of the evening curled up on her couch, staring into the cold fireplace, her kitties snuggled beside her, wondering about the cosmic irony of it all. She'd awakened with a kink in her neck and Bandit happy-clawing in her hair. She'd been ten minutes late opening the shop and had had a steady parade of leaf-peeper traffic all day.

And now?

She felt like someone had ripped the Band-Aid off a wound, and she'd been walking around all day trying to protect it.

The ironic thing was, she'd believed she was over it all. It wasn't as if she'd spent the last thirteen years wallowing in self-pity and what-ifs. She'd moved on. Grown up. Opened a business. She had friendships and support groups and family and her fur babies. Life was full.

So why did she feel so raw?

Because, deep down, a part of you still loves him.

She sighed. She hated when that little voice inside her spoke, because as quietly as it said things, they resonated like giant gong strikes.

As much as she'd like to deny it, it was true. How could it be otherwise? Their love affair had been brief and intense and tragic... all the things that make for good Shakespearean drama. The fall-out from such an experience would last a lifetime.

She picked up a lilac sachet and inhaled, the scent always reminding her of her mother.

"I'd do anything to fall *out* of love with Jeff Dayton," she said, whispering the words out loud.

"People talk about falling out of love, but I don't believe it happens that way. As if a person can take just the right step this way or that and be free of all that tangled emotion. Once you've been in love, you're mixed up together, whether you want to be or not."

Separating again would be like trying to unstir the eggs from brownie batter so you could eat it without risk of salmonella poisoning. Can't be done. From that point forward, every bite comes with the risk of gut-wrenching pain and regret.

She set the sachet down again and blew out a breath. Listen to her, all melancholy and philosophical. As if a sachet was going to help her move on in life.

Someone pounded on the rear door behind the stockroom, setting the bells on the inside handle to tinkle excitedly.

"We're closed!" she called out.

The pounding came again.

She sighed, walked to the back room and pushed the door open. Her breath caught.

"Jeff?" He stood in the alley behind her shop looking hot and annoyed, hands on his jean-clad hips. She moistened her lips with her tongue and then flushed when she recognized the unconscious gesture for what it was.

"Yes?" she said.

"Why isn't this locked?" he demanded.

She shoved her hair off her face and shrugged. "I must have forgotten to relock it after the delivery this afternoon." She flipped the key protruding from the inside of the lock. "There."

"I warned you about there being break-ins in this neighborhood. You need to keep this locked twenty-four seven."

All right, so being reprimanded by your heart's desire wasn't exactly a turn-on. "Thanks for your vigilance," she said, "but I don't feel in any danger."

"You don't *feel* in danger?" He glanced up and down the back alley like some B-movie spy. "I think I'm a better judge."

"I think you're programmed to believe there's danger where none exists. It's not your fault. It probably comes with the training."

"It comes with experience."

"This is Sugar Falls. I'll be fine."

"Don't fool yourself. There's a dark side to everywhere. Just keep it locked, okay?"

"Okey-dokey. Will do." She moved to close the door in his face.

He blocked it open with the palm of his hand. "Give me a break with the attitude, Grace. I'm just doing my job."

He blew out a long breath, and it was then she noticed the tension in the lines around his eyes, realized he was still checking on things even when he wasn't in uniform. He rubbed a palm over the tendons in the back of his neck with his free hand.

She didn't want to admit that she was more afraid of what he made her feel than any random stranger with nefarious intent. Just because her feelings for the man were all tumbled contradictions wasn't his fault. Well, not entirely. Mostly, since he'd come back to town, she'd felt gutted and blindsided, as if something she hadn't realized had been missing suddenly opened up like a giant Florida sinkhole, the once solid ground of her existence eroded and falling away overnight, exposing a fragility she didn't know she had.

At least, that's how she imagined it, being a born and bred New Englander. Surely Floridians felt the same way. But every time she went to the grocery store or pumped gas, she felt exposed, as if at any moment he might appear, rocking her world and not in a good way.

"You want some iced tea?" He startled at that, probably as surprised by her about-face as she was. She pulled the door wider in invitation and blew out a breath. "You look like you could use some."

He shrugged and followed her into the stockroom, closing the door behind him. "Sure."

The air hung in the room, still and close from the heat of the day. If she were honest, she'd been tempted to block the back door open to allow the cooler air blowing in with the impending storms to come in. She was glad she hadn't now, because she could only imagine what Officer Worrywart would have said about that. No doubt, it was her subconscious desire for fresh air that had led to leaving the door unlocked.

She reached into the little dorm-sized fridge they had in the kitchenette area and pulled out a jug of iced herbal tea. She poured him a glass.

"So," she said, "why are you lurking around the back of my shop when you're off-duty?"

"I saw something when I was headed home. Thought I'd check it out."

"Probably Casper."

"Casper?"

"My ghost. He likes to slink around the back alley casting suspicious shadows."

"Now you're just yanking my chain."

She found herself smiling ever so slightly. "Maybe. Maybe I'm annoyed you don't trust me to take care of myself."

His eyes darkened. "There was a time you didn't mind me looking out for you."

She swallowed, hating that he'd refer to the past so casually, as if he hadn't been the one to push *her* away. "Were you? Looking out for me? Funny how I don't remember it that way. Well, at least I'm at peace with myself and not skulking around back alleys imagining bogey men around every corner."

"At peace, eh?" he stepped closer, his eyes challenging. "Something tells me that's wishful thinking." He strode into her darkened shop as a flash of lightning lit up the interior. Looked like the storms were closer than she'd thought. Little Luna hated storms. She'd be hiding under the bed at home for sure. "You talk the talk with your ocean wave CDs and herbal tea and healing circles. You seem to make a decent living off all the promises of peace and tranquility." He turned then and his lips tilted without humor. "But you don't believe in any of it, do you?"

"Excuse me?"

"Face it. If you were so 'at peace' with yourself, you wouldn't jump every time I walked into a room with you."

"You don't know what you're talking about. I'm fine. My friend, Maddie, just got married and all because of a visit to my shop. So, clearly, I'm helping people."

"Maybe you should start by trying to help yourself."

"What does that mean?"

"Have you ever gone for counseling?" he asked.

"Of course not. I'm fine."

"Sure you are. Perfectly at peace."

She frowned, regretting her iced tea charity. "I'd appreciate it if you'd keep your opinions to yourself.

"I've tried that for two years, Grace. It's not working."

"What's not working?"

He gave her a long, weary look, his mouth tightening in one corner as if he didn't know whether to laugh or frown. "Nothing. Nothing is working."

"For whom?"

"For either of us."

Something broke in her then. Not a dam of emotion, but a small easing of the tightness she'd held onto for so long. It was as if the stillness inside her she'd held so rigidly, shifted, moving freely again for the first time in too long, rusty gears being asked to turn once more.

She swallowed over the thickness in her throat. "I work just fine," she said.

"Liar."

He was right. It was a lie. She hadn't moved past it, spent every anniversary of *that* night going back to that place where she'd cried ugly tears into the earth, wishing she could go back to when she was innocent again in so many ways. Throughout her childhood, she'd believed that life had sent her all the bad luck it was going to. What is worse than losing both your parents?

Life had felt charmed. She was loved and doted upon.

It didn't seem fair that life would steal a baby from her, too. It wasn't her fault she'd been too young to appreciate the gift. The universe hadn't given her time to grow into appreciating it; instead, it took the gift back just as she was growing to love it.

And ripped her happy ending right out of her hands in the process.

Her hand went to her throat then, protectively, her fingers seeking something that hadn't been there for years. His eyes followed, the creases around them growing deeper.

She dropped her hand.

"I wouldn't expect you to still wear it," he said. She didn't ask him what he was referring to. "It was my grandmother's, you know."

Her eyes flew to his. "I didn't know."

"Yeah, well, she's dead, so she doesn't care."

Grace stepped closer, but he put a hand up, wiping it down his face. "Jesus. Haven't thought about that locket in years. If you find it, you can give it to Mauri. She'd probably like to have it."

"I can't. I... lost it."

He let out a small sound, not quite a laugh. "Figures."

She pressed her lips together, knowing the truth about the little locket he'd given her, a picture of them on one side, a little slip of paper with a question mark on the other. She raised her hand to her throat again as if the gesture could bring the locket back then dropped it once more.

Another flash of lightning lit the shop's interior.

Jeff drained his glass and set it on the counter. "Thanks. I should get going. Just, lock up behind me, all right?"

"I will. And Jeff?" He paused, an energy pulsing off him she hadn't felt in a long, long time. An answering hum sang softly inside her. "Thanks for caring. Even after all this time."

A flicker of raw emotion passed over his features before he schooled them into impassivity. "What makes you think I ever stopped?"

CHAPTER TWENTY-THREE

Jeff sat in his truck, the to-go bag on the seat beside him, wishing he could turn his brain off and go home.

Wishing he could forget.

There was a time he'd imagined a much different future, one where he'd been a hero for real, not by accident, one in which he'd been happily married. Hell, just happy.

Not that he wasn't happy, per se. Police work kept him busy saving people from themselves—from their own hurry, greed, addictions, neglect or stupidity.

In a way, it felt like penance.

There wasn't a lot of glory in being a small-town cop. Most people didn't even know the crap he saw on a daily basis. It was invisible to them, the dark underbelly of human existence. Most people remained blissfully unaware of the alcoholic mom driving home drunk from her boyfriend's house with her eighteen-month-old in the back seat. Or the elderly man with no family who couldn't keep up with eating but refused to leave his trailer. Nobody saw the teen who'd attempted suicide or the guy trapped on his roof when his dog knocked over his ladder.

But he saw it. Every day he saw it.

And every day he tried to fix it.

He cleared his throat and stretched a kink in his neck. He should go home and beat the storm whipping up. He pulled out of the Silver Birch Inn' drive.

A few random splats of rain hit his windshield as he passed the entrance to the hiking trails on the outskirts of town. He slowed when he saw a car parked there. Who the heck would be hiking after dark? And in this weather?

He pulled off and parked behind the vehicle and frowned.

Grace?

He shrugged into a light jacket, the rain falling a bit more steadily now and slammed the door shut. He flashed a light into the interior of her car. Empty.

A hum of adrenaline snaked through his veins as he flashed his light around the small parking area and at the entrance to the trailhead.

Hadn't he just been thinking about saving people from their own stupidity? What the hell was she up to now?

Shaking his head, he set off toward the trailhead. Maybe she'd gotten out to pee, but it was a damned odd place for a pit stop considering her house was on the *other* side of Sugar Falls.

He didn't bother with his hood as he picked his way up the trail. He might have pooh-poohed Grace and her 'feelings' earlier, but some sixth sense told him exactly where he would find her.

He took a left at the fork. Within a few minutes, he entered the clearing under the pines. Strange that after all these years it was still here, almost exactly as he remembered it.

He flashed his light around the perimeter, the beam zeroing in on a hunched form near the far side of the clearing.

"Grace?"

She ignored him. Or maybe she hadn't heard him. Instead, she knelt on the ground, ripping at the earth with her bare hands.

She only startled and paused when he stepped close enough to rest a hand on her shoulder.

She shrugged off his touch. "Go away." Ah, so she knew it was him.

Her voice sounded hoarse. The wind blew the leaves above them, a spattering of rain falling through to the forest floor.

"What the hell are you doing?" he asked.

"None of your business."

"Grace." It was a warning.

"Looking for something. Go away."

"What are we looking for?"

She scratched at the ground, clumps of mud flying as she ripped at the earth. Her actions were clearly not rational. Grace had always marched to her own drummer, but this wasn't just odd behavior… it was alarming.

"Grace, tell me," he said softly. It was the same voice he used to calm people he thought might do themselves harm.

She shook her head. "It's something I left here… a while ago."

"What?"

Then, he watched her shoulders relax as she tugged something free of the earth. It dangled from her fingers for a moment before she wrapped it in her palm and sat back on her heels.

"I can't believe it's still here," she breathed.

177

Then it hit him what it was she'd just pulled from the ground. *Buried*. Not lost.

"Grace, I think you owe me an explanation."

"There's nothing to explain," she said, meeting his eyes for a moment before glancing away. "You know what it is."

"But why is it here?"

She stood, letting a long breath fill her lungs before replying. She uncurled her fingers, shaking her head as she looked at the contents of her palm. "I told you I lost it," she whispered.

"You didn't lose it. You knew right where it was."

She sighed and looked off at the forest canopy as if seeking something. "I'm not talking about the necklace."

"Then what are you talking about?"

She looked at him then, her eyes weary. "What do you think?"

"I have no idea! That's why I'm asking."

"Our baby," she said. "I'm talking about our baby."

"So that's what this is all about?" He blew out a breath. "Well, I guess I'm not surprised. After the choice you made, it's only natural—"

"There was no *choice,* Jeff. I didn't *choose* anything. I miscarried. I lost the baby. I lost it," she repeated.

The last words were barely a whisper but they hit him in the gut like a roadside IED, the truth exploding, roaring in his ears, bits of him and her and their past tearing through his emotional armor, ripping apart everything he'd believed about them. Everything he'd built the last decade of his goddamned life believing.

And then the dust began to settle, leaving him broken and raw in the aftermath, waiting for someone to help pick up the pieces. Waiting for someone to notice that amid all the commotion, he'd been wounded, too.

"You lost it?" he said. "You lied about having an abortion?"

She shook her head. "I never lied. You jumped to the wrong conclusion. And then you decided it didn't matter... I just never corrected you."

His jaw felt tight as he stared at her. "A lie of omission, then. You've always been good at those."

Her shoulders slumped. "Does it matter now?" She turned to leave, but he grabbed her arm.

"It mattered *then*," he said. "It mattered to *me*."

"Why? The truth wouldn't have changed anything. She was already gone."

She? "You knew it was a girl?"

178

Grace shook her head. "No. I've always thought of her that way, that's all."

He nodded, letting her go. He didn't want to touch her after all. She'd done this to them. *To him.* "Maybe knowing the truth wouldn't have changed what happened, but it would have changed what happened to *us.* Did that not occur to you?"

"I doubt it. Would you have come home again? *Not* asked for immediate deployment? Nothing I said seemed to factor into any decision you ever made. It was like you were cutting me out of our future before we ever had a chance. Not to mention, you made it very clear what you thought of me when you jumped to the wrong conclusion."

"I was nineteen, Grace. *Nineteen!* Give me a break for not having a fully-developed prefrontal cortex!"

"Stop yelling at me. Do you think you were the only one confused and hurt? I was scared. I didn't want to be pregnant, and yet I wanted her with every cell in my body. I was only sixteen. Just a kid. Just a scared, overwhelmed kid..."

"We both were."

She grimaced, the fight going out of her. "Exactly. Don't you see? We were too young to be so... so *much.* It only proved what we should have known. Things were moving too fast. I was afraid we'd jump into things we weren't ready for, and you'd end up resenting me."

"Resenting you? I wanted to marry you, Grace. I had the ring and everything. Baby or no baby."

"You had a ring?" Her face registered some emotion he couldn't name.

"Yeah. I got it in that antiques shop that used to be downtown. I'd been carrying it around for days. When you told me you were pregnant, I figured it would just move up the timeline."

"I can't believe you bought me an engagement ring."

He shrugged. "It wasn't anything big, just silver flowers and little blue stones. But I think you would have liked it."

"Sapphires," she breathed, as if she could picture it, although he knew she couldn't. He'd never shown it to her, had pawned it just before he'd left for basic training. "Forget-me-nots."

He stared at her dirty hands, her slim fingers gripping his grandmother's locket. It didn't surprise him that she'd know what kind of flowers decorated a ring she'd never even seen. Grace had that knack for saying things that turned out to be true.

He'd forgotten that about her.

Or maybe he'd been too damned afraid to believe in her. Even then.

179

"Yeah. Forget-me-nots." He glanced up at her. "They seemed meant for you." He shook his head at the memory. He'd been so certain.

She'd once told him he was The One. She'd almost had him convinced. But that was a long time ago.

He shook his head, his mouth twisting with regret. "Do you think, if things had been different, we would have made it?" He couldn't say what possessed him to ask the words. They tumbled out. Some masochistic side of him that felt the need to flog himself with what-ifs.

She raised one shoulder. Not so much an expression of uncaring but of weariness. "We'll never know."

"No. I guess not."

He swiped at the rain on his face and turned away.

"I named her Faith," she said, her voice a whisper.

He closed his eyes.

"Not that it matters," she said.

He swallowed, and a swell of something innocent rose up inside him. It felt like hope. "It matters."

CHAPTER TWENTY-FOUR

His words whispered over her. *It matters.*

Somehow those two small words soothed the open wounds no one could see, made her feel less alone. She was no longer the only one mourning what might have been. After all these years, at least now he knew the whole truth. That was something, right? It was the first step in dealing with all the unfinished business between them so they could finally find closure and move on.

"I'm sorry," she said, even though she wasn't sure what she was apologizing for. Maybe everything.

He turned, his dark eyes haunted, his shoulders uncharacteristically slack. "Me, too," he said. His tongue darted out to moisten his lips as he moved toward her. "Me, too," he said again.

He stood apart from her, close enough to see the steady tick of a muscle in his jaw as he watched her, far enough away to wish he'd close the distance between them.

It had always been that way, the longing to be connected to him, as if they were tied together with some invisible force.

His shoulders rose and fell with a silent sigh and he grimaced.

Now what?

She shuffled her feet, keenly aware of the grit under her fingernails, the mud soaking the knees of her jeans.

He reached a hand toward her, palm up. The rain fell more heavily. "Come on," he said. "Let's go home."

"Home?"

"Yes." He closed his eyes for a moment and she thought he wasn't going to say anything else, but then he said the one word that gave her pause. *"Please."*

"Why?"

He laughed then, a choked sound, his hand still held toward her. "Maybe because we don't have a history of making good decisions while standing in the rain. Or maybe because... I've always wondered, if I hadn't forced your hand, how things would have played out between us."

She stared at his palm. "Me, too," she said. She took his hand.

He gave her a soft smile. "So, come on."

Fifteen minutes later, he pulled into a parking spot outside the old woolen mill and cut the engine. She hadn't known this was where he lived, but it made sense he'd choose a low-maintenance apartment near downtown. She was glad for the dark interior of the vehicle. Now that he knew the whole story, she wasn't sure what to expect.

He said nothing, just glanced over at her, then got out and closed his door. Her door swung wide, and he handed her out. She thanked him with a small nod and followed him inside. He opened the inner door of the vestibule and glanced around the hallway.

"Looks like Mrs. Finch is asleep. You'd hear her TV if she wasn't." His voice echoed off the walls of the empty vestibule like laughter at a funeral.

She waited while he unlocked the door to his apartment and held the door for her to precede him. He'd always been a gentleman that way, holding doors. It had been something that had made her feel special, cherished, despite the outrage of her inner feminist.

She toed off her sneakers on the mat inside the door and lined them up against the wall. Back when they'd been dating, she'd toss off her sneakers, and he'd make a show of lining them up on the mat together, toes to the wall. She'd laughed at him then, but she'd liked looking down at their shoes, his so much larger than hers, shoulder to shoulder, as if they would always be walking the same course and the same direction.

She waited as he removed his shoes. After a moment's hesitation, he set them next to hers. She fought the urge to fix them so they'd face the wall together.

She bit her lip instead and glanced around at the sparse but functional furnishings of his living room. He turned to face her.

Neither of them spoke.

Finally, he shrugged out of his wet jacket and hung it on a hook. He cleared his throat. "Can I get you something to drink?"

She shook her head and moved toward the front windows overlooking downtown. Rain caused puddles on the road under the streetlights. She pretended to find the view engrossing, as if she'd never seen rain or puddles before. Meanwhile, the nerves in her stomach were turning somersaults "No, thank you. I'm good."

He moved around behind her. She could feel his energy burning in the air. She fought the urge to shrug her shoulders.

Why had she come? After all these years, what could they possibly have in common except for a terrible mistake and hard feelings? But maybe this was the start of finishing up old business between them. Shedding the cocoon so they could finally be free of the past.

She sucked in a breath and turned around. "I wouldn't mind freshening up a bit." She held her hands by her sides, her dirty fingers curled into her palms.

"Sure. The bathroom is down the hall. First door on the left."

"Thanks." She strode down the hall, glancing briefly over her shoulder to see that she was alone. He'd gone to the kitchen.

She exhaled long and slow. She needed a moment to herself to collect her thoughts and emotions before facing him again.

...I've always wondered if I hadn't forced your hand how things would've played out between us...

Funny how she'd always felt she'd been the only one playing the game of 'what if.' What if he'd stayed around a bit longer? What if he'd been home for the miscarriage? What if she hadn't dropped the towel?

Would they have still made love that night?

She walked further, past the bathroom, a desire to put some distance between them overcoming her need to wash hands. Before she knew it, she stood at the threshold to his bedroom. The light of the hallway cast the room in shadows, but a large, multi-paned window overlooking the falls the town was named for, drew her. She stepped into the room, her stocking-clad feet silent on the thick carpet, like the hunted hiding in a cave.

The muffled sound of the falls was both peaceful and wild all at the same time. Like her emotions. Adrenaline ran high in her veins, making her feel buzzy and skittery.

She pulled herself away from the window. She had the thought that it would probably be best if she didn't allow herself to get caught wandering around his apartment like a poorly trained houseguest, but then she came face to face with the largest, most masculine four-poster bed she'd ever seen. It looked like it was a football-field wide, with a massive headboard and deep blue linens.

It was the kind of bed that invited you to attempt the backstroke in its depths.

Grace allowed herself a moment or two to imagine swimming and Jeff and this bed.

Someone cleared their throat behind her.

She turned, her face flushing hot.

Jeff stood in the doorway, one arm resting against the frame, a slight, knowing smile curving his lips. "Bathroom is back there," he said, hooking a thumb over his shoulder.

"Yes," she said, "of course. I was just—"

Except she couldn't finish, her face flushing even hotter as she struggled to come up with an explanation of why she was clearly standing in his bedroom and fantasizing about being on his bed with him. Not that he knew *that* part.

Except one look at his face told her he probably knew exactly what she'd been thinking.

"You have a big bed," she finally said.

"Why, thank you," he replied, a bit of laughter warming his voice. Oh, he loved to fluster her. He always had. He knew she was as green as they came despite her reputation for being a flirt.

But she wasn't the same girl she'd once been. She knew, at least in theory, what a big bed like his was good for.

He shrugged and took a step into the room, and her pulse kicked up another notch to a heavy, steady drumbeat. "After so many years squeezing myself into skinny army cots, it feels good to sprawl."

She glanced back over to the bed. Great. *Now* she was imagining him *sprawling* on it. Naked. Because, heaven knew this man wouldn't do anything constricting. Or fully clothed.

Or maybe that was her.

He grinned. She knew this, because she could hear the humor in his voice. "You're welcome to try it out," he said. "It's got one of those memory foam toppers."

She blinked away the image of his naked, sprawling magnificence. "Oh, no. Not necessary. Besides," she gestured vaguely to her body, waving her fingers in the air. "I'm all dirty."

His eyes danced. "Maybe I like it that way."

Her expression must have been comical, because he laughed out loud. "Relax. I'm kidding. Mostly."

She shook her head, darting a glance back at the ginormous bed. "I don't think that's a good idea."

"What's not a good idea?"

"What you're thinking."

He stepped another foot closer. "And what am I thinking?"

She swallowed. "That we should pick up where we left off."

He grimaced. "I'd rather not."

"Good," she said with relief. At least she thought that feeling was relief, that sense of emptiness inside her.

"I'd rather start over," he said.

She took a step back. "What?"

He stepped closer still, trapping her between his wall of a chest and his bed. Her gaze slid down to where his shirt clung damply to his chest. "I'd rather start over. Here. Now. We aren't two kids playing at being grown-ups anymore. We're adults who want to put the past behind us…"

Her face went slack. They both looked at the bed. "I'm not the kind of woman who thinks of sex as a casual thing."

"Who said anything about casual?" His voice dropped down to a frequency that hummed along with something deep and non-casual inside her, the part that believed in true love and happy endings. "I'm very, very serious."

"I'm not going to fall into bed with you."

"I'm not asking you to." *Yet.* He didn't say it, but she heard it nonetheless. Or maybe that was the voice inside her along with the parts of her that always went soft and willing when he was near.

She frowned. "You're not?"

His lips quirked again, and she found she missed all that he could convey with the tiniest of movements of his mouth. He had no idea how expressive he was even when he'd trained his other features to go blank. His mouth always gave him away. "No, not asking." His eyes sparked again, this time with self-deprecating humor. "More… hoping. But I'm not the one standing in front of my bed."

He grinned again, all this talk of sex making her hormones run amok inside her like they were on some sort of sugar high. She didn't like the feeling, as if she were one careless leap into an enormous four-poster away from disaster.

She flexed her fingers in front of her and shook her head. "I'm going to clean up now."

She stepped abreast of him, the size of his body surprising her. He'd gotten… bigger over the years. The lanky teen he'd been somehow becoming *more*. It unnerved her how much she liked it. He turned as if to follow her. "I think I can find the bathroom on my own," she said over her shoulder.

"You've already missed it once," he reminded her.

She ignored the wise-ass comment and found the bathroom without incident, thank you very much. She turned on the tap. Normally, she'd glance around, check out the décor, the kind of shampoo he used, the usual getting-to-know-you stuff, but she knew him already, knew he was *right there.*

"Is this the stalker behavior you police people are supposed to watch out for?"

"I'm not stalking you," he said, his voice low as he leaned oh-so-casually against the doorframe. She was wound so tight she thought she'd pop. "I'm trying to figure you out, that's all."

She kept her eyes on the water as it ran into the sink and waited for it to heat up. "There's nothing to figure out."

"You've changed."

"Thirteen years will do that to a person." She flicked her fingers into the stream of water. Still cold.

"Right."

"I'm still me inside," she added for no particular reason.

"The old you was a lot less uptight as I recall."

She raised her chin at that. "The old me has learned some hard lessons." She glanced toward him. "I made a mistake coming on to you in that motel room. I was too young to understand what I was getting myself into."

"Right." He nodded slowly, digesting her words, and she hated that he'd agree with her. She blew out a small breath that tried to trap itself inside her.

"No. *Wrong,*" he said, stepping into the small room beside her. "You knew perfectly well what you were doing. We both did."

"We were just kids," she said.

"Horny kids," he said, a slight smile tilting those damned fine lips of his. She stared at them, her face growing warm again.

"Speak for yourself."

He laughed then, a low rumble deep in his chest. "Not to name names, but I do believe one of us was naked first. And it wasn't me."

"Yes, well, that was then…"

"And this is?" He quirked an eyebrow, the corner of his eyes going all crinkly with humor. He hadn't had those fine lines before. She found she really, really liked them.

"This is now. I'm not a horny kid anymore."

The crinkles deepened. "You stripped in front of me when you got sprayed with a skunk."

"That was different. That was an emergency. I didn't want to bring skunk smell into the house."

"And here I was hoping it was because there was something about me that made you want to get naked."

She thought about him and being naked, and a flash of heat scorched her like a lightning bolt. She grabbed the bar of soap and shoved her hand under the water, yanking it back at the scalding heat. She clutched the bar tightly in her hand, reflexively, and it squirted out and up into the air.

Jeff's hand shot into her peripheral vision and grabbed the soap from the air.

Grace jumped back, landing against the solid wall of his chest. Her breath came short and fast, and it had absolutely nothing to do with scalding water or flying bars of soap and everything to do with her sudden awareness of the man behind her.

His laughter reverberated low, the vibration of it speaking to parts of her body that only spoke in trembles. "Troubles?"

"No, just a bit hot…" *Oh, dear Lord.* "I mean, uh, slippery." She squeezed her eyes shut in embarrassment. Hot and slippery? *Seriously?*

Jeff reached forward, his chest pressing into her back, making her hyper-aware that the man worked out in fabulous and delicious ways. "Allow me," he said, and he adjusted the tap and held the bar under the water before grasping her hands and working the lather over her skin.

She couldn't breathe as she watched his fingers stroke between hers, felt the smooth heat of his hands rubbing up and down her palms.

After a few moments, he urged her hands under the spray to rinse them, and she shook her body to rid herself of the trance she felt overcoming her, to push his heat away from her so she could *think* again and stop seeing the act of hand washing as some metaphor for sex. "I can do it," she whispered, quickly rubbing her hands under the water and smacking them dry on the hips of her jeans.

She stood up straight, keenly aware of the fact that he hadn't moved from behind her. She glanced down at his fingers as they gripped the edge of the sink on either side of her then up at their reflection in the mirror.

His gaze met hers, and she caught her breath as she watched his dark head lower, felt his warm fingers, still damp from the water, gliding over her neck as he reached up and moved her hair aside to press his lips to her nape.

He closed his eyes at the last moment, and that was her undoing. That one moment of vulnerability, of giving in.

She let her own eyes flutter closed as his lips played softly over her skin, the sensation too much and not enough all at the same time, and then he stopped, shifted, and she looked up again only to see him watching her as his hand slid back and to the sides of her hips, his fingers splayed as he urged her to turn around.

She did. God help her, she did.

She expected he would kiss her again, but he didn't. He just stood there looking at her, watching her, a hot, pulsing energy radiating off him, searing her where his hands still gripped her hips. Then he moved, sliding his hands slowly up her arms, then down again, up and down. Up and down. His eyes grew hooded as his gaze followed the movement of his hands, and then his hands rose again, his fingers digging into her shoulders ever so slightly.

"I want to kiss you," he admitted.

"Then kiss me."

"I don't know if I can stop at a kiss," he said. And he raised his eyes again, and she felt oddly powerful seeing the need reflected back at her there.

"Then don't kiss me," she said, and she pulled his hand from her shoulder and pressed it against her heart. "Just, touch me for now."

He frowned, staring at the hand she held against her, and then his fingers opened, splaying, curving around her breast. "Er, kissing is good," she said, heat flooding her face as well as other parts of her anatomy.

He squeezed, a low groan rising up between them, and she realized it was her.

"Grace." He breathed her name, his other hand stroking her cheek, her neck. He leaned in again, his lips poised above the skin at the opening of her shirt, but then he paused and looked up at her and smiled before dipping his head to touch his lips to her skin.

A jolt of something primal shot through her, and her fingers sank into his hair of their own volition. His hair was shorter than it used to be, but the feelings that swirled hot and needy inside her were just as she remembered them.

"I don't know what we're doing here," she murmured.

His lips curved against her and then he pulled back to meet her gaze. "If you don't know what I'm doing, then I'm doing it wrong."

"But, what if... what if something happens?"

His eyes grew hot, and those crinkles appeared again. "Grace, something's already happening."

"No. I mean, what if we do it again and..." she wiggled her eyebrows meaningfully, her face flaming to her hairline.

"You mean have sex?"

"That. Right. What if we do and... something happens? Like last time."

The humor left his face as he caught her meaning. "Then we're careful."

"Mistakes happen. Even when two people are being careful."

"Then we're flexible in what we do so mistakes don't happen."

"I don't—"

His mouth covered hers, lightly, teasing her inhibitions out of her with soft, leading kisses.

"I refuse to think of this as a mistake," he murmured.

Grace moaned, her fingers gripping his shoulders as his mouth slid lower, his hands moving deliciously over her. Dear heavens, the man was *genius* with his hands.

He stroked down the curve of her back, the swell of her backside, and then one tricky hand plucked open the button of her jeans. She was *this* close to getting naked in front of this man—again—when she yanked back hold of her senses. "Wait!" The panting breath that followed made her feel ridiculous, but she needed to think.

"Wait?"

"I, uh…" She glanced around the room, her eyes alighting on the toilet. "I need to pee."

He stepped back then, his hands leaving her body with big, gaping cold spots on it. "Oh. Sure."

"I'll be out in a minute."

"No problem."

She closed the door behind him and blew out a long, steadying breath. Classy. Real classy. *I need to pee?* She couldn't just say she needed a minute? Now he had a vision of her peeing in here, which, *ew!*

She turned to the mirror, horrified by the flush of lingering passion still staining her cheeks. She looked mussed. And horny. She ran the water again and splashed cool droplets on her hot cheeks.

Think!

She should go home. She should suck up her tattered dignity, thank him for a lovely, er, evening and march out that door before things got any more out of control.

Except he'd driven them here, and she'd need him to drive her back to her car.

Why hadn't she thought that through?

She avoided meeting her own gaze in the mirror, because the truth would only be staring back at her. She *had* thought it through. Just like that night in the motel all those years ago, she'd known *exactly* what she was doing every step of the way. Call it following her heart or her hormones, she'd asked for exactly what had happened.

She'd wanted to bind herself to Jeff Dayton as no one else had.

Irony was getting what you most wanted.

When she met him in the living room a few minutes later, he had his back to her. The windows were open, cooling night air flowing in along with the distant sound of the falls.

"Faith is a beautiful name," he said, then he turned to her, pinning her with that dark, unyielding look of his. "Why did you choose it?"

She swallowed and forced herself to step further into the room. She'd expected an onslaught, but not an emotional one. She shrugged. "You'll think it's silly."

"Try me."

She lifted her chin. "Because I have faith that one day she'll come back to me."

He shook his head, his eyes softening. "She's never coming back, Grace—"

She felt her heart pinch. "I knew you wouldn't understand."

He let out a slow breath, still not letting her drop his gaze, and he stepped into her personal space, invading all of it with his pulsing energy and hot eyes. "I mean, she's never coming back... unless you're with me."

"What's that supposed to mean?"

"It means she was a product of us. Not just anyone. *Us.* She can't come back unless there is an *us.*"

"There is no *us.*"

He smiled then, just the tiniest bit, as he raised his palm to her cheek and pulled her toward him. "That's where you're wrong." He leaned toward her, his lips poised above hers, his breath mingling with her own as she waited for what would happen next. Then his gaze grew dark and brilliant, refusing to let her look away. "There's always been an *us,*" he said.

Then he kissed her, a hot, searing contact that felt nothing like the playful sensuality they'd shared a few moments before. He was drinking from her soul. And just the fact that she was thinking those words made her sure she was losing her mind.

She pulled away, pushing her palms against his chest even though the action felt like ripping duct tape off her bare skin. "Stop vampiring me."

He blinked. "What?"

"Stop saying things and... doing things. It's too much too soon."

He raised one dark brow. She hated that eyebrow. It mocked her. It seemed to know she was falling under his spell. It knew she loved what he was saying and doing too dang much.

"Did you just say 'stop vampiring me?'"

"Maybe. Yes."

He chuckled and she hated that sound even more than his all-knowing, all-seeing eyebrow. "What does that even mean?"

"You're all... intense. It's overwhelming. I can't breathe when I'm near you."

"The feeling is mutual."

"See? Don't say stuff like that! I can't think when you say stuff like that. I just picture you and that porn-bed of yours, and I start babbling..."

"Go on..."

"See? No. I will not go on. You can't make me confess all my secrets just because..." Hell. Just because she already *had* confessed all her secrets? There was nothing left to say. It was all out there as naked as when she'd stood in front of him all those years ago and dropped her towel. At least then, she'd held onto her dignity.

Only she still had one secret left.

Jefferson Ward Dayton didn't know she still loved him.

And for her own sanity, she had to keep it that way a little while longer.

"I want to go home," she said.

He blew out a breath and stepped back. "You do?"

"Yes."

He looked disappointed, but he nodded. "All right. Just give me a minute to change out of these wet clothes, then I'll take you back."

She watched him disappear down the hall and let out a long, aching breath. It was better this way. Better to step back and not get all tangled up again. Especially *now,* right? What with the festival coming up and all, it would only make things awkward if she and Jeff started up again.

She needed to step back and figure this out before someone got hurt again.

She paced by the window, an antsy, unsettled feeling pushing her to scan Jeff's CD rack for a distraction. She smiled to herself. His tastes hadn't changed much. She recognized some bands he used to listen to back when they'd been dating. A few indie rock groups had made it into the collection. She popped open the CD player to see what he'd been listening to, her chest squeezing in as she read the label.

That band had been playing on the radio back when they'd made love in the motel.

She heard Jeff in the hallway and quickly pressed buttons to close the player.

Except she pressed the wrong button.

As Jeff rounded the corner from the hallway, the stereo speakers declared their desire to 'make love.'

Grace froze. "That was an accident."

He stared at her. "You once told me there are no accidents. Just fate waiting to happen."

"I say a lot of things I don't mean."

The base beat of the song matched the thudding of her heart.

"Does that mean you don't want to go home just yet?" He stepped into the room. "Because I'll be honest. I don't want you to go."

"You'd only be disappointed if I stayed."

He ate up the distance with two strides. "I highly doubt that." He turned off the stereo and turned back to her.

She swallowed over the nerves in her throat and bit her lip. His gaze zeroed in on the movement, and he reached up to rub his thumb over the spot, his palm splayed over her cheek like a brand. He leaned toward her, that delicious mouth of his descending...

"They call me the Ice Princess," she blurted before his lips could touch hers again.

"What?" He pulled back slightly. Frowned. "Who is *they?*"

She shrugged. "You know. People. Men." She sighed. "Guys I've dated."

His brow furrowed. "You mean Joe Sedowsky? Because if you're taking some wiener's opinion—"

"No! We never... Just... other guys."

"Well, whoever they are, they obviously don't know you very well."

"You can say that again."

His gaze narrowed. "What does that mean?"

"I'm saying," she said, because—*hello!*—it would be incredibly obvious in about, oh, thirty seconds anyway if they kept going in the hanky-panky department. "I kind of freeze up when things get too, um... hot."

The hand that had been stroking up and down her arm stilled. "'Freeze up?'"

"Yeah. I can't go through with... *you know.*"

"With what?"

She made herself spit out the word. "Sex."

He blinked. "Ever?"

She shook her head, face flaming. "Not since you... and I..."

He blinked and let out a choked sound of disbelief. "Wait. You haven't had sex since you were *sixteen?*"

She shook her head, too mortified to speak.

"Wow. That's not the Grace I remember. The Grace I remember—"

"Isn't the Grace I am now."

He looked at her thoughtfully. "I wouldn't bet on that. A woman as sensual as you? You're too sexy to be frigid."

"It's an illusion."

"I assure you, it's not."

She made an awkward, horsey bark of laughter. "I think I know whether I am or am not sexy." *Sheesh!*

He had the nerve to laugh. "Sweetheart, even crying and wallowing in skunk, you ooze sex appeal."

"I do not!"

"The way you roll your hips when you walk, the way you stroke your fingers through your hair when you're thinking, the way you look at me, like that... All hot as hell."

Did she do all that?

"I'm just looking at you," she said, trying not to unwittingly stroke or roll anything.

He bit his lip, his teeth drawing her attention to his mouth. "Oh, yeah, you are."

"Stop that. That's not fair. You're leading the witness."

He laughed and tugged her hips against his. The movement was new and yet oh, so, familiar. They fit like a puzzle, which was horribly clichéd, but true. He pulsed against her.

"I have no idea who told you you weren't sexy, but they're idiots. Ever since you dumped that ice water down your front to get my attention, you've had it."

"That was an accident."

"I prefer to think of it as fate," he said. He leaned closer again.

"I'll freeze up on you, too," she warned. "I won't want to, but I can't help it."

He didn't answer. Instead he kissed her again, a firm, heart-pounding kiss that had her snaking a steadying palm up between them.

His hand came up to cover hers, and then he paused, inhaling long and deep, and stepped away.

"Okay," he said. "I'll take you home."

She blinked, certain she'd misheard him. "What? Why?"

"Why? You're pushing me away, that's why."

She stared at the palm she still held over his heart, surprised to see it there. "That was just reflex," she said. "It doesn't mean anything. I was enjoying the kissing thing. Really."

He gave a half laugh. "Weren't you the one that always said that our bodies know more what we want than our minds do? Well, your body is telling me loud and clear we should put the brakes on."

"That's not what it's saying," she said, a bit desperately. Oh God. It was like Zach and all the other men from her past all over again! She pulled her palm off his chest and linked her fingers together. "It's saying, '*oooooh.*'"

He cocked one eyebrow. "Is it? So you're ready to get naked and bump uglies right here on this sofa?" He pointed to the sofa in question.

She blanched.

"I thought not."

"Not because I don't want to, but because that was just crude," she said.

"I know. But if you were really into me, you'd be up for it."

"No. When we make love again... I mean... when we have sex again..."

She swallowed. Why was he *looking* at her that way?

"Grace," he said. He ran a hand through his short hair, his bicep doing that twisty, humpy thing that seemed uniquely choreographed to turn a woman's insides to mush. "We jumped into bed together once, and it ended badly. Maybe..." He laughed, a sort of choked sound. "I can't believe I'm saying this, but maybe we should take it slow this time."

"How slow?"

"Like actually go on a date before we have sex."

"Are you asking me out?"

"I think so. Yes."

"Okay."

"Okay to the dating or okay to the sex?"

Her heart fluttered in her chest. "Okay to the date." *For now.*

"Just checking," he said. "Come on. I'll take you home."

Jeff drove in silence back to where she'd parked her car, which she was grateful for. Too many thoughts swirled in her head.

He stopped, and they kissed. Soft kisses of promises and anticipation as they leaned across the center console toward one another.

After a little while, he pulled back. "It's getting late."

She nodded and slid away, resting her head on the headrest, not quite ready to go. The earlier storms were now a soft pattering of rain on the windshield.

"Thank you," she said.

"For what?"

"Coming to my rescue so often. I swear I'm not usually as accident-prone as I've been the last few months." She smiled shyly. "You're like my own, personal hero."

He grimaced. "I wish you wouldn't say that."

"Why not?"

"It's not true."

"You're the Hometown Hero. Of course it's true."

"No I'm not. That was some crap made up by the press."

"You didn't rescue that couple?"

He leaned back against his seat and raked a hand through his short hair. "It doesn't matter now. I don't know why I said anything."

"No. Tell me."

He sighed, a long exhale that filled the dark interior. "It was dumb luck I stumbled across that couple."

"Their luck," Grace said. "They would have died of exposure if not for you."

"Hell, we all would have."

"I don't understand."

"I was lost. The only reason I found them is because I'd lost my way myself. My dad had blown me off for some gig at the last minute, and I was pissed, so I took off without him... and got lost." He let his head roll toward her on the headrest. "My apologies for not being the hero you thought I was. Then or now."

"But... you gave them your tent and hiked all the way down and led rescue crews back..."

"I was a kid running on adrenaline, that's all. Not a hero."

"You saved that couple. They got married. They invited you to their wedding!"

"They're divorced now."

Grace sat back in her seat, nonplussed.

"So now you know. I didn't want to do search and rescue because I felt like a hero; I decided I would do it, because I knew the fear of being lost in the goddamn woods."

He huffed out a breath. "I'm sorry. I don't know why I said anything."

She reached out to rest a hand on his forearm. He flinched but didn't move away.

So they'd both made mistakes.

"I have to say, I'm rather relieved," she finally said.

He glanced over at her. "Why?"

"Here I thought I was always the more impulsive one."

He turned toward her. "You are." A slight smile curved his lips. "But I like it that way."

He pushed his door open without another word and walked around to open hers for her.

She wanted to kiss him again, to ease the slightly awkward awareness that swirled around them now, but she wasn't sure if she should. It was almost as if they both wanted to be closer and run apart all at the same time, as if everything was new and yet burdened with a lifetime of overwhelming emotion and secrets held too long. It felt almost as if divulging their secrets after all this time had left them both with enormous caverns inside they weren't sure how to fill.

"Thank you," she murmured, "for a, ah, lovely evening." Oh, dear lord. She'd *thanked* him? She might as well have thanked him for his amazing hands or sexy lips.

"You're welcome," he said, just as inanely.

She didn't want to untangle her fingers from his. It was still all so new, and part of her felt like it would disappear in the light of day. I mean, really, where did they go from here?

What would he do if she blurted her last and only secret? *I love you. I've never stopped loving you. I want to make babies and get married and have the future we should have had but didn't.*

Probably too much too soon.

He waited while she got into the driver's seat of her car and motioned for her to roll down her window. "I'll follow you home," he said.

"That's not necessary," she said.

"A lot of crazies out at night," he said.

"I have a shovel."

His eyes crinkled, and even though she was already head over heels, she fell a little more in love with him. "That's why I'm following you home."

He paused, his hand still on her open window, as if he were weighing his next words. "I'm really looking forward to tomorrow," he finally said.

The part inside her that spoke in sighs swooned. She nodded.

"Eight o'clock?"

She nodded again, like a human bobblehead.

And as he walked back to his SUV, his tight, gorgeous ass convinced her that no matter how high-handed and overbearing it was to have him trailing her across town, she knew she liked it.

Scratch that.

She *loved* it.

A lot.

CHAPTER TWENTY-FIVE

Grace absently scrunched her hair and tugged at the hem of her skirt as she stared out at her backyard, the sun sinking low on the horizon. She shivered despite the moderate temperatures for mid-September. What if starting things up again with Jeff was a mistake? What if she were just opening herself up to more heartache?

What if things worked out?

She silenced the tiny whisper inside her with a firm shake of her head.

There was no predicting the future. Or was there?

She pulled a deck of oracle cards from the desk drawer. He'd be there in five minutes, and she was too nervous to stand around, waiting. Taking a few calming breaths and cleansing her mind of her own intentions other than to listen, she spoke the question upmost on her mind: "Am I on the right path with Jeff?"

She shuffled the deck. A card flew out and landed on the floor in front of her. She stooped to pick it up, then flipped it over.

The Butterfly. It meant transformation. Rebirth. Leaving the old self behind.

She shoved the card back in the deck and slid them all into the pouch with shaking hands.

Either it meant she was meant to leave the past behind and be reborn into a new relationship with him… or she was shedding the suffocating cocoon that was all their baggage to be reborn again and fly away. Well that was annoyingly ambiguous.

A knock sounded at the front door, and she dropped the deck into the drawer again.

She wore a black skater dress, black heels and, yes, heaven help her, a red scarf. From the look Jeff gave her when she opened the door, he approved.

He wore a pair of dark jeans and a white button-down.

She thought she'd spontaneously combust as he escorted her to his car.

They made small talk on the way, senseless chatter about things like the festival and the weather. She couldn't say what they discussed, but she was acutely aware of the raw energy pulsing off him like sexual radioactivity.

He took her to the little Mexican place on the edge of town.

After the waitress seated them, Jeff popped open his menu and peered over it at her. "I thought you'd have a better chance of finding something you like here. Hope you don't mind. I missed their beef enchiladas. Army chow was sometimes… hard to swallow."

"This is perfect. I mean, yes, I like the food here. Thank you."

"Good. When I got out, I told myself I'd never eat another crappy meal again."

She nodded. It made sense now why she saw him getting fancy take-out so often.

The waitress delivered chips and salsa and took their drink order. Grace crossed her legs. Uncrossed them.

Jeff leaned back and studied her. "I know I've said it before, but you really have changed over the years." She wasn't sure where he was going with that, so she stayed silent. "Used to be you'd order a Reuben every time we went out. Now you're a vegetarian."

"It's healthier," she said.

"I've seen your cart at the grocery store. That's not why you're a vegetarian."

He watched her in that silently knowing way cops have. She frowned and tried not to fidget in her seat. "Is it such a shock that I care about the living creatures of this earth and don't want them to die for me to eat?"

He paused, his salsa-drenched chip hovering over the white tablecloth. "Huh. It all makes sense now. The vegetarian thing, the roadside burials, the whole peace and love act you've got going… I get it now."

"I doubt you do." She didn't like the way he was looking at her, like she was a bug pinned to a specimen board. Or the fact that he'd just called her lifestyle an 'act.' "I happen to be at peace with myself. I'm sorry if that surprises you."

"Bullshit."

"Excuse me?"

"If you were so 'at peace with yourself' you wouldn't be flogging yourself with pity dates with guys like Joe Sedowsky."

"That wasn't a pity date. I went out with him because…" She paused. Damn. Why had she? She'd been about to say because Jeff had been nearby and she'd wanted to show him that even though he was clearly over her, she was still in demand by other guys, but that sounded pathetic. And wrong. What had Joe ever done to become some unwitting pawn in their love/hate relationship? Not that she and Jeff *had* a relationship. They'd gotten no further than any of the other umpteen dates she'd been on over the years.

And despite their physical chemistry, this might very well end the same way.

She *had* changed. She'd become the Ice Princess, and it didn't take a rocket scientist to figure out why.

And *that*, ladies and gentlemen, was the real problem.

"Joe is a loyal, caring, trusting man and he's good company," she said.

A muscle began to tick in Jeff's jaw. "You just described a Beagle."

"What do you have against him, anyway?"

He took another bite of tortilla chip. "Nothing. I'm just making an observation. You've been dating guys like Joe with no intention of letting them get close enough to hurt you, because you're scared of hurting anything including yourself."

She hated how close to home he'd gotten, like she was a fish and he'd just filleted her on the counter. "So you think I'm lying to Joe and the others about their chances with me?"

"Yes."

"I would never do that. That would be cruel. I genuinely liked him. *Like* him. For your information, I called him and told him about you and tonight. I said we were getting together to work out our past so we could get on with our lives. *That's* the truth. So no stringing of anyone along."

He frowned, the forgotten chip dropping a blob of salsa on the tablecloth. "Get on with our lives? Are you saying you're not sure about us?"

"No. I'm not."

"Why not?" he demanded, which seemed pretty harsh for someone who'd told her they'd take it slow and not jump ahead of themselves.

"Because..." She grasped for an explanation he'd accept, because the truth was she wasn't sure she could pinpoint anything. "Okay. Fine. You never said goodbye."

"What? When?"

"Before you were deployed. You never said goodbye."

He stilled. "And when I came home again and tried to explain everything, you refused to see me."

"I was hurt."

"I know. I get it, but…" He ran a hand over his face. "Do you think we could not rehash this all now? Can't we just make tonight about moving forward?"

"Can we?" she asked. What was that saying? That people come into our lives for a reason? What was the lesson she was supposed to learn from Jeff?

"I want to put it behind us. Lord knows I do. But, I don't know. Something keeps pulling me back. It feels as if… everything I need to know hasn't been revealed. And until it is, I can't make promises about the future." She forced herself to look him in the eye. "Is there something else? Something that will help us move forward once and for all if we just get it out there?"

He frowned and then glanced away, his jaw going stiff. He swore under his breath. "How did you find out?"

"Find out what?" she asked sipping her water.

Jeff let out a breath. "That I slept with your cousin."

Water spewed across the table. *"What?"*

For one awful, stunned moment, Grace felt like she was going to throw up, but then he continued. "It was years ago. When I came home on leave…" He let the words trail off, thank God. Grace didn't think she could take a play-by-play recounting of it.

So he'd slept with Rachel.

She picked up her water again, hoping the normality of the action would help her process the enormity of what he'd just said. But maybe it was only enormous to her. To him, it was something in his past he regretted, not a revelation blowing a hole in her fragile memories or current composure.

He'd screwed Rachel.

She took another sip of water, pleased with how calm she was able to keep herself despite the way her hand shook. See? This was how mature adults behaved when the crap hit the fan. She glanced around the restaurant. Glanced back. She took in a few even, measured breaths. "What?"

"That's it?" he said. "You're not upset?"

No, upset would come later when the entire restaurant wasn't witness to her coming out party as the 'spurned woman.' No way, no thank you. She had enough of a reputation to live down after nearly killing Joe last week. Not to mention her reputation as the Ice Princess.

"So, Rachel, huh?" she said.

He watched her warily. "Yes. It was brief, then it was over."

"Poor Doug."

"They were on a break," he said, as if that somehow made it all right.

"Doug has never for one minute been on a break from Rachel and you and I both know it." She sipped more water hoping it would make it through the narrow opening in her throat where her subconscious seemed to be constricting her ability to speak the words.

Rachel.

She kept waiting to feel righteous anger toward her cousin, because—*hello?*—it takes two to tango. But it was Jeff, for cryin' out loud. Every hetero woman on Earth had a thing for this man.

And really, it wasn't a surprise. Hadn't she in her heart of hearts suspected as much? She'd had weird vibes from Rachel way back when, had known Rachel had seen and talked with Jeff when he'd come home that time on leave, but now that it was confirmed...

"Why?" she asked, amazed at how calm her voice sounded. Eerily calm. She liked the fact that she wasn't going psycho on him. She liked that she could have control over her wayward emotions for once in her life. "Why Rachel? I'm curious."

He grimaced, looking uncomfortable. "It doesn't matter..."

"I deserve to know," she said with a little more force.

The pulse in his jaw thumped hard at her tone, and she smacked down the part of her that found it sexy. "Do you? Do you *deserve* to know? Does it help assuage your own guilt to hear how she came to see me when you ignored my calls when I'd come home from the other side of the goddamned world hoping to see *you?* Does it help you feel *even* somehow to know that I initiated it with her? That all she did was hug me when I cried over you, and she smelled of your perfume or shampoo, and the next thing I knew..."

"*Stop.*" Grace's chair scraped back as her legs involuntarily pushed away from the images. "That's enough."

"Why? Can't handle the honesty, Grace? I thought that's what you wanted. What this dinner was all about. Clearing the air and all that crap. If this is what's between us, then by all means, let's get it out there."

"What I can't handle is knowing that we've been reduced to this," she whispered.

And then, without even fully realizing what she was doing, she shoved up from the table, turned, and fled out of the restaurant, past all the prying eyes and into the cool night. Great. *Another* restaurant she was never, *ever* going to eat in again.

Home. She had to get home.

She looked up and down the deserted road, pulled her scarf tighter around her shoulders and started walking.

The door to the restaurant slammed. Jeff's footsteps pounded the gravel drive.

"For God's sake, Grace, let me drive you home."

She kept walking, her heels sinking awkwardly in between the stones with a horrible feeling of déjà vu. "I'll walk."

His hand touched her arm and she whirled on him then. "Don't touch me!" she spat. "You lay another hand on me, and I'll file charges."

He raised his palms up in the air. "No touching. Just talking."

"I'm done talking to you, too."

"It was years ago, Grace. Rachel and I…"

She turned again and shimmied between the parked cars. "I don't want to hear it! You screwed my cousin. *Yes*, we weren't dating, and, *yes*, it was years ago, but it's all new to me right now, so if you could at least give me the courtesy of processing this, I'd appreciate it."

She resumed walking, grateful for the relative dignity of reaching the paved road. Her heels tapped out her anger. Yes it was a long walk home, but she'd sooner wear her heels to nubs that get in a car with him at that moment. She'd never imagined he was a saint before or after they'd dated, but somehow this was… personal… as if he'd chosen the one way to drive the stake into the heart of their love affair that would prove most painful.

"I imagined it was you!" he said to her back. "The whole time, I imagined it was you."

She stopped and whirled to face him, hot, burning emotion inside her chest. *"This is supposed to make me feel better?"*

He swiped a palm over his face. "No. But it's the truth. I'm not proud of it, but it's the truth."

She stared at him, letting the godawful silence stretch out between them. She'd done this. She'd told him she was tired of all the lies between them, but *really?* She hadn't wanted *this*.

"When you got pregnant… I panicked a little. It was like my parents all over again, but I wasn't going to be that dad that flaked out on his kids."

"We're not them."

"I know that now."

"I'd already made one mistake," she said. "I didn't want to make another."

Something pained crossed his features before his eyes went dark. "You think marrying me would have been a mistake?"

She didn't answer.

"I see," he said after a long, silent minute. He had the nerve to look gutted.

"Do you? I didn't return your calls when you came home on leave, because you never let me have a say in what happened to *us*. You just kept making decision after decision, pushing me further and further away. You never gave me time to catch up to where you were. You left me behind. So I let you go."

"You kept making excuses for not wanting to get married," he said. "And after you'd been so sure of us from the beginning…" He ran a hand through his hair, spiking it. "I thought you were pushing *me* away. I thought you didn't care."

"I cared too much, damn you! *Too much.*" And then, damn it, she began to cry.

He blew out a long, shaky breath. "Well, shit."

They faced each other, the air heavy with all the pain unleashed into the air between them. "We'd planned how it would go, how you'd wait for me," he said. "I was happy when you told me you were pregnant, because it meant I had an excuse to marry you sooner. Relieved! Can you believe that? But when you told me the baby was gone... I couldn't believe you would throw it all away like that. That you could care so little about *us*."

She hadn't, of course. They both knew that now, but it didn't prevent her from wanting to kick him, to lash out and hurt him back for enlisting so soon and getting deployed and sleeping with her cousin. *Aargh!*

But they couldn't go through the rest of their lives beating each other up.

And she couldn't keep blaming him for something she'd been a part of creating.

Damn it.

Being an adult sucked. She sniffled and willed her tears to stop.

She hitched her scarf around her shoulders again and nodded, a small, objective, painfully adult part of her acknowledging her part in the mess that was and wasn't their relationship. She hated that small part of her, hated that everything she'd hoped to have with this man was so hopelessly, thoroughly ruined because of a series of assumptions, half-truths and regrettable actions.

And just like that, the anger left her like a deflated balloon forgotten at the end of a party. "I hate the truth," she finally said. "I hate thinking this is how it ends between us."

"Yeah." He laughed then, just a bit, just enough to relieve a bit of the tension between them.

"I suppose I should thank you," she finally said.

"For what?"

"For all the years Rachel has been amazingly generous with my birthday and Christmas gifts. Now I know why. I may not tell her I know. It would serve her right."

He nodded, the brief humor gone from his face. "We were kids, Grace. All of us. Trying to be adults and doing it very, very badly."

"I know." She met his eyes and wished it were an option to start fresh without knowing all she knew. To be innocent again. To stand at the opening of all the possibilities that lay before her and savor them for what they were. Possibilities. Paths untaken. Dreams unawakened. To look into this man's eyes and *not* have them reflecting years of hurt and regret back at her.

"Sometimes," she said, "the truth is we're just human. We're doing the best we can. We make mistakes. It happens. We need to learn from them. Learn from them and move on with our lives, because rehashing everything over and over… it hurts. And I'm done hurting."

She turned away and walked back to the passenger side of his car.

He spoke to her back. "You said once I was The One. Did you mean it?"

She glanced at the door, her feet like lead on the gravel drive. In that moment, she wanted to tell him how much she loved him, had always loved him. But what would it change? No amount of love could erase the hurt they'd inflicted on each other over the years.

Was he The One?

He was silent, and she glanced up and looked at him, *really* looked at him.

What did she know about identifying The One? Did she even believe there was one best soulmate for every person? Did she even believe in soulmates?

She squared her shoulders and reached for the door handle, and even though tears were blurring her vision again, she let the truth bubbling up in her heart be heard. "I meant it."

Relief flooded his features. "So?"

"So, what? What can I say? I meant it, but… Don't you feel, if we were meant to be together, it wouldn't be this hard? Maybe this should be telling us something. We're drawn toward one another, because we're meant to learn something from each other. Not be together."

"Do you really believe that?"

She shook her head.

She was out of answers.

But as he drove her home, she knew one thing.
If she had to do it all over again, she's still drop the towel.

CHAPTER TWENTY-SIX

Dee Barrett had a cup of coffee and a cupcake waiting for him on his desk when he arrived at the station the next day. As if a cupcake would make up for a shitty mood. He'd made a mess of things on the date with Grace, and for the first time in his life, he didn't have a plan for what his next step should be.

"The answer is 'no.'"

"I haven't even asked you yet. It's a tiny favor."

Jeff slid into his desk chair, rocked back and plucked the cupcake off the blotter. He took a giant bite off the top. He was a standup guy as a rule, but he'd slept like crap the night before and wasn't feeling charitable. "They're never tiny," he said around a mouthful of chocolate. "And bribery is illegal."

Dee rolled her eyes and slid her hand through her short brown hair until it stood up in awkward spikes. Her eyes looked sunken.

"You look as tired as I feel."

"Dad had another bad night," she admitted, chugging her own coffee.

"Sorry to hear that," he said. "Wait. Isn't this your day off? Why are you even here?"

Dee nodded. "I have a private security gig over at the closing sale for Lamont's. If you'd take over for me so I could go home and crash, I'd be forever grateful."

Jeff stuffed the rest of the cupcake in his mouth and sighed. Eventually Dee and her brother would need to figure something out. Just last week, Mr. Barrett had been driven home by a neighbor after he'd gotten 'too tired' to walk home again. Whatever was going on, he clearly needed help, but it wasn't in Jeff to tell her so. "Have you asked Derrek? He's usually up for extra money."

"He's already working this shift."

Jeff rocked his chair forward again. "Fine. I was just doing paperwork anyway."

She gave him the details, pulled a bakery box full of cupcakes out of her bottom desk drawer and set it on his blotter. "You're a prince among men, Jeff Dayton," she said. Then she smiled, grabbed her keys and left before he could change his mind.

He nabbed a second cupcake, stashed the bakery box in his drawer and prepared himself to make some easy money. Hell, it was better than sitting around brooding.

~ * ~

Jeff chose to walk the half mile to Lamont's. The morning was cool, a hint of autumn in the air, but he knew by noon it'd be warmer again. Might as well enjoy the cool temps while he could. His phone chimed with a text alert.

Mauri: *Well?*

He stopped on the sidewalk, because as much as he wanted to, his big fingers wouldn't let him text and walk at the same time.

Him: *What?*

Mauri: *What's the deal with dad? Did u talk?*
Jeff punched in his sister's number and waited.
"I'm in a meeting," she said upon answering.
"Then stop texting me," he said.
He could hear movement and apologies. She was excusing herself. Jeff waited.
"It's been days," she finally said. "I'm calling to see if you've made any progress on Operation Stop Dad."
"We never agreed to call it that. That's stupid."
"Fine. Any progress? Anything to report?"
"No."
"No, there's no progress or, no, there's nothing to report?"
"No, I'm not doing this for you, Mauri. This is something you need to suck up and handle yourself."
There was a pause. "Wow."
Jeff's stride got longer as he vented his frustration with every step. "This is New Hampshire, Mauri. Nobody gives a crap about Dad and his band. Hell, there are states with a lot more colorful characters already in office. You're blowing this all out of proportion, because you and Dad have never dealt with you and Dad."

207

"You're wrong. The voters are a whole lot more conservative than you think. I've made my platform all about safety. Sure, public sentiment is all for getting rid of distracted drivers, but heaven forbid we try and pass a law about texting while driving. Then it's all, 'don't dictate to me what I can and can't do.' It was a hell of a lot harder to get support for that bill than you might think.

"And now Darrell Witherman is organizing rallies about preserving our heritage... which boils down to his being in a snit over the town moving his 'historic fieldstone wall' so they could put in a culvert and not have the road wash out every spring. Since when did a pile of rubble thrown to the side by tired farmers become historic artifacts we can't disturb? But who do you think is getting all the front page press for being patriotic and preserving our agrarian roots?" She paused for breath.

"This isn't about Witherman or his bill."

"No, it's not! It's about why I went into politics, because I want to improve the lives of those around me, not dictate my own personal bias onto them. There are limits to how much government should intrude, I agree, but when your freedoms interfere with *my* safety, that's when the law needs to be clear about what's okay and what's not okay!"

"It's okay to be sad."

Maureen went silent. He heard her take a ragged, steadying breath. "I should get back to my meeting."

"It's only been a couple years."

She gave a derisive snort. "Yes, well, I'm young and need to move on."

"Who the hell said that?"

"Chair of the State Democratic Committee. Apparently he didn't approve of my naming the distracted driving bill after Christopher. Said it was 'too personal' and he 'has doubts I have the objectivity to lead our state at the gubernatorial level.'"

"He's a dipshit. People name bills all the time. It makes it easier to garner support."

"He said it wasn't as meaningful because Christopher wasn't a kid. Apparently, if Chris were an adorable three-year-old instead of a thirty-year-old, it would be okay, but because Chris was an adult with a clear party affiliation, it doesn't skew well with all voters."

"Seriously? What an ass."

"This is what I'm dealing with, Jeff. Dad is just one more pain in my backside."

"I've tried. Unfortunately there's no law against his going on tour again."

"If only." She sighed, letting the silence fill with the sounds around him of traffic and the occasional crow flying overhead. "Thanks for trying," she finally said.

"We're only human," he found himself saying. "We're doing the best we can. Sometimes we just have to accept the shit as it happens and move on. I've done everything I can think of to help you."

"I know. Thanks for arranging the announcement at the festival. It'll be good to come home for that." There was another long pause and then a gruff, "I gotta go."

She hung up.

Jeff's phone chimed with a text message.

Mauri: *Thx. Trying not to cry. I know ur doing ur best. I'll make it up to u. Promise!* <3

~ * ~

Grace hurried down the aisle in Lamont's, flipping through clothes hangers as she went. An older woman, her arms loaded with appliqued sweaters pushed past. Grace edged aside and continued looking.

Lamont's had never been this crowded before, but as soon as they had announced a liquidation sale, the bargain shoppers had come out in force. It was like one of those sample wedding dress sales, only with mothers with strollers and older women with walkers thrown in for added adventure.

Why was she even here?

Because Meg had less than graciously pointed out that a bit of shopping therapy would be less damaging to her health than staring into the bottom of another empty Ben & Jerry's container hoping it would reveal the clarity she craved.

Was she supposed to forgive him? Herself? Learn to look before leaping? What? What was the universe trying to teach her?

She stared at the bedazzled blue jeans in her hand and tossed them carelessly on the giant stack in her arms.

The spiritualist she'd listened to that morning had said that in order to truly forgive, one needed to let go of the past. *Pfft.* As if all she had to do was uncurl her fingers and let the wind take the past away like so many dandelion seeds in a summer breeze.

Grace sighed and threw a skirt on top of her pile.

Appliqued-sweater woman was on her way back by, and she was carrying comforters.

Grace scooted out of the way to find a changing room.

The line to the changing room nearest *Accessories* snaked around the back of *Women's Separates* and into *Sportswear*. Good grief. She'd be lucky to get out of here before the Harvest Festival.

She glanced across the store at *Menswear*. Lucky bastards probably had a changing room big enough for an army. As if any guys would care about a store closing sale. Or trying things on for that matter.

Grace gave the snaking line one last glance and turned toward *Menswear*.

Moving quickly so as to not lose her nerve, she swept through the door into the men's changing room, her selections piled in front of her face so she didn't unwittingly see anything she shouldn't.

"I know I'm in the men's room," she proclaimed loudly through the pile, "but the ladies' room is swamped, and I need a mirror."

The door squeaked behind her. "Grace, what are you doing?"

Grace's stomach lurched. "Jeff?" She tried to see around the mound of clothes in her arms. Failed. "Is there a bench or something I can set these on? I need to try these on, and my arms are giving out."

"Grace, you're in the men's room."

"I know, but it's a mad-house out there, and I need a mirror. Just tell me where I can set these down."

"You're not supposed to be in here," he said in his police voice. She hated when he used that voice. It got her anxious and excited all at the same time.

"Stop yelling at me."

"I'm not yelling."

She stifled her impatience at a universe that delighted in throwing them together. *Give it a rest already!* How was she supposed to let go of the past if it kept hurling itself in her way? It was like when a chipmunk dashes into the road. There were only so many times one can swerve before a collision—and tears—are inevitable.

"Why are you even here?" she asked, juggling her load. "Are you following me?"

She heard Jeff's long exhale through the puffy skirt of a cocktail dress she'd grabbed at the last minute. As if she'd be wearing crinoline any time soon, but it was a gorgeous shade of royal blue she thought she should have in her closet. "For the last time, you can't just walk in here with a pile of clothes—"

"Please. No one is paying any attention to the limits today. I swear I think I saw someone trying on a bathing suit right in the middle of an aisle. You should be giving them a lecture and be glad I'm in here."

"Grace."

One large, manly hand compressed the ruffles in front of her face. She glared into Jeff's eyes. "Don't start with me. I need to get back so Trish can pick her kids up from school on time."

"You are in the men's room," he enunciated slowly.

She rolled her eyes. "I'm well aware of that, considering I walked through the door with the little pants-clad guy on it. The line for the women's changing—"

The next instant, he lifted the clothes from her arms, and she saw *exactly* where she was. "Ohmigod! I'm in the *men's* room? I thought I was in the men's *changing* room!" She choked on the horror and irony of it all. It seemed rather poetic that they should meet in the crapper, to put it indelicately. "Oh, to hell with it. Just watch the door for me."

Jeff stared at her. "Come on, Grace. Just bring these back to the sales floor, and this'll be the end of it."

"I think not!" she said, grabbing the pile back. "I've been out there for forty minutes getting poked... shoved... cursed at... even fondled by a blind woman who wanted to know if I was the same size as her daughter. This is not the end of it!"

She was losing it, she knew she was, but she'd spent half the night alternately crying and ranting over this man—*again*—until all four cats had hidden in fear, and now he was just staring at her like she was some homeless person he was trying to figure out what to do with...

"Why don't you just leave me alone?" she asked.

"I can't."

"Can't or won't?"

He stared at her, weariness etched into the lines around his eyes.

Something inside her snapped, that little barrier between common sense and throwing caution to the wind, and suddenly she was tired of being mature and forgiving and *handling* it all. "You know what sucks?" she said, grabbing a pair of jeans from the top of the pile. Fine. If the universe kept throwing them at each other, she wasn't going to let it trip her up. She'd keep moving forward and do what she came in here to do. "What sucks is that we still have to live in this town, pretending we're perfectly okay, that we're just two people who once knew each other and who occasionally cross paths..."

He continued to stare at her. Silent.

Her words trailed off. She hated that silence—the emptiness that remained after they'd spoken all the ugly truths that had come between them. Maybe that's why she was afraid to let go of the past. Maybe she was afraid that once it was gone... there'd be nothing left.

Why wasn't he talking? Did he not even hear her? Did he not care?

She unbuttoned her shorts and jerked them to the floor.

She yanked on the jeans and stood on tiptoe to pivot and look at them in the mirror over the sinks. She met his eyes in the mirror. "But that's a lie, isn't it?"

She tugged the jeans off and tossed them over his shoulder before grabbing a skirt from the pile. She yanked it up, the fabric swirling around her thighs. "Where's the top that goes with this?" She rummaged and found the top, pulling her t-shirt over her head.

He shook his head. Silent.

"It's a lie," she said. "Because we're not just two people who once knew each other. We're two people who once l-loved each other..."

Jeff cleared his throat. "Grace," he said, his voice barely audible, "don't do this."

She paused, the clingy beaded top still bunched above her breasts. She pulled it into place. Swallowed. "But even though we loved each other," she whispered, "we didn't love each other enough, did we?"

"Is that what you think? That I didn't love you enough?"

She couldn't answer. She couldn't, because there was more than enough blame to go around on that score.

Oh God.

She had a wall plaque in her shop that read: *Tears are the shovel that dig the well for future happiness to fill.* If that were the case, she had a hell of a lot of happiness coming her way.

Tears threatened the backs of her eyes.

"No. The problem was, I loved you too much," she whispered.

He watched her, a muscle jumping in his jaw, the sequined butt of a pair of jeans twinkling on his broad shoulder. "And now?" he asked.

She stared at him, nearly drowning under the urge to run and hide. What the hell was she doing here? She hated how unsettled and confused he could still make her. How bruised and raw and alive all at the same time.

"I—" She shook her head and, realizing what she was wearing, yanked off the beaded top and skirt with hard, jerky movements. She grabbed her shirt from the pile and pulled it on.

"And now?" he asked again.

She stared into his eyes, eyes with dark circles to match her own, and figured there was no reason not to tell him.

"I still do," she said.

He stared at her, wordlessly, his face unreadable.

Her lips compressed. Well then, so that was it? She pushed past him to head for the door.

His voice stopped her. "Grace, wait!"

She turned.

His eyes crinkled. "You might want to put some pants on first," he said.

She glanced down at herself, then up at him, and all the emotion roiling in her gut burbled up and out of her...

And she began to laugh.

And the tears that had been tears of frustration moments before turned to tears of another sort.

"Damn you! *This* is what you do to me," she said. "Because of you, I'm now officially the woman that walks around half-naked!"

Humor tugged at the corners of his mouth now. "I hate to break it to you, but you've always been that woman."

She let out another chuckle, like somebody had shaken all the laughter loose inside her and it was burbling to the surface.

She let her palms rise and fall in a helpless gesture and shook her head as she began to sober. "I don't know what comes next," she said.

"Me, either."

"Then how do we move forward?"

He tossed the clothes onto the top of a trash can, ignoring the fact that half of them slid to the floor, and stepped closer. "One step at a time?"

"What does that mean?"

"Just... let things play out, I guess."

"That's not your style."

"Maybe I want it to be."

She pressed her lips together, kind of wishing she were wearing pants, but not wanting to interrupt the moment.

Her arms began to tingle.

"Maybe I like having some things planned out," she said.

"Then we'll plan another date." He stepped closer. "Tonight?"

She grimaced. "I have my Healing Circle."

"Then we'll leave things open," he said.

"Really?"

"Really."

She stared up at him. "Aren't you going to kiss me?"

"I'm on duty."

She stepped closer. "So what does that mean?"

"I'm not allowed to do anything that's not in an official capacity. But if a random, half-naked woman wanted to kiss *me*... well there wouldn't be anything anyone could say about that."

She grinned and pressed herself closer. "Like this?"

"I may have to restrain you if you get out of hand," he said. He winked. "Please get out of hand."

She laughed again, a flirty, happy burst of joy she hadn't felt since those early carefree summer days so long ago.

She rose up on tiptoes, her hands on his shoulders and leaned in for a sweet, happy kiss.

The door to the restroom creaked open.

"Oh, pardon me. I'm so sorry— *Grace?"*

Grace hid her face in Jeff's chest as it shook with mirth against her cheek. The universe was having a *field day* with her lately. She lifted her hand to wave a mortified hello.

"Hey, Joe."

CHAPTER TWENTY-SEVEN

Jeff gave a hearty wave to Mrs. Finch and shoved open his apartment door. To think he'd gone into today feeling frustrated and confused and ended it with Grace pressing her sweet, half-naked body into his.

She still loved him?

He'd wanted to grab her and kiss her senseless, but then Joe had waltzed in, and he'd been laughing too hard to do anything but ask Joe to give them a minute.

Grace had blushed three shades of crimson, yanked on her shorts and bolted. If that woman ran away from him one more time, he'd recommend she sign herself up for a Nike endorsement.

After she'd left, he'd bought the beaded top and skirt she'd tried on. It was his new favorite outfit for her.

He glanced at the clock. He had less than an hour to shower, change and drive over to his mom's for dinner.

He would have begged off, but Mauri was driving up from the coast and staying in town through the festival. Not that he really wanted to see her. He'd failed to do anything about the dad situation except make his father as pissed at him as he was annoyed with everyone else.

Happy, normal family they were.

At least things with Grace were on the upswing.

He punched the play button on his answering machine and grabbed a soda from his fridge. He popped the lid and guzzled half a can.

The first message was Mauri telling him she had a surprise for him.

The second message nearly made him drop his soda.

... from the Wyoming State Parks and Cultural Resources... Ranger position... We'd like to arrange an interview...

The woman had left a phone number, but he wasn't really listening.

What the hell?

He finished his soda and decided he'd get some answers soon enough.

He strode up the walk of his mom's house. He planned to eat, get answers, and go home.

He knocked lightly on the front door. There was no reply. Mom was probably still finishing dinner. Maureen should pull in any time. He opened the door, "Mom? It's—"

A scream from the kitchen followed by the sounds of a struggle and something breaking on the floor had him tossing the door wide, his body going into high alert. He ran across the living room and smashed the kitchen door open with one hand while reaching for his service revolver with the other.

"Police! Stand and put your hands in the air!" he shouted.

A man scrambled from the floor, his pants around his ankles, his hands dutifully stretched toward the sky, the family jewels on full display.

"Dad? *Mom?*"

Peggy Dayton, popped up behind the island and hastily grabbed a placemat to cover herself. It was not, Lord help him, opaque.

"Oh, Christ!" Jeff whirled away, his nerves jangling like a rookie's as he re-holstered his gun and tried to mentally erase what no eyes should ever have to see. He stumbled over the fragments of pottery strewn across the tile floor—a casualty of their sexcapades, no doubt—and all but dove for the kitchen door to escape.

A light hand on his shoulder made him jump with adrenaline. "I'm so sorry, honey. You're early."

Jeff froze at his mother's voice, his eyes squeezed shut. "It's ten of. You said dinner would be at six."

"Well, your father stopped by, and I lost track of the time…"

"I see that. Saw that." Jeff groaned and swiped a hand down his face. Three tours of duty and two years on the force and only *now* could he say he'd seen it all. "I'll be in the living room."

"We'll just be a moment, Son."

"Take your time, Dad."

Jeff met his sister in the front yard.

Mauri slammed her car door shut, her black pumps clicking smartly on the front walk as she strode toward him. "You look like hell," she said in greeting. "You got the flu or something?"

"Dad's here."

Mauri rolled her eyes. "Again? What does he want?"

"Some questions are better left unasked."

The front door swung open, the creaky hinge screaming like the little voice inside Jeff's brain still crying out, *No! For the love of God, no!*

"Jeff? Oh, Mauri! Hi."

Maureen's gaze narrowed as she looked from their mother back to Jeff. "Oh, for the love of… seriously?"

"It's not what you think," their mom insisted. "Please, I can explain. It's not like last time. Just... come in the house, all right?"

Jeff shrugged, glanced at his sister, and made a gesture as if to say, 'after you.'

He stopped on the threshold and turned to his mother. "Your shirt is on inside out."

"At least I'm wearing one now," she whispered back.

He nodded and reluctantly entered the living room.

His father stood on the other side of the room. Thankfully, his pants were now zipped, although it was hard to take the man seriously knowing he had sex with his socks on.

Never in a million years would he be able to erase that image.

"I'm glad you're both here," their mother said, flitting a hand over her hair to smooth it. "Your father and I have news."

Mauri sucked in a gasp. "Please tell me you're not having a change-of-life baby."

"No," his dad said. Maureen audibly exhaled in relief. "I've asked your mom to marry me."

"And I've accepted!"

His mom thrust her left hand forward and held it aloft.

Maureen scowled. "Isn't that your old engagement ring?" She turned to their dad. "You couldn't even spring for a new ring?"

Their mom snatched her hand back. "He did, but it's the wrong size, so I'm wearing this in the meantime." She smiled up at their dad and gripped his arm as if they were Romeo and Juliet standing up to their disapproving families.

"I can't believe this," Mauri said. "Mom, you're smarter than this. Fine, I get that at your age you might still want to..." she swallowed "...hook up from time to time, but marriage? There's a reason you two didn't work out the first time."

"Yes, there was," their mom admitted. "I didn't believe in us strongly enough."

Jeff frowned, but Maureen had on her placating, reasonable expression now, so he let her run with it.

"Sure you did. But you were wise enough to recognize that that life wasn't conducive to raising a family. You made the right choice."

"But that's no longer an issue. I'm not raising a family. You're both successful adults in your own right. And now, I can do what I want without worrying about what others think."

"Don't you think you might be rushing into things?" Jeff said. From the bass-mouthed expression Maureen was sporting, he guessed it was

217

time for him to step in. "You have a history of breaking up. Things don't last."

"That's my fault," his parents said as one, then they laughed and clung a little more tightly to each other as if shared guilt was endearing instead of a portent of disaster.

"I let my family influence me when I should have followed my heart," his mom said.

"Grandma and Grandpa have always had your best interests in mind," Maureen said a bit desperately. "Didn't they step in to help when we were little?"

"I was talking about you two."

"Us?"

"You're always so negative whenever your dad and I are together. I begin to doubt it's worth the effort to fight with you all the time and put up with your disapproval."

"We're not the ones acting like teenagers," Jeff said.

"Maybe you should try it some time."

Jeff held his breath in his lungs. He didn't want to think about acting like a teenager. For one thing, that hadn't worked out so well for him. For another, it made him think of Grace and second chances and damned if it didn't make him feel a bit of sympathy for the shoeless man standing next to his mother.

"Just once," his mom said, "I'd like you to consider what would make *me* happy."

"Stability," Maureen said firmly. "Stability makes you happy. Knowing what bed you're going to sleep in each night. Your students at the school!"

"No. This man," she said, beaming up at their dad, "*this man* makes me happy."

"I love you," his dad murmured down at his mom.

"I love you, too," she whispered back.

"Get a room!" Maureen all but shouted. "I can't stand to watch this. It's a train wreck waiting to happen." She grabbed her purse and jacket from the couch and shuffled from behind the coffee table, trapped by floral upholstery.

"Maureen, stop." Rodger's voice reverberated throughout the small room.

"Why?" she whirled. "Why should I listen to you? You're about to break her heart again, and I can't stop it, but I sure as hell don't have to watch it. All my life it's been about the band and your career. It was always more important than being there for any of us." She turned toward their mom. "You think it's all hunky-dory, but just wait. Something will come up, something important to you, and then you'll see who comes first in his life."

The door slammed behind her.

Jeff blew out a breath knowing he was caught between an uncomfortable silence with his parents and going after his sister. "I'll talk to her."

He found Mauri on the front walk, hands balled into fists, pacing.

"I thought you were leaving," he said.

"Just getting some air," she said. She glanced up at him, her eyes shining with hot emotion. "We have to stop them. This is insane."

"I admit I think it's ill-advised, but they're adults. They're allowed to make their own mistakes."

"Really? You approve of this?" She waved a hand accusingly at the door.

"You heard mom. She thinks *we're* the reason they never worked out."

"That's an excuse. If they were meant to be, they would have been together by now. It's too late for them. Don't you see? It's too late!"

And then Maureen did the one thing he least expected.

She burst into tears.

He stepped forward and wrapped her in his arms as she soaked his shirtfront with her sobs. He patted her back. "This isn't about Mom and Dad, is it?"

"Of course, it is!" she hiccupped.

He gripped her shoulders and held her apart from him until she met his gaze. "Mauri?"

"People like that don't deserve a second chance," she said.

"What do you mean, 'people like that?'"

"People who throw love away when they have it. I would never have done that with Chris. Never. When you have a love worth fighting for, you don't let it get away because of a little rough spot. You won't let it go until death rips it from you."

He dropped his hands. "Don't you think that's a bit judgmental?"

"Oh, come on! They're making excuses! Our disapproval? Really? That's what kept them apart? I *never* would have let something so trivial get between me and Chris."

"You were kids, Mauri. Just kids. You have no idea what you would or wouldn't have done."

"He was my soulmate."

Jeff shook his head. "You really believe that?"

Mauri nodded. "Yes."

"Maybe Mom and Dad are soulmates. Maybe their timing was just off before."

"For years?" she scoffed.

"Yeah."

"You really believe that?"

He paused a moment, reflecting, because if he lost hope for his parents, he lost hope for himself. "Yeah. I do."

"It's not fair," she finally said. "It's not fair they get so many tries to get it right."

He smiled, a wave of something bittersweet and hopeful rising up within him. "Some of us aren't lucky enough to get it right the first time. Are you really going to begrudge them another shot if there's a chance they could be happy?"

"What about your happiness? And *mine?* You know this is going to impact all of us."

"I thought you wanted an intact family. I thought that was what your PR people always harped on."

"I want a *normal* family. This circus is anything but."

"Welcome to the Big Tent, sis."

She sniffed and wiped her nose most indelicately, then squared her shoulders.

"You know I love you," she said.

He grinned. "I know." She hated this. Hated the uncertainty. The problem was, Mauri had a heart as big as they came. She wanted it all to go according to plan, neat and tidy, everyone safe and happy in the end.

Life wasn't kind to people like Mauri. There were no guarantees your heart wouldn't get broken.

The trick was knowing whether it was worth the risk.

Grace was a bit like that.

He just needed to convince her it was worth the risk.

Mauri put a hand on his arm. "Oh! Did you get my surprise? I called one of Chris's old college buddies. Pulled a few strings... They said they'd call you."

"Right. About that..."

"I know. It's not the job you gave up to come here, but it's a start. It would take you away from all this," she waved her hand in the air, "crazy. You'd have to go through the application process, but just between you and me, you're as good as in if you want it."

"I see."

"I know this small-town stuff makes you bonkers. There, you could get away from it all, helping people who are hurt or injured when needed, just like you always dreamed of doing."

He nodded, thinking about what it would be like if he had the courage to chase his dreams after all these years. Was it too late to be happy? Truly happy? Was it worth the risk?

The answer slammed into him, clear and sure: *yes.*

"I'll think about it. For now, let's go face the crazy."

"Do I have to?"

He draped his arm over her shoulders. "Come on. We can do this. We can wish them well."

They re-entered the living room, all awkward civility as his mom offered them iced tea and finger foods like it was some ladies luncheon.

Jeff's cell phone chimed with a text.

Mauri: *Thxgiving at my house?*

He glanced up to meet her eyes across the living room, saw the faint hint of laughter straining to come to light from beneath the stress and sorrow.

He nodded.

She smiled.

He fumbled with his phone again.

Jeff: *Just us, right?*

Mauri laughed out loud then and accepted her glass of iced tea, and he knew, somehow, they'd work it out.

CHAPTER TWENTY-EIGHT

"Hi, Lydia. Meg." Grace nodded and pretended everything was normal despite the fact that she felt like a baby bird who'd been pushed from the nest. She was flapping her little wings of hope, praying she was actually flying and not hurtling toward certain doom.

She flipped the store sign to 'closed' and froze, her heart skipping a happy beat. She quickly unlocked the door again as Jeff crossed the street to the door of her shop.

"Hey," she said. "Missed you last night at the Civic Pride meeting. Everything okay?"

"Sorry about that. I was out on a call," he said.

She nodded. "Um, I'm sorry, but it's Healing Circle night."

"That's why I'm here," he said. "I was hoping Lydia Sweet might be here?"

Grace nodded and opened the door wider. "She's in the back."

She walked toward the back of the store, acutely aware of the man trailing behind her.

Grace watched as Linda fidgeted on her yoga mat and pulled off her sweater. "Oh, God. Having another hot flash. Somebody open a window."

Sandi leaped to turn on the little fan Grace kept for activating the wind chime display and turned it toward Linda who raised her armpits and billowed her shirt between pinched fingers.

Grams leaned forward, her yoga pants riding down in back. Grace prayed Jeff wasn't looking. "You need more orange," Grams could be heard saying to Linda.

"Oranges?" Claire asked. She was still trying to pull her legs under her ten minutes after everyone else had settled.

"No 'orange.' Her sacral chakra is out of whack. You need balancing," Grams said, waving at Linda's flushed face.

"I need a spa day and year-round air conditioning," Linda said, fanning herself with a book on medicinal herbs she'd pulled from the display behind her.

"She's right," Sandi chimed in. "I don't know why I didn't think of it sooner. Your sexuality is all clogged because of this ongoing turmoil with Jerry, plus all the chemicals and surgery. You need a cleansing."

"Just send her in for a colonoscopy. That'll cleanse her," Claire snorted.

Grace paled. Dear God. Why did every Healing Circle seem to devolve into a discussion about bodily issues or the political crisis du jour?

Lydia fluttered her hand in front of her to get their attention. "If her sexuality is blocked, I think the best thing—"

"You know what?" Grace cut in before Lydia could, heaven help them, complete her thought. "I think we need to meditate on this."

"On Linda's sex drive?" Claire asked.

"No. On finding balance within ourselves," Grace said. *Sheesh.* There was more sexual innuendo and snickering going on with these women than a group of boys in middle school Health. It didn't help that they were crammed together like sardines tonight.

Peggy had given her regrets, something about big news she'd share next week, and an impromptu visit with her parents in upstate New York. Grace wasn't disappointed not to have to face Jeff's mother when she'd spent half the night dreaming about him and his, er, handcuffs.

"Lydia," Grace said. "You have a visitor."

Jeff cleared his throat behind her. "Good evening, ladies."

A tittering like she hadn't heard since junior high dances rose up from the ladies as they all stopped to turn and gawk at the newcomer.

Jeff stood at the periphery of their little circle in full uniform like a stripper at a bachelorette party.

Okay, so maybe he was simply standing there looking all navy blue and slightly cocky, but Grace was imagining him as a stripper.

Again, thank God his mother wasn't there.

Embarrassment flooded her face at her own thoughts. Would she never be immune to this man?

"I'm sorry to interrupt. Lydia, I was on my way home and thought I'd check and see if you'd discovered anything missing after all," he said in that booming low voice.

"What? Why is he asking?" Grams wanted to know.

Lydia's cheeks pinked up as she waved her hand. "Oh, nothing. It's fine. I swear, I probably left the service door ajar by accident. I'll be more careful, I promise."

Grace sat in her usual spot which, thank goodness, kept her far away from Officer Hot & Spicy. (If he were to have a stripper name, that is.)

"Join us!" Lydia said, scootching away from Grace to make space.

Grace whirled toward Lydia to see what possessed her to say such a thing. She ignored Grace's stare.

Jeff shook his head. "Thanks, but I don't mean to intrude." He looked at Grace with a hot, melting stare and then focused on Lydia. "You'll let us know if it happens again, okay?"

"Absolutely."

Jeff touched his forehead in a small salute. "Grace. Ladies."

"Do join us," Linda said. "It'll be fun to have a man with us for a change."

Jeff stalled, clearly weighing his options.

"It's kind of a women's thing," Grace said.

Grams made a *pfft* noise. "I think Officer Dayton is plenty man enough to handle us."

Oh, great. Grams was being inappropriate again.

"I only meant he might prefer not to—"

"You know? Why not?" Jeff said, stepping over yoga-pant clad legs to reach the open spot of carpet next to Grace. "I'm curious."

"Are you sure?" Grace said, as he folded himself into the spot beside her, his energy strong and hard, filling the space and pressing down on her. His elbow pressed into her right breast for a thrilling moment before moving away as he stretched his legs out in front of him.

"I think I'm man enough," he murmured under his breath. "Don't you?"

She shivered involuntarily and shrugged to cover up her body's response. Oh, Kris Kringle. Yes. Yes, he was, and that was definitely a problem when she was trying to be professional and all.

Grace pasted a serene smile onto her face and nodded at the ladies as if her pulse hadn't just rocketed into the stratosphere.

"Very well, then. Let's get started. We'll start with deep breathing exercises today."

Grace sat cross-legged on her mat and waited silently while everyone quieted. The gentle sound of ocean waves played over the sound system, and she willed herself to let the rhythm of the waves regulate her breathing.

Jeff shifted next to her. His knee cracked. He picked up the pillow near his hand, looked at it, and tossed it to the side.

"Welcome, everyone" Grace said quietly. "For those of us who are new, I invite you to join us all in allowing your breathing to flow with the sound of the waves. In... and out... In... and out..."

The sound of heavy exhales and deep inhalations filled the space. Jeff coughed then cleared his throat. He did that when he wasn't entirely comfortable. She liked knowing he wasn't any more relaxed than she was.

"And now I invite you to allow the intentions of your heart to speak to you in the silence between your breaths. This may be a time for you to release worries or burdens you may be carrying or secrets that are weighing upon you. You may voice them or allow them to speak silently in your heart."

Jane Alexander, a relative newcomer, cleared her throat. "My eldest left for college a couple of weeks ago." Her voice caught. "I miss him so much, but… is it wrong to be happy he's doing his own laundry now?"

Words of consolation and support rippled around the circle.

"We hold Jane in our hearts and support her son as he embarks on his journey of growth and independence," murmured Grace.

"I've been struggling this week with an, um, infection," Linda whispered. "*A woman's thing*," she added unnecessarily. "I'm so tired of feeling tired. I want to be strong again."

"We imagine the waves lifting Linda up with strength," Grace intoned.

Grace exhaled long and slow. "Let us hold hands, joining ourselves in collective hurt and collective healing." Lydia grasped her hand on the left, Jeff on her right.

Grace flexed her fingers within his grasp, but he held fast. Why had she suggested holding hands for Pete's sake? She almost lost her train of thought.

"Some of you may resist the flow of healing energy from your neighbor, but this is natural. We will continue to hold together as a circle until we feel the free flow of energy one to another, until we breathe as one body."

Red hot heat pulsed from the thick pad at the base of Jeff's thumb as it pressed against her hand, and Grace's sole awareness zeroed in on that one point of contact.

As she'd spoken the words 'one body,' Jeff had glanced at her briefly, an intense heat darkening his eyes, and for a moment, it was as if they were alone, facing each other.

Warmth crept up her neck, and she was grateful for the low lighting.

Jeff leaned toward her ear. "Is this when the miracle happens?"

She slanted a look at him and fought the urge to laugh, and suddenly the tightness inside of her broke loose, and a flood of heat spilled out, radiating through her.

"I'm finding it very hard to relax with you here," Grace whispered.

"I feel a disturbance in the force," Sandi said, opening one eye and grinning at Grace.

"And now," Grace said, "We can let go of each other and our concerns."

"Is it snack time yet?" Grams asked. "I smell brownies."

Grace waved a hand. They'd been on the mat all of ten minutes, but she was ready to head for the hills, because if she sat here one more second, she'd be proposing deep breathing exercises of an entirely different variety. "Yes. Let's take a refreshment break before we learn the Chi Gong moves Jane was going to show us." The ladies stood and rushed toward the brownies leaving Grace and Jeff alone.

Grace stood from her mat and brushed imaginary lint from her yoga pants.

Jeff's eyes followed her hands down her thighs.

"Now would be a good time to duck out. I'm sure you don't really want to be a part of Healing Circle," she said.

"You're right. I'd really rather be home."

"You would?"

"With you."

"I wish I could…" she let her words trail away.

"I understand," he nodded. "Too much, too soon."

He let out a long breath. "Well, goodnight ladies. I'm going to head out."

He waved, murmurs of disappointment and good wishes followed him out the door.

Grace watched him leave, her heart squeezing in her chest.

"You can't just let him go."

"If it were me, I sure as heck wouldn't still be eating brownies."

"I don't need to learn Chi Gong tonight…"

Grace turned to the ladies as they stood over the brownie platter. "He said it himself. It's too much, too soon."

"Don't be stupid," said Lydia. "Now go after that man and tell him how you feel."

"He knows how I feel, Lydia." She watched Jeff's retreating back. "But, what if it doesn't work out?"

Lydia offered a small smile. "Oh, Butterfly, what if it does?"

"What did you just call me?"

Lydia shook her head. "I'm sorry. I don't know where that even came from. Brainfart, I guess."

Grace blinked, the universe slamming home its message with crystal clarity.

She didn't want to merely *exist* through another fifteen years—not if there was a chance she could make it work. It was time to stop beating themselves up and beating around the bush.

She shook her head, a rush of something strong and sweet and hopeful pushing her limbs toward the door and out onto the sidewalk in her bare feet.

Jeff stood outside his cruiser, leaning against it. He pushed upright when he saw her.

"You didn't leave," she said inanely to him.

He smiled, just a small tilt to his lips. "You came."

She nodded, her pulse kicking into overdrive as he took four long strides across the road to meet her.

"I don't want to take it slow," she said.

He chuckled then. "Haven't you learned there's only one speed when it comes to us? It's always been that way."

She nodded. Tears swimming in her eyes. She blotted them with her fingertips.

"I thought I needed to be the butterfly," she whispered. "That I needed to fly away from all the stuff that went wrong..." Her hand waved jerkily between them as she struggled to find the words. "And start over."

"Maybe being the butterfly doesn't mean flying away. Maybe it means becoming the you—*the us*—we were always meant to be."

The tears overspilled at that.

"Don't make fun."

"I'm not. I promise." He reached out and rested his hand against her cheek.

"You called my spirituality Voodoo," she said.

His shoulders slackened, for once giving in to the weight he seemed to perpetually carry around on them. "I love your Voodoo," he whispered. "I don't understand it, but it beats the crap out of what I've seen and heard over the years. It gives me hope to believe your reality is real. I want to believe it's real. But I can't believe it on my own. I need you."

"I need you, too," she said.

He grinned then, a smile that crinkled his eyes. "Then come home with me. Now."

She glanced over her shoulder. The ladies were less than subtly crowded near the front of the store, pretending a sudden interest in her window displays.

"Ditch them," he prompted. "I have a feeling they'll understand."

Lydia pushed open the door, giving up all pretense. "Gracie? You want us to lock up?"

Grace's arms hummed. Yup. She was on the right path. "Could I at least come get my shoes?" She turned back to Jeff, going on tiptoe to press her lips to his and then smiled. "Ten minutes. Your place," she said.

He squeezed her fingers in his before she stepped away.

"We're doing this?" he said as if he expected her to back out.

"We're doing this," she promised.

~ * ~

After a flurry of well wishes and hurried departures, Grace locked up and drove the short distance to Jeff's condo. Mrs. Finch's TV was blaring when she entered the foyer. For some reason this made Grace smile. She knocked on Jeff's door.

She was doing this.

Here.

Now.

The door swung open, and before she could even think of a segue to ease the awkward transition of standing on his doorstep, before she could formulate a stilted 'how are things since we just decided to give it a go ten minutes ago?' speech, he'd hauled her over the threshold, swung the door shut, and pulled her tote bag off to swing it to the floor beside them.

"What took you so long?" he asked, wrapping her in his arms and burying a kiss in her hair.

He was no longer wearing his uniform shirt, his plain tee pressing against her nose, and she inhaled the warm, musky scent of him.

"Well, I—"

But he didn't wait for an answer, thank goodness, just tilted her chin up with his knuckles and kissed her silly until they were both breathless.

"Take your shoes off," he ordered, between kisses.

"Why?"

"Because I plan to carry you down that hallway in exactly three seconds, and you don't need your shoes where we're going. One..." He kissed her neck. "Two..." He kissed her ear.

"Okay, okay!" she said, toeing off her sneakers.

"Three!" He swung her up into his arms and she laugh-yelped, because she hadn't really believed he would.

And then they were in his room, near that ginormous bed of his, and her nerves started humming, and not in a good way.

She pressed a palm against his chest. "Wait."

"Nuh-uh," he said in that deep voice of his. "I'm done waiting."

She squirmed away, and he let her go with an audible sigh. "Now what?"

She flapped her hand. "It's just… I'm scared," she whispered.

"Of me?"

"No. Of what might happen. I mean, what if we have sex and… I get pregnant?"

"We'll use protection."

"What if it fails?"

He stepped closer without touching. "Then we make a family."

Her voice wobbled. "But what if I lose it?"

He reached out then, his palms warm on her shoulders. "Then we keep trying."

Waves. Waves were crashing into her, over her. He was saying and doing everything she'd dreamed of hearing for so long, and yet it felt like she was drowning. "Oh God. Wow. You know what? I don't know if I am ready for this. I don't know if I could do that again. What were those ways you were thinking of that we could be flexible? You know, the ones you talked about last time I was here?"

He chuckled and brushed his lips softly over her forehead. "Hey, didn't you name her Faith because you believed she'd come back to you?" She nodded. "Then believe. You can't believe in her and not believe we're meant to try again someday. So let's try. Practice makes perfect."

He pulled her stiff body against his warm, solid strength. She squeezed her eyes shut. "You're right," she said. I know you're right."

He leaned in and kissed her again, his lips firm and warm, and she felt the worry ease inside her just a bit. His palms brushed over her back and lower, pulling her toward him. She could feel him pulse against her. She wanted this. She wanted to move forward with him physically and emotionally, but she hadn't let go in so long.

Years, in fact.

He let out a quiet breath. "We don't have to do this tonight if you're not ready."

"No. I'm good," she insisted, pushing herself against him. "So ready. I'm just, um, out of practice." She kissed him again to prove her willingness to keep going. Keep trying.

He held her face in his palms as they kissed, and it felt like that first time they'd stood in the rain, lightning all around. Yes. This was good. This was how it was meant to be.

She threw herself into kissing him back, letting her hands remember him all over again. His palm gripped her hip and then slid up, under her shirt, higher, the heat scorching her bare skin until he slid his palm over her breast and squeezed.

She froze.

His hand slid away, leaving her breast cold.

"No, wait! It's okay. You just surprised me," she said. She grabbed his hand and pushed it up under her shirt again.

He pulled away. "Stop. This isn't going to work," he said.

She could feel the tears crowding her vision. "No. I promise. It will work."

"Forcing it isn't the answer," he said. He held her loosely, an energy she'd never felt before radiating from him. She thought she might ignite. She could do this! What was wrong with her?

He kissed the top of her hair, then, so sweet and understanding...

No. She *would* do this.

"I'm not giving up. We're doing this," she promised, and just to prove how committed she was, she yanked off her shirt and yoga pants and tossed them aside. When she was down to her underwear she scurried over to the bed and crawled between the covers, lay on her back and squeezed her eyes shut. "Ready," she said.

After a few moments of silence, she opened one eye. "Aren't you coming?"

He nodded, but his face held an odd expression as he slowly removed his own clothes, methodically peeling off his shirt and pants and socks. He slid off his underwear, his arousal clearly evident, and not breaking eye contact, walked over to the opposite side of the bed and pulled the covers back.

Wow. She'd forgotten how amazing he looked naked. Something hot and dark and sweet stirred inside her. She had a sudden craving for Dr. Pepper.

"Hey, what happened to your arm?"

He glanced down at the neat white bandage on his right bicep. "Just a kitchen injury. I fell on a pizza cutter."

"Ouch. You're getting as clumsy as me. Next time order take-out," she said.

His mouth tilted with humor, and then he slid between the sheets beside her, the mattress sinking toward him. She shifted as his skin brushed against hers.

She waited.

After a few moments, she opened both eyes and stared at the ceiling, swallowed and tilted her face toward him. "Um. Aren't you going to kiss me?"

He stared at the ceiling. "No."

"No?"

"No."

They lay in silence a bit longer. She shifted, her foot making brief contact with his shin. The hair on his leg tickled her. She liked it.

"Aren't you going to hug me then?"

"No."

She raised herself on her elbow to look at him. "We're not going to touch at all?"

A muscle pulsed in his jaw. "I didn't say that."

She leaned over him now. Heat radiated from him. "If you won't kiss me or hug me, how is this going to work?"

His eyes met hers. "You're going to touch *me*."

"I don't understand."

"You're in charge, Sweetheart. We're never going to move past this until you decide you're ready to take the risk again. I can't push you over this hurdle. You have to leap it on your own."

"You're not going to help at all?"

"I'll meet you on the other side."

She reached toward him and then stopped, her hand hovering over his bare skin. "You mean, you're not going to touch me at all?"

"Not unless you ask me to. You're in control."

"But—"

His eyes flashed hot across her chest before he turned his face toward the ceiling again, the muscle in his jaw pulsing. "Look. You're scared because you feel like you didn't have any control over what happened in the past. And I'm sorry for that. So I'm giving it back to you... as much as I can."

"Don't go all psychoanalytical on me."

"I'm not. I'm seeing a woman who wants desperately to control the future, but you have doubts. What happened to the woman who dropped her towel?"

"*Pfft.* Dropping the towel is the easy part."

"Maybe. But standing there afterward? That's the part that takes guts. I'm telling you to make your move. Control what comes next."

"I can't control everything."

His eyes crinkled. "You have more control than you give yourself credit for."

She let her gaze slide down his torso to the sheet draped low over him. The sheet moved once, then twice. She glanced up at him, and he grinned despite the tension still in his jaw. "See? You've got powers."

She glanced back at the tented sheet again. "I don't know where to start," she said.

His lips tilted in a strained smile. "I think you'll figure it out."

Heat flooded her cheeks… and other places.

So it was up to her now.

She let her finger trail lightly down the center of his chest toward the vee of hair that disappeared beneath the sheet then leaned forward to let her tongue follow suit. Jeff sucked in a sharp breath and let it roll out of him in a half-laugh, half-groan, his voice rumbling over her, deep and dark and sexy.

She lifted her face and worried her bottom lip. "Is something wrong?"

His eyes bore into hers, hot and piercing. "So. Damn. Right."

"So I should keep going?" she whispered. Okay, the control thing was a bit intoxicating.

He moaned and bit his lip, and she bent down to soothe it with her tongue before pressing her mouth to his. She paused and pulled away. "What's wrong?"

"Nothing."

"You're not kissing me back."

"You haven't told me to."

She huffed out a breath of frustration. Okay, this was taking things a little too far. "Kiss me back," she ordered.

He turned toward her. "Can I use my hands?"

"To kiss?"

He nodded.

"Sure," she said.

Before that one short syllable was out of her mouth, his arms hauled her down on top of him, his lips crushing hers as he drank her in, lifting his head from the pillow to meet her mouth, his hands sinking into her hair.

They kissed like that for a long, long time.

Finally, Grace pulled back with frustration. "You can touch me other places, too, you know."

His eyes crinkled, and her heart tumbled in her chest. She loved this man so hard it hurt. "You hadn't told me I could yet."

She huffed out a breath. "Touch me," she said lifting herself over him to straddle him. "And don't make me ask you again."

He flipped her onto her back in a maneuver she was pretty sure the Army hadn't envisioned being used in quite that way, but she didn't mind.

He hovered over her, his breath hard and heavy, but his eyes crinkled. "I wouldn't dream of it."

CHAPTER TWENTY-NINE

Grace smiled and waved hello as *The Jolly Rodgers* set up their equipment on the stage they'd erected behind the main barn at the Burgess's farm. She was so giddy, so full of hopeful joy, she wouldn't have been surprised if she'd looked up the word "happy" in the dictionary and a picture of her own face was smiling back at her.

She should be exhausted. What time they hadn't spent, er, practicing, she'd spent staring at Jeff's beautiful, sleeping face like Bridget Jones watching a slumbering Mark Darcy. But she didn't need sleep when she had this sweet, heady joy pulsing through her.

Meg waved a hello, her daughter, Amy, in tow.

Grace smiled down at the girl. "I see someone was first in line at the face-painting booth. It's beautiful."

Meg laughed. "Thank God I found some stencils to use. Sandi is much better at drawing butterflies and ladybugs free-hand."

Grace winked at Amy. "I'm particularly fond of sparkly butterflies."

Meg leaned toward her as they watched townspeople gather in for the festivities. "How are you doing? I can't believe how calm you look. I'd be a wreck after what happened to Jeff."

"Something happened to Jeff?"

Meg pulled back. "Yeah. Wednesday. He didn't tell you?"

"No."

"Some cook at the Silver Birch Inn went off the deep end and threatened to kill himself. He even threatened a waitress—Angela, I think—when she tried to stop him. Jeff was there for hours talking this guy down. And then when the guy finally agreed to go to the hospital with them, he grabbed a knife or something and tried to kill himself anyway. Jeff had to tackle the guy to stop him."

Meg swam before Grace's eyes. *"Oh God."*

"I know. Horrible isn't it? Thank God everyone was all right. One of my client's works there, so I got the whole story."

...kitchen injury. I fell on a pizza cutter...

Dear God. He'd been injured in the line of duty? He could have been killed...

Meg continued, oblivious. "They say he just got out. PTSD or something. That's got to be awful. Can you imagine being his family? I hope he gets help."

Grace nodded, feeling numb. "Yeah. Definitely."

"I can't believe Jeff didn't tell you."

"He probably didn't think I'd want to hear about it."

"I guess so. How do wives of cops do it? Living with the fear? It's got to be awful."

"Yes. I imagine so."

"Well, looks like the face-painting line is growing again. I'd better go. See you for Healing Circle!"

Grace nodded and watched Meg hurry away.

She took a few deep breaths to steady herself, but didn't have the luxury of going to a quiet spot to cry grateful tears of relief that Jeff was safe and sound.

Peggy Dayton jogged over, smiling broadly. "I can't believe it," she said. "My whole family, all together, doing what they love to do. I can't tell you how happy that makes me. Thank you for making this festival happen."

"It was a team effort, but I'm glad you're enjoying yourself."

Peggy's grin widened, her cheeks pinking prettily. "We're engaged, you know."

"I'm sorry?"

"Rodger and I. We're getting remarried. I hope you'll come to the ceremony."

"Me?"

"Of course! I credit the Healing Circle gals with helping me finally focus on what's best for me, and forgetting all of the old expectations. Rodger is what makes me happy. I know it will sound silly, but even when we were apart, I felt connected to him."

It didn't sound silly at all. It sounded... lovely. "Congratulations."

"Thank you." Peggy watched the men set up their equipment on the outdoor stage. "To think that my fiancé—I can't believe I'm saying that!—and my daughter will be sharing that stage tonight. Momentous occasions for both of them."

She turned toward Grace with a knowing smile. "Of course, Jeff also has his big news, but that's not official yet."

Grace fidgeted. Had Jeff mentioned their reunion to his mother? Already? What had he said?

Something warmed inside her nonetheless. No, it wasn't official, but it was promising. "I have a good feeling things will be official sooner than later," she said, her own silly smile, no doubt, matching Peggy's.

"No doubt. Mauri said that job is as good as his if he wants it."

"Job?"

"With the Parks Service. In Wyoming. What did you think I was talking about?"

The roaring in Grace's ears made it difficult to hear. First he'd been hurt and now *this?* "That. I meant that. Sorry. Too many things to keep track of with the festival and planning and stuff…"

"It would mean his moving away, of course," Peggy said, oblivious to the knife protruding from Grace's heart, "but he's put his own life on hold long enough, don't you agree?"

"Yes. Of course." She could feel the words sliding over her lips, the socially acceptable responses coming of their own volition.

"And I wouldn't blame him. Police work is so dangerous, even in a small town like Sugar Falls. I'll miss him terribly, but you can't fight destiny, can you?"

"No," she said, barely able to force the word over her lips. "No, you can't."

He was leaving?

He hadn't breathed a word to her, but surely he'd take the job. Peggy was right. Jeff had never wanted to be a cop, had always talked about being out in nature, joining search and rescue efforts to help find lost hikers and wandering children. He'd never wanted to deal with teen drug addicts or elder abuse or any of the other crap she knew from talking to Dee he must face day in and day out. And it *was* dangerous, being an officer. Even in sleepy little Sugar Falls. She knew there was a dark side to life even here, though, for the most part, she'd been shielded from it.

But Jeff had seen that dark side. Apparently he'd seen it just two days before.

He'd gone into the Army with the sole intent of coming home and becoming a ranger… of saving people without the risk of being shot at anymore… or run at with kitchen knives. Of course, back when they'd made those plans, Grace had always intended to go with him, not set down roots and build a business right here in Sugar Falls.

But now… Good God. How could she deny him that? The relative safety of moving away from law enforcement? Could she see herself as the wife of a cop? Never knowing whether he was one road rage/domestic violence/escaped convict incident away from becoming another tragic statistic?

236

The worry of losing him to far-off Wyoming morphed into worry that he might actually stay to be with her. Surely grizzlies and snowy-mountain rescues were safer than heroin-addicts with nothing left to lose?

Peggy disappeared through the growing crowd leaving Grace to pull the blade of Peggy's words out of her wounded heart. She needed to talk to him. But when?

"I hope to hell you know what you're doing here."

Grace glanced up, the late afternoon sun making her squint. Jeff was in full uniform, his aviator sunglasses completely masking his expression. "What would make you think I didn't?"

There. That sounded natural. Casual. Not at all like she'd just been creamed by a semi like so much roadkill.

Honestly, what had she expected? That the universe would neatly deliver her One True Love and a shiny ring and all the loose, messy ends of life would suddenly weave together in a magic carpet to fly them away to their happily-ever-after? She was spiritual, not delusional. Surely if she and Jeff were truly meant to be, these roadblocks wouldn't keep falling in their way like great cosmic landslides blocking the path to happiness.

She needed to face facts. The truth about their past was out there now. Everything between them all out in the open. They'd worked it out. All their unfinished business was... well... finished.

They'd even forgiven each other.

Then they'd had sex. Wonderful, amazing sex. She was no longer the Ice Princess, for which she was very, very grateful.

And if she had to, last night could last her another fifteen years. By then she'd be middle-aged. And middle-aged people rarely had sex, right? So she was all set.

Jeff could go and live his life, and do what he'd always planned to do with it, and she would stay here in Sugar Falls and live hers. If he came home for the occasional booty call visit they'd both be fine. At least he'd be alive.

She at least knew this hell she was in. She knew how this felt. She could still get up each morning. She could still breathe in and out. She could at least *exist* like this.

But if she lost him...

She looked up at him, the love of her life, and she finally knew what the Butterfly card meant.

Jeff's lips twitched a bit at the corner as he turned to scan the crowds. "It always makes me a tad nervous to see a minivan with llama heads sticking out the windows. I thought we discussed the whole llama thing."

Her gaze drank in everything about him. His close-cropped hair. The lean, loose way he held himself. His scent. She'd soak it all in, because she loved him so much it hurt, and yet, she loved him too much to hold him back in a dangerous job he'd never wanted.

He was a hero whether he felt like one or not. The fact the whole rescue way back when had been precipitated by his getting lost wasn't something to feel guilty about. It was clearly the universe showing him both the panic of finding yourself off track and alone and the grace of helping another find safety. That trip wasn't a mistake—it was Jeff's destiny. Just like Peggy said.

And, yes, she was sure he was The One, but that only meant he was the one she was destined to love forever, not necessarily that they'd be together.

Eventually, cocoons could suffocate if you remained in them too long. She needed to trust that as fragile as she felt right now, she could fly. They both could.

It didn't mean they would necessarily fly in the same direction.

Having finally run out of platitudes, she took a deep, cleansing breath and shook her head.

"We did," she said with forced brightness. "I chose to ignore you. Your main worry was that they'd get loose, so I arranged for them to be driven directly into the petting corral, the gate will be closed and locked, and no one has a key to the gate except for me and Hank." She dangled the key in question before him. "So, relax. I've got this."

"Good. Mauri will have my hide if this becomes a circus."

"I'm more capable than you give me credit for. Now, shoo. Your energy is all nervous and uptight tonight, and I don't have time to fix that right now." Or the will.

His eyebrows appeared above the frame of his sunglasses for one moment. "I know a way you could get me to relax."

She turned away, biting her lip, knowing exactly what he had in mind. Suddenly the energy emanating from him was of an entirely different sort.

"Stop. Don't you have traffic to direct or something?"

He shrugged, hands clasped behind him. "Dee and Derrek are on traffic duty for now. I'm supposed to be milling about and keeping an eye on the crowds, but until the teens arrive after sunset, things are bound to be quiet."

Dee's brother, Kevin, walked by with his dad. Mr. Barrett's bright red flannel shirt was probably as much for warmth as to keep an eye on him in the crowds.

"Good afternoon, Kevin… Mr. Barrett," Jeff nodded.

Grace said her hellos and dropped her clipboard to her side. She reached out to shake the older man's hand, whistling a short tune as she did so.

Mr. Barrett's face went from distant to alert. "Ha! Blue Danube!" His eyes focused on Grace. "Have we danced to that before?"

"Many a time," she said, pulling him into a quick waltz through the dried grass. "You were always so light on your feet."

The older man's eyes twinkled back. "Light fingers and light toes they used to say," he laughed. "Good to see you."

Grace nodded and let her hand fall away from his shoulder knowing he didn't remember her name. It was all right. He remembered enough. Funny how music was still one of the things that could break through the fog that had settled over him more and more.

She turned to Kevin. "I hope you enjoy yourselves tonight."

Kevin nodded, the strain of life etching faint lines around his mouth and eyes. "We'll try. Dee's neighbor, Trudi, is coming up later to take him home. I may head over to Lucky's for a bit after that."

"It'll be good to get out," Grace said.

Jeff clapped Kevin on the shoulder. "Let me know if you want to go fishing some time. My pole is getting rusty."

Kevin grimaced. "Maybe next spring," he said.

They both looked toward the red plaid shirt headed toward the games stalls.

"Looks like we're on the move," Kevin said. "Thanks for organizing this, Grace. I know Dad will enjoy seeing everyone."

Squeals of delight came from the ball pit. Someone announced the pie-eating contestants should gather, and the clang of a cow bell at the top of the portable climbing wall signaled another successful ascent.

"Quite the turn-out," Jeff said, scanning the growing crowd.

"Don't sound so surprised."

"I'm not." He laughed. "Just relieved. Mauri will be pleased. A wholesome, family-style event." He turned toward her again. "Thanks."

"Hang on a moment while I let that compliment soak in." She closed her eyes and raised her face toward the sky.

He chuckled, the warm echo of it reverberating through her. She tried not to cry, but so much of tonight felt like an ending. Especially now that she knew.

She slanted a look at him, wondering if he was thinking about the job offer. They'd be crazy to let him get away. He'd be crazy not to take it.

No doubt he was waiting until his sister had made her announcement and the festival was over before springing the news. Surely Maureen couldn't complain about his move from law enforcement to actual rescue personnel. It's like having Mother Theresa donate a kidney. To an orphan. Who grew up to be a doctor who treated children with birth defects in third-world countries.

Basically, he couldn't be any more of a hero.

Grace grimaced and made a mental note to greet the ladies from Healing Circle. They'd invited a palm reader in, and from the looks of the line waiting to have their destinies read, she was doing a brisk business.

"I should go check in with Dee," Jeff said. "Looks like the back field is filling up fast with cars."

Grace nodded and watched him stride off, his powerful body eating up the ground as he moved away from her. Dang, he was fine with his navy uniform pants hugging his lean, muscular thighs. She wanted, desperately, to make her way back to a place where she could act on that desire with as much carefree abandon as she once had.

As hard as it would be to watch him go, it was no doubt for the best for both of them to start fresh, without all the baggage they both brought to the relationship. If they could even call it that. What did thirteen years of history and one hot night make them?

Well, at least she was no longer the one-night stand he'd promised her she'd never be.

She watched *The Jolly Rodgers* mount the stage at the back of the barn, the broad red wall behind them twinkling with little lights. Rodger Dayton winked and waved, looking happier than she'd seen him in a long time. He blew a kiss to his ex-wife/fiancée and then launched into the first set without an introduction, the familiar tune moving through the crowd and catching people's attention like a ripple in a pond.

Lydia pushed through the crowd and clasped her hands before her excitedly. "They sound just as good as they always did," she said.

"Better," Grace said. The lyrics spoke of friends and time and changes, and the importance of family. Jeff had never liked this song when they were teens. He said it was hypocritical coming from a guy that divorced his mom to pursue a dream, and yet, listening now, Grace heard the hopefulness in the song, the acceptance. She wondered, wherever Jeff was, if he heard it, too.

As the song wrapped up and the crowd cheered, Chief Russell, Maureen Dayton and some other prominent townspeople took the stage. Chief Russell thanked everyone for coming and asked them to please enjoy themselves responsibly and then made an announcement that they didn't have the license number, but they'd gotten a report of a silver minivan with a dog inside chewing on what appeared to be an iPad. A dozen harried parents hurried toward the parking area.

Jeff stood just off the stage, facing away from Grace, his mother standing near, her navy cardigan with pearl buttons looking very proper next to her tattooed ex-husband in torn jeans and a tee with an American flag across the front.

Rodger waved them on stage and took the microphone. "May I introduce my baby girl, Maureen Dayton!"

Maureen visibly paled, her body going rigid for one tense moment before she pulled her public visage into place and smiled broadly, taking the stage near her father. "Thank you." She turned toward the crowd looking polished and approachable all at the same time.

"It's good to be home," she said, "and a pleasure to hear my dad back where he belongs."

Lydia leaned in toward Grace. "I'm sure she's thinking it's anything but. That girl should watch out, or she'll grind her teeth to dust."

Grace *shushed* Lydia as Maureen continued working the crowd.

"...you know that Sugar Falls is where I've experienced many firsts. The first time ice skating on the common when I was six... My first job at Swift Grocery... My first car from O'Connell Auto... Sugar Falls sent me to my first session as an elected official, and I've worked hard to..."

"How long is this gonna take?" Grams asked.

"...and so, it seems only natural, fitting, in fact, that it is here among friends and family and those who have supported me through the years that here is where I first announce," she paused for dramatic effect, "my candidacy for Governor of the great State of New Hampshire!"

Her dad's band broke into a patriotic tune, and Jeff and his mom both paraded onto the stage to clasp hands with Maureen as the crowd dutifully cheered.

"Lordy, you'd think she'd invented the Internet or something." Claire trundled up beside Grace and Lydia, and sucked loudly off a water bottle.

"I'm proud of her," Lydia said. "She goes after what she wants." She glanced pointedly at Grace who rolled her eyes and turned away.

Lydia meant well, but she had no idea.

As the cheers quieted down, Maureen introduced the town's glee club who proceeded to sing the school's fight song, making it sound way more peppy and less intimidating that it probably was meant to sound.

The crowd cheered some more, Maureen and her aides exited stage left, and *The Jolly Rodgers* began another set. Grace blew out a sigh of relief. There. Like a well-oiled machine.

"Grace!"

Grace turned, Kevin pushing through the crowd to her side. "Have you seen my father?"

"No. I'm sorry."

Kevin swore and ran a hand through his hair worriedly. "He was right here. Right by my side, and I turned to buy us some fried dough, and then he was gone."

Grace placed a calming hand on his arm. "How long has he been gone?"

"Just a couple minutes."

"Okay, I'll see if we can make an announcement. I'm sure he's not far."

"Don't," Kevin said. "Not yet. I don't want to embarrass him."

"Kevin, I don't think it's a good idea to wait."

"Just a few minutes. Like you said, he can't have gone far. If we find him, we'll ask *The Jolly Rodgers* to play *Sweet Road Home* as a signal. Agreed?"

They nodded and quickly divided quadrants of the festival to search.

Grace's heart rate shot up as she worried about sweet Mr. Barrett. She hoped he hadn't wandered far. It was nearly dark. If he wandered beyond the lit edges of the fields, he could end up in serious danger. It was late September. It wasn't unusual for nighttime temperatures to dip below freezing.

She knew Kevin didn't want to embarrass his dad, but after what Dee had revealed the other day, safety had to come first. Grace felt a wave of relief when she spotted Chief Russell near the livestock barns. He'd radio Dee and they could decide the best course of action.

Grace began to run toward the barns.

The crowd began running toward her.

It was like swimming upstream amid screeches and laughter and an ungodly racket of bizarre squeaky honk-like noises. Grace struggled to make headway as the crowd rushed forward and scattered into the dark.

Grace came to a halt. A panicked llama charged toward her, those in its path alternately lunging for the animal and stepping aside. She covered her face with her arms and braced for the impact.

The llama veered at the last moment, its broad, wooly side slamming into Grace before it trotted off through the crowd. She landed hard on her backside. Strong hands grabbed her from behind and hauled her to her feet again before she could get trampled by the melee around them.

She turned to thank her rescuer, but the words died on her tongue.

Jeff stood over her, his face clearly expressing his displeasure at this unfortunate turn of events.

"The llamas are loose!" he yelled at her, as if this point were under some disagreement.

"I see that," she said, slapping the dirt off her jeans. "We'll have to find Hank. He must have some way of calling them."

"You said this wouldn't happen!"

She pushed past him toward the corral. "Call Dee on the radio and tell her to have your dad ask everyone to quiet down a moment as we collect the animals. They're probably terrified with the commotion."

"You think?"

She spotted Hank and waved him down.

"I'm sorry, Miss Grace. I don't know how this could have happened! I swear the gate was locked."

"I believe you. How do we get the llamas back?"

"Apples. They love apples."

She turned to Jeff. "Tell Dee to have people bait them with apples from the orchard stall and lead them back here to the barn."

He nodded, relaying the info to Dee. Soon the band came to an abrupt halt as they asked for help in corralling the loose llamas.

Hank hurried off to retrieve two of his wandering herd.

Grace turned to Jeff. "Don't even start."

"A gate doesn't just unlock itself," Jeff said.

But Grace ignored him, because at that moment, she spied a red plaid shirt disappearing around the corner of the farmhouse. She had other issues. "Call Dee and have her tell the band to play *Sweet Road Home!*" she yelled over her shoulder.

"What?"

"Just do it! I don't have time to explain!" And she high-tailed it around the corner after Kevin's dad.

~ * ~

"Thank you." Dee and Kevin each hugged Grace and expressed their heartfelt relief at having their dad with them again. He sat at a nearby folding table enjoying a cup of cider with Grams and the other ladies.

Kevin wiped a hand down his face. "I shouldn't have brought him. I just... I wanted to get out of the house, you know? I thought he'd be all right."

Grace patted his shoulder. "You couldn't have predicted this."

"He hasn't done anything like this before," Kevin assured her.

Dee winced. "Actually..." she glanced toward her dad and back at them. "It's happened a couple of times. That I know of."

Kevin blanched. "Why didn't you say something?"

"Because... I don't know. Denial? I didn't want to admit how bad things had gotten."

The band closed their set, the mood decidedly more somber than it had been earlier in the evening. Grace nodded toward their dad. "He's safe now. Time enough to think about what to do in the morning."

Dee nodded and gave Grace a hug. "Thanks. Sounds like it's bonfire time."

"Hey, we're holding a special Healing Circle under the full moon tonight. You're welcome to join us."

Dee backed away and shook her head. "Thanks anyway. I'm looking forward to the end of my shift and a tall cool one. I think I've earned it tonight. And Kim from the ambulance crew is working the Touch-a-Truck exhibit. I thought I might, um, go see if I could Touch-a-Truck later."

Kevin flushed bright red. "Words I never again what to hear from my sister."

"Then close your ears, little brother, because I'm off duty here in, oh," she checked her watch, "ninety minutes, and after tonight, I'm ready for some distraction."

Grace waved goodbye to Dee and headed over to the table. The ladies tittered over some story Mr. Barrett was telling, looking like his old self again.

Peggy, Linda, Sandi and Meg had also gathered near as Meg's little girl prepared to light the bonfire. Amy stood flanked by her paternal grandparents, her silvery blonde hair in pigtails, a flaming torch stretched out in front of her.

Okay, so maybe someone could have rethought that part.

The crowd cheered as the flames licked up the side of the pyramid of stacked pallets, brightening the night sky. The band started their final set, the mood festive and electric.

Lydia grinned and grabbed Grace's hand. "Come with me!" she said. "I found just the place to hold our Healing Circle."

Lydia waved the other women over, and they made their way down the slope of the field in the dark, the bonfire alight behind them, a primordial sense of connection to earth and land and elements sparking in the air around them.

Grace decided she couldn't make her living believing in destiny and fate and spiritual guides and fight this any longer. It was past time to ride the waves and trust they wouldn't drown her.

She shivered as the band of women made their way toward the edge of the bonfire's light, away from the bustle of the festival. Lydia stopped at an intersection of walls, the tumbled stones having formed a misshapen circle maybe ten or twelve feet around. Lydia invited each woman to take a seat as they carefully picked their way over the uneven ground.

Once they were settled, Grace thanked Lydia and asked them all to hold hands.

The noise of the fire and the crowd felt distant now, and as they sat, Grace lifted her face to the full, lush moon above. What she had planned was probably a bit dramatic, but she didn't care. Tonight felt bittersweet. She imaged herself pushing out of the past and leaving her cocoon behind.

"We gather here, with our sisters, refreshed in a lustrous sea of moonlight. The moon speaks to us softly. It guides the seas and oceans, and yet it does not dictate. It lights the way, yet does not blind us." Murmurs of agreement rose from some of the women. Lydia's hand tightened on hers. "I invite each of you gathered here this night to follow the moon's light to reconnect with yourselves. To welcome healing. To be open to the tug of the divine in your lives as it pulls forth the message you are meant to share with the world into the soft light of acceptance and honesty. Find strength in one another. Find strength within yourselves. And in this quiet stillness, find your voice. Find the courage to speak your truth. Recognize you are a unique gift made to share your wisdom with creation. Be heard!"

Grace paused for dramatic effect, waiting. She hadn't planned her words, instead letting them tumble out. She hoped they made sense.

She stood, pulling up the hands of those nearest, and the women stood with her, rippling up like a wave. They watched her expectantly.

She squeezed Lydia's hand. "Be heard," she said again. "Speak the truths you've been holding inside yourselves."

Peggy cleared her throat. Grace nodded her encouragement. This woman's life was filled with acceptance and forgiveness and love. She... "I sleep with my ex-husband. A lot."

Grace blinked.

Peggy continued. "After we get married again, I'm going on the road with him."

A murmur of congratulations rippled around the circle, before an expectant hush fell over them again. Well, moving on then...

Meg's hand grew tense in Grace's. "Tommy cheated on me," she said. She lifted her chin. "Our entire marriage."

Okay, that was another bombshell Grace hadn't expected.

"The good for nothing'..."

"I never liked the look of..."

"I'm not surprised..."

Rumbles of support rippled through the circle of women as they squeezed hands.

"I never filed taxes in 1963," Lydia blurted. Then she shrugged. "I forgot."

Oh, good lordy.

"I smoked a reefer once." This from Grams. "At least I think it was. Might have been a clove cigarette. I stole it from my older brother."

"I once kissed Frank Sinatra. On his knee!"

"Claire!" Grams said.

"Why only his knee?" June wanted to know.

"I was being dragged out by security. It was all I could reach."

Sandi piped up from the far side of the circle, "I didn't wear a bra for a whole year."

Linda half-laughed. "I haven't worn one since my surgery. So that's more than a year."

A squeeze of hands rippled around the circle.

Linda spoke again. "I miss wearing a bra."

"No you don't," Sandi said. "You miss *having* to wear a bra."

"True."

The group grew quiet. Grace watched the crowd up by the bonfire as the flames licked into the air. It seemed all of Sugar Falls was here for the festival, and yet they were oblivious to the small group of women whispering their secrets in the dark.

"I hate how I look," said Linda.

Some teens whooped near the bonfire.

"You're beautiful," Grace insisted. "You're a miracle of survival."

"Easy for you to say," Linda replied. "You're a walking Venus."

"I'm not perfect," Grace said.

"Neither am I," Sandi agreed. "Old boobs ain't pretty."

Grams snorted. "You want to see old boobs? Mine are friends with my belly button."

Lydia pulled her hand out of Grace's, and it was only then Grace realized it was because Grams had pulled *her* hand out of Lydia's.

"Grams, what are you doing?" gasped Grace as she watched her grandmother's stiff fingers fumble with the buttons on the front of her shirt.

"Showing Linda none of us is perfect."

"That's right," Lydia said, "but we're still beautiful." She pulled her own blouse out of her waistband and began to tug it over her head.

"Lydia! *Grams!*" Grace said.

"Oh, screw it. I haven't had this much fun since Sinatra."

Grace whirled.

Claire already had her husband's ugly old bowling shirt fisted in her palm and was working at the back clasp of her bra.

Meg's laughter sounded behind Grace. Grace froze at the sound of a zipper.

"Meg?" she gasped.

Meg yanked off her jacket and threw it on the ground. "Tommy was always looking at naked women on the Internet, but did he ever look at me?" She ripped open her shirt, a couple small buttons flying past Grace's head into the darkness beyond. "What's wrong with me, anyway? Why didn't he want this?"

The women turned and gasped.

"He was an idiot!" Sandi nearly shouted. "You're magnificent!"

"Beautiful!" June concurred. "His loss!"

"We're *all* beautiful!" Lydia insisted, her silver bangles jangling. "What have we got to be ashamed of? These are our bodies made for us to use as we see fit. Own it, girls! Like Grace said, be heard!"

Linda stood, her body visibly shaking as she stepped toward the center. "Dammit. I *am* beautiful. I never *stopped* being beautiful. Jerry will just have to suck it up and deal with it!"

"That's right!" Sandi agreed.

Peggy stepped forward. "We'll do it together, Linda. On the count of three. One, two… *three!*"

And then they were all half-naked, shirts and bras flying in the air, as they whooped and laughed and began dancing inside the stone circle, elbows linked, cheering for one another and declaring their inner beauty and connection with spirit.

Oh, dear Lord. She'd done this. She'd encouraged this.

Grace clasped a hand over her mouth too flabbergasted to move.

CHAPTER THIRTY

"Sorry about the llama escape," Hank said for the thirtieth time as Jeff closed the minivan door on the last of them.

"Well, I'm just glad no one was seriously hurt."

Hank nodded and motioned for Jeff to open the gate so he could drive out of the corral. Jeff fingered the lock as Hank drove past, and something small fell to the ground. Jeff clicked on his flashlight and ran it over the packed dirt. "Well, I'll be damned," he said, reaching down to pick up the short length of wire. "Somebody picked the lock."

"Goodnight, Jeff," Kevin walked by.

Jeff straightened. "I thought you'd already left."

"Dad wanted to see the bonfire, so we stuck around a bit longer."

Jeff raised his hand to wave goodbye to Kevin and his dad, the red flannel of Mr. Barrett's shirt reminding him of who had been near the gate when the llamas had gotten loose...

Damn. No wonder Dee and Kevin had had such a time keeping their dad safe! He'd been a locksmith his whole life, even performing Houdini-like shows for the library and schools when Jeff was a kid. Something told him the break-ins around town and Mr. Barrett's walks were more than coincidental.

Jeff chuckled to himself. Life in a small town was never dull. He rather liked that, though. It kept things interesting. And the best part was, he got to sleep in his own bed at night.

Hopefully with Grace beside him.

He grinned to himself as Mauri strode up, her aides and advisors tagging along nose-deep in their smartphones.

"I think we're heading out, too." She smiled. "Thanks for making it all go off without a hitch."

"You're not staying?"

"Got a rally to attend in the morning. Besides, it's too dark for pictures now."

"And the campaigning begins," he said.

"Don't you know it." She sighed as they listened to one of *The Jolly Rodgers'* more well-known hits. "I really wish I didn't like this song so much."

"It's gonna be all right, Mauri."

She nodded and kissed him lightly on the cheek. "I should go. Love you, big brother."

"Love you, too. Take care."

Jeff watched her walk away with Scott and a couple others as they headed for the parking area. He let out a sigh of relief, glad the evening was nearly over. He could finish up here in a couple of hours, maybe meet up with Grace for a while. Just another quiet night.

"Jeff!" Derrek yelled, stumbling toward him over the uneven ground from the direction of the bonfire. "Jesus, Mary and Joseph. Jeff, you gotta see this." Derrek gasped for breath, and then Jeff realized it was because he was laughing so hard it made it hard for him to breathe.

"Tell me it's not a group of underage drinkers, because I don't want to have to call in a police van tonight."

"Just... come see."

Derrek didn't wait but turned back toward where he'd come from, pushing through the crowd. Jeff sighed and followed, preparing to make the call for back-up transport.

But then his hand stilled as the Dionysian scene unfolded before him.

At least a dozen women frolicked in the far side of the field, half-dressed, twirling bras in the air, yelling about how beautiful they were, and declaring themselves free as a couple dozen teens cheered them on from the sidelines. Meanwhile, a few sane adults scurried behind, ineffectually attempting to throw jackets over the women and shouting at them to behave themselves and show some decency.

Jeff wiped a hand down his face. "Derrek, let's get these women under control, but try not to, um, touch anything. Got it?"

One of the grandmothers danced by, brilliantly illuminated with moonlight. Derrek's face paled. "Got it."

"You go corral the older women, and I'll get..." *Oh, dear God.* "My mother."

~ * ~

Grace shook herself out of her stupor and grabbed someone's discarded shirt. It was all fine and dandy to declare oneself free and another to do so within range of half the cell phone cameras in town!

She stumbled after Grams who shrugged her off with uncharacteristic strength. "They're just *breasts,*" she said, as if she hadn't been the one to scold Grace for wearing Daisy Dukes to the Independence Day parade just two years before.

Grace turned, shock and relief warring within her as she heard a low baritone order the women to quiet down and cover themselves.

Jeff strode toward the melee, his focus on Grace. She stopped trying to throw shirts at people. No one was listening to her anyway.

Jeff shook his head. "I should have known you'd be in the thick of this."

"I didn't start it, I swear."

Just then his mother leaped by them, laughing, her pale skin like an apparition in the moonlight. Jeff winced, his face contorting comically. "Jesus, mom! Put your shirt on!"

"No!" she said, dashing away. "I'm free! I'm beautiful! *I will be heard!*"

"Peggy!" Rodger Dayton came jogging down from the bandstand.

"Dad!" Jeff grabbed his father's arm. "Get her under control!"

His father grinned and chased after his ex-wife. "I'm on it, Son. Don't you worry!"

Grace watched the happy couple as they disappeared into the dark. She felt a pang of envy poke her.

Or maybe that was Lydia stabbing her with a bright pink fingernail in the shoulder.

Lydia flapped her hands like a terrifying butterfly, a colorful shawl trailing from her naked arms. "Grace, join us!" she called out as she swooped away again. "I've never felt so alive!"

Jeff gave Grace a warning look. "Don't."

Something inside her rebelled against the censure in his eyes. She'd done nothing wrong. Why was he being short with *her*? "Why not?"

"It's my job to keep order."

"Not for long."

He'd been about to step by her and snag the nearest streaker when he paused. "What's that supposed to mean?"

"It means, I know about the job offer," she blurted. "Your mom told me. I know you're leaving."

"I haven't decided."

"What's to decide? You've wanted to be a ranger ever since I've known you. Now's your chance. There's nothing keeping you here."

He turned, his shoulders rigid, a note of exasperation in his voice. "*You're* keeping me here."

"Don't make this about me." Tears burned the backs of her eyes. "Don't make me the bad guy again."

"You're not the bad guy, Grace—"

"If you don't take the job, you'll only resent me." She lifted her chin. "I know how you got hurt. This… this job is too dangerous."

"Right now it's frustrating," he said as he lunged for a passing grandmother. Grace watched as he tripped on a clod of dirt, June Hastings escaping into the dark. "We can work something out," he said.

"How?" she asked, dogging him as he strode around the perimeter of the circle, presumably to assess how to contain the situation. "How will we work it out? I have a business here, and you have a chance of a lifetime there. How is this supposed to work out?"

She saw Derrek stumble to his knees, a half-naked woman leaping over him. "We'll figure it out. I don't know. But now is not—"

"I won't let you stay because of me," she said. "I won't be responsible—"

"Hey!" Jeff shouted to some nearby teens. "No pictures!"

Grace stepped in front of him, and went rigid in the midst of the swirling, shouting mayhem. "It's time I shed my cocoon and trusted my own wings."

Jeff blew out a frustrated breath. "I have no idea what you're talking about."

"I know, which is why I know you should take the job."

"Grace, I've learned my lesson. There's nothing you can do to make me not factor you into this decision," he said, pulling out his whistle.

"Nothing?"

"Nothing," he affirmed. "Now step aside. We'll talk about this like rational adults when everyone has their shirts on."

"No," she said. "We won't."

"Grace. Don't."

He paused, the whistle poised in front of his lips, and she heard the warning in his voice then the shrill sound of the whistle piercing the night air.

It sounded like a wake-up call. Or maybe a call to action.

It occurred to her, then, that it would only ever be like this between them, this struggle between what drew them together and what pulled them apart. It was like they were two magnetic poles forever trying to get closer despite the fundamental laws of nature that prohibited it.

They were too different.

Her heart felt tight, as if it had expanded too much and slammed into the walls of her chest.

There was only one way to let it free.

She looked up at the furrow of tension between Jeff's eyebrows, the way his close-cropped hair could still look mussed, the strong, broad hand holding the bright, silver of the whistle.

He turned and shouted to Derrek and others who had come to help corral the women, fanning out to shield and contain the revelers. She watched him stride forward, loving each strong step, the timbre of his voice as it carried across the field.

Yes, he was The One. He'd always been The One and always would be.

She smiled at that, bittersweet emotion tugging at her lips.

"I love you," she whispered.

He turned back to her and met her gaze even though she was sure he couldn't have heard. Then she pulled her shirt over her head, let it drop to the ground and dashed into the dark.

CHAPTER THIRTY-ONE

"This way, ladies. Gentlemen." Jeff held the door. Grace followed the somber procession of women into the station, Jerry Andrews and Rodger Dayton at their heels. They were all instructed to leave their handbags and empty their pockets as Derrek took inventory. Finally, they were herded into neighboring cells, men into one, women into another, the men refusing to abandon their wives' sides by waiting in the lobby.

Grace sniffed at how touchingly romantic that was.

She didn't regret her dalliance into semi-nudity, not one bit. Lydia had been right. It had felt freeing. Like she had nothing left to lose. She realized she would always be this person who lived life a bit impulsively, dashing through the dark under the moonlight just because she *could.*

The cell door closed with a solid clank.

Okay, maybe she had dignity and a clean criminal record to lose.

Grace sank to the floor in the far corner, hugging her knees.

Meg slid down the back wall beside her and grinned. "Well, that was fun."

Grace nodded, silent.

"I mean, it'll cost me, but I don't care. I'm glad we did it. I don't think I walk around topless nearly enough."

Grace hugged her knees tighter.

"Oh, honey," Meg said, leaning forward. "Are you crying? What's wrong?"

"He's been offered a job in Wyoming," Grace whispered.

"Who?"

"Jeff."

"*What?* He can't leave you!" Meg said, far too loudly.

Grace shushed her. "Be quiet. His mother is right there!"

Meg glanced up with mama-bear ferocity. "Well she should know what an idiot her son is."

"Grace, what's the matter, honey?" Lydia pushed her way through the crush inside the cell to the back.

"Nothing—"

"Jeff is leaving," Meg supplied. "He's taking a job out west."

"No!"

"Yes, I'm afraid so," Peggy Dayton said, turning toward them. "Sorry, hon. I couldn't help but overhear. I didn't realize things were as serious as all this with you two. I've been in my own little bubble."

Grace buried her face in her arms, embarrassment coursing through her. It was bad enough Jeff and she were probably over and caput, but did she have to suffer the heartbreak in front of his mother?

"He's an idiot." This from Jeff's father as he peered through from the neighboring cell. "And I'll tell him so."

Grace struggled to her feet. "No! Please don't. I know you all mean well, but I'd prefer if no one said anything. I mean, if it were meant to be between us, things wouldn't be this hard. He *should* take the job. I want him to be h-happy."

"But what about you?" Meg asked.

They all fell silent at a commotion down the hallway.

"What do you mean, you've got them all in here?"

"We couldn't leave them running around the bonfire half-naked."

Chief Russell came down the hallway, shaking his head. "Just bear with us folks. We'll get this all straightened out."

Jeff stopped in the corridor. His eyes met Grace's. "They willfully disobeyed an officer of the law. Plus, there's the public nudity."

"Breasts are beautiful!" Lydia shouted back.

"Yeah. Since when is it against the law to show your nipples?" Grams demanded. "Women can breastfeed in public, and that's not a crime."

Chief Russell nodded. "She has a point," he murmured.

"Really?" Jeff asked. "You think Grace's grandmother is lactating?"

"Work with me here, son. We can't put the whole dang town in jail. For one, fire regulations. We're above capacity already."

Jeff ran a weary hand down his face.

Linda stepped toward the front of the cell, her hands on hips.

No one breathed.

"I had a double mastectomy. No one can claim that I'm lactating, but I didn't show any nipple, either."

Chief Russell's mouth twitched. "What say you to that, Officer Dayton?"

"I don't care if you think I'm ugly. I am not ashamed of myself!" Linda said.

Grams stepped forward in support. "You're beautiful, Linda, and don't you let anyone tell you otherwise. Not even Jerry."

Jerry, Linda's husband, stiffened and straightened from where he'd been slumped on the metal bench in the neighboring cell. "I never said she wasn't beautiful. You're the most beautiful thing I've ever seen," he insisted.

Linda made a face. "You don't have to lie."

"I'm not lying. I love your baby blues. I've always said so."

"I'm not talking about my eyes," Linda whispered, gesturing toward her shirt.

"What? I don't care about your chest."

"See?" she said, turning toward her husband. "That's what I'm saying! You don't even want to look at me anymore."

Jerry stared at her, dumbstruck, then pulled his fist out of his pocket and shook his head, reaching through the bars to tilt her chin up with his fingers. "I don't care about your chest, because every morning that I wake up and can look in your beautiful eyes—and have you looking back at me—is a good day."

Those eyes he spoke so highly of welled with tears.

"Oh, Jerr. I thought you were just checking my pupils to see if they were dilated."

"You nut," he said fondly. "I love all of you. Every precious bit. I'm sorry I wasn't showing you that enough."

She sniffed and her hand crept up to grip his tightly. "You're showing it. Trust me, you're showing it just fine."

And she began to sob as they clutched hands, Jerry seemingly oblivious to the hot man-tears falling to his big burly chest.

The chief's mustache twitched. "The worst kind of riff-raff you've got here, Officer Dayton. I'm glad you're keeping our streets safe."

"Sir—"

"Listen, nipple exposure isn't a crime. We generally define indecent exposure as," he wiggled his thick white eyebrows, "*down there*. So unless there was intent to cause 'affront or alarm' or willful disruption of the peace—"

Derrek poked his head through the connecting door. "Chief, you have a phone call."

"I'm busy here."

"It's Mrs. Chief."

The Chief raised a finger. "I'll be just a minute, folks."

Grams pulled a deck of cards out of her pocket as the Chief hurried off. "Looks like we'll be here a bit longer. Who wants to play a round?"

"Where'd you get the cards?" June asked.

"Well he didn't frisk me."

"Pity," Lydia added. They gathered around, and Grams began to deal.

Jeff stepped toward the bars. "Grace…"

She frowned and stepped toward the front of the cell, her arms crossed protectively across her body. "What?"

"You know what. We need to talk."

"There's nothing to say. You should take the job. You never wanted to be a cop. You've only ever talked about being out in nature, doing search and rescue. It's who you are. Don't ask me to take that away from you. You're meant to be a hero. It's your destiny."

"Hero? I was a seventeen-year-old kid in the right place at the right time. It was a coincidence, not destiny. I was scared shitless the whole time."

"Being heroic isn't about not being scared. It's about being scared and stepping up to do the right thing anyway. I've always admired you for that. Now it's time to let me step up and do the right thing, too. We both know you'd only come to resent me for holding you back. You'd feel trapped, and I… I love you too much to do that."

"Now who's making decisions without consulting the other?"

She ignored him, plowing on. "And staying here… this time it turned out all right, but I hear the horror stories from Dee. Being a cop is dangerous work. You need to go," she whispered.

He shook his head. "No."

"It's safer for you."

He choked out a hard laugh. "You don't think doing a remote rescue in avalanche country is dangerous? Look, I'm sorry I didn't tell you about the other night, but there was no point. It was over. I could just as easily get hurt crossing the street. There are no guarantees in life."

She pressed her lips together. No. There were no guarantees. Sometimes bad things happened. Bad things could happen to *him*.

"Maybe I'm not the one that needs to be a hero here," he said.

She frowned. "What?"

"If what you're saying is true, if being a hero is acting despite your fear, than do it. Be a hero. For me."

"I don't under—"

"Accept that I'm staying here in Sugar Falls. For good. Accept that I'm a police officer and sometimes that means dealing with crazy women running around half-naked and sometimes that just means dealing with crazy people. If you love me, you'll still be afraid. I get that. But don't let that fear stop you from doing what needs to be done and sticking by me."

"What if I'm not strong enough to handle what needs to be done?" she whispered.

He looked at her then, at least she thought he did, because her vision blurred as tears flooded her eyes. Would she ever get through an emotional discussion without tearing up?

Then a single, stupid tear spilled loose and trickled down her cheek and he cursed and stepped back. He pulled his keyring from his waistband.

"What are you doing?" she gasped, alarm shooting through her.

"I'm coming in," he said.

"What? Why?"

"Because this nonsense has gone on long enough. Derrek!" he barked. "You're in charge now."

Derrek stared at him as if Jeff had lost his marbles. Grace was sure she had the same expression.

"Officer Dayton?"

Jeff unhitched his service belt and handed it to Derrek as he swung the cell door open. "I'm going in."

"Sir?"

"There's something I should have done before now, but I refuse to do it through the bars of a jail cell."

"Yes, sir."

The cell door shut behind him. Everyone shifted aside to let Jeff through.

Grace sucked in a breath and watched as the man she loved more than anything in the world got down on one knee.

"What are you doing?"

"Shush, I'm still figuring this out, so just listen, will you?" She nodded. "I love you, Grace McIntyre. I've loved you since you first threw a glass of water on yourself to get my attention. I love that you'd do anything for a slice of cranberry-orange cheesecake. I love that you bury squirrels and play with beanbag cats and believe in things you can't see or touch.

"You once told me my own gut held more truth that any words..." His voice trailed off, and he swallowed. "It saved me more times that I want to count, listening to my gut." His eyes bore into hers. "You have something, Grace, something special I want in my life. You inspire and balance me, and I love that you're willing to let me follow my dreams."

He reached into a pocket and pulled something silver out that glinted as he clenched it in his fist. "I know you're scared, but you're the only one I ever dreamed of making a life with, and you'll have to work a whole hell of a lot harder to shake me loose, because I believe I'm The One for you just as much as you're The One for me. And don't you dare ask me to explain it, because I can't, but I still know it's true, because I feel it here." He jabbed a finger at the wall of his chest and then opened his palm. A silver locket shined up at her. "It was as close to my grandmother's as I could find. Over a decade in the dirt wasn't friendly to the original."

"I'm sorry."

"It's okay." He held the necklace toward her. "Please. There's no one else I'd rather make my family with than you. I can't guarantee anything, but I can guarantee I'll love you as long as I breathe."

Grace took the necklace with shaking fingers and hiccupped over the sob that threatened to follow the tears already rolling down her cheeks. Etched across the front of the locket was a single word: *Faith.* She popped it open. Two pictures, one of Jeff as a teen and one as a man, smiled up at her.

He looked up at her. "Well?"

She nodded, the tears flowing freely now. When had he even had a chance to have this done? To an orphan who'd only ever dreamed of making a family as idyllic as the one she could barely remember, she couldn't think of anything he could have said that would mean more to her. "Yes," she said.

"Yes, to what?"

"To all of it."

He stood and crushed her in his arms as the others laughed and congratulated them.

She caught the hint of lilac as she slipped the locket around her neck and felt it slide into place over her heart.

"Are you sure?" she asked, pulling away. "You'd trade your dream job for all this? The crazy small-town life? You'd give that up for me?"

"For us," he corrected. "For us. Either way," he said, "I'm saving people. But here, I get to be with you."

He kissed her soundly then, cupping her face in his palms, his eyes crinkling knowingly at her. Her body hummed. "There'll never be a dull moment with you, will there?"

"Likely not," she said.

His eyes crinkled more. Her heart thudded happily in her chest.

"Good."

Then he grasped her hand in his big, warm grip and turned and nodded to her Grams. "Deal me in," he said.

"Oh, I feel good about this!" Lydia clapped excitedly, her bangles tinkling. "You two are going to make beautiful babies together!" Then she stopped and threw her hand over her mouth.

Grams, June and Claire all looked at her. Grams paused in dealing. "Lydia Sweet, do you know something we don't know?"

Lydia swallowed and glanced at Grace in panic. Grace felt the hum in her bones sing happily. *No. It couldn't possibly be! For heaven's sake, they'd only had sex yesterday!*

Lydia's old eyes crinkled joyfully as she gave Grace an almost imperceptible nod. "Let's just say I have faith in them."

"So when is the wedding?" Claire wanted to know.

Grams elbowed her old friend. "He hasn't proposed yet."

"What's he waiting for?" June Hastings asked.

"Probably less of a crowd," Grams muttered, although she smiled. "Though the Good Lord knows that never stopped the others. It's all about the spectacle nowadays."

"Maybe he doesn't have a ring yet," Claire guessed. "Although I wouldn't wait if I were them."

"Why not?" Linda asked, getting in on things.

Claire shrugged and picked up her cards. "I've seen that smirk on Lydia's face before."

Grace's left hand slid to her stomach. She blew out a breath and met Jeff's eyes. "I've always liked November," she said.

He grinned and pulled her in for another kiss. "And here I was thinking October."

The door at the end of the hall banged open, and Chief Russell's voice echoed off the concrete walls. "Okay, folks, you're all free to go home!" He nodded as he opened the cell and they began to file out. The Chief frowned at Jeff, his hand still tightly holding Grace's.

"What the....?"

"Officer Dayton wanted to speak with Miss Grace, so I took his gear, sir." Derrek handed Jeff back his service belt with a wink.

The Chief slapped Jeff on the shoulder and pulled him close. "I'm not going to ask, but if you ever pull another stunt like this, I'll demote you on the spot. Got it?"

"Yes, sir. I needed to speak to—"

"Not that," the Chief said, smiling at Grace. "Hauling all these good folks into the station. I'll be doing paperwork until next Tuesday thanks to you, and the missus wasn't pleased I was suppressing a women's empowerment demonstration."

"Sir?"

"Your sister has quite the PR people on her staff."

Jeff grinned. "Yes, sir."

"Now get out of here while I'm still in a good mood."

"Yes, sir."

"And for the love of God, I hope you proposed to this woman."

"Not yet, sir." He winked at Grace, and it sent another warm thrill through her that sang *The One!* "But I plan to, sir. I plan to."

CHAPTER THIRTY-TWO

Two weeks. Two weeks is all it took to turn her world into a magical land filled with rainbows and unicorns, or at least that's how it felt. As much as she loved the sound of the falls behind Jeff's downtown apartment, her place was bigger, and her cats had quickly adjusted to another warm body to sidle up to and ask for ear rubs. She didn't blame them one bit.

It shouldn't have surprised her how quickly Jeff could pack up his belongings, but it didn't take more than a handful of pick-up loads and car trips. Her brothers raised an eyebrow or two at the ginormous bed she insisted they help haul up her stairs while Jeff worked his shift, but she was deliriously happy and not interested in explaining yet again how she knew it seemed fast, and yes they'd had their rough patches, but she was sure this was the right move and no, he hadn't proposed yet, but she was sure he would, because she had a tingly feeling...

Joe Sedowsky had taken the news of her reunion with Jeff in stride and confessed that the rep for a wheelchair distributor had asked him for drinks the last time she'd been in town.

By evening, Grace was exhausted and sweaty despite the cool early-October temperatures. She thanked her family again for their help, promised to invite them to the housewarming when things were settled and firmly shut the door behind them.

"They're gone," she said.

Jeff stood at the other end of the hall by the living room, looking sinfully gorgeous in a pair of faded, ripped jeans and some old concert t-shirt with a psychedelic butterfly on front. He'd arrived in time to unload the last pickup load. "I thought they'd never leave." He dropped the box he'd been carrying on the couch and strode toward her with purpose in his dark eyes.

She knew that look. She'd seen it a lot over the past two weeks. She put a palm out and let it flatten against the heat of his chest. "I'm too sweaty. I need a shower. And food."

"I'll get food. You shower."

"Deal."

"Leftovers?" he asked as she headed for the stairs.

She grinned and nodded happily. Fettuccine Alfredo and cranberry-orange cheesecake. Jeff had insisted they go out the night before to celebrate his moving in. Grace had worn red. Angela had been nice to her. She'd even *smiled.* Clearly, the universe had upended itself.

"I'll be ten minutes," she promised.

She showered quickly. Would it always be like this? The light, sweet happiness inside her? The giddy anticipation? No doubt it would quiet down with time to a soft, steady hum. But now...

She stepped out of the bathroom, one of Jeff's plush bath sheets wrapped around her. The man had not scrimped on the luxuries of bed and bath when he'd gotten out of the Army, that's for sure. Steam billowed out the door behind her.

Jeff set a tray of food on the dark comforter.

"Are we eating up here?" she asked.

He cocked an eyebrow. "It seemed a good idea. Let me just wash up, and I'll be out."

She snaked a hand out to grab his arm as he slid by. "Give me a kiss first."

He leaned toward her, but she frowned. Something was wrong. If she didn't know his expressions so well, she would never have noticed the slight tightening around his mouth when she grabbed him. The mouth never lied.

"What's wrong?" She gripped harder. He closed his eyes.

"Easy, love," he said.

Her eyes went to where her fingers gripped his left bicep. She pushed up his sleeve and gasped, her eyes flying to his.

She tried to speak, but the words tumbled forward, all crowding on her tongue at once, and she couldn't have assembled them in order anyway, because one word was staring up at her from the arm in front of her. *Faith.*

The ink was so fresh, the skin around it still red and puffy, but she knew what it said. She looked at him for explanation.

"I got it after my shift. I figured this way, she'll always be with us. Whenever I hug you, whenever I hold you in my arms, she'll be there... until she's back between us where she belongs."

Tears hot and stinging flooded Grace's eyes, and she let the fabric of his sleeve slide back over the fresh tattoo.

"That's so..." she said, but the words choked up in her throat and he raised her chin, his fingers warm and firm on her skin.

"I was scared, too," he whispered. "What nineteen-year-old plans to be a dad? But I don't want you to ever doubt she was wanted. She was very much wanted. As are you."

Grace managed to bob her head once, twice, before lifting her lips to his. She squeezed her eyes tight.

His big arms crushed her to him, his heat radiating through her as he met her kiss, his lips firm and soft and heartbreakingly eloquent. His kiss told her his emotions, his regrets and his hopes, and then his hands slid up to cup her cheeks the way he did that made her feel loved and treasured and needed, because he cupped them like a stranded, thirsty man cups fresh water from a stream. Gratefully. Greedily. As if he could drink forever and never get enough to slake his thirst.

Like she could never get enough of him.

"I love you so much," he said.

"I love you, too," she whispered.

"Thanks for giving me a second chance. I'm sorry I screwed up our first for you."

"I guess it's a good thing I made sure you'd be my first and my last." And she smiled, big and wide and happy.

His eyes lit up, and if she didn't know any better, she could have sworn they grew a little bright. "I planned to wait. I told myself I wouldn't rush it—I'd hold off until the timing was right—but I want the rest of my life to start now." He dug in his pocket and pulled out the little silver and sapphire forget-me-not ring and slid to one knee before her.

Grace froze.

This was the memory she'd have to share with everyone when they asked for her proposal story? That she was a blubbering, indecent mess dressed in a towel? No! She couldn't let him do this while she was naked and unprepared with tears streaming down her face! It was bad enough they'd declared their love in a jail cell of all places.

What would they tell their children?

They'd made too many mistakes. She'd be damned if they wouldn't at least get *this* right.

So, she did what any butterfly in control of her own destiny would do. She smiled.

And then she dropped the towel.

He could propose later.

Dear Reader,

In all honesty, I struggled with this story. The sad truth is, despite the statistics of how common an experience it is, we *don't* openly talk about pregnancy loss. It is the one source of grief too many bear in silence.

I felt it was time to end that silence. But while I bring personal experience to the writing of this story, I still worried whether I would do the subject matter justice. Would it ring true? Would readers relate to Grace and Jeff? In the end, though, this isn't a story about loss so much as a story of hope, and *that's* the story I wanted to tell. Because even when loss has come to define where we've been in life, there's still room to have hope for (and faith in!) a happier tomorrow.

Speaking of happier tomorrows, yes, this is the final 'Betting on Romance' book—but don't worry. I'm not done with Sugar Falls yet. Look for more quirky, fun, small-town happily-ever-afters in the *Lucky Charm* spin-off series starting with Jack and Helen's road-trip adventure in *The Runaway Cupcake Queen.*

Plus, don't miss out on exclusive contests or info on new releases. Sign up for my mailing list at www.cheriallan.com today!

Sweet regards from Sugar Falls,

~ Cheri

About the Author

Cheri writes kissing books about love and other shenanigans from her charming fixer-upper in rural New Hampshire. She is often distracted by social media, reality television, and a menagerie of cats and dogs. If you find her whizzing down the slopes at the nearby mountain with her family or inadvertently killing perennials in her garden, bring her coffee. She will gratefully provide the conversation and chocolate.

Cheri loves to hear from readers!
E-mail her at cheri@cheriallan.com.
Friend her at facebook.com/cheriallanauthor.
Or, visit her website and blog at www.cheriallan.com.

If you enjoyed this book, please consider telling other readers by writing and sharing a review. (It's ridiculously helpful and makes an author happy!)

Look for all the all-new *Lucky Charm* books—more great romances set in beautiful Sugar Falls!

Be sure to start where it all began, with Jim and Kate, in Book One of the 'Betting on Romance' series:

LUCK OF THE DRAW

If only life had a refresh button...

Kate Mitchell never planned to be a 31-year-old widowed single mom, but when her soon-to-be-EX husband up and dies, her dreams of finishing college and starting over are thrown in the air like a game of 52 pick-up. When she's given a leave of absence from work and told to "quit or recommit," Kate retreats to idyllic Sugar Falls, New Hampshire, to figure out whether she can discover her passion and pay the bills. Cue the fresh air, summer sunshine and one sexy local contractor.

Tall, dark, and handy...

Volunteer fireman and all-around hunky guy in a toolbelt, Jim Pearson has sworn off complicated women with messy baggage. They cling to his nice-guy stability and skills with a power saw just long enough to straighten out their lives and move on... but then he meets the cute single mom staying at Grams' lake house for the summer.

While a sizzling attraction draws them together, Jim's distrust of complicated women and Kate's incredibly complicated life threaten to pull them apart. But forces beyond their control—match-making grandmothers, the lazy backdrop of summer, and their own reckoning with the past—conspire to make them risk it all... and bet on love.

Our match-making grandmothers are at it again, *Stacking the Deck* against Liz and Carter in Book Two of the 'Betting On Romance' series:

STACKING THE DECK

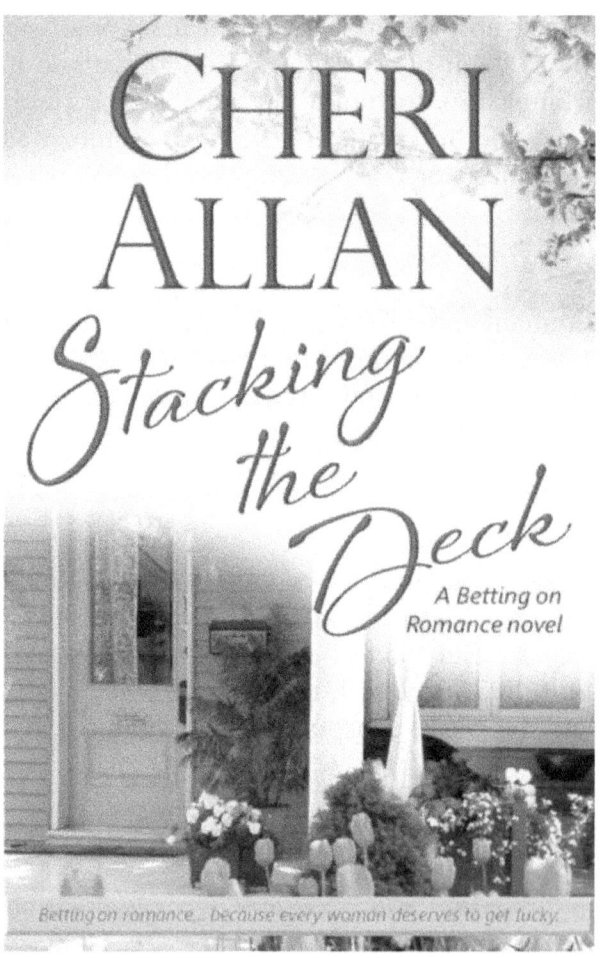

Who said coming home is easy?

Liz Beacon has life all planned out—prioritized, color-coded *and* cross-referenced. She long ago traded in the geeky high school nickname, teenage pounds and dysfunctional family for a fab career, killer abs and a man every woman would envy. Okay, so her sex life is non-existent and her almost-fiancé is technically a coworker. Life, if not perfect, is still on track. But then, Liz is called home to Sugar Falls, NH, to prepare her childhood home for sale. She's spent ten years denying her insecurities and hokey lawn-ornament roots. There's nothing she'd rather do less than face all she happily left behind, including her embarrassingly one-sided high school crush.

Carter McIntyre has sailed through life on his winsome smile… and by the skin of his teeth. A college drop-out with ADHD, he's learned it's safer to play the carefree charmer than step up and take over his uncle's landscaping business. But then his class valedictorian returns to Sugar Falls and hires him for some home improvements. Now Carter's wondering if it's too late—to grow up, take a chance and win over the only girl who ever believed in him…

Cheri Allan

Book Three of the 'Betting On Romance' series:

ALL OR NOTHING

"Smart, funny and emotional!"
—Julia Kent, New York Times and USA Today bestselling author

CHERI ALLAN

All or Nothing

A Betting on
Romance novel

Betting on romance... because every woman deserves to get lucky.

When finding Mrs. Right goes, oh, so wrong...

Self-made tech millionaire Ian McIntyre has suffered through a reality dating show only to return home to idyllic Sugar Falls, New Hampshire, empty-handed, swarmed by paparazzi, and hounded by a Hollywood producer determined to deliver a Happily Ever After. But then his home is invaded by a sexy, snarky local staging it for the season finale, and Ian finds himself more interested in the cute and scrappy hometown girl dusting off his action figures than the audience's favorite southern belle.

Auto mechanic Bailey Adams grew up on the wrong side of the tracks and is struggling to patch together enough odd jobs to buy a garage of her own. When the Golden Boy of Sugar Falls entangles her in his disastrous season of Happily Ever After, they both discover that some long-held dreams are only as 'real' as 'reality' TV. Now, with the deal on her dream garage in jeopardy and her unlikely love affair with America's favorite geeky hunk playing out on national TV, Bailey must decide if she's willing to risk it all for love... or be left with nothing.

All or Nothing is a 2015 Golden Leaf Award finalist for excellence in romantic fiction.

www.ingramcontent.com/pod-product-compliance
Lightning Source LLC
Chambersburg PA
CBHW071130170626
46809CB00002B/563